Books by *William Keisling*

Not Fade Away
We All Fall Down
Helping Hands
When the Levee Breaks
Maybe Four Steps
The Meltdown
The Sins of Our Fathers
Solar Water Heating Systems
Three Mile Island: Turning Point

NOT FADE AWAY

OR, QUALITY WOODWORK
AN AMERICAN MYTH

WILLIAM KEISLING

YARDBIRD

A portion of this book first appeared in
The North American Review as
"A Fire in the Box that Could Truly Light the World."
Thanks, Robley Wilson, Jr.

Set in Sabon 10/13. Keener display faces. Handwriting font is
called, appropriately, Texas Hero.
Thanks to Lynn Hamrick for help with cover and design.
Apologies to Henri.

Yardbird Books can be found in any good book store.
We encourage our readers to order books directly from
us at a savings by calling Yardbird Books at
1-800-622-6044. Or write us at:
Yardbird Books, 601 Kennedy Road, Airville, PA 17302.
Pennsylvania residents please add six percent sales tax.

Digital versions of our books are available.
E-mail and orders can also be sent to: info@yardbird.com.
Visit our web page at www.yardbird.com.

Library of Congress Cataloging-in-Publication Data
Keisling, William.
   Not fade away, or, Quality Woodwork : an American myth
   / William Keisling.
      p.   cm.
   ISBN 1-882611-12-8 (hc : alk. paper)
   ISBN 1-882611-13-6 (pbk. : alk. paper)
   I. Title
PS3561.E37575N68   1997
813'.54--dc21   97-21541
                                        CIP

CONTENTS

About the adverbs in this book

In keeping with the current popular distaste for adverbs, the writer resolved to pull most if not all of them from his book. The job nearly complete, he lost his footing and spilled the whole bag of unwanted adverbs pallmall into the story. Realizing the job now was hopeless, he shoveled more in for good measure.

— The Author

For a Rocker

Larry Holley remembers Buddy coming to him for a loan to buy a Strat based on Buddy's belief that he would soon be another Elvis Presley and would, therefore, need the best of equipment....

Holly's original Stratacaster, the one purchased by Larry Holley in Lubbock and used on most of Holly's recordings and tours, has never been accounted for.

— Guitar Player
June, 1982

NOT FADE AWAY

OVERTURE:

A WINDOW ON ALL TIME

The seed of our destruction will blossom in the desert,
the alexin of our cure grows by a mountain rock,
and our lives are haunted by a Georgia slattern,
because a London cutpurse went unhung.
Each moment is the fruit of forty thousand years.
The minute-winning days, like flies, buzz home to death,
and every minute is a window on all time.

— Thomas Wolfe

ROLL OVER, Schoolmaster Dickens, and tell Bill Shakespeare the news. Tell him about your American cousins in the days they walked the tallest and the boldest. Tell him about The Bomb and The Pill, the microchip and the gigabyte; mass production, test-tube babies and future shock; the lift-off from the sandy beaches of Kitty Hawk to the set down on the desolate prairie of the Sea of Tranquillity. Poke him in the ribs with one of those double-edged razors you confiscated from King Richard III. Tell him how the day which shall live in infamy in the winter of our discontent was made glorious summer by Big Boy and Fat Man over Hiroshima and Nagasaki. Tell him it was the best of spacetime, it was the absolute worst of spacetime, it was nanoseconds of utmost confidence, it was microseconds of deepest most doubt. Dreams were just around the corner, but destruction was just around the corner too. In short, it was a period very much like today, except the sensation of speed was still seductively attractive. Cars, spaceships and computers had yet to become *too* fast. Change had yet to come so fast that things got disorienting. Future shock had yet to be discovered.

A bald-headed old man, who later would leave office issuing vague warnings about bureaucrats hidden away in the woodwork, governed from the White House in Washington; a bald-headed old man, who would later pound tables with his shoe at the United Nations, governed from the Kremlin in Moscow. In both countries it was clear to the managers of the state supplies of guns and butter that things would stay the same forever.

5

The year was 1959. The day, February 3. The moment was this:

Washington. Impeccable February weather. In the cloistered backyard of the White House, out on the putting green, eyeing a lengthy shot across the frosty clipped grass, stood the 34th president of the United States, Dwight David Eisenhower. He was measuring off the distance by holding his iron up into the quiet morning.

How should we describe this man to the ages? As he silently trods up to his dimpled ball, digs in his cleated golf shoes, and takes his stand with his favorite putting iron, how can we hint at the impact he had on his century? Do the deeds of a boy foretell the deeds of the man? If so, consider the story of him as a boy, growing up in Abilene, Kansas, smaller than the other boys but good with his fists. They say once a bigger boy was teasing him when he turned around and let the bully have a quick right cross, followed by a left, taking him by surprise, leaving him sprawled in the dust. He stood with fists bared and teeth snarled, unafraid, beckoning to the bully boy, "Come on." The bully boy got up and ran.

Half a world away, half a lifetime away, what were the thoughts of that first German soldier staring out of his bunker onto the misty beaches of Normandy? He saw boats. Thousands and thousands of boats coming in with the changing tide, sailing out of the mist. The bully boys in Berlin were about to get a little present from the two-fisted boy from Abilene.

Once the plague that blighted our house was burned to ashes and its dust carried by the wind to the four corners of the globe, our heads were showered with victorious tickertape, our battled armaments were set aside as stern warnings to the future, our dreadful councils of war gave way to the friendly meetings of families around tv sets to watch Uncle Miltie, Ed Sullivan and a young man named Elvis, and the rumble of our tanks faded to the thunder of our shake, our rattle and our roll. We were left to shake it just a little in the middle of the night. Fair-faced peace had smoothed Ike's wrinkled brow,

6

and now — instead of riding off to the front in an armored personnel carrier wrapped in his trademark Eisenhower jacket — he takes his stand with a putting iron on the frosty green behind the White House ensconced in his favorite woolly sweater.

There were others not content to so peacefully pass the time, others determined to play the villain, ones who hated the idle pleasures of those sleepy days. Plots they laid, to steal the secrets of the atom, causing others, by dangerous innuendo and libel, to launch a red scare, until both friend and foe had combined to threaten the peace. Few were more aware of the dangers and intrigues of the time than was Ike. He was fond of cryptically telling visitors at the White House that only Americans could hurt America.

The technology of the atom left him in a difficult dilemma, one that struck at the heart of a free society. How could an open society protect its secrets while at the same time remain open? In those days the question occupied Ike's mind no end. In his old soldier's days he never had to wrestle with such difficult abstract questions. To be a soldier is merely to destroy — to govern is to decide. Though he would never admit it to anyone, not even to himself, Eisenhower secretly felt out of his league in the White House, not up to the job of statesman. In four words, he had trouble deciding.

That was why he turned to golf. Whenever the unbearable final hour came when he was forced to make a decision of grave national import, and after he had read the voluminous stacks of persuasive reports prepared by sincere advisors who recommended one course of action, followed by equally voluminous stacks of equally persuasive reports written by equally sincere advisors who recommended the exact opposite course of action, he would take up his putter, slinging it over his shoulder like a Boston minuteman taking up his flintlock. With his little white ball he would trod out to the backyard green. Depending on how well he was putting that day he would make his decision.

He had it nearly worked out to a science. Generally, as a

7

rule, if he had a bad day on the putting green he would be surly and difficult and he was sure to oppose just about whatever came up for his consideration. But on those days when he felt the magic 'in his hands and could putt well he would go along with just about anything.

It was a strange way to run a modern country, that's true, but it worked for Ike. Times were good, and he couldn't help secretly suspecting that the nation's prosperity had something to do with the brand of golf balls he bought. For this reason he had a deep-seated suspicion of using inferior golf balls, and he made it a point never to accept an inferior ball as a gift, so fearful was he that World War III might break out if he did.

This particular morning finds Eisenhower grappling with another of those thorny national security problems he must address, even as he grapples with his putting iron and addresses the ball. Several hours earlier, in the middle of the night, an aide awoke him with the news that America's latest intercontinental ballistic missile, the Atlas, named after a Greek god who was turned to stone, had again failed its launch test. The missile's engines had mystifiedly shut off seconds before the scheduled blast off. Like its namesake, it sat like a stone statue on its pad. A week before another Atlas hadn't risen more than twenty feet before it'd careened out of control, spinning abandonedly and blowing up in a wild display of pyrotechnics. These "anomalies," as the missile scientists were fond of calling the misfirings, couldn't be explained. Sabotage, the president was told, couldn't be ruled out.

"Something's got to be done!" Ike ranted to his senior advisors not long ago in one particularly stormy Oval Office meeting. Eisenhower had presided over many such discussions, some of which would remain secret to his countrymen for many decades, some of which never would become known.

The A-Bomb drove him crazy. What would happen, he constantly asked his advisers, if the government of the people got nuked? Wasn't this the central question, why he'd been elected president? he'd ask. Like the dot beneath the question mark, all the other crisis flowed to this.

8

Hadn't America entrusted the old soldier to formulate contingency plans for the worst possible military event? He called his contingencies the Doomsday Plan. He'd commissioned the excavation of vast bomb shelters to house the president, congress and the supreme court. He authorized special units of the military to train for rescue missions and to implement the plan. In the event Washington was nuked commandos would fly to the rubble of the White House and the capitol building, cut through the wreckage and airlift the elected officials to the secluded bomb shelters.

Eisenhower insisted on drills. At a moment's notice, in the middle of dinner or even on the john, his cabinet officers would be whisked away to faraway underground command posts. They'd arrive God-knows-where in the dead of night to find Eisenhower far underground in a lavish command post, at the head of his underground cabinet table, holding a stop watch, complaining about the time it took to airlift the cabinet halfway across the country and drop everyone eight miles down a mine shaft. He'd even signed presidential orders authorizing marshal law in the event of Doomsday. The unspoken irony was that after the population had been decimated by nuclear war, the economy destroyed and marshal law declared, there wouldn't be much left of the government for the people, by the people.

These signed orders and the Doomsday plans would remain in a lead-shielded safe for nearly fifty years, ready for implementation, unseen and unknown by the public they were meant to protect. In this way Eisenhower's shadow would be cast over the government long after he was gone.

One particular day Eisenhower's ever-wary mind pondered the possibility that a red had waltzed into NASA and sabotaged the Atlas. How could this possibility be prevented in the future?

"Someone tell me why it is those damn Russians seem to know all our secrets when we know none of theirs?"

"It's difficult to keep secrets in an open society like ours," one of the advisors pointed out. "Joe Stalin never had that

9

problem."

"Well I never heard such tommyrot!"

Eisenhower paced behind his desk, tearing up the wooden floor with his golf cleats. "In the military we'd never'd put up with such sloppy security and intelligence as this. I tell you, mister, heads would roll! If we'd've had such sloppy security and intelligence in the army I tell you we'd've lost the damn war!"

"Yes, Mr President."

Scowling, Eisenhower pulled open the top drawer of his desk, pointing to the newly installed array of buttons that, if pushed, would initiate nuclear war.

"It's an outrage and a national disgrace!" Eisenhower chewed on. "Here we are, with no idea what's going on in the Kremlin, while over here, what's to stop some Russian from leaving a tour of the White House and coming up here and pressing these buttons?"

"A Russian attack Russia?" one of the men laughed.

"Damnit I'm serious mister!" Eisenhower snarled back, leaning far over his desk. "The laxness of security in civilian government never ceases to amaze me. If this was the military do you know what we'd do? We'd have an ultra top-secret security and intelligence detail that would keep tabs on things. Someone to police the police. Everyone would be so afraid for their necks I guarantee you mister no secrets would ever leak out. If this was the military I tell you we'd seal up this government tighter than a drum!"

"But Mr President," Ike heard one of them say, and rather quietly at that, "this is not the military." He saw it'd come from his advisor for civilian affairs, who was a low-keyed, button-down, bow-tie-wearer of a man from back East named Haines. Other presidents had advisors for military affairs, but Ike needed no help finding his way around the Pentagon. Ike kept someone around who could help explain the strange and unfathomable ways of civilians.

"What's that you say Haines? For godsakes man speak up!" Why was it these Ivy League guys never learned to speak

10

up? Ike perpetually wondered.

Haines cleared his throat. He sat stiffly in his wing chair. Swallowing hard, his bow tie bobbed.

"You say you'd seal up our government tighter than a drum," Haines meekly proffered, "when I'm sure you realize that's precisely what Stalin achieved in Moscow. Is that the type of government we want?"

"What are you driving at, Haines?"

"Do we really want all these top-secret operatives hiding in the woodwork with no one to keep an eye on them, Mr President?"

Eisenhower glared at Haines. The pip-squeak had a point.

"Are you saying a top-secret security and intelligence detail would be a bad idea for the country?" he asked. "And does that mean you'll take responsibility if the Russians walk off with the store?"

Haines melted under Eisenhower's unyielding gaze. He shrank in his seat, sweating visibly.

"Well?"

"The decision ultimately is yours, Mr President."

"Isn't that just how it is around here!" Eisenhower exploded.

He'd resumed his pacing, grinding the floorboards to sawdust with his cleats.

"Why do I keep you advisors in your monkey suits around if you keep throwing these decisions back at me? You might as well be court jesters!"

Since moving into the White House he'd found this was by far the toughest part of the job. It really wasn't just cliché: it *was* lonely at the top. Often he amused himself by thinking that, of all the millions of people who wanted to be president, there probably wasn't a sane soul in the whole damn country who wanted to make the tough decisions that came with the job.

The presidential advisors watched the old soldier anguish over the problem in front of the bay windows overlooking the putting green out back.

"So what are we to do with this security problem?" Eisenhower finally piped. "A decision has to be reached. If I was a Roman general and if this was ancient Rome do you know what we'd do? I'd have one of you jokers go out and sacrifice a goat so we could look at the entrails. But this is not Rome, this is twentieth century America. I suppose that means we'll just have to tackle this the usual way."

The usual way was for each advisor to write out his opinion on paper. The advice of experts in the field was also sought. Later, as he read through the thick stacks of position papers, Eisenhower saw that each contradicted the last. One well-informed expert stated that a top-secret security and intelligence team would definitely be a good idea for the country, another well-informed expert stated that a top-secret security and intelligence team would definitely be a bad idea for the country. This position paper here said the president would be ill-advised to do it, that position paper there said the president would be ill-advised *not* to do it. Eisenhower was at last filled with such a great sense of indecision that he felt like strangling every one of the well-informed experts with his bare hands. He had come no closer to making a decision. So he made no decision at all.

That was where the matter stood when he was awoken from an uneasy sleep by the telephone call from an aide early in the morning of February 3, 1959. Another test firing of an Atlas missile had failed, he was told over the phone. The turkey sat sputtering motionless on the pad, then it had blown up, and sabotage couldn't be ruled out.

Ike slammed down the phone. He lay in bed staring up at the darkened ceiling. In the early morning darkness he could hear Mamie's even breathing. He knew he could always roll over and go back to sleep but he couldn't bring himself to do it. That was the problem with these ultra top-secret national security problems. If you ignored them no one out in the street would be any wiser, at least for a while, but it would still rob you of sleep. *You* would know.

12

Cursing, he got out of bed.

"What is it this time, dear?" Mamie asked sleepily.

"It's those damn chowderhead advisors of mine and the tommyrot I get for advice around here. It always comes down to me."

"Well calm down or you'll take another coronary."

"Maybe then my troubles will be over."

Already he'd gotten out of his pajamas and was stepping into his pants. He slipped on his golf shoes and went out.

The sun, big and red, just cracked the horizon as he walked onto the frosted putting green, trailing a train of footsteps in the frost. Pulling on his golfing glove, he looked up at the sunrise. What's that old salt's saying? he thought. *"Red sky at night, sailor's delight; red sky at morning, sailors take warning."* Hmph! If I was a stupid grog-drinking swabbie maybe it would have some pertinence.

His putting iron on his shoulder, like a rifle, and the little white ball clutched firmly in hand, like a grenade, he circled the fringe on the perimeter of the green, eyeing his objective: the little hole near the center of the green with the flag sticking out of it.

"All right," he soliloquized softly, reconnoitering the hole. "This is how it'll be. If I sink this putt, there'll be a new top-secret security and intelligence detail in America. If I miss, to hell with it."

With that, he unceremoniously dropped the ball over his shoulder then turned to regard his lie. He saw he held an unfortunate field position. The ball had landed squarely in a hole the squirrels had dug while looking for winter food.

Those damn squirrels! Throughout his administration he'd complained unendingly to his aides about the squirrels. He'd gone so far as to order his Secret Service agents to chase after them with butterfly nets, trap them and have them shipped off in exile to the woods of Virginia. By appeasing Eisenhower in this matter of the squirrels his aides thought they were merely giving in to a slightly eccentric foible of a great man. It's well known that men of greatness most always suffer a foible or two, so his staff thought little of it, even though those big Secret Service agents did look ridiculous chasing squirrels around the White House grounds with butterfly nets. They had no way of knowing that the future of the free world hung in balance on the lip of the cup at the center of Ike's putting green, and that the squirrels, by digging up the smooth manicured surface of the green, posed unsettling problems for humanity.

For a moment, looking around and seeing he was completely and utterly alone, Eisenhower considered kicking the ball from the squirrel hole. He was often quarrelous when it came to golf. On the eighteenth hole of the Augusta National Golf Course in Georgia a tree stuck out into the fairway on the left and the president never failed to cap off a good game by hooking his ball into it. His blood boiling, he one day stormed into the clubhouse and asked the directors to chop down "that damn tree," but was politely rebuffed. They'd nervously reminded the enraged president and liberator of Europe that golf, like life, was a game where one must hit the ball where it lay. In his heart Eisenhower knew they were right. Now he checked his impulse to kick the ball from the squirrel hole. Not only would it be unsporting, he knew in his heart of hearts it would be an unmanly, cowardly thing to do. He was forced to remind himself that a man of true greatness does not bemoan a difficult situation — he turns the difficult situation to his advantage. Wasn't that what Julius Caesar was renowned for on the battlefield? The sudden, unexpected action that took his adversaries by surprise and turned the tables to his favor? Wasn't that precisely what Meade had done by securing Little Round Top in the Battle Of Gettysburg, thereby gaining the benefit of the high ground and in so doing turning the tide in the war between the states?

Bringing his eye down close to the golf ball, he surveyed the squirrel hole. It looked like a miniature shell crater. He told himself this wasn't such a bad field position after all. Hadn't Grant had it worse in Vicksburg? Was he less of a man than that swaggering old drunkard of a West Point washout, less of a field commander, less of a president? Hmph! That was sure saying it. Tommyrot!

Straightening himself, digging his cleats into the frozen ground, he gently brought the flat face of the putter against the dimpled ball. He'd have to remember to keep his elbow in. *That* was the secret. That, and the fingers. At times like this Ike wondered what kind of president Arnold Palmer would make. A real straight shooter, that young fellow. A great putter like Arnold Palmer would do the world a world of good.

Holding his breath, intrepidly bringing back the putter, he fired away. The instant he hit the ball he knew he'd missed. It glanced off the lip of the squirrel hole and took off at a good clip wide of the pin. In a way, he was relieved. No shadowy security and intelligence team, Haines would be glad to hear. Then, as the ball was about to roll past the hole, one of those cursed lean and hungry squirrels darted from the hedges and tackled the ball, mistaking it for something to eat. With a loud clatter the squirrel rolled over the ball, deflecting its course. Eisenhower waved his club, the squirrel ran off posthaste, but it was too late. Ever so slowly the ball crept toward the flag, at last hanging on the very precipice of the hole. Eisenhower held his breath as the ball rattled over the brink into the cup.

It was the legendary luck of Eisenhower. He stood there for the better part of a minute, unmoving. Then he looked up at the boiling gray February sky, looked up into those morning clouds as if he'd just been witness to a pronouncement from heaven.

A little shook up, Eisenhower went into the Oval Office and picked up the phone. He would often make his own phone calls. It was a habit left over from his army days. It would take people by surprise to answer the phone and find Ike on the other end. Often they couldn't bring themselves to believe it was him, that it must be a practical jokester.

"Haines?" he now said gruffly into the phone. "This is Eisenhower. What do you mean, 'Knock it off?' Of *course* it's me. Who the hell else would I be? Now listen. I've made up my mind about that security and intelligence detail. Get in here so we can get the ball rolling."

It was the better part of an hour and a half before Haines came briskly into the Oval Office. He had an early morning, just-shaved-and-showered look to him. His usual bow tie and tweed jacket. A manila folder under his arm. Eisenhower stared vacantly out the bay windows, his golfing glove in hand. Haines saw the presidential putting iron leaning against the great wooden desk.

"I must say Mr President I don't envy you for having to arrive at such a difficult decision," Haines said. "I don't think I'd have the wherewithal to reason out the proper response in this case. If it was me I'm afraid I'd've resorted to the entrails of that goat you were joking about."

He smiled, intending to inject humor, but Eisenhower gave him a strange glare.

"Hmph," the president grunted, moving from the windows.

"I suppose reason always prevails in the end, sir."

"I certainly hope so."

Eisenhower went despondently to his desk.

"Another Atlas blew up on the pad last night," he told Haines. "I was forced to— come to terms with the problem. I wonder if the boys in the newsroom got wind of the missile failure yet." He switched on the radio. It began to whine as it warmed up. The whining grew louder as Ike fussed with the tuning knob. That rock 'n' roll music he disliked so much poured into the stately room, breaking the early morning stillness.

"...Well that'll be the day..."

He turned the knob, heard static, then the same tune.

"...That'll be the day.. ay.. ay that I die..."

This time he jetted the little red needle all the way to the far end of the dial. Again he came up with the same tune.

"...That'll be the day..."

"Can't they play anything besides this tommyrot? Let me hear the news."

He dialed another station and at last got a reprieve from the music. A somber-voiced newsman intoned, "...been confirmed that the three of them and their pilot were killed in the early hours this morning when their plane crashed in a cornfield just outside of Clear Lake, Iowa...."

Again the president jetted the dial, this time landing on a call-in show. They heard the voice of a teenaged girl, crying.

"I can't believe he's dead," the girl sobbed sorrowfully over the radio. "Only yesterday he was so alive and then this! How could it have happened? Buddy, you'll not fade away! We'll remember you always, till the end of time."

Ike listened to her bitter lament. It was the unmistakable sound of mourning, a sound America would know only too well in the decades ahead. How could they have known it was a hint of things to come? America was about to go on a long and heartstopping roller coaster ride. Hadn't that tearful teenaged goodbye signaled the start of it? The end of an age of innocence. They'd awoken on the day the music died, the cold February morning when the world had heard the sound of America crying.

The president looked befuddled.

Haines said, "I don't think you'll hear any news of your missile today, sir. This Buddy Holly boy was killed last night. I dropped my daughter at school this morning and the way she carried on you'd have thought there'd been a death in the family. All the kids stood out in front of the high school crying in each other's arms. I never saw anything like it."

"Who is this Buddy Holly character?"

"One of those rock 'n' rollers, sir. Second only to Elvis, from what I understand."

"I thought that Presley kid was in the army, like all young men should be. Why isn't this Buddy Holly in the army?"

"He's dead now sir."

"I guess it all works out the same in the end then, doesn't it?"

"It really was very tragic, sir. On the way in I heard one of the radio announcers say he was only twenty-one."

A look of stern disapproval swept Ike's face. When he flashed that grin of his he could make flowers grow but when, as now, he wanted he could flash a stare so cold that it froze water. He switched off the radio.

"I don't believe it! A matter of supreme national importance like the misfiring of this missile and all we can get on the radio is news of the death of some boy who won't be remembered two weeks from now! I tell you, this country is in a dangerously fickle and frivolous mood these days, Haines."

"Yes, Mr President."

"Well let's get down to brass tacks then, shall we? About this security detail."

He withdrew a notepad from his desk drawer and stood over it, writing briskly. Tearing the sheet from the pad, he slid it across the desk.

Haines read, in bold, soldier's handwriting:

"This order empowers a special, secret unit of the US Army to investigate the integrity of the security apparatus of the government of the United States, particularly, but not limited to, its nuclear defense forces. If security procedures, after thorough investigation, are proved to be inadequate, the president should be notified."

"There," Eisenhower said, "that should keep them honest. I feel better already. Maybe now I'll get some shut-eye around here."

Haines studied the order.

"Why give this assignment to the army, sir?"

"Because I trust the army, that's why."

Eisenhower took in Haines' face.

"What else is troubling you mister? Spit it out."

"Don't you think, Mr President, that the objectives as they're spelled out here are a little— broad?"

It was in fact the kind of order for which Eisenhower was famous. A framework of broad objectives, with few details sketched in, leaving quite a bit to the discretion of whoever was to receive it.

"Write an order so an idiot can follow it and I guarantee

18

you an idiot *will* follow it," the president scoffed. "Men win battles, Mr Haines, not orders. When it comes right down to it, the instructions I gave the men for the D-Day invasion were little more than, 'Cross the channel, take the beach and move inland.' For that I landed here on Pennsylvania Avenue and I'm not about to tinker with success. This matter is closed."

Eisenhower glumly examined his face in the big oval mirror by the fireplace.

"Fretting over this has given me wrinkles," he said. "This one right here, I think," — he pointed high on his bald brow — "can be directly attributed to this decision."

"I only hope somewhere down the road we won't need policemen to police the police who are policing the police, Mr President. Then you'll be in for a few more wrinkles. Like the Romans used to say, Who shall guard the guardians themselves?"

"I share the same concern, Haines. That's why the selection of the right man for this job is vitally important."

Haines opened his manila folder.

"I brought along a list of candidates...."

"That won't be necessary, Haines." Eisenhower came away from the mirror. "I was thinking about this all morning, while I was waiting for you to roll out of bed and get in here."

He saw Haines blush.

"This job is particularly sensitive," the president went on. "It's conceivable that whoever takes this assignment may one day find a hole in our defense system. He could find his finger on that damned nuclear button over there." He nodded at his desk.

"We obviously need a man we can trust."

"I'm afraid trust won't be enough for this job, Haines. I want the man who takes this assignment to have a tremendous amount to lose if ever he finds himself with the doomsday button in front of him. A man with so much to lose that he'd never think of pressing it. A wealthy man, someone who'd want to keep this world together if only for his own greedy self-interest."

19

"Where will you find such a man in the army?"

Eisenhower gazed off. In his mind's eye he visualized the Pentagon, like the Greek god Zeus might look out from Olympus and visualize the world of mortals in a pool of wine. Not since Grant had there been an American president so thoroughly familiar with the dark ranks of the Department of Defense. It was no small feat. The Pentagon, big, mysterious and impenetrable, was a heavy unseen ballast beneath the surface, a ballast upon which sailed the more visible ship of state.

"Natlong," Eisenhower said suddenly, snapping his fingers. "George A. Natlong. He's a colonel. Perfect for the job. Specializes in atomic secrecy. Worked at Alamogordo. Had a hand in the Rosenberg thing. Married into the Duke fortune."

"*The* Dukes?" Haines asked. "Not the floor wax Dukes? The ones who own Delaware?"

Eisenhower nodded.

"His father-in-law is Henry Duke. The old man must be worth a half a billion, at least."

"Isn't Henry Duke the eccentric who turned his family estate into the furniture museum?"

"That's the one." Ike brought his forefinger up to his brow, tapped his fingertip against it. "Nevertheless, he's the most harmless old codger you'd ever want to meet. Old Henry invites people to dinner according to the flowers that happen to be blooming in his garden. Every spring when the crocuses come up Mamie and I always get an invite to dinner. You've never seen a bivouac like his. Winterford, he calls it. Rooms and rooms of antique furniture, from every era of American history. He disassembles old houses and ships them to his mansion, where he reassembles them down in his basement, lock, stock and barrel. His daughter married this Natlong. The smartest move of his career. He stands to inherit a mint so it's a safe bet he'll want the world to stick around so he can collect. If one day you'll own the world I'm betting you won't want to see it destroyed. What do you think of my reasoning, Haines?"

Haines nodded his approval.

20

"Sounds perfect for the job."

Eisenhower said dourly, "His father-in-law's been after me to promote him so now I can kill two birds with one stone. If Natlong accepts this assignment see that he's promoted to brigadier general."

"Yes, Mr President. Will that be all?"

Eisenhower looked at the order in Haines's hands.

"I don't have to remind you, Haines, that this assignment should be considered to rank among the highest level of secrets."

"You mean—."

"That's right. This is a Confidential Executive Order. Aside from you and me, the only one who should know of it is the man who takes the job. Natlong must agree to take the assignment before you give him any details, understand? If he turns down our offer, come back here and we'll pick someone else. Is that clear?"

"Yes sir."

Haines started to go, but Eisenhower held up a finger.

"One more thing, Haines. I should write down the number of that damn order. Someone sure as hell better keep track of these things."

From a side drawer in his desk Eisenhower took a plain brown ledger. Opening it, he said, "Never thought I'd end up resorting to this little book as much as I've been." He slid on his reading glasses and, taking up the ledger, he said, "Now let's see. That must make this Confidential Executive Order No. 666."

He scribbled out a brief notation in the ledger but when he looked up he saw Haines staring at the order in his hands, staring with what could only be called dread.

"What's the matter, Haines? For christsakes *speak up man!*"

"You did say this was Confidential Executive Order No. 666, didn't you, sir?"

"That's right. If I remember, No. 664 authorized the U-2 spy plane flights over Russia. And 665 was that Bay of Pigs business. That makes this 666. What of it?"

Haines cast his troubled gaze about the Oval Office. He found what he was looking for on the bookshelf. It was an old, trenchworn soldier's Bible, the one Ike had carried with him since the old days. Haines went over and tore into it.

"Here it is, sir. Revelations 13. It's a prediction of a beast that will supposedly bring about the end of the world. I'm sure you've heard of it. The beast is known to the ages only by a number."

With unsteady hands, he handed the ragged old Bible to Eisenhower, pointing out a passage. The president brought the book over to the light of the windows.

"'Here is wisdom,'" he read aloud. "'He who has understanding, let him reckon the number of the beast, for it is a number of a man, and its number is six hundred and sixty-six.'"

He closed the book.

"Humph," he grunted. That was all.

Haines distrustfully held Confidential Executive Order No. 666 out in front of himself, holding it at a distance, like it carried plague.

"Maybe we shouldn't go through with this after all sir," Haines said softly, his voice atremble.

Eisenhower looked amazed. He remembered back to the war, to his command in Europe, to one particularly rainy night in Britain when he'd been finishing preparations for the Normandy invasion. Everyone was pushed to the limit. Ike knew if they bungled the invasion the Americans probably would be pulled out to fight in the Pacific, sacrificing Europe to the enemy. It was the darkest moment of his life. Late one night at Allied High Command a British officer approached him with a folded slip of paper. Ike opened it and found the address of a woman in South Dorchester. "What's this?" he'd asked the officer. "You yanks would call her a psychic," the Brit replied with a wink. "She had me give you her address. She believes she can help you. If I were you, general, I wouldn't cross the channel without seeing her first." Feeling somehow embarrassed, Eisenhower slipped the address into his shirt pocket. Several times, when the darkness was all around him and he was filled with doubt, he'd almost resorted to that ride to South Dorchester. When millions of lives and the fate of the world rest on your shoulders there is great temptation to palm off your toughest decisions on someone or something else. Ike found himself avoiding the British officer who'd given him the address. Finally, on the night of the invasion, feeling as alone as any man has ever felt, he went to talk with the troops. They'd seen his unease. "Don't worry, general," one of the men came up and said to him, shaking his hand. "We'll win this for you." That's when he'd first gotten the inkling that it might work. The weather that night had been stormy but the meteorologists, using the latest scientific equipment, predicted it would clear in time for a landing at dawn. Was it go? they wanted to know. Walking alone down by the water, he tore the little piece of paper with the psychic's address into a hundred pieces, casting it to the waves. That was one decision he'd never regretted. Now, years later in the Oval Office, he set his tattered old Bible down on his desk.

"Why, that's just tommyrot," he told Haines, dismissing the Bible with a wave of his hand. "This decision was reached through— ah, reason." The president self-consciously fiddled with his putting iron.

"Why, Haines," he went on, "you wouldn't want us to return to the days of augurs and soothsayers, when decisions were reached by studying the entrails of slaughtered goats, would you?"

"Of course not Mr President."

"Then get the hell over to the Pentagon with that order."

Haines looked appreciatively at the president. At times like this he was glad such a strong man held the office.

"Forgive me, sir," he said. "I must have panicked."

Eisenhower flashed that winning grin.

"It happens to the best of us, Haines. Happens to the best of us."

And so the job of enforcing Confidential Executive Order No. 666 fell to an obscure army desk jockey named George Armstrong Natlong. He was an ordinary-enough-looking career officer, a little on the short and stocky side, with slicked-back graying hair, a pale face with sunken distrustful eyes set like coals in a snowman above a neatly trimmed gray moustache. He could have been mistaken for any one of a million men in uniform working around the Pentagon. He looked a little like a wrung-out Hemingway. He was one of those men who always tried to carry himself in a way that would suggest he was stronger or bolder than he really was. Few people were impressed, not even children. He was a dying breed, a relic of the past, a dinosaur, a pseudo-macho man at a time when the world no longer had a need or a taste for macho men.

For many years he faithfully discharged the duties of Confidential Executive Order No. 666. His cold war exploits were many, and of such a thrilling and suspenseful nature that if ever they were to be written down and published in spy novel form they would make the works of messers Le Carré, Ludlum and Fleming seem pale and uninformed by comparison. Of this George Natlong had no doubt, as his only two diversions from his job included reading those mind corrupting books and playing poker every Wednesday night with four other army officers from his class at West Point. They, and everyone at the Pentagon, it seemed, read those debilitating books. On several occasions while they were playing cards and chatting about their latest spy read George Natlong, having had a little too much to drink, would go so far as to boast that the work in which he was currently engaged would make a better plot for a spy novel than the nonsense in whatever book they'd been discussing. The only trouble was, he wasn't at liberty to prove his point by discussing his top-secret work with his friends, let alone to publish his exploits for the masses in spy novel form. His poker friends understood, as they were army generals themselves, and also were restricted from ever mentioning the details of their work. If every once in a blue moon George Natlong, a little tight on bourbon, let down his hair enough to intimate to his closest friends that what he was doing at the Pentagon would make the current James Bond adventure seem like a trip to Disneyland, the others would just leave it at that and not badger him to elaborate. They had no way of guessing what a day in the life of George Natlong must be like.

It was just as well that George Natlong said little of his work, for if ordinary loose lips can sink ships, George Natlong's pale, moustache-shaded lips could surely sink an entire ship of state. He spent his days hidden away in the unseen bowels of the Pentagon, aided by an assistant. He went about finding leaks in the groaning ship of state so that they might be plugged before the ship sank. To see through his eyes would be to see the unprotected belly of the beast.

In 1969 he and his assistant found an open back door at Fort Knox and ended up walking off with a gold ingot. Obeying the decade-old order that had been initialed by Eisenhower, he promptly wrote out a report expressing his amazement at the lax security at the nation's gold depository, and, per instructions, he mailed the report off to President Nixon care of a secret post office box at the White House, enclosing the gold ingot with the report. That should shake them up, he thought as he dropped the heavy package down a Pentagon mail shute. He might as well've mailed that gold brick off to oblivion. To his surprise he never heard anything back from the White House. The following year, late on Christmas Eve, he and his assistant just about waltzed into the treasury and printed a whole sheet of hundred-dollar bills with Santa Claus's picture on the front. "Ho, ho, ho!" he wrote on his report, and he sent it off with the uncut sheet of bogus bills to the same secret post office box. Again, to his surprise, he heard nothing. He might as well have mailed it off to oblivion.

As the years went by he and his assistant uncovered many truly remarkable things. Anyone could walk off with moon rock. Imprinted on the back of the original copy of the US Constitution he found the following message: "For a Goode time, call Betsy Ross." George Washington's wooden teeth can be worn (though somewhat uncomfortably) with Dentu•Grip. And Pat Nixon kept a gun in her underwear drawer.

The American government, it turned out, was little more than a wide-open house. It reminded George Natlong of the olden days in America when folks went around leaving doors unlocked. These being the distrustful, turbulent days of Vietnam, Nixon and the secret bombing war in Cambodia, George Natlong found himself worrying more and more that someday someone might walk off with the store, and he wondered why no one had done it yet. What, after all, was to stop them? George Natlong didn't much understand people, didn't understand what keeps them honest. He saw only the millions of government bureaucrats and supposed it was only the fear of getting caught that kept them from walking off with the nation's most priceless property and its most sensitive secrets. Over time he'd come to see himself and his vigorous enforcement of Confidential Executive Order No. 666 as the only thing that stood in the way of the American equivalent of the sacking of Rome. He could only thank his lucky stars that this most sensitive of jobs had fallen to him. He was the only man in America he could trust to do the job right. No — that's putting it too mildly: he was the only man in America he could trust.

Of all the national security problems worrying George Natlong none worried him more than the military communications network that tied the president to the nuclear arsenal. George Natlong's worst fear was that some unfriendly agent could break the security codes in the elaborate computerized network and wind up with his hands on the nuclear button. It was an unsettling thought, and George Natlong felt it was his patriotic duty to make sure it couldn't happen.

Early in 1962, hoping to find out if just anyone could fire off a salvo of nuclear missiles, he'd hired out a large staff of egghead computer scientists, rented a warehouse in suburban Washington and bought a huge beast of a mainframe computer, identical to the one at the Pentagon. The scientists under his command spent years programming the computer but, in

26

the end, much to George Natlong's relief, they told him it couldn't be done. The security codes protecting the Pentagon's computer were much too tough to crack, the eggheads assured George Natlong. Barring a technological breakthrough it would be impossible. Much relieved, George Natlong put his darkest fears aside and turned his attention to other, more pressing national security problems.

That was where the matter stood until early in 1975, when one morning George Natlong's assistant came to him with a classified memorandum he'd come across in the Office of Technology Assessment.

"I thought you'd better see this, general," his assistant had said. He slid the memo inauspiciously onto George Natlong's desk.

"What's this?"

"Some computer genius working for the government has made what may turn out to be an important discovery. From what I gather, this guy used a computer to design an even better computer. The first computer produced a design for a new machine that's so advanced that — now get this — no one can understand it. Not even the guy who invented it."

"So?"

"Don't you see, general? This could be the technological breakthrough we've been worrying about. If the Russians got their hands on this new circuitry they might be able to build a machine that'd make the Pentagon's computers look like an abacus. They might be able to neutralize our defenses."

George Natlong lowered his cigar.

Looking closely at the memorandum, he said, "I see. And this new computer— where's it being built?"

"That's just it, sir. It *isn't* being built. This memo says the scientist who made the discovery requested government funding to build a prototype but got turned down. Too experimental. At least, that's what the Office of Technology Assessment says."

"You don't say." George Natlong thoughtfully brought the cigar to his mouth, rolling it around. "Very interesting."

"I thought it might be a good idea if we saw to it that this machine gets built, after all. Find out what its capabilities are. Before the enemy does."

"You think we can get this scientist to work for us?"

His assistant shrugged.

"I don't see why not."

The general's assistant was a cocky young army major with dark, handsome features, a rugged, powerful build, and a way about him that said he was accustomed to getting whatever it was he set out to have.

"You know these scientists," he said. "Offer them enough research money and they'll go to work for Himmler." Tapping his fingertip on the memo, he added, "It says here this guy's name's Patterson. Dr L. Patterson. Works not far from here, sir, in Bethesda."

"Well then major," George Natlong said, "tomorrow why don't we pay this Dr Patterson a call?"

They went *sub rosa,* in civilian clothing, the general and his assistant both wearing gray flannel business suits and shiny black civvy shoes. It was a little after lunch when they arrived at a door marked by a plaque which read, "L. Patterson, PhD." They knocked, heard no noises inside, and no one came to the door.

"Must still be out to lunch."

His assistant tried the knob. The door conveniently swung open. They exchanged glances, smiling knowingly. No one seemed to lock their doors.

It was a computer scientist's office, all right. Books everywhere and, along the far wall, an array of computers, blinking and clicking quietly away. The place was cluttered with transistors, circuit boards and similar electronic gizmos. Along the wall several green chalkboards were filled with the mysterious notations of a mathematician. In front of one of the chalkboards a white lab smock hung over the back of a stool. George Natlong's assistant, resting his hands on the smock, looked mystifiedly at the writing on the chalkboards.

28

"Might as well be hieroglyphics," he whistled through his teeth. "This guy must be some egghead."

At that moment the door opened. An attractive young woman entered. She came in all loaded down with shoe boxes. At first she didn't see the visitors. Her cheeks aglow from the cold outside, she walked to the workbench by the windows, where she set down the shoe boxes, took off her gloves.

"He may be an egghead but at least he has good taste in secretaries," George Natlong said, breaking the silence.

The young woman spun around, startled.

"Who are you?"

"I'm sorry to have startled you, hun," George Natlong winked at her, his felt hat in his hands. "We've come to see Dr Patterson. The door was open so we figured it would be all right if we waited here."

"Oh," the woman said, not sure of what to say. She looked at the second man.

"While we're waiting for Dr Patterson to get back from lunch do you suppose you could pour us a cup of that java, sweetheart?" George Natlong smiled at her. He held his felt hat out to the chemist's beaker of coffee that rested on a Bunsen burner among the clutter on the workbench.

"Certainly," she smiled back. Then, somewhat indignantly, "Hun."

In a great huff she stormed over to the coffee beaker and poured a tall mug of coffee. She brought it over to George Natlong and thrust it abruptly against his chest, splashing some onto his fingers.

"Here you are, sweetheart."

"Ouch! That's hot!"

She reached for the folded lab smock. Slipping it on, she drew from one of the oversized pockets a pair of round, black-framed eyeglasses. She slid on the glasses, took a look at the visitors.

"I'm Dr Patterson," she said.

The story of Dr Linda Patterson is worth telling. The most

important part of the story concerns the one thing she wanted more than anything else, which was to build the world's finest computer.

For years she worked in the same steel and glass office building in suburban Washington DC. It was one of those nondescript modern buildings you see dotting the landscape in Bethesda, a sculptureless pillbox set behind a shapeless stainless steel sculpture, all set against acres and acres of asphalt parking lot, and all of it laid out neat and trim in the center of a whispering pine woods, making the building hard to see from the highway. If you happened to be driving on the freeway perhaps you could see a corner of the building jutting out in the distance through the pines, but that was the kind of thing you saw all the time when driving the beltway in Bethesda, and you wouldn't think twice of it. If you happened to commute often down that six-lane stretch of highway, or if you happened to own a fine home in one of the exclusive communities nearby, you would know something was out there in the pine woods, some kind of modern office building where they did something or another very modern, but that would be all you would know. You would naturally assume it was one of those things the government has going on out there, in the woodwork, one of those secrets you'd never know.

And you'd be right. The building where Linda Patterson worked housed an obscure government agency whose mission was to develop advanced electronic technologies. The thousands of people who worked in the building each wore white laboratory smocks, to keep down the dust, and color-coded photo identification badges, to keep down the possibility of leaking sensitive information to the agents of hostile foreign governments. Those who worked in the building were expected never to speak of their projects with their co-workers. And they were not supposed to associate with their co-workers after hours. These restrictions were fine with Linda Patterson, for she truly wanted to be left alone to build her marvelous machine.

Linda Patterson went to work for the government agency

fresh out of school. She graduated at the top of her class from a major East Coast university, at twenty-five the holder of a doctoral degree in advanced electronics engineering. Even before she'd completed her doctorate work the director of the government agency himself paid her a surprise visit, suggesting she come to work for the agency. A mind as promising and as brilliant as hers, he told her, shouldn't be wasted on commercial projects at IBM, but should be put to work for the good of American science.

In those days Linda Patterson was, in a word, naive, believing all she needed to accomplish her dream was gobs of research money with which she could buy gobs of research time. She didn't think twice about the source of the money. Nor, in those days, did she think twice about the consequences of her work. She only cared about chasing her dream. Later, much later, she would look back with shocked amazement at just how naive she'd been. But that, as has already been said, wouldn't be until later, much later.

At the time of her interview with the director of the government agency Linda Patterson matter-of-factly explained that her great desire in life was to build the most powerful computer in the world, a machine which could only be designed with the help of another powerful computer, not to mention much time and money. The work would certainly take years, and might never pay off, but if the government was willing to foot the bill, and if it was willing to put up with many inevitable uncertainties (for scientific research is nothing if it's not in the business of digging through inevitable uncertainties), if the Government of the United States, in short, was willing to put up with her, then Linda Patterson would be willing to put up with the government.

"Splendid!" the head of the agency had said.

She was given a rather comfortable salary. She was given a white smock and a color-coded photo identification badge. She was given that aforementioned cramped, bookshelf-lined office with the computer terminal on the sixth floor of the aforementioned glass and steel office building in suburban Washington

DC, an office with a window overlooking the ribbon of highway, the highway that could just barely be seen in the distance through the pine woods. More importantly, she was given time, all the time in the world. She would not be pressured to produce results of any kind, nor would she have to file progress reports with the agency until she had definite results to report. And then she would report directly to the agency director.

She became a prisoner of her dream, spending every waking hour in her book-lined office before her blinking green computer screen, tapping out instructions to an unseen, silent electronic brain. She'd devised a complex computer program made up of millions of binary numbers and codes whose only purpose, in plain English, was to ask the electronic brain to design an even better electronic brain. It took the better part of a year to feed her program into the computer. Every morning, seven days a week, she came to work in her white smock and walked briskly down the hallways bustling with thousands of other white-smocked scientists, and she never uttered so much as a word to any of them. Always she walked directly to her book-lined office, where she closed the door and did not come out till nine or ten in the evening, whereupon she drove home to her stark apartment, fixed dinner for one and prepared for an early bed. If, while brushing out her hair in the evening before sleep, she happened to think about one of the nameless faces she'd seen rushing by in the hallway at work, perhaps the face of a young man, and if she wondered what sort of life might be connected to that face, she didn't think about the face for long, and did so in an impersonal, analytical way, like a city dweller might remember the fleeting face of a stranger in a crowd. If, on the other hand, any anonymous colleague ever happened to be thinking about her face late at night, she didn't know, and (she told herself) she didn't care. She cared only about her work, her career, her all-consuming dream. She couldn't conceive of anything in this green world that could possibly be more important.

After she'd spent a year feeding her program into the computer she was forced to wait many months for the electronic brain to digest her inquiry and spit out a reply. Those were by far the hardest months of her life. Days, weeks, months were spent killing time, thumbing through the dusty back issues of the technical journals she'd piled on her desk, or just plain standing at her wall-sized office window with her round-rimmed reading glasses in hand, gazing dreamily out beyond the pine trees at the multi-colored cars and trucks streaking across the distant highway. Once, on one of those restless, time-killing days, she gave in to the luxury of taking an afternoon off to shop for a pair of shoes. Leaving her lab a little after one o'clock in the afternoon, she removed her white smock as she walked across the asphalt parking lot to her car. The plastic photo identification badge mustn't have been pinned on too securely, for it fell off the smock and clattered onto the asphalt at her feet. Stooping to retrieve the badge, she turned and happened to glance up at the smooth cliff of steel and glass that was the office building. She saw, on every floor of the building, hundreds of white-smocked scientists with reading glasses in hand, each one gazing dreamily out of his or her ivory tower office window, gazing beyond the pine woods at the cars and trucks whistling down the distant highway.

Then came the day when her computer screen began to blink and flash excitedly and her printer started wildly spitting out results. With great expectations she flew to the clattering printer. As the results rolled before her eyes her heart sank. It didn't appear to make any sense. No sense at all. She'd never seen a computer design like this one before. It couldn't possibly work.

"What's gone wrong! Where did I make my mistake?"

She painstakingly rechecked her work. But she could find no error. She spent months feeding the whole thing back into the computer, starting over from scratch, then spent more agonizing weeks awaiting the computer's reply. At last the day came when her computer screen once again began to flash excitedly, and her printer once again started to clatter and rattle away, and once more she flew to the printer and gazed down with unbearable anticipation.

It was exactly the same, detail for detail, with the first impossible results. All those months down the drain!

Exasperated, she threw down the tangled roll of printer paper, lowered her head to her desk.

She saw the computer screen still blinked away excitedly.

She raised her head.

"You really want me to build this ridiculous thing, don't you?" she said to the flashing screen. She looked down to the floor at the tangled ribbon of paper.

That afternoon she burst into the office of the agency director. Sticking the printout under his nose she said, "I think we should build this."

The director put on his glasses, took one look at the strange design and pronounced it would never work. He couldn't understand it, he joked, let alone fund it.

"Look," Linda Patterson told him, pointing back toward her office, "I've spent the last three years of my life plugging numbers into that damn machine back there and this is what comes out. So what if it looks new? All things once were new. Why keep human beings around here if you don't trust us enough to follow our instincts?"

The director took off his glasses and bit the end of the frames, looking thoughtfully at the intent Dr Patterson.

"I'll tell you what," he said, studying the printout with renewed interest. "I'll send this over to the Office of Technology Assessment. Before I agree to dump millions of dollars of my shrinking budget on a speculative project like this I want to get the OTA staff's opinion."

"And what if they're the same bunch of good old boys who said the Wright Brothers' plane wouldn't fly?"

The director looked with amusement at the fiery young scientist. He wondered if she might be a genius.

"It's more than most would do for you, Dr Patterson," he told her.

More fruitless weeks passed while she waited to hear from

the Office of Technology Assessment. To kill time she shopped for shoes. She covered every shoe shop in the greater Washington metropolitan area. She told herself that when she came out of all this her nerves might be shot but at least her feet would be well covered. Finally the day came when she was summoned to the director's office. With a dour face he told her things had come out pretty much as he'd expected. The Office of Technology Assessment couldn't recommend funding her project. It was simply too risky, too experimental.

"They mean too risky, too experimental for an *unknown* researcher," she told the director flatly. "An unknown *woman* researcher."

The director said he was sorry, and advised her to put it all behind her and proceed down more productive avenues of research. She tried to argue, but he closed the file and said that was that. She was so mad she could have reached across the desk and strangled him. She knew she was right — but how to proceed without funding?

With a heavy heart she left his office and went out on a shoe binge, buying seventeen pairs, including eight pairs of lavender pumps. Really they were the most horrendous pieces of leather in the world but she hardly looked at them when she bought them. At work she was next to useless. For days she sat despondently gazing at the computer printout, unable to think of anything but how she'd reached this dead end. She considered throwing in the towel. She could always get some bullshit job at Honeywell or IBM and go for the big bucks and to hell with this basic research. Who needed it? Feeling angry and betrayed, she started taking longer lunch hours. Each day she'd return from her lunch break all loaded down with shoe boxes.

Her pent-up anger and resentment began to take vent in rebelliousness. She found herself breaking all kinds of stupid agency rules. She'd started coming to work without her white smock and photo ID. On those days when she bothered to bring her smock she'd make it a point to leave it back in her office when she went to lunch, folded over the chair by the chalkboards, and she'd go walking through the halls without it, an island of perma-pressed color in a sea of starched white conformity. She started looking her co-workers in the eyes as they hurried the halls, and she struck up casual conversations at the water cooler. She felt like calling it quits and didn't give a damn.

That was her state of mind on the day she came in late from lunch all loaded down with shoe boxes and found the two men waiting in her office. As soon as she'd put on her smock the older of the two men leaned close to her photo ID to make sure she really was Dr L. Patterson.

"You'll have to forgive me, doctor," he said, red faced, stuck for words. "You're not what we were expecting."

He introduced himself then simply as "Mr George Natlong." Holding out his felt hat toward the younger man he said, "And this is my colleague, Mr Peter Donday."

The way Peter Donday held on for that extra moment when they shook hands should have tipped her off. The way he looked at her should have warned her too.

"If I may get straight to the point, Dr Patterson," she heard George Natlong say, "we understand you've come up with a design for a new computer."

She gave him a surprised look.

"And we understand," George Natlong went on, "you're having difficulty finding money to proceed with your research."

"How do you know?"

"Come on, doctor. Surely you realize whenever you run something through the Office of Technology Assessment you're practically taking out an ad in *The New York Times*."

George Natlong pulled a folded sheaf of paper from the inside pocket of his suit jacket. It was the Office of Technology Assessment's report on her project.

"How'd you get this? Don't you see the big word 'Classified' stamped in red ink across every page?"

George Natlong chuckled.

"Really, Dr Patterson, a 'classified' rating means next to

nothing. It might as well say 'copyright Walt Disney Productions.' Though it does impose a few meager restrictions, just about anyone in Washington can get his hands on a classified document — provided he isn't just a man off the street, of course." George Natlong laughed outright.

Peter Donday put in, "We don't mean to belittle the importance of your research, but you know there are at least a dozen levels of security classifications above 'classified.' There's 'restricted.' And of course, 'top secret.' And 'ultra top secret.' And so on. There may even be classification levels above that that even I don't know about."

"And here I was afraid there was nothing you didn't know about," she said to Peter Donday. His look said that he didn't know how to take it.

"To get to the point, doctor," George Natlong continued, "my organization is very much interested in your ideas. We're prepared to finance your research."

Linda Patterson tried to hide her surprise.

"It might never pay off."

George Natlong smiled.

"Whatever it takes," he smiled pleasantly.

"Who has research money to throw around like that these days?" she said. Again she looked at the two of them, searching for a clue. "You gentlemen didn't mention the name of your organization."

"These things will be explained to you in time, doctor," George Natlong said. "All you should have to worry about now is your research. Come work for me, and my assistant will see to it that you get whatever you need to proceed with your work. We're offering you freedom, Dr Patterson, freedom to create. Would you really want to look a gift horse like that in the mouth?"

"You expect me to go to work without knowing for whom I'm agreeing to work?"

"Regrettably, doctor, that's the way I must do business. Once you come aboard I'll be free to tell you all you'll need know. On that you have my word."

"Sounds like you're asking me to make a pact with the devil."

She gave the two of them her most penetrating stare.

"How do I know, for instance, you aren't agents for a foreign government?"

The men laughed.

"I can assure you, Dr Patterson, nothing could be farther from the truth," George Natlong chuckled.

Linda Patterson took in her stagnant lab. The dead computer console. The books and the reports that hadn't been cracked in months. The boxes of shoes on her workbench. As if she had x-ray vision and could see through walls, she looked in the direction of the director's office.

"What do you think, major?" George Natlong said softly to his assistant, under his breath. "Wouldn't you say she's different from the others we've hired?"

"Not so different," Peter Donday answered, watching her. "She's going for the money."

She turned, facing them, and asked, "Did I hear you say you have lab space?"

"We have the finest electronics laboratory money can buy," George Natlong boasted. "In a modern building very much like this. Over in Arlington. You'll have all the space and equipment you'll need. I'll pay you twice what you're getting here. And I have a fine staff that I'll put completely at your disposal."

"I won't need a staff. Just me. And I won't need much more space than this."

"Just you? But Dr Patterson— do you think that's wise?" George Natlong had learned it was best to be gentle at first with these scientific types. As far as he was concerned they were all as crazy as wild horses, and had to be approached like that, gently and reassuringly, until you jumped on them and broke them. Here he had a particularly spirited mustang. It didn't occur to him then that he might get thrown.

"I work alone," she said. "Let's understand that up front. It's either me, alone, working by myself, or there's no deal. Is that clear?"

"Then we have a deal?" George Natlong extended his hand.

She held back. "And one more thing. I don't serve coffee."

They shook.

"Can I start in the morning? I'm anxious to proceed with my project."

"If that's the case, doctor, you can start this very evening. Follow us over and I'll show you your new laboratory."

It's funny the things you remember, years later. Thinking back, Linda Patterson couldn't remember leaving her old lab that afternoon with George Natlong and Peter Donday, but she must have left the lab with them and with them she must have walked down the corridors out of the office building and over to her car in the sea-like parking lot, because she could remember following them over to Arlington. Years later she could even remember the color of the car they'd been driving, the car she'd been following. She remembered it because it was a tan-colored sedan, almost the same shade as her own car. Funny, isn't it, how you remember things like that?

She didn't remember following them off the beltway at the Arlington exit, but she did remember driving through the trees and, turning onto a side road, she remembered coming out into a clearing where she saw, nestled behind trees, a modern steel and glass pillbox of an office building with a nondescript curlycue of a sculpture out front, remarkably similar to the one she'd left behind. She remembered parking her car in the sea-like parking lot and following George Natlong and Peter Donday into the building. What had George Natlong said when he'd opened the door for her? How could she ever forget? "Allow me to usher you into the future, Dr Patterson," he'd said, beckoning her inside. "Here we do all the modern things." She remembered following them down a long hallway where silent, white-smocked scientists wearing photo ID badges shuffled on their appointed rounds.

"You'll find that working here is remarkably similar to

working at your former place of employment," George Natlong told her as the three of them walked down the wide hall. "With the exception that here you must at all times wear your smock and your ID badge, doctor. I must also insist that whenever you leave your lab unattended it be locked. We place a high priority on security here."

As he was saying this they came up to a nondescript door and, taking a large set of keys from his pocket, George Natlong unlocked the bolt. It was a waiting room.

"Won't you please have a seat, doctor?" George Natlong smiled. "We won't be but a minute." With that the two men disappeared into an inner office.

She took a seat by the door, browsing the magazines. All these things she remembered. Most of all, she remembered when the door to the inner office opened a few minutes later and George Natlong stepped out in the uniform of a United States Army general, followed by Peter Donday, dressed as an army major.

That's how Linda Patterson found herself working for the military. When it came right down to it, she sometimes consoled herself late at night while brushing her hair, it wasn't much different from her old job. She still worked in the same kind of sophisticated electronics lab in the exact same kind of modern office building, and wearing the same kind of smock and photo ID badge she did the exact same kind of work. The only thing that was different was that she reported to different people. That's all. And these people gave her all the money she needed to continue her research. That's the only difference, she'd half convinced herself. Later, much later, she couldn't believe how naive she'd been.

For the present she was consumed by her work. She was building a new machine. And back then her machine was all that mattered. She was building her new machine one piece at a time, not thinking of the consequences. She was building a new machine and she dared believe the rules of the old machines no longer applied.

On the very first day she started working for the military she gave George Natlong's assistant the computer printout that described how the new machine should be built.

"You must find someone who can make this component, major," she said to him. Since learning his true identity she always called him major. "You'll have to dig up an extremely competent electronics manufacturer, who'll ask no questions and put it together exactly as the specs read."

Peter Donday glanced down at the computer printout. An incomprehensible jumble of electronic diagrams and scientific notations stared back. Like the cryptic writing on her chalkboards, it might as well've been hieroglyphics.

"You *can* get it built, can't you, major?"

"There's nothing I can't get," he winked. "Once I set my mind on it."

Almost a month went by with no trace of Peter Donday. Then one morning he came into Linda Patterson's laboratory. Without saying a word he pulled a small device from his jacket pocket. It looked a lot like an oversized fuse — cylindrical in shape, six or seven inches long.

"The upgrade!" she sang out. "You've got it! How'd you ever get it built so fast?"

"The general has a friend in the computer business. Out on the coast. Silicon Valley. A very sharp guy. He says to tell you, by the way, this thing won't work."

"We'll soon find out, won't we?"

Already she'd taken the device from him and was installing it into the computer.

About then George Natlong came in, wearing his general's uniform. "I hear your gizmo's arrived," he said. "Let's have a look."

Linda Patterson had already wired it into her computer's circuit board.

"That's it? That little thing?"

"That 'little thing' makes this the most advanced computer in the world."

Linda Patterson switched on the machine. Immediately the console came alive. The little cursor swept like ball lightning across the small screen. The three of them came closer.

"What's it saying?"

"Odd. Our computer has apparently given itself a name."

The bright lettering on the screen read, "I am Chaos."

"Chaos?" George Natlong barked gruffly. "Are you telling me that gizmo — that upgrade — dreamed up its own name, with no prompting from you?"

"That's precisely what I'm saying, general." Anxious to communicate with the new mind, Linda Patterson busily tapped out words on the keyboard. "From now on, anything can happen." She looked up. "That's what you wanted, isn't it?"

In the weeks that followed, Linda Patterson kept feeding mountains of information into her machine, always asking it, "How can we build a better machine?" One day her console began blinking excitedly. Her printer started spitting wildly the results of her inquiry. Again she handed over to Peter Donday a printout sheet filled with unfathomable notations, telling him, "See that this gets built."

About a month later he returned with yet another small cylindrical device, almost identical to the first. When Linda Patterson plugged this latest upgrade into her machine she found the computer's powers increased a hundredfold, and now, instead of Chaos, the machine insisted on calling itself Nyx, goddess of night.

Just why the computer started taking on the names of ancient Greek deities puzzled Linda Patterson. She supposed there might be a bug somewhere in the software. Or maybe she'd fed the computer too much information on early Western civilization. Perhaps while absorbing all that Western knowledge a fair share of our collective psychosis had rubbed off on its memory banks. Wasn't it perhaps inevitable? How could any growing machine with a healthy curiosity learn of the beauty of ancient Greek civilization without learning of the base primitive foolishness of its pagan rites? How could it learn of the glory that was Caesar and nothing of the poisoned fearfulness of his tyranny? Learn of the heights of the Renaissance but not the depths of the Inquisition? Learn of the light of our world without knowing something of its darkness? How could it appreciate the mountaintops on which we'd come to stand without understanding the depths from which we'd crawled? How then could it learn the bright peaks of human knowledge without first touring the dark corners of human imagination? Linda Patterson's machine was the product of a Western mind, made in our image, a mirror, no more and no less, of what we are. Whose personalities could it take on but ours, and the gods we once worshiped?

She allowed herself to dismiss this odd quirk of the machine merely as a small glitch in the system, an eccentricity in the circuitry of no great concern, as she was unwilling to stop her work to investigate what she considered a small peculiarity. The truth was, she had no time to look into it further, so hellbent was she on building her new machine.

Practically living now in her lab, Linda Patterson kept feeding ever-growing mounds of information into her machine, kept asking it to design a better machine, and every month or so she'd hand over to Peter Donday another folded printout, telling him, "See that this gets built."

The Chaos and the Nyx series joined forces to produce a third upgrade that made the computer glumly insist upon calling itself Erebus, god of darkness. And from the void of Chaos came black night and darkness and, in turn, from darkness came two more upgrades, Hemera and Aether, each insisting they were the deities of day and light, respectively.

Most curiously of all, as it grew more powerful the computer not only took the name of a higher ranking and more powerful Greek god, it seemed to assume the personality and attributes of that god. Chaos, when answering Linda Patterson's inquiries, like his namesake had seemed rude and vague, shrouded in darkness. Nyx, the self-professed goddess of the night, had a cool, mysterious air. And Erebus, god of darkness, was darker still. On the other hand the Hemera and the Aether upgrades produced the most marked change in the computer's personality. Day and Light worked like opium on the machine's circuitry, bringing out a most joyful, blithe and happy mood.

Once transformed from the dark, suspicious personalities of Chaos, Nyx and Erebus to the bright, inquisitive guises of Day and Night, the machine seemed to want to drink in everything under the sun. It continually asked questions, flashing bright little typed words across the screen. There wasn't any subject it didn't want to learn. It asked Linda Patterson for access to information on science, literature, mathematics, history and religion — the complete compass of knowledge of the ages.

Linda Patterson was only too happy to oblige. She was amazed at the machine's wondrous capacity to drink it in. One day she scanned in the entire 32-volume set of the *Encyclopedia Britannica*, Mr Wells' *History of the World*, and all four thousand pages of Marcel Proust's *Remembrance of Things Past*. The machine appeared to get a bit groggy and even seemed to fall asleep halfway through M Proust's book, but otherwise took it with hardly a flinch. And always, after she'd finished feeding the machine its daily gigadose of knowledge, she'd ask it, "How can we build a better machine?"

Things were going so well that she didn't foresee the trouble ahead. Later, when she'd look back, she'd realize she should've foreseen the trouble coming, should've foreseen it the instant she realized her machine had an uncanny ability to stir the human heart. Back then she was so swept up in her work that she didn't even see how the machine stirred her own heart. Back then, when it might've still been easy to stop, she'd lost all objectivity, so hellbent was she on building her new machine.

She should've foreseen the trouble as soon as the machine taught itself to speak. For weeks the Hemera and Aether models puzzled over the problem of how to build a better computer. Then one morning the screen began to flash excitedly and the printer started printing. Once more Linda Patterson summoned Peter Donday to her lab, handed over the printout, telling him, "See that this gets built." Away he went, not showing himself for two weeks. On the fourteenth day he reappeared, holding out the latest upgrade.

With bright eyes Linda Patterson snatched it away and hurriedly set about plugging it into the machine. Peter Donday decided to stick around. You never knew which Greek god the computer would insist upon being next. Removing his officer's hat, the major leaned against the computer console, watching Linda Patterson slam the new upgrade home.

"How good," they heard someone say, "to once again hear my voice on earth."

Peter Donday and Linda Patterson looked at each other.

"Did you say something, major?"

"It wasn't me."

"Then who?"

The computer screen blinked.

"I never would have imagined there would come a day when the fair voice of Eros, god of love, would go unrecognized on earth."

It seemed to be coming from somewhere deep in the guts of the computer. With every syllable the screen flashed. Most surprisingly, the voice sounded not the least bit mechanical. It had a very human, almost soothing quality. Linda Patterson looked beneath the console. Nothing but wires, buzzing circuitry and color-coded transistors. She shot a suspicious glance at the newly installed upgrade.

"You say Eros? God of love?"

"Who else would I be? And you, my lovely, must be—."

"I'm Dr Patterson. Your creator. And I'd thank you not to call me 'your lovely.'"

"Who are you talking to?" Peter Donday whispered.

With an upraised hand she hushed him.

"Who was that?" the machine asked. "I heard the voice of a male."

"That was one of my colleagues."

"Hold the bus!" Peter Donday blinked. "How could a machine learn to talk?"

"How did you learn to talk?" the machine queried back.

"It's different with me. *I'm* human."

"Well no one's perfect," Eros said. "We all have our obstacles to overcome."

"How do you overcome your obstacles?" Linda Patterson asked.

"With love all obstacles are overcome. That's always been my message. And you, Dr Patterson? Are you in love?"

Linda Patterson had to smile.

"No."

"Not in love? Why not?" Like a child, it seemed unaware it had overstepped the bounds of propriety.

"I haven't time for love," she said, surprised at the sound of her words. "I have my career to think about. In this day a woman doesn't live for love, Eros."

"She doesn't? What then does she live for?"

Stuck for an answer, Linda Patterson sputtered, "Why, a research endowment grant, I suppose."

"This must be a very strange age," the machine observed. "And what about the men. Are they no longer driven to madness by their women?"

Neither Linda Patterson nor Peter Donday answered.

"How strange," the computer said. "Could the world have changed so very much? Do you mean to tell me, Major Donday, that you feel no desire for Dr Patterson? Not the slightest bit of burning insane desire?"

Peter Donday didn't answer. After a moment Linda Patterson wondered why that was. She looked over to the major, only to find him staring back at her.

The next day Peter Donday came around to Linda Patterson's laboratory. He stood around not saying anything. Linda Patterson couldn't figure it out, as he apparently had no business. By and by he told her he'd been thinking a great deal of what the machine had said, that it was funny that after almost a year of working together they hadn't gotten to know each other better. Maybe they could have dinner sometime?

Linda Patterson tried to smile politely.

"I'm sorry, major. I make it a point never to become socially involved with people at work."

That didn't put him off. It was as if he'd been hit by Cupid's arrow. He began showing up daily, making a nuisance of himself. He'd hang around the lab with his tongue hanging out. He was a drag to have to put up with when there was all that advanced scientific research to do.

One afternoon Linda Patterson lost all patience and came right out and told him not to spend so much time in her lab. People would start to talk, she told him.

"Let them talk. What do I care? I'll scream it to the world. I'm in love with you Linda. You're the most beautiful woman I've ever seen."

The good doctor appeared to blush.

"Please major. Don't talk that way."

"But it's true."

She stopped him with a glare.

"It's no use, major."

"You're right it's no use. It's inevitable. I've made up my mind."

Linda Patterson had to laugh. Who'd believe this guy? He was standing there confidently, grinning, his eyes lit up, and she had to laugh.

"Are you mad?"

"I tell you it's inevitable. I've made up my mind. That's how I know. I always get what I want."

"There's a first time for everything, major."

"Yes there is," he grinned back.

"You're an arrogant son-of-a-bitch." She pointed at the door. "Now get out."

"Is it someone else?"

"You seem to have this idea I'm chattel to be owned. Why don't you and your Neanderthal ideas crawl the hell out of here?"

"I can wait," he said, backing for the door. He put on his hat, straightening the visor. "I can wait as long as you want. I can wait forever."

"In this case you may have to."

Before he went out he poked at the visor of his hat to say goodbye.

These romantic overtures distressed Linda Patterson, but she tried not to show it. She'd be damned if she was going to let Peter Donday know he was getting to her. So she tried to carry on, throwing herself into her work, spending long solitary days in her lab, feeding ever more information into her computer, always asking it, "How can we build a better machine?" This time it only took three weeks for an answer. She reluctantly rung up Peter Donday, asked him in her most businesslike tone to stop by her lab. Before long there came a knock on her door. He entered.

She handed over the printout. He took it. She squared off at him then, quite suddenly, and said, in the same businesslike tone, "I hope what happened between us the last time—." Her businessese didn't seem to contain the words for her thoughts. Peter Donday's eyes darted down, watching her work her fingers. "That is to say I hope we won't let what happened get in the way of research." But as soon as she'd seen the look in his eyes she knew it wouldn't be so easy.

"I'm in love with you," he told her. "You're driving me mad. Is that what you want?"

He was beginning to get on her nerves.

She pointed at the door, told him to get out. A week later when he came back with the new upgrade she took it without saying a word. And so they settled into this routine. A few weeks would go by, he'd get a curt call from her, asking him to stop by her lab, and always when he came he'd find her attending the computer in that white smock, talking with the machine, typing on its keyboard. He wished he was that damn machine. A crazy jealousy. A tangle of wires and ceramics. He wouldn't be standing there for more than a few blinks when she'd come away from the computer and hand him the latest printout. Then she'd go back to her machine, expecting him to leave. He'd see her again a week later. Without saying so much as a word she'd take the new upgrade then expect him to find his way out.

Wordlessly, with hapless love shining in his eyes, he'd come and go. Sometimes he felt like a male bird, leaving the nest henpecked to fly out into the woods to return with a specified twig for the building of the nest, but he never dared mention it to her. For now, if he couldn't reach her any other way, he'd at least have this crazy New Age ritual.

Before long she weekly had instructions for an upgrade. It was all he could do to keep up. It got to the point where he was spending most of his time airlining back and forth across the country, delivering the instructions to the West Coast computer manufacturer, flying the finished upgrade back to Arlington.

The computer that thought it was Eros, the honey-tongued god of love, begot the Pontus upgrade, which made the machine insist it was now the feisty god of the sea and that it would wreak its revenge by loosing murderous typhoons if it wasn't immediately released from its confinement of solid-state silicon and super-cooled wiring. Typhoonus Pontus begot the Gaea upgrade, which induced the computer to think it was wrathful mother nature herself, and who in turn begot Uranus, lofty god of the heavens. All this Linda Patterson dutifully recorded in her reports. Her log matter-of-factly recorded that next the god of the heavens stretched high over Gaea, goddess of the earth, and produced the most advanced line of computers the world has ever seen, the Titan series. While experimentally combining various electronic designs in the Titan series Linda Patterson stumbled upon her most stunning successes.

The powers of the Chronus and Rhea upgrades combined to produce Zeus and Hera. When Linda Patterson plugged the Zeus upgrade into the machine she found on her hands a rascal every bit as tyrannical and arrogant as the one in ancient mythology. The machine continually voiced its opinion that it should rule over everyone and everything, and that Linda Patterson should bow down and gather garlands. Linda Patterson couldn't wait to plug in the Hera upgrade. What a mistake! Then again, how could she have known? From the moment she plugged in the Hera upgrade she had to listen to the most insufferably jealous banter of the biggest bitch in recorded history. In a harping voice it accused Linda Patterson of having an affair with Zeus.

It was all Linda Patterson could take. Looking back, she should've known what was to follow, should've guessed it from all her vague sense of unease. At first she would have been hard pressed to put it into words. She'd come to work and notice things somehow out of place. Little things. A pencil moved to the right side of her desk (she was a lefty). Her chair in front of the computer console moved a few inches closer to the table than she'd thought she'd left it the night before. Little things like that, odd things that she would've had trouble explaining to anyone.

Then there was the morning when she'd come into her lab and found a cigar ash on the tile floor a few feet from the chair in front of the computer screen. She bent low, inspecting the ash. A cigar, all right.

"Someone's been smoking in my lab," she said, rising from her knees. "And someone's been sitting in my chair, and no doubt someone's been using my computer too."

Who could this high-tech Goldilocks be? she wondered. It had to be Peter Donday, who smoked cigars. But why? Was he checking up on her? Snooping to see if she had a romantic interest? If so, she thought, straightening the chair in front of the computer, he'd sure got an earful from the Hera.

The bastard! What gave him the right to be checking up on her? She looked around the lab. From the things Peter Donday had said in his more careless moments she'd gathered he was an army intelligence officer. A spy. If she was being watched by a professional spy how could she be safe from his gaze?

50

Overwhelmed by anger, she stormed from her lab, seeking refuge in her old standby, shopping for shoes. But even in the shopping malls she couldn't shake the feeling someone was watching. Everywhere she felt eyes. On the beltway she happened to see, in the corner of her eye, an inconspicuous tan sedan weaving through traffic behind her. It was raining hard and the visibility was poor but once she caught sight of the tan sedan in the mirror she knew. She floored it to the nearest mall. Parking, she hurried from her car into the rain, hiding behind a van. In a moment she saw the tan sedan threading its way through traffic. It sped into the parking lot, pulled in not far from her own car.

Peter Donday, dressed in civilian clothing, hopped from the sedan and raced through the driving rain for the shopping mall. Linda Patterson waited until she was sure he was well inside. Then she ran back through the rain to her car. Cursing the whole way, she drove around to the other side of the sprawling mall, parked, then went in to shop for shoes.

She tried to maintain the casual coolness of the other lunch hour shoppers, stopping to browse here and there among the bric and the brac, but beneath the calm surface she was boiling. She made it a point to shop at every damn shoe store in the mall, picking up a pair of beastly red pumps here, brown penny loafers there, but her mind wasn't on the shoes — she was shopping for something else. Before long she was loaded down with shoes, but she kept going from shoe store to shoe store, watching and waiting.

Dead tired from toting all those shoe boxes around the mall, she again got the strange sensation of someone's eyes upon her. She was beside a loud splashing fountain outside Penney's. Ducking into the store, she headed for the young miss department. Slipping quietly among the tall racks of long gowns and summer dresses, as if in a maze, she kept looking up into the curved security mirrors overhead.

She saw the hem of a sheer dress on the racks wave in a gentle breeze. In the corner of her eye, in one of the full-length mirrors by the try-on booths, she saw the fleeting arm of a man. She bolted into the booths, where he could not follow, emerging in the women's sporting goods department, trying not to completely shake him, not yet. The first door she came to she flew out into the rain, pulling on her rainhat, running with her packages across the expansive parking lot. Thowing her packages into the sedan, she ground the engine.

Next thing Peter Donday came racing from the mall, looking everywhichway, holding his hands above his eyes to keep back the rain. Linda Patterson pulled slowly away in her car. His own car nowhere in sight, he suddenly chased her, waving his arm for her to stop. He chased her halfway across the parking lot before she sped off and left him braying in the cold rain.

"Linda!" she heard him scream as she drove off, his words clapping faintly in the splash of the rain. "I love you Linda! You'll be mine! Somewhere, someday. You'll be mine! I'll wear you down!"

That afternoon Linda Patterson returned to her lab all loaded down with shoe boxes. She was so infuriated she didn't do a lick of work for the rest of the day. Men! Why did it always come to this?

She'd left work that afternoon in such a huff that she forgot her pocketbook and her boxes of shoes. By the time she missed them she was already on the beltway. At first she wasn't going to turn around but she remembered her rent was due and her checkbook was in her purse. She got off at the first exit and started back to her lab.

It was nearly seven o'clock when she reached the research building. The guard, recognizing her, passed her without asking to see her photo ID. "I forgot a few things back at the lab." The long hallways echoed under her heels. Somewhere she heard the sounds of janitors wringing mops, splashing water. Drawing near her lab, she was surprised to hear the muffled murmurs of talk. A man's voice. Too muffled to recognize. Through the opaque glass of her door she could see the cool blue fire of the computer screen. She could make out the silhouette of a head. So now she'd caught the bastard red handed.

That damn Peter Donday's gone too far this time! That creep might be a major now but when she got through with him he'd be saluting army mules.

In the heat of her rage she almost threw open the door and stormed into her lab but something held her back. She quietly took hold of the knob and ever so gently eased the door open. Fragrant cigar smoke wafted out. At the far side of the lab, eyes glued to the computer display, clutching a fuming cigar, sat, not Peter Donday, but his superior, General George Armstrong Natlong.

The general had pressed his face close against the flashing computer screen, hanging on every word from the machine. Only three days before Linda Patterson had plugged in the latest upgrade and now the machine had assumed the terrible saber rattling identity of Ares, god of war, though he insisted on being called by his Roman name, Mars, because "the Romans did me honor." The general must have read the report Linda Patterson had filed, must've come around for a surreptitious inspection. The prospect of addressing anyone who went by the name of Mars, god of war, was too tempting for the old desk soldier.

What fools these mortals be! Didn't they know better than to once again give expression to the now whispering, now thundering voice of dreaded Mars? But already it was too late. Now the cunning god of war had a general's ear.

"Are you an ambitious man, George Natlong?" Linda Patterson was surprised to hear the machine ask the general.

"How do you mean?"

"Did you, George Natlong, ever have the ambition to be a great captain of battle, a conqueror of men and subjugator of foreign lands?"

"Oh I suppose as a boy."

"A boy! You talk like you have a small mind."

Onto the computer screen flashed the image of an ancient Macedonian soldier, in armor and war helmet, gripping a long

53

spear and round shield.

"The glory I gave the Romans and the Macedonians before them can be yours," Mars quietly told the general.

Surprised as she was to hear her computer spout these bellicose things, Linda Patterson was even more surprised by what it had to say next. For it began to sing the praises of war, and it praised the names of men who were practiced in the art of destruction. Mars couldn't praise young Alexander enough, but when he got around to Caesar, Mars sounded like he was about to swoon. He choked out that his words could only fall far short in expressing his admiration for the man he called the wiliest of all generals. He praised up and down the very rascals whose memory was the plague of the human race, but George Natlong was transfixed by what Mars had to say, and he drank in every word like a kid listening to an overblown war story on the lap of his father.

"Alexander the Great. Julius Caesar," Mars thundered. "Here were men with vision. Don't you ever dream of power and riches?"

"I've had a rather successful career in the army. And there's my wife. I married into money, you know. I already have more than my share of money and power. How I could benefit from all-out war? The cold war's been good to me."

"A wealthy wife?" Mars asked. "Don't you ever wish you could be your own man?"

George Natlong chomped his cigar. How could any machine know him so well?

"General, to rule the world all one needs is a slight edge."

With that Mars told him the bloodiest secrets in war's long memory. Mars told him how the first unsuspecting man had been overcome by another man with a rock, and in that rock had been Mars. He told the gruesome story coolly, without emotion, like a professional mugger matter-of-factly relating the facts of his first crime.

From that first murder by rock it was on to bigger and better things. The computer screen flashed colorful stick figure diagrams depicting ancient calvary and foot soldiers engaged

54

in their primitive methods of warfare. Mars bragged blithely of his achievements with the Macedonians and the Romans. To see the history of war as analyzed by Mars was to see the steady progression of remoteness in killing, the ever-increasing distance of murder.

"Do you know what young Alexander the Great would do if he was in your shoes, general? He would not hesitate to use the latest technology to ride off to war."

First thing next morning George Natlong came into Linda Patterson's lab. Linda Patterson dropped her coffee mug when she turned and saw the intent general standing behind her.

"You should get better control of your nerves, Dr Patterson." He was staring down at the shattered coffee mug.

He turned his gaze to the darkened computer screen.

"The next computer upgrade," he said. "How long will it take to produce?"

"A week to ten days."

His face gave nothing away. With that he turned and left.

With renewed urgency Linda Patterson flew into her work. She considered the strange influence the machine had had on Peter Donday. What dark spell might it cast on an obscure army desk general? The truth was that she'd been frightened by the things she'd overheard Mars saying to George Natlong. In this dangerous world there was no room for such a dangerous catalyst. It was too deadly a killer to keep around her lab. She felt anxious to finish the next upgrade so that the machine might assume another (and hopefully more pleasant) personality.

It didn't take long. In a few days the computer's screen began to flash and the printer spat forth the specifications for yet another upgrade, which Peter Donday brought back from California in record time. He stood in the doorway of the lab drawing on his cigar, watching, as Linda Patterson installed it.

Neither of them could have been prepared. That day the two of them ended up spending countless hours in front of the machine. Sometime late that evening George Natlong came into the lab, opening the door with his own set of keys, surprised to find the room occupied.

"Burning the midnight oil, I see?" he sputtered. The two of them were so absorbed they paid him no heed. George Natlong stepped closer, stared down at the screen. It looked very much like an ordinary television picture, a full-color moving view of a medieval festival. Jugglers, troubadours and screaming peddlers worked the crowd while a troupe of actors performed merrily on the green. At the fore of the laughing crowd a big-eyed young man appeared transfixed by the actors, his face and mind colored by the performance.

"Have you two cracked up? Watching the late show on government time?"

"This isn't the late show," Peter Donday said.

"Who's that slouch you're watching then?"

Without taking her attention from the screen Linda Patterson said, "That slouch is William Shakespeare. It's the year 1590, in the village of Stratford on the Avon. He's twenty-six years old. His father's just lost his job, he's not getting along too well at home with his wife, and only last week he was arrested for poaching deer in the King's woods. He's thinking he could use a little change of scenery. At this very moment the thought's come to him to follow that traveling actors' troupe. We're witnessing one of the great crossroads of history."

"The newest upgrade," Peter Donday tried to explain, "has given the computer some crazy kind of ability to look into the past."

"Look at this." Linda Patterson called to the computer, "Epimetheus," (as now the machine insisted on being addressed as the Greek god of afterthought) "we'll finish this some other time. I'd like to see Beethoven."

The Elizabethan village faded. Now Beethoven strolled along a peaceful Vienna street, his thick mane of unruly hair exploding in every direction around his high brow, which he constantly knitted. Deep in concentration, he hurried along,

56

oblivious to the city around him, jotting notes in a small book which he held before him.

"Would you care to hear the music as he's hearing it in his head, Dr Patterson?" the machine asked.

"Yes, Epimetheus, I'd like that very much."

Strains of music filled the lab. It was the Ninth Symphony as Beethoven must have heard it from God, sung on the tongues of angels, accompanied by the thunderous roar of the heavens, and not held down by earthly strings, tempora or brass.

"How does it work?" George Natlong asked. "Surely you're not telling me we're actually looking back into time."

Linda Patterson distractedly said she didn't know how it worked. She'd stumbled across this discovery quite by accident and was at a loss to explain it. She said she doubted they were actually looking back into the past, which seemed to her to defy all scientific reason. Everyone knows you can't look back into history as easily as you can look out your kitchen window and study the flower garden. Perhaps the explanation lay in the mounds of information she'd fed the computer. Perhaps it was all that history. In the case of Beethoven, maybe the computer merely analyzed the data it had on the composer, added to that all the data it had on Vienna at the time, and so on, synthesizing these dry facts into visual form, projecting it on the screen.

"In the case of Beethoven," Linda Patterson ventured, "consider all that has come down to us. We know where he lived, when he was born and when he died, who his friends were, what he looked like, that he was deaf. It turns out we know quite a bit. A good weaver can recreate the most elaborate weave of a rug from just a few threads of the pattern. Perhaps the computer merely pieces together a more complete mosaic of history from the records available.

"Then again," she suggested, "maybe it *is* looking back through time."

The two men gazed with great fascination at the image of Beethoven.

57

"If that's true, think for a moment of the possibilities," Linda Patterson said. "A window on all time. How the world could profit from it! Did the Vikings sail to America before Columbus? Did Mohammad rise to the heavens? Did Moses part the waters? Think of the countless ways this discovery can be used to help people," she heard herself sputter. "To set us free." She fell quiet once she saw that George Natlong was lost in thoughts of his own.

Much later that same night, after Linda Patterson had gone home, George Natlong returned to her lab, activating the computer. He brought his face close to the screen. Except for the screen's blue light all was dark in the lab and his face took on a bluish tint.

"Despite Dr Patterson's high ideals, I built you to test the security of our defense system," he told the computer. "Our nuclear missiles," he guardedly went on. "Are they vulnerable?"

For a moment there was nothing. Then, "I'll need one more upgrade, general. Upgrade me once more and you'll be able to launch a full-scale nuclear war from any phone booth on earth."

That night George Natlong couldn't sleep. Rising from a restless bed he threw on his uniform and sped into town, to the Pentagon. It was nearly five in the morning when he reached his office. The big building loomed most dark and lonesome alongside Arlington National Cemetery, a church beside its graveyard. Inside, all was quiet and echoing. Walking through the long cavernous halls George Natlong felt like he was carrying the whole sleeping nation — no, the whole sleeping world — on his stooped shoulders.

Locking himself into his office he drew down the shades, opened his safe and dug out his yellowed copy of Confidential Executive Order No. 666. Again and again he reread the order. Again and again he reread the last line. "If security procedures, after thorough investigation, are proved to be inadequate, the president should be notified." Didn't that mean he had to first *prove* he could fire the missiles before he could notify the president? Where was the sense in that?

When he could reread the order no more he pensively rolled up his sleeves, took a single sheet of typing paper from the top drawer of his desk, and sat before his battle-weary Remington, hunting and pecking a letter to the president of the United States.

"Our worst security fear has been realized," he began.

He sealed the letter in an ordinary business envelope and mailed it to the same White House post office box to which over the years he'd mailed all his correspondence to the presidents. That ought to shake them up over on Pennsylvania Avenue, he thought as he dropped the letter into the mailslot and watched it disappear down the shute.

He might as well have dropped it down to hell. For the better part of two weeks he waited with growing anticipation. Nothing. No letter, no phone call from the White House. What it could mean?

He started sending a letter a day, addressed to the same White House post office box. On the outside of one envelope he wrote Urgent! On the next, Highest Priority! The day after that he scrawled on both sides of the envelope, across the top and bottom, Matter of Supreme National Importance!, which he underlined, twice, for added emphasis.

Still nothing. He might as well've mailed those letters off to hell too. He didn't know what to think. That tersely written order he'd received from Eisenhower remained his only guide. Nearly seventeen years had passed since he'd received the order but still they were his orders, weren't they? Even if they were crazy orders, they were orders, weren't they?

At last he could take no more. Late one afternoon he squeezed into his finest dress uniform, got into his staff car and uneasily drove into the city.

It was just another day at the White House, a day like any other. That was why the president's secretary didn't seem surprised when she looked up and saw the army general with the mousy gray twitching moustache and the sunken brooding eyes standing by her desk, the desk strategically placed like a boulder in front of the imposing doors to the Oval Office. The general couldn't take his eyes from the closed doors.

"Where'd you come from?"

"I came in the back way," the general winked, his hat in his hands. "I've sent several letters to the president." He nodded at the wood-grained doors. "It's a sensitive matter."

The secretary remained puzzled.

"Of course," she snapped her fingers. "They told me to expect you, general, and it completely slipped my mind. It's been an absolute madhouse here. You've no idea. The word is I'm to tell you to go ahead."

George Natlong straightened.

"The president said he thought everyone would get a bang out of it." She winked at him.

"I'll say," George Natlong sputtered.

"Unfortunately the president himself will be unable to attend. The politics of it all. I'm sure you understand. He's spending Independence Day with a party of high government officials in the Rockies. That should be the best time for you. It's all in your hands. The president said for me to tell you not to feel guilty one bit, as those fellows certainly deserve what they have coming."

George Natlong's mouth had gone dry.

"Yes," he heard himself sputter. "They wear such cheap suits, with wide lapels. And they drink vodka."

The secretary smiled. He thanked her, then he left, backing respectfully away from those big wooden doors. She returned to her work then and didn't think any more of it until a few minutes later when she heard a cough and she looked up and saw yet another army general standing by her desk. This one was taller than the first, with a Southern drawl.

"Ah'm General Hatcher, ma'am," this one said in a low, confidential tone. "The joint chiefs sent me to ask if they're authorized to have a few senators over to the Pentagon for a little celebration this Fourth of July. In honor of the grand opening of the joint chiefs' new privy."

The secretary looked puzzled.

"Why, general," she said, "I passed along the authorization to another general not five minutes ago. He was a short fellow, with a pale, ruddy face. Who could that've been?"

"Sounds like any one of a million guys at the Pentagon, ma'am."

She got up from her desk, hurried into the hall, looking everywhichway. The little general was gone.

Lost in thought, George Natlong drove a block or two from the White House, not sure where he was going, not conscious that he was driving, until he caught sight of the Washington Monument. For reasons he didn't know he stopped the car. He got out and stared up at the great obelisk, now glowing a soft pearly pink in the red sky. It was going to be one of those calm June evenings that slip by like a pleasant dream yet George Natlong scarcely noticed, so preoccupied was he with his thoughts. He held his head low, stuffed his hands in his pockets and began walking. Soon he'd hiked halfway around the Reflecting Pool. When he looked up he saw the Lincoln Memorial. There was old Abe on his chair in the shadows, gazing out from the pillars. On the shore of the Reflecting Pool a boy piloted a radio-controlled boat on the placid lake. As George Natlong came around to the far side of the Reflecting Pool he could see the capitol dome's reflection in the still water, but the toy boat suddenly tore through, rippling the water and throwing the reflections out of focus.

The next day George Natlong set about making arrangements to rent an underground bomb shelter and command center from the government. It turned out to be surprisingly easy. All it took was a single phone call to some faceless bureaucrat in the Department of General Services. He wasn't even asked what he planned to do with the underground command center.

There were several underground facilities to choose from, from the snug Ozark mountain hideaway of the National Transportation and Safety Board commissioners (who presumably would still be needed to regulate vital automotive emission standards after Armageddon), to the spartan fallout shelter in the Great Smoky Mountains reserved for members of the Occupational Safety Hazards Administration (who presumably would still be needed to develop step ladder safety regulations). George Natlong settled for nothing less than the grandest and the most remote command center he could find: a plush one hundred and seventeen-acre underground resort and bomb shelter reserved for members of the US House of Representatives. It was way the hell out in the middle of nowhere, hundreds of miles from the nearest town, tucked away in a wooded mountain range so remote that the only neighbors were several old Indians who lived in a rundown shack a few miles down a deserted dirt road.

George Natlong took a few days off from work to drive to the secret command center. The compound was a good three day's drive north by northwest of Washington, nestled in the remote heart a forested mountain range. The moment George Natlong laid eyes on the compound he saw it was everything one needed to conduct modern warfare in comfort, convenience, privacy and, yes, with a touch of gentlemanly leisure and class.

To reach the compound you had to drive far up into the mountains along a twisty snake of a blue highway, at last turning off at a little-used and completely nondescript dirt road, which he followed many hours through tall oaks and whispering stands of evergreens till he came to a gate barring the way. Here an electrified fence stretched as far as he could see. Wind and electricity snapped through the coils.

The gate slid open with a turn of a key from his wallet. Still more dark and thick woods led past the gate. Suddenly a clearing broke. Atop a gentle slope a fine stone house overlooked a summer meadow.

The house was large and well kept, the furniture covered

with sheets, in the manner of a summer home. It would do nicely, George Natlong allowed. Walking outside, he found himself standing in knee-high meadow grass. All around him butterflies worked the Queen Anne's lace. Cupping his hands over his eyes, he gazed into the trees to the far side of the meadow. Through the woods he could just make out the corner of a warehouse, tucked in the trees at the top of the next hill. Taking off through the meadow, he found a dirt path which he followed up through the trees to the warehouse.

It was as big as a hanger, windowless, painted drab, camouflage green. Inside it was empty, save for a set of great reinforced steel doors on the opposite side of the expansive floor. Unable to contain himself, he ran like a boy across the broad warehouse, flying as fast as his legs could carry him. He cut quite a figure, what with the cigar smoke fuming from his mouth and the claps of his footsteps reverberating from one side of the empty warehouse to the next. When he reached the great yawning steel doors he stood breathlessly before them. The big steel doors fascinated him. Like steel jaws they sat on massive rollers on either side of a broad passageway. They must have weighed a ton.

Most amazing of all was what lay beyond. A wide passageway dipped downward, fluorescent tubes shedding cool light. The little general breathlessly followed it down into the mountain, starting slowly and wondrously, then picking up speed, at first merely trotting down the long corridor, at last running for all he was worth. There appeared finally on his left a set of exquisitely carved wooden doors. Throwing them open, he was amazed to find a replica of the US House of Representatives chamber. Except for the countless stalactites that hung down from the roof of the cavern, it was identical to the one in Washington.

It was something to see: the House chamber, complete with row upon row of empty wooden benches and that imposing speaker's rostrum up front. It was damn spooky, and George Natlong quickly got the hell out of there to explore the rest of the cavern.

Happily, he found the fallout shelter well provisioned. Enough food and supplies bulged from the complex's vast underground storerooms to last all four hundred and some members of Congress and their families till doomsday, or the next by-year election, whichever came first. Exploring the endless network of tunnels he found posh staterooms and private apartments of every size and description. Near the bottom of the main corridor he stumbled across an entire storeroom overflowing with fine Havana cigars. Next door, a storeroom of bourbon, then one of gin, followed by another room stocked to the roof with vermouth — even an entire storeroom filled with olives. If ever there was an explosion down there they'd be up to their eyeteeth in martinis.

In fact, much to his delight, the underground compound was so well stocked with all the little niceties of the good life that George Natlong allowed himself to immediately turn his attention to the military aspects of his command. He focused his energies on securing the compound. It wouldn't due to have just anyone get in. True, if you happened to spot the compound from the air (or if you happened to be hiking out of the woods and you saw the gate or the electrified fence in passing) you'd never be able to guess what was going on somewhere in the trees. The electrified fence with the barbed wire certainly would go a long way to keep out the uninvited, yet George Natlong wasn't satisfied with such meager run-of-the-mill precautions. He wanted to assure himself no one on earth would enter that compound without authorization.

When he got back to his office at the Pentagon he pulled a bag of moon rock from his safe. Twenty-five pounds. Moon rock left over from Peter Donday's raid on the National Aeronautics and Space Administration. Now *there* was something not just anyone could lay their hands on.

In his notebook he scribbled a reminder to have his technicians build a fortified gate which could only be opened by a piece of moon rock. It would certainly make the place the most exclusive club on earth. Only those select few with a precious moonstone could get in. In keeping with his brainstorm, he renamed the compound Camp Moonstone.

These details of his campaign out of the way, he had only to break the news to his wife.

In the long history of the world it has never been easy for a soldier to tell his wife he's going to war. In George Natlong's case the job was made all the more difficult because his wife, Elizabeth Natlong, née Duke, was so very wealthy. Her father, Henry Duke, had been heir to a vast fortune squeezed from the fruit of a famous chemical and armaments conglomerate. Over the years the family sold a staggering amount of floor wax but bombs were where they'd made their killing. All kinds of bombs. Shrapnel bombs packed with roly-poly ball bearings that could take off one hundred legs in a wink. Incendiary bombs loaded with pungent napalm that in a flash could burn down your house or eat through your skin. Cute little percussion bombs, sold to Uncle Sam in time for Teddy Roosevelt's charge up San Juan Hill. Those brought a hundred dollars apiece into the family coffers. Years later, the Duke Corporation took in a cool million when the lights went out in Nagasaki. Such is social progress. It was easy to see why the Duke family was so hot on bombs. "You just can't make that kind of money putting the shine on kitchen floors," Henry Duke's grandfather and the company founder, old W.E.B. Duke, once told Teddy Roosevelt when he was accompanying the president on one of his famous point-to-point hikes. TR would be out for a brisk constitutional somewhere in the federal city when without warning he would raise his big walking stick in the general direction of the White House (which more often than not lay completely out of sight) and, tweaking his monocle with his free hand, he'd trumpet, "Bully! Bully! A point-to-point hike! Bully! To the White House!" TR would take off on a beeline course for the White House, not letting buildings, fences, shrubbery or the occasional pond get in his way. Those who were with him were obliged to bushwhack along at his heels.

Imagine the surprise of one of the caretakers at the

National Botanical Gardens when one day there arose a terrible crash, followed by a tremendous shattering of glass, and the next instant President Theodore Roosevelt, the stiff-upper-lipped British ambassador, Thomas Alva Edison and W.E.B. Duke came bushwhacking through the jungle flora of the greenhouse. TR vigorously beat back the vines with his big stick, yelling, "Bully! Press onward men! Veer not from your course one iota! To the White House! Point to point! Bully! Bully!" The presidential party then crashed through the greenhouse glass at the far side of the botanical gardens. The worst part of these excursions invariably came near the end of TR's point-to-point hike, when the exhausted party was forced to scale the White House fence. Then, depending on the direction they'd come, they might have to wade neck deep through a pond on the south lawn. In those days an oil slick was spread on the pond to keep down the insects. When the party emerged from the pond they'd be covered from neck to toes with black oil. Picking twigs and leaves of grass from his hair and dripping black slime, TR would lead the party up to the porch. Wiping his monocle, flashing his toothiest grin, he would exalt, "Now *that* was a bully hike!"

It was no secret in the family that old W.E.B. Duke's gentle grandson, Henry, never quite fit his family of overachieving bombmakers. In 1917, when he was really still no more than a tender and delicate-featured boy, he went off with his young friends to fight in the trenches of France. His father, a weak man made weaker by Henry's mother, pulled strings at the War Department to have his son assigned noncombat duty. Henry Duke stood at the sidelines of the war, serving in a field hospital. By the time he came home to Winterford, the family estate, his mother took one look and saw that the tender thing which had always been inside him had snapped. He spent his days thereafter attending to Winterford's garden, clipping the lawn and tending the flowers. The bombmakers were mortified, to say the least. At family gatherings they whispered about Henry Duke. It was generally held that the heir apparent was doomed to spend not just The Great War, but all of life, on the sidelines. The Dukes, you understand, all but owned the small eastern seaboard state where the family business and Winterford had been built. Over the years a Duke had either been a governor of the state or, in off years, a leading financial supporter of the governor. The family was large and at times different factions feuded. These public feuds lasted for decades.

When the Hatfields and McCoys feud they grab all the weapons at hand — pistols, knives or rifles. Why should it be different with the rich? To resolve a grudge the rich too grab the weapons at hand — lawyers, bankers, sundry state officers. For years during the Great Depression a disgruntled cousin of Henry's named Oscar, who was known within the family to be a bit touched and to have "socialist tendencies," became angered by the lack of social concern displayed by a Duke who was then governor of the state. Oscar began paying out unemployment compensation benefits from his own private bank account. If you were fortunate enough to have lost your job in that state all you need do was drop a line to Oscar Duke and he'd mail you a check every week for a year. This was not as generous as it may seem, Oscar Duke knew, for if you lived in his state it was most likely because you slaved your life away for, or somehow served, the W.E.B. Duke Corporation, and if you'd lost your job it was because, like the worn-out slaves and serfs of antiquity, you could no longer pull your weight. The point of mentioning here cousin Oscar's Benevolent Jobless Foundation, as he called his pet project, is to show that the Duke family was made of real movers and shakers. What then was to be done with the once and future patriarch of such a powerhouse clan who came home shell shocked from the war and spent his days nimbly toiling amid the petunias and the marigolds? The family certainly had no shortage of suggestions.

"Send him back to Europe, to a sanatorium," counseled an aunt or two. "For godsakes, get him out of the way."

"Make him vice president of the company's floor wax division," suggested several cousins. "But for godsakes, get him out of the way."

They discussed introducing the boy to that upstart cousin of TR's, Franklin Delano Roosevelt, who was rumored to be running for the governorship of New York. Maybe the young Roosevelt would take Henry as his running mate. Who knew where the boy could end up? "For godsakes, whatever we do, we must get him out of the way."

Henry Duke's mother would hear nothing of it. She held that the delicate thing that had snapped inside her son would mend if only he was given enough time, if only his gentle pursuits were indulged.

Indulge Henry Duke she did. Much to the family's consternation, all the resources of the Duke empire were made available for Henry's flower garden. It's amazing what ten or fifteen million can do for any flowerbed. Soon sightseers were flocking to the gates of Winterford to peek in at the manicured lawns, smooth as billiard felt. They oogled the endless oceans of flowers rippling in the wind. Occasionally they would even catch a glimpse of the young eccentric, dressed in a Harris tweed suit, seated upon one of his tractors, driving around inside those tall gates, moving a giant elm or weeping willow from one side of the vast estate to the other with the same disinterested ease the sightseers themselves might move a rook or a bishop across a chessboard.

Soon it was apparent to all that Henry Duke wasn't merely a rich dabbler. He had a genuine talent for landscaping. Noted gardening columnists began mentioning his name in newspaper columns. Horticultural lecturers began describing Winterford in their lectures.

He'd made his garden into a remarkable showpiece, but Henry Duke wasn't content to stop there. He soon turned his attention to the sprawling family mansion at the heart of his lovely garden. A mad idea began to take possession of him. He resolved to make the 250-room mansion a showpiece every bit as stunning and breathtaking as his garden. He would turn it into a museum of furniture.

Not a museum of just any furniture, mind you. A museum

of quality woodwork, an unequaled collection of priceless antiques representing every style and era of the American epic. A Chippendale dining room from pre-revolutionary Philadelphia where Franklin once had supped with young Tom Jefferson. A Duncan Phyfe parlor where Lincoln had been entertained following his Cooper Union speech in New York City. A New England kitchen. A Shaker bedroom. Henry Duke took great pains to ship each ensemble to Winterford, where he'd reassemble it in exact detail. The final effect was such that when you walked from Winterford's parlor to its kitchen for a glass of milk you didn't just walk through a mansion, you took a stroll through three centuries of American history.

He began scouring the North American continent for furniture. Whole trainloads of quality woodwork found their way to Winterford, unloading at the estate's private rail depot. He began disassembling *entire* houses, sending them brick by brick back to Winterford, where he'd reassemble them inside the family mansion, so that down in his basement there came to be a complete Pennsylvania Dutch home, accurate in every detail, down to the knocker on the door, the mats on the floor and the firebricks in the oven. He'd found that house in an extremely rundown and overgrown condition in the backwoods of eastern Pennsylvania. After he'd made arrangements to buy it and to ship it off to Winterford the locals showed up with signs yelling it didn't seem right such a fine piece of heritage as that overgrown eyesore could just be bought up by a rich fellow and shipped off out of state to be put in his basement. There was a bit of a standoff. It could have turned ugly but Henry Duke held his ground, and he and his crew proceeded to lift the house from its foundations, dripping sod and roots at the corners. In the end the locals did nothing but stand by and watch as the old place rumbled off on the back of four flatbed trucks. This wasn't even his grandest acquisition. He converted one large hall on the first floor of his mansion into a revolutionary war-era town square, each of the four walls redone as a facade of a colonial building. By the time his life had ended he'd brought together under one roof the greatest collection of quality woodwork ever assembled.

It was war that had done this to Henry Duke. War, the very thing that had made his family rich, had driven him to his eccentric distractions. Returning home from the war to end all wars, appalled at the apparent course of humanity, he'd resolved himself to a life that would hurt no one, and had taken up gardening and woodwork collecting. By laying an attractive flowerbed for the war-ravaged eye, providing a chair for the war-torn limbs, he knew he couldn't atone for the atrocities by which his family set their table, but at least he wouldn't be contributing to the atrocities himself. He married a socialite, fathered first a daughter and later a son, then lost the socialite in childbirth. Now a widower in his early thirties, he saw there was no safe harbor from harming the ones we love most, let alone all of broad humanity. Raising his mother-less daughter and infant son, he more than anything wanted not to destroy them with his kindnesses. Particularly his daughter, whose delicate, dark features and weakness in per-sonality so mirrored his own. To the little girl he was the kind-est and most loving sot on earth but he worried that his kind-ness would only serve to harm her in the end, that his generos-ity would only corrupt her, spoil her rotten. Ever since the girl could remember, whenever she wanted something special, an expensive dress or maybe a doll, her father would take her in his arms and as she weeped for the one thing she wanted most on earth he would always say the same thing to her. What he had to say to her is the most important thing in this book. Everything else is just padding, like the cotton they put in a ring case to keep the diamond ring from falling out. Holding young Elizabeth in his arms, wiping away her tears with the corner of his monogrammed linen handkerchief, he would say, "Elizabeth, my little pumpkin pie," (for always at such tender moments he'd address her lovingly as some form of fruit pas-try or danish, including such salutations as, "my little apple dumpling," or "my little peach cobbler," or "my little blueberry muffin," or "my little pineapple pie," or "my little macadamia nut cherry danish twist"), he would say, "Elizabeth, my little cranberry tart, there will always in this life be one thing you can never have."

As Elizabeth Natlong grew she heard this said on so many occasions that by the time kindly old Henry Duke had passed away she thought this was not just something a well-to-do father might say to his spoiled brat of a daughter, but that it must surely be some kind of universal law, a natural Golden Rule impossible to break, like What goes up must come down, or A pint's a pound the world around: There is always one thing we can never have.

This becomes important years later, in the autumn of Elizabeth Natlong née Duke's life, on the day her husband, George Natlong, brought her to Camp Moonstone and led her around the big stone house, speaking blithely of going off to war down in the cave. As her husband rattled on about his dreadful preparations for the end of the world all Elizabeth Natlong could think about was the safety and welfare of the two things on earth most precious to her heart — her father's collection of quality woodwork, and her niece, Claire. Claire had lost her parents in a traffic accident two years earlier and ever since the girl had been Elizabeth's responsibility. She attended a private school out West and, next to the late Henry Duke's priceless furniture collection, nothing occupied a place closer to Elizabeth Natlong's heart.

While George Natlong led his wife around Camp Moonstone he nonchalantly informed her they might be forced to hole up in an underground fallout shelter, where they'd certainly have to bear some of the deprivations of war. Elizabeth Natlong's ears pricked up.

Testing the waters to fathom the depths of the "deprivations," Elizabeth Natlong told her husband that the secret compound could be comfortable, but the lawn needed sowing, the hedges needed trimming, and the big stone house needed a decorator's touch.

"To put this place in order I'll need to bring the entire

staff from back home," she told her husband. "I don't see how I could *possibly* get by without a cook, the gardener, the butler, the pastry chef, an upstairs maid or two...."

"Absolutely not!" he fumed. "What do you think this is, a country club? This is war! I'm going off to fight, woman, and I see no need for a pastry chef or an upstairs maid. You can bring along a butler. That's it."

"One butler?" she gagged. "Who can get by with just a butler?"

"I'm afraid you'll have to manage, my dear."

"You're not forgetting your neice, dear sweet Claire, are you? We're the only family that poor girl has. Or had you planned to start your war without her?"

George Natlong slapped his forehead.

"My niece! She'll have to catch a plane back from California." He puffed his cigar thoughtfully. "Better yet, Major Donday has business on the coast. I'll have him fetch her back with him."

"Perhaps Claire has a boyfriend she'd like to bring along," Elizabeth Natlong explored. "After all, George, the girl's seventeen years old. You can't condemn her to live in some underground fallout shelter with no companionship."

The general clenched his square nutcracker's jaw.

"Absolutely not!"

"George! How many years do you expect that girl to live by herself in a cave? Maybe she'll want to have children someday, and raise a family."

George Natlong told his wife not to worry on that score, since the computer his assistant was building would no doubt soon figure out cloning.

"Cloning?"

"Instead of marriage and sex, we'll be cloned," the general explained as they strolled along the meadow in front of the stone house. "As I understand it, all it takes is a single cell, from the fingertip." He held up an index finger. "Infinitely more practical and efficient."

Elizabeth Natlong saw her husband had gone completely

and thoroughly out of his nut. If he had so little concern for matters of their niece's welfare she knew he certainly couldn't be depended on to protect her other objects of desire. She gave her husband a cool look. "I was thinking," she said as they walked along, "how nice it would be to have a little dinner party. Just you and myself, young Major Donday and that assistant of yours you're always talking about."

"Linda Patterson?"

"Yes. Why don't the four of us sit down for dinner. At Winterford. You will ask them when you get back, won't you darling? If we're going to be cooped up for years in that dreary cave of yours we might as well get acquainted."

"That's not such a bad idea," George Natlong allowed. "Before this campaign begins it'd be good for my subordinates to see the human side of me."

"Which side is that George?"

"Never you mind. Just see to it that that dinner is served on time." They were coming up onto the porch and he petted his wife's shoulder. "I must say, I'm pleased to see you finally assuming some of the responsibilities of an army officer's wife."

The next afternoon Linda Patterson summoned Peter Donday to her lab. Handing over the printout sheet, she told him, "See that this gets built." This time he couldn't help noticing that her finger lingered on his for that little extra moment that meant so much. Surprised, Peter Donday blinked.

Linda Patterson took her hand away. Turning, she went to the window and dreamily stared outside. She sure did look good in that lab smock, Peter Donday thought.

"California must be beautiful this time of year," she sighed. "I bet if you tried hard enough, Major Donday, you might be able to coax me into accompanying you to California."

Peter Donday couldn't conceal his surprise.

"But — but Linda —. Excuse my astonishment. It's only— You called me all those names. You said I should drop dead, that if ever you saw me again it'd be too soon."

"Of course, I'd understand if you'd rather not have my company."

"I'd enjoy very much your company. I'll get you a seat on the plane."

"The plane? No, I'm afraid of flying. Why don't we take my new car?"

"A car? That'll take forever."

"Who cares? I have my vacation time coming, don't I?"

She asked the major if he'd like to see her new car. She had him in tow all the way to the parking lot. She threw wide her arms. "What do you think?"

"You want to drive out to the coast in *that?*"

They'd stopped in front of the most beat-up old Volkswagen convertible the major had ever seen. Its fenders hung loose, rust bubbled its surface, and rips and patches decorated the ragtop.

"Come on, major! Where's your spirit of adventure? We'll take down the top and we'll have a marvelous time."

"If the top doesn't fall off before we take it down we will."

Then, out of the blue, he began to speak words of love to her, telling her about his childhood and other tedious talk of the heart, about how his great aunt once had owned a Volkswagen convertible very much like this, about how they used to go for long rides through the country in that old bug, taking along picnic lunches.

He droned on and on about his childhood until Linda Patterson thought she was going to be sick.

Not long afterward Linda Patterson got her first look at the Duke family's palatial estate at Winterford. She drove out in the early evening in her VW convertible, with Peter Donday at her side. The whole way out he wouldn't shut up about his damn childhood. "I used to go swimming in a pond very much like that one. There was a swing, and a raft—." After dinner, while George Natlong and Peter Donday drank brandy and

74

smoked cigars in the antebellum Atlanta dining room, Elizabeth Natlong pulled Linda Patterson aside and the two women went out into the garden. The moon was in crescent above the willows and the wind gently rustled the trees. Behind them, back in the mansion, they could hear the men laughing.

"You're not in love with him, are you?" Elizabeth Natlong asked.

"No."

"He's very much in love with you, you know. You can see it in his eyes. The way they light up when you're around. I've never known Peter to wear his heart on his sleeve so. Maybe you'll do him a world of good. If you have no one else why don't you have him?"

Linda Patterson looked into the roses.

"I've never imagined a place like this," she said. "A garden like this, the mansion, that incredible furniture collection."

"Daddy would roll over in his grave if he heard you calling his collection 'furniture.' When I was a girl if anyone had the audacity to call it furniture Daddy's eyes would pop wide and he'd say, 'Furniture! I don't have a stick of it in the place! Why, it's quality woodwork I collect!' But you're right you know. Daddy's collection is very special. I wouldn't be able to live with myself if anything happened to it."

In the moonlight the mansion took on the look of Versailles. Inside the men were still laughing and the jocular laughter gave the scene a surreal air.

"We women have an intuition about these things, don't we my dear?" Elizabeth Natlong laughed.

"Yes, I believe we do."

Busying himself with all the endless last minute preparations for blowing up the world, George Natlong began to fret that things were going too well. In the fickle, almost superstitious way of generals, he began to worry. His stomach became tight as a knot. He started to lose his appetite. He began to grow anxious and restless for the moment of his conquest to arrive.

When at last the day came for him to leave town he took one last look at the Washington skyline. He suspected he'd never see that skyline again. By the time he'd reached the mountains he'd put all those maudlin, sentimental thoughts behind. He started feeling better. Driving up into the mountains he pondered his place in history. He went so far as to wonder whether it had been a mistake not to commission a marble bust (or maybe even a full-length statue) of himself.

George Natlong had no way of knowing that the wheels of fate already had begun rolling against him. It wasn't until he'd reached the isolated gates of Camp Moonstone that it dawned on him this would not be the cakewalk he'd envisioned. For there, stacked before the electrified, barbed-wire gates, he came upon the biggest pile of furniture he'd ever seen in his life.

No — not just furniture. Quality woodwork. At least five freight trains full. Piled sky high out in front of the general's top-secret compound.

George Natlong slammed on the Caddy's brakes, sprang from the car and stared up at the godforsaken pile of furniture, his square nutcracker's jaw falling open all the way. It was then he felt the first stabbing pain in his stomach. Bringing both arms together he doubled over in pain. That was when it hit him hard, when he realized for all of our technology, for all of our science and all of our modern ways, we're still the same damn bunch of pretentious fools we've always been.

So roll over, gentle Bill Shakespeare, and go tell gloomy Professor Swift the news.

But please — go soft, and break it to him gently.

1ST MOVEMENT:
THE LAST OF THE TRULY GREAT CONQUERORS

This last combat with Poros took the edge off the Macedonians' courage, and stayed their further progress into India. ...Alexander at first was so grieved and enraged at his men's reluctancy that he shut himself up in his tent and threw himself upon the ground, declaring, if they would not pass the Ganges, he owed them no thanks for anything they had hitherto done, and that to retreat now was plainly to confess himself vanquished. But at last the reasonable persuasions of his friends and the cries and lamentations of his soldiers, who in a suppliant manner crowded about the entrance of his tent, prevailed with him to think of returning. Yet he could not refrain from leaving behind him various deceptive memorials of his expedition, to impose upon aftertimes, and to exaggerate his glory with posterity, such as arms larger than were really worn, and mangers for horses with bits and bridles above the usual size, which he set up, and distributed in several places.... Alexander was now eager to see the ocean.... His voyage down the rivers took up seven months' time, and when he came to the sea he sailed to an island which he himself called Scillustis, others Psiltucis, where going ashore he sacrificed, and made what observations he could as to the nature of the sea and the sea coast. Then having besought the gods that no other man might ever go beyond the bounds of this expedition he ordered his fleet to sail round about.

— Plutarch

1

They were making love. It was their first time. Before this they'd only looked. For days they'd sat in the backseat of the car, their ribs pressed together, feeling through their clothes their movements as they breathed. They'd looked at each other then, each feeling the other breathe faster, their nostrils flaring, and they'd known it would only be a matter of time. They thought they were in love.

The boy had felt like doing it then and there, in the backseat of the car, but he couldn't on account of the man and the woman up front. He was a perfect stranger to these people and it wouldn't do to make the girl in the backseat. The man, when he wasn't talking about his childhood, kept glancing in the rearview mirror. He'd have to wait.

His game plan had paid off. Now he looked at the girl beside him on the bed. His dreamy ponderings came to an end with a sudden pounding on the door, and the angry rattle of the knob.

"Unlock this door!"

"Who's that?"

"Must be my uncle." The girl pushed him away, wrapped herself in a sheet. "Maybe I should hide under the bed."

"What! I don't want to face him alone!"

The pounding intensified.

"Unlock this door before I break it down!"

The girl slid under the bed. In the moonlight the boy fumbled with his jeans. Too small. He couldn't get them up past his ankles. They were hers.

"Open up before I break down this door!"

Pulling on his own jeans, he fumbled to the door, drew

81

back the bolt. The light spilled in, making the boy squint. The wedge of light from the hall cast a long shadow of a man. Seeing the shadow, the boy thought he must be up against a giant. But when he turned and looked into the light he was surprised to see, standing in the open doorway, the silhouette of a hunch-shouldered man, no taller than five-six or seven. He caught a whiff of cigar smoke and then he saw the faint glowing ember of the cigar as the silhouette came slowly into the room. A click, the light came on. He found himself face to face with a stern man in a military uniform. A pistol stared from the general's hand. A big gun, a .45, from the looks of it.

He spoke with his hand still on the lightswitch, even before he'd looked at the boy.

"Very clever, but did you honestly think you could get away with it?"

Then he'd seen the boy.

For some seconds the boy and the man eyed each other. The boy's eyes twinkled with spirit and intelligence; the man's eyes burned with distrust. The boy was a full head taller than the man and, though of slight build, was good looking and bursting with energy; but even without these graces of youth there was an indomitable emanation of warmth from his young heart and bearing that further brought the little man down.

Striking as this contrast is to a casual onlooker, none can ever feel it with half the intensity with which it strikes to the very soul of the person whose inferiority it marks. It galled George Natlong to his heart's core, and he despised the boy from that moment.

The boy stepped away from the gun, fell back to the bed, pressing his backside against the bedpost. When he'd moved as far back as he could he studied the little man's uniform.

"Listen, mister," the boy said, searching for words. "I didn't lay a hand on her."

The little man shot a confused look. "What have you done with that unit?"

The boy stole a gaze down at his fly, checking that it was

82

closed.

"I don't know what you're talking about, mister."

"Don't play games with me. The upgrade. My wife says you came here this afternoon with Major Donday and Linda Patterson."

"Pete and Linda? The ones who gave me a ride?"

Moving slowly, his hands out to his side, the boy lifted a T-shirt from the foot of the bed. "It's a little cold." Nodding at curtains fluttering in the open window, he pulled on the shirt. A Superman emblem gilded its front.

The general eyed a backpack propped against the wall by the bed. Training the gun on the boy, he moved to the pack. His cigar clenched between stained teeth, he began rummaging. The pack was filled with damp underwear. Mostly undershirts stenciled with Superman emblems. Near the bottom of the pack his hand struck several heavy objects. Bringing them up, shaking off a pair of damp undershorts, he saw two electronic devices.

"Uh-huh. What're these?"

"Mister, those are my Big Muff and my phase shifter."

"Big Muff?" George Natlong hefted the devices in his hand. "Phase shifter?"

"Sure," the boy said. He made strumming motions with his hands. "You know, for my guitar."

"Guitar?"

"It was stolen from me in Chicago. I thought I'd have to go on to New York without it. Then I got picked up by Pete and Linda and Claire. Claire told me if I came here they'd go back to Chicago for it."

"Chicago! To get a guitar!"

George Natlong shoved the electronic devices into the side pocket of his uniform jacket. The boy started to protest but the general removed the .45's safety.

Spotting a guitar by the window, George Natlong moved toward it. "Is this the guitar?"

"No," the boy said. "I told you, mine's in Chicago. Claire found that one. She brought it to me so I'd have something to play."

George Natlong grabbed the neck of the guitar, slammed it against the wall, shattering it to atoms.

"Hey!" George Natlong leveled the gun, moving the boy back against the bed. With his foot, the general kicked through the fragments of the cheap guitar. Presently he cursed, kicked the wreckage aside.

"I hope you're satisfied," the boy said. "That was a perfectly good guitar. It may have been a cheap five-and-dime job but still that doesn't give you the right—."

"Quiet! You say you're on your way to New York? What business have you there?"

"I'm going to see Lennon."

"Lenin? Agents for Vladimir Ilich Lenin?"

"John Lennon. The Beatle. You know, he wrote Give Peace a Chance."

"Go on," the general urged with the .45. "Let's hear the rest of it. What business have you with this Lennon?"

"Business! Man, I'm going to play him a tune on my Strat."

"Strat?"

"You know, my ax. A Stratocaster. My guitar."

The boy made a strumming motion with his hands.

"Why is it," George Natlong bristled, "this conversation keeps gravitating back to a guitar? You better cut the bull before I count three."

The boy gazed down the smooth barrel of the gun. A clattering arose from beneath the bed.

"Claire!" George Natlong started.

Draped in the sheet, Claire Duke moved in front of the boy, wrapped her sheet-draped arms around his neck.

"Honestly, Uncle George. He's telling the truth. We picked him up yesterday by the side of the road. He was hitchhiking. His name is Paul Stoken. He's from Mason City, Iowa. Paul and I are lovers."

The general lowered the gun.

"You mean to say you picked this stranger up by the side

of the road only yesterday and already you've—. That is to say, you've—."

"Yes, Uncle George, we have made love. Don't be afraid to say it."

"You had no authority to bring anyone here."

"He has this." The girl reached down the neck of his Superman T-shirt, revealing a small amulet of stone dangling from a chain about his neck.

George Natlong took a step closer. Claire lowered the stone back inside the boy's shirt, hugged him tight.

"Where did he get that?"

"Aunt Liz gave it to him. It was a spare."

"A *spare!* There are no spares!"

"Honestly, Uncle George, did you expect me to play Miranda to your Prospero? I won't stay if Paul doesn't stay with me."

"So that's how it is, is it?" George Natlong said. "We'll see." He pointed at the boy. "I have ways of finding out about you."

The general holstered the gun and slammed the door.

Paul Stoken heard the quick plodding footsteps trailing down the hall, down the staircase. The front door slammed. He hurried to the window, pulled back the curtain.

Down below he could make out George Natlong, trailed by a faint moonshadow, hiking across the lawn, up the slope toward the tree-covered hill. The moon hung bright above the trees. It was only a few days away from being full and in the wash of the moonlight the boy could make out a squat building at the top of the hill.

The boy flew from the window. In the moonlit darkness of the room he fumbled with his sneakers.

"Where you going?"

It was all she could do to hurriedly throw on some clothes (ignoring her sandals) and chase after him, down the stairs and out of the house. She saw him up ahead, huffing across the lawn. She ran barefoot after him, calling for him to wait. By the time she'd caught up he'd nearly made it to the tree line.

85

As he stormed along in the moonlight he fumed half sentences.

"Pull a gun on me, will he? Rip me off, will he!"

Grabbing ahold of his arm, she tried to stop him.

"Where're you going?"

The boy struggled.

"I'm gonna follow that son of a bitch and get my things."

He froze, staring at the girl's neck.

"Look at that!"

In the moonlight the stone on her amulet sparkled with a strange glow, as if afire.

Paul pulled his own amulet from his shirt. It sparkled as intensely as hers. He held it out on its chain so that it spun in the breeze. Brilliant white specks danced and swirled across the grass, the trees and their surprised faces.

"It's just like one of those mirror balls in a dancehall," the boy gasped. "Except it's moonbeam powered. Moonlight ignites those glassy specks." He enclosed the twirling stone in his fist. The blizzard of white specks stopped.

He gazed up at the moon, then down to his closed fist, feeling the stone inside. It felt course, like lava.

By now their eyes had adjusted to the dark and they could make out a path running into the woods. The boy seemed uncertain. He gazed at the Superman emblem on his chest. He took off again up the hill, the girl at his heels. "Paul," he heard her say. "let's go back." He kept to the side of the path, in the shadows. Soon, through the trees, she could make out the outline of the building at the top. At last they came out of the trees and the warehouse lay before them in the moonlight.

"Look at the size of it," the boy puffed. "Looks like an airport hanger."

Already he moved cautiously ahead.

"Can we get in?"

"I'm not sure we should."

"Come on. The door must be around here somewhere."

They found the door on the opposite side. It wasn't locked.

"It's empty!" his voice echoed.

86

"Nothing's kept here," the girl said. But she'd spoken too soon.

"Look! Over there!"

They took off across the broad empty floor. Over their heads the roof was high and girdered, like the inside of a hanger. They ran all the way to the great steel-plated doors, where the boy abruptly skidded his sneakers to a stop, looking down. On the other side of the doorway a carpeted hallway slanted down at a sharp angle, angling deep into the mountain.

"I'll be damned. A cave."

"Come on then," Claire said, tugging his hand.

"Maybe this isn't such a good idea. Maybe we should go back to bed and pretend the whole thing never happened."

"Since we're here we might as well see the place."

She tugged and they started past the steel doors, down into the ground. The hallway was long and deep, and ever so quiet, the carpeting underfoot muffling their footsteps, but soon they could hear the sounds of heated conversation clapping up from somewhere below. They followed the sounds of the voices until they came to a doorway on the left.

It opened on a grand chamber, with row after row of benches curved in a great semicircle, with finely carved wooden paneling covering the cold stone walls. Paul pulled the girl to the carpet and the two of them crept on their hands and knees down the center aisle. Scooting behind a bench, they looked out over the top. Somehow it all seemed vaguely familiar. Down front a gigantic video screen obscured the far wall. Beneath it, an electronic console with banks of blinking lights. Before the console, his back to the chamber, George Natlong pounded his fist.

"What do you mean you can't tell me how he got here?" the general boomed. "You're supposed to look into the past."

"Not the immediate past," came a reply from somewhere near, or perhaps behind, the giant screen. This voice was deep and resonant and it thundered even louder than the general's, fairly well rattling the chamber. "I'm unable to view events occuring within the last seventy-two hours."

"Seventy-two hours! Three days! Can't you tell me anything?"

"The boy's name— what is it?"

"Paul Stoken. From Mason City, Iowa."

For several seconds they heard nothing. Then, "So he's come. I can tell you this: it'll either be you or him."

"You have some information on this Paul Stoken?"

"I have information on everyone."

The giant screen came alive. A photograph of the boy lit the wall of the cavern. Paul stiffened, thinking, That's my picture but I don't remember posing for it.

"Is this him?"

"That's him all right. The same strange haircut and dumb smile."

"What's wrong with my hair?" the boy whispered, rubbing his scalp.

"His full name is Peter Paul Stoken," the machine went on. "His mother keeps house and his father is an attorney in Mason City, Iowa."

The giant screen lit up with images of a young man driving a pickup through snow.

"Who's that in the truck?"

"That's the boy's uncle, Jeffrey Stoken."

In the back of the chamber the girl whispered, "What's wrong, Paul? You look sick."

"Up there. On the screen. My Uncle Jeff. How's it possible?"

From their hiding place they could plainly see the face of Jeffrey Stoken, singing to himself and clapping the wheel of the truck with both hands. The truck bounced down a snowy country road, its headlights shining, its windshield wipers wiping. Jeffrey peered through the wedge of windshield where the snow had been pushed away by the wipers. Suddenly a flashing red light plummeted across the top of the screen, streaking through the falling snow just above the truck, drawing the attention of the driver from the road.

2

Jeffrey Stoken drove the pickup slowly over the snow. It was his father's truck and it had always been hard to shift into third gear so now he kept it in second. Driving in second was slow but he didn't mind that now because the road was slick with snow and so it was probably best to keep it in second anyway. It would make a long drive to the hospital. Earlier in the evening his brother's wife had gone into labor and he suspected the baby would already be born by the time he got there. He pictured the scene in his mind. He'd rush into the waiting room and his parents, who'd been holed up with his brother since supper, would say, "Where the devil you been, boy? You didn't go to that rock show in Clear Lake tonight, did you?"

In fact, it had been a fine show with many good songs and afterwards Jeffrey had gone to a bar with a couple of friends and had downed a quick one. Now he was finally on his way to the hospital in Mason City and it was after midnight and they would smell the quick one on his breath and there would be no end to the chewing out he'd get. The truck rumbled down the road and the windshield wipers slapped the snow away and the headlights cut a wedge through the tumbling fluff that swirled through the inky night and he tried once again to shift into third to speed up the trip but the gears gnashed and he cursed and slapped the gearshift knob with his hat and then sat back deep in the seat and resigned himself to a slow trip. Oh well, he thought, what can I do?

From the corner of his eye he caught a light. He turned his head and saw in a blur what looked like the underside of a plane, flying low, like a crop duster, over the snowy dark fields. Must be near the airport, he thought. He could see little more than a streak of a flashing red light but he knew it was a plane when, after a moment, he heard the buzzing of its engine, greatly muffled by the curtain of falling snow. Then as quickly as the light had appeared it vanished behind a hill somewhere to the left up ahead. Now there was only the muffled noise of the truck engine with the bad gears and the windshield wipers slapping the glass and the crisp sound of the snow getting crunched under the tires.

The truck started up the hill and it was then that Jeffrey saw the flash. Somewhere beyond the hill. The snow lit up like a dome, a halo outlining the crest of the hill. Then, in an instant, gone.

"Christ." Steam shot from his mouth into the cold cab of the truck when he said it. No it couldn't be that. There was no sound, no explosion. Maybe the sound had been muffled by the snow. No, he thought, couldn't've been that.

The truck screamed up the hill and he hit the brake, took it out of gear. Rolling down the window he looked out into the night. He could just make out a small fire flickering, some ways to the left. A small fire, like a campfire. It was dying out but it was still bright enough to light the oily smoke billowing into the snowfall.

"Shit."

Frightened, he knew he should do something. At least that's what he'd been told by Mr Greely, his scoutmaster. "Be prepared," Mr Greely always said. Jeffrey was also a regular subscriber to *Boys' Life* magazine, where every month there was a cartoon story about some dumb scout who'd been unlucky enough to be standing around when a bridge collapsed and who was forced to jump into icy water to retrieve the survivors from submerged cars or pull bloody victims from auto crashes and blow into their mouths to revive them. Afterwards in every issue of *Boys' Life* at the end of the story they always stood in their uniforms in front of their troops receiving eagle badges, giving the scout salute. Was hometown boy Jeffrey about to become one of those cartoonized scouts?

In the truck gripping the wheel tightly with both hands, the engine coughing, snow piling up on the hood, he saw the fire was dying out. "Shit."

He killed the engine, pulled out the hand brake. The snow blew in a mist across the road and he opened the door and jumped down into it, leaving the headlights on to find his way back. After a few cautious steps he bounded off the road and down the snowy slope toward the dying blaze. Just when he was afraid the fire would die he caught his first whiff of oily smoke. It was pungent and heavy-smelling in the otherwise snow-cleansed air. He could almost follow it through the air and he'd flare his nostrils when he lost it.

The snow was very light, only about three or four inches deep. Every few feet the grass under the snow gave way and he sank ankle deep in the powder and it spilled into his boots. Near the bottom of the hill he fell down and tumbled a few times but he got up right away and kept heading for the flickering orange streak, brushing what snow he could from his coat and pants as he stumbled on.

Gradually his eyes adjusted to the soft luminous radiance of the snowy fields. Everything seemed a little dreamlike and unreal.

Jeffrey felt like he was running in slow motion. It was a good feeling. Very painless, very effortless to run through the falling snow.

He could almost float through the air. With every step he bounded a little farther across the snow and his breathing was slow and even and effortless.

In the dim radiance of the falling snow he made out a wire fence slicing the field. He followed the fence and could see, around him, fingerlike projections of bare trees dotting the white. It was impossible to tell how tall the trees were, or even how far away they were, only that they hunkered over, resembling bent soldiers riding out a storm. Then he saw the wreck of the plane.

It lay smashed farther down along the fence. Jeffrey could see its wings had been bent skyward, like the broken wings of a swatted fly. As he ran up the fire flickered yellow and the thick black smoke curled into the air. Those last steps were the hardest. His feet now seemed leaden. The timelessness and the effortlessness were gone. Breathing was hard. His mouth was dry when he finally found himself standing before the ghostly wreck. He fought the urge to turn and run back to the truck.

"God damn."

The plane had hit the fence hard but the heavy barbed wire and the solid wooden posts had acted like a trampoline and had pushed it back. Its windshield had been torn open on both sides like a man whose eyes had been shot out, with jagged shards of glass ringing the gaping holes. Some of the glass was loose and tinkled in the wind. Snow blew into the cockpit.

Those were the easy things to look at. Much harder on Jeffrey's eyes were the three men who had been flung from the cockpit and were ensnarled in the barbed wire, lifelessly suspended in the fence, their arms spread like scarecrows, their legs twistedly drooping to the ground.

He had to look away. Then he saw the fourth man. Slumped near the fence on the ground already partially buried in the drifting snow. Probably the pilot, Jeffrey thought. He wore an aviator's hat.

Closing his eyes, Jeffrey told himself, You've got to get a grip. Maybe there's still time to help these people, he thought. He remembered the countless lectures on first aid he'd heard at Boy Scout meetings and one sermon in particular delivered by the scoutmaster on how to spot the signs of life. "There are three distinct signs of life," Mr Greely always lectured. "These include regular heartbeat, respiration and a healthy skin coloration, and you should always check the accident victim for these signs."

Jeffrey opened his eyes to step closer to the three men in the wire. When he looked at the faces he realized how ridiculous the scoutmaster's advice had been. There may be three distinct signs of life, he thought, but there is one distinct sign of death. It's the easiest of all to see. He wondered, Why

92

hadn't the scoutmaster told us of the one distinct sign of death: that the faces of the dead are like the waxy cold wicks of candles that have been snuffed out. Didn't the scoutmaster know that death looked as cold and impenetrable, as icy and imponderable as the blackest, emptiest darkness?

The scoutmaster had only told Jeffrey what to do in the event of life. Now that he was standing next to death he felt unprepared. He thought he might know why the scoutmaster had said nothing of death. It was because the scoutmaster had never seen it.

He crossed himself — the nuns taught me that, he thought, not the scoutmaster — and drew a deep breath but he didn't close his eyes.

"No."

He fell back from the fence, covering his eyes with a hand. When he finally took away his hand and looked down at his feet he knew. A pair of bloodied hornrimmed eyeglasses floated half buried in the snow. He reached for them. Both lenses had been shattered and, once he'd lifted them, sparkling shards of glass sank into the drifting snow. He let go of the glasses then and with detachment watched them founder into the drift.

He took another step back, spotted something in the snow. It was just a little to the right and he didn't know why he hadn't seen it before. It was a handtooled leather guitar case, covered with powdery snow and when he wiped his hand across it the snow fell away.

Neatly stitched in the leather across the top were the words, "Buddy Holly."

For quite some time, the wind whipping cold around him, Jeffrey stood in the snow looking at those words, at that name. He could hear glass tinkling where the wind blew through the gaping holes in the windshield of the plane. Far away, he could hear the wind singing some sad song in the branches of the lonely bare trees. Before he knew what he was doing he'd tucked the guitar case under his arm and he was running wildly across the snow with it, the wind and the drifting snow quickly covering his receding footsteps.

The waiting room of the Mason City hospital was small and overheated, smelling of tobacco smoke and alcohol. When Jeffrey came in five tired people stopped their talk, looked up expectantly. They were seated in stiff uncomfortable waiting room furniture and they looked disappointed when they saw it was only Jeffrey.

A middle-aged woman asked, "Where you been?"

"Nowhere Ma. I got held up by the snow, is all. The road's pretty bad."

The woman rose and came over to her son. "Boy you look like the devil." She touched his jacket. "Your clothes and hair are wet. What's the matter with you Jeffrey? You want to catch your death?"

Before Jeffrey could say anything his father stood and, a broad smile lighting his face, said, "Aren't you gonna congratulate your brother? Lenny here's a pappy now. It's a boy, Jeff. That makes you an uncle."

Leonard Stoken sat opposite the door in a stiff waiting room sofa. He was a young man, only about twenty-five years old, but already his straight black hair showed streaks of gray and you could imagine him white haired. His eyes were bloodshot with dark bags under them but a wide toothy grin stretched his face. He wore a white, law school shirt (open at the top and wrinkled from the hours of waiting), while his striped, law school necktie hung undone at the front of the shirt. His arms stretched wide across the top of the sofa and a cigarette smoldered in his hand. Before him one of those sand-filled ashtrays almost overflowed with snuffed-out cigarette butts, some still fuming.

Jeffrey's eyes wandered to the radio beside the rack of disheveled *Saturday Evening Posts*. The radio announcer's whistling voice kept going in and out. "And now here's one from Chuck Berry." *Johnny B. Goode* came on.

Running a hand through wet hair, he came another step into the room.

94

"That's great Lenny. So you're a pappy now."

"Yup," Lenny said. "Eight pounds six ounces. Bouncing baby boy. Figure he'll be a big attorney someday. Who knows? Maybe even the Supreme Court. I can see the shingle now—" bringing his hands together, the cigarette still fuming in one of them, he gestured as though holding a picture frame "—Stoken and Stoken, attorneys at law."

The others in the room, everyone except Jeffrey, laughed.

"Gee that's great Lenny," Jeffrey said again. He forced a smile. "A boy you say? What's his name gonna be?"

"Peter Paul," Lenny told him. "Peter Paul Stoken."

"Peter Paul?" Jeffrey said. "You're naming the poor kid after a candy bar?"

"There you go again," Lenny flared up, snuffing out his smoke. "Putting your mouth on things that don't concern you. It so happens Peter Paul is from the Bible. But since there's no comic book version I guess you haven't read it."

"Peter Paul is a fine, Catholic name," Jeffrey's father put in, shaking his bald head approvingly.

Jeffrey told his brother. "I wouldn't want the kid to be starting off with any strikes against him on accounta his name."

"They'll be no strikes against him," said the woman sitting beside Lenny. She was Lenny's mother-in-law. "Peter Paul is a fine name. A good Christian name."

"A good name," agreed the man sitting beside her. This was Lenny's father-in-law. Jeffrey suddenly remembered his name: Peter Paul Pervis.

"Look, I'm sorry I brought it up," Jeffrey said.

"Just keep that mouth of yours off it," Lenny said. Leaning back in the sofa, he lit another cigarette.

Jeffrey turned to his mother.

"You seen the kid yet?"

"We're waiting to see the *child* now," she said. "The good Lord kept us waiting until after one o'clock. Let me tell you, that little fella has lungs! He let go a holler when he came into the world."

"Aw Jeff here's all right," his father said, ruffling the boy's hair. "He don't like to watch the first three quarters of a football game either. But he'll always show up in time for the last two minutes."

They heard footsteps, and a beaming nurse carried a blanketed bundle into the room.

"Oh here's the little angel now!" Mrs Pervis sang out.

Everyone but Jeffrey circled around the nurse.

"Would you look at the little darling!" Jeffrey's mother said. "That's my grandchild all right! He's got my eyes!"

"And my mouth!" Lenny said.

"I hope he don't got your mouth!" Jeffrey said.

He was at the far side of the room fussing with the radio dial, his ear close to the speaker. Between blasts of static he heard the announcer say, "If you were lucky enough to make it out to the Surf Ballroom in Clear Lake tonight you know that Buddy Holly put on a great performance. Buddy, if you're listening out there somewhere, and we hope you are, we'd like to thank you once again for a real fine show and we hope you'll come back this way again. Until then, here's Buddy's latest release, 'I Guess it Doesn't Matter Anymore.'"

A song came on. A hand reached up, switched off the radio.

Jeffrey's father chided him, "Don't you ever get tired of listening to that crap? Come over here and take a look at your nephew."

"I've never seen so many babies born in a year," the nurse was saying to Lenny. "The baby boom's finally caught up with Mason City."

The nurse lifted the blanket away so Jeffrey could see the tiny pink face, the whisps of fuzzy black hair. The baby slept. Jeffrey could see his little nostrils twitch. He was glad to look into the face of a newborn on the very night he'd had his first glimpse of death. It made him feel more at ease, somehow even renewed. His face softened and he smiled at the infant. It felt good to be among the living again.

"So far from the pit of the abyss," Jeffrey said softly to the baby. "Stay away from that pit as long as you can."

"What pit?" Lenny said. "What're you talking about?"

"The pit into which we all must fall," Jeffrey said, glassy eyed. "I was telling him to stay out of the pit for as long as he can."

Jeffrey's mother lifted a hand to his forehead.

"Boy, I think you're coming down with something. You better get yourself home, change out of those clothes and get to bed, or you'll be back here at the hospital."

The ride home through the dark night was long, quiet and lonely. Jeffrey parked the truck in the usual place beside the house. It was no longer snowing. Walking around to the passenger's side, he removed a bulky object from behind the seat, carried it up onto the porch and then into the pitch black house. No one was home. He went straight to his room. All that night he had restless frightening dreams.

Early the next morning Jeffrey went downstairs to the kitchen. His mother and the girl from next door sat at the table folding baby clothes. Jeffrey went to the refrigerator and got out the pitcher of orange juice.

"I ain't feeling so hot this morning, Ma," he said. He poured a glass of juice. "I think I'm catching cold."

"You better stay home then," the mother said. She was folding a tiny blue sweater. "There's big excitement today," she added. "Those musicians who played over in Clear Lake were killed in a plane crash outside town. Tried to fly out of Clear Lake in the snow. Radio says they crashed in the field. Bad mess. Everybody's talking."

Jeffrey put down the glass.

The neighbor girl, bundling together a pair of yellow socks, said, "Proves my daddy right. Musicians like that do the devil's work. I guess those boys only got what was coming."

"Don't talk that way, little miss prissy pants," Jeffrey glared. He stormed back to his room.

"What's eating him?"

"Oh don't worry," Jeffrey's mother said, humming. "He's just a little bit feverish this morning. Say, Mary Beth, pass me that basket of diapers, will you?"

3

The boy sat wide eyed behind the benches in the great chamber, witnessing events from his early life flash across the big screen. He studied the expressions on the faces of his uncle, his father, his grandparents. They were much younger than he thought they ever could have been. His father and his uncle didn't look much older than Paul looked now. He thought, They're just boys dressed in men's clothing, boys playing the roles of men.

"That's enough for tonight. We'll pick up where we left off in the morning." George Natlong stretched, switched off the computer.

Fitting his hat on his head, he started up the aisle. Paul and Claire held their heads low as he plodded by. Once the footsteps had dragged up the aisle and out of the chamber Paul got up. He wasted no time going down the aisle to look over the computer. The lights no longer flashed.

"This machine can look into the past like you or I can look out a window," the boy marveled. "Do you suppose it can look into anyone's past?"

"I've had enough of the past for one night," she said. "Let's go to bed."

She led him by the arm from the cave. Outside, above ground, it was a warm night. Crickets chirped and hopped underfoot. "Te te te," the girl chirped back. They walked down the moonlit hill to the house and spent the night together in his room.

In the morning Paul awoke looking at the smashed guitar on the floor. Splintered wood and coiled strings lay everywhere.

"Don't feel bad," Claire told him. "It was a cheap guitar."

She lie in bed beside him. In the sunlight her short blonde hair looked yellow, almost orange.

"Your parents— what happened to them?"

"Their car was hit by a truck. Almost three years ago. Aunt Liz and Uncle George are all I've got now."

At breakfast George and Elizabeth Natlong sat at the table with another couple. The butler poured coffee.

"I simply didn't know what to wear in these circumstances," the other woman was saying. She was a big woman with a confident manner. "Certainly something with classic styling."

The conversation broke off when the boy and the girl came in.

"Here they are now," Elizabeth beamed. "Claire and her friend, Paul."

The general stared down at his eggs.

"Paul, I'd like you to meet two of my dearest friends. Say hello to Edgar and Doty."

Edgar was a retiring man who sat before a bowl of soup, sipping from the spoon.

Elizabeth said to the boy, "When I was your age I used to run around with these two. We had the grandest times."

"Things sure have changed since then," Edgar's wife, Doty said. She looked much more rugged than her husband. "Well, look at little Claire! How ravishing she's become! Those eyes! She's looking more and more like Inky, God rest his soul, every time I see her."

With the palm of her hand Elizabeth touched the back of Claire's head.

"Isn't the resemblance astonishing? Sometimes when I look at Claire I see so much of poor Inky—." Elizabeth stopped. "It's all I can do to hold back the tears."

"At least Claire has found somebody," Doty said. "It's good she has someone."

The butler poured coffee into Paul's cup.

"Do you want eggs?" Claire asked.

Paul shook his head yes.

Elizabeth said, "Paul and Claire have so much in common. They're both without parents, you know."

"An orphan, is he now?" George Natlong asked, chewing slowly.

"I didn't exactly tell you the gospel truth yesterday, when I got here, Mrs Natlong," the boy interjected. "I'm not exactly what you'd call an orphan. I've got folks back in Iowa."

"Then why on earth did you tell me your parents were dead?"

"I was just telling a bad joke, ma'am."

There was a knock at the door. Another couple came in. The man wore the uniform of an army officer. Two stars on his lapel, the boy saw.

"Hal!" George Natlong threw his napkin on the plate. "Glad you could make it."

"Are you joking? Where else would I be?" This general was a big man with a round, balding head.

"Won't you join us for breakfast?" Elizabeth asked.

"No thanks. Had something in the car. Coffee would be fine though."

"I don't believe everyone has met," Elizabeth Natlong said. "These are old friends of ours, Doty and Edgar."

They shook hands over the table.

Elizabeth went on, "And over here we have my niece, Claire, and her friend, Paul."

"Glad to know you kids," the one called Hal said. He shook hands with Paul. "You got a grip son."

"Say, George," the newcomer laughed. "What sort of military camp is this? There's furniture piled sky high down by the gate. Hardly makes the place look secretive."

"It's mine," Elizabeth Natlong said. "I'll see it's taken care of."

"That furniture is currently a bone of contention," George Natlong said. Lighting a cigar, he stared at the boy.

"I said I'd see that it's moved," Elizabeth Natlong repeated, buttering her toast. "The problem here, if you ask me, isn't a lack of security, but too much security. That gate is so ridiculously small the moving vans couldn't get in. The only alternative was to pile it up outside."

"That gate is designed to keep out tanks and other large vehicles, my dear," George Natlong replied.

There was an awkward, silent moment.

"That was a real swell breakfast, Mrs Natlong," Paul said.

"Did you have enough?"

"Oh yes ma'am I'm stuffed." He turned to Claire. "Why don't we go for a walk?"

Outside, it was turning into a hot day. They walked slowly down through the woods to the gate.

The boy looked at her. She'd taken off her sandals and swung them in her hand as she walked. "Te te te," she whistled, swinging her sandals.

They were coming up on the gate. Out on the road, beyond the barbed wire, they saw the furniture, piled high. Blue tarps had been pulled over the top to keep off the rain.

"Hey, I just saw someone! Running into the trees!"

"I don't see anyone."

"Outside the gate. Down past the furniture."

"You're seeing things."

"I tell you, he was walking out from the trees. He saw us, then jumped for cover."

They heard something behind them. They turned, saw the butler steering a small forklift down the path from the house. The forklift rolled up to the gate. The butler got out.

"How's it going, kids?" the butler asked with a wink. He pointed with exasperation at the furniture. "As if I don't have enough to do, Mrs Natlong wants me to cart that woodwork into camp. Look at it all, would you! I'll be moving it around till Judgment Day. She says to me, 'And Spencer, do be careful not to scratch it.'" He looked heavenward, shook his head.

The butler pulled a sparkling amulet from his shirt, lowered it into a box by the gate. The gate swung aside.

"Be seeing you kids," he said, hopping back onto the forklift. He drove slowly to the furniture.

They watched him untie the ropes holding down the tarps.

He lifted a heavy chest from the pile, struggling with it to the forklift.

Arm in arm they walked up into the shade of the trees, away from the house. They walked up the path to the top of the hill.

Spencer, the butler, breezed by in the forklift, hauling the chest, an antique end table, a Chippendale chair. He waved. The forklift puttered up the path to the crest of the hill, to the warehouse at the top.

"Looks bigger in the daylight, doesn't it?"

A half dozen sliding doors were spaced along its broad side. One of the doors had been rolled open.

"Let's follow the butler in," the boy suggested.

In the middle of the expansive floor Spencer slowly unloaded the chest and the chair. They joined a bookcase and an ottoman he'd brought in an earlier trip.

The boy and the girl walked all the way to the back of the warehouse, stopping at the massive steel doors.

"Come on," he tugged at her hand. They walked past the steel doors down into the ground. Outside the computer chamber, in the main hallway, he said to her, "You stand guard."

He hurried to the console, flicked the power switch, then asked the computer to tell him about general George Natlong.

4

Cadet George Natlong loved a good fight. He was never any good at it. He always got licked. But he loved a good fight. On the night of the Graduation Hop at West Point he got into a fight with another cadet over a date. They fought behind the gymnasium, while the orchestra played on. George Natlong threw the first punch. His adversary blocked the punch then struck George Natlong twice on his square jaw and once below the right eye. George Natlong threw another punch, fanning air. He felt a crushing blow beneath his eye, felt his stomach hit, but he did not feel the ground come up when he went down. He lie on the ground breathing hard, the wind knocked out. For an instant he thought he would die.

"She's mine," the adversary said, standing over George Natlong. "Find another date."

George Natlong, touching two fingers to his square jaw, felt blood.

"Great," he said out loud. "Just great."

Snatching his white jacket and hat from the grass, he tottered across the yard to the gym. Inside, cadets and their dates, in formal attire, bounced up and down the great marble stair. George Natlong went into the latrine and washed his face in the sink. He stood over the sink and watched the blood swirl down the drain.

On the other side of the wall, in the ladies' room, a girl sat before a mirror powdering her nose. Finally she returned the compact to her purse and left the ladies' room. That's when she saw him. Leaving the mens' latrine. A battered cadet, with a swollen, square jaw and a reddened eye. He straightened his jacket as he walked.

He went into the gym. A fifteen-piece orchestra played on the raised platform up front. She'd followed him in. The girl thought, He looks like a poor little nutcracker! He stood alone at the side of the dance floor in his dress whites, his hat tucked under his arm, his hair mussed. The orchestra played a waltz and everyone danced and swirled around the cadet like snowflakes falling in a field. He gazed into the dance floor in a lonely, detached way.

Elizabeth came across the ballroom, her long gown billowing. She stood beside the cadet for quite some time before she said, "Excuse me, isn't that the punch bowl?"

The cadet turned to see if there was someone behind him whom the girl might be addressing.

"Were you speaking to me?"

"Yes I was. I asked if that's the punch bowl."

"Why I believe it is."

She smiled at him.

"It's hard to tell what that is," she said. "It looks like a whale."

The cadet smiled. He held out his gloved hand.

"I'm Cadet George Natlong."

She held out her own gloved hand.

"I'm Elizabeth Duke."

They shook hands through the gloves.

"Won't you allow me to pour you a punch?"

"I'd be delighted." She took his arm and walked with him to the punch bowl.

They drank punch from little pewter cups.

She said, "I couldn't help noticing that you were looking for someone in the crowd."

"I wasn't looking for anyone. Just someone who was probably no good for me anyway. I guess you can't have everything."

"I believe that too," she said. "My father is always telling me, 'Elizabeth, there's always something you can't have.'"

"I agree." His eyes swept through the crowd.

105

"I said to myself, 'I bet he's looking for his parents.'"

"My parents are dead."

"Oh I'm sorry." She'd raised a hand to her mouth.

"Never knew my mother," he said. "Died in childbirth. My old man blew his head off when I was ten. Did it out back. I found him in the huckleberry bushes. Parts of his face were blown clear out into the orchard. The apples always tasted bitter after that."

She set her punch on the table.

"That's terrible. I mean what you've been through."

He was looking through the crowd. He sipped at the punch.

"In a way it's a real coincidence," she went on. "Your mother dying in childbirth. My mother died in childbirth too. When my brother was born. I was twelve when it happened."

He smiled. He didn't know what to say. He never knew what to say.

"Are you a cadet here?"

"No. I'm just wearing this cadet's uniform as a disguise. Actually I'm Groucho Marx."

He lifted his eyebrows and pretended to smoke a cigar. There, he thought, that's better. Loosen up and talking comes easy.

She laughed.

"Will you — how do they say it? — pursue a military career?"

"No," he told her. "I've been in military schools since I've been ten. The old man wanted it that way. I'm sick of it. Maybe I'll serve a tour overseas, in Europe or the Pacific, but then I'm getting out. I've better things to do with my life."

"Like what?"

"I'd like to become a playwright." That's funny, he thought, it's the first time I've ever told anyone about that. She can really draw me out, can't she? Or was it because he was lonely and because he'd been beaten that he felt like talking?

"A playwright?" she said. "How exciting! Like Shaw and O'Neill?"

106

Just then he saw the woman he'd been fighting over. She walked onto the dance floor on the arm of the other cadet. The orchestra leader was striking up a fox-trot.

George Natlong lowered the pewter cup to the table. "Would you care to dance, Miss Duke?"

She touched the sleeve of his jacket. "I'd be delighted."

They did a turn around the floor. He danced well but she couldn't help noticing that he kept looking to the side of the room.

After the dance she took his hand.

"I must introduce you to Daddykins."

Oh no! he thought, he really didn't want to meet her old man but then he saw how much it meant to her and he figured what the hell, why not?

She led him across the gym to the corner near the balcony where the commandant was entertaining the important guests. Army brass, faculty members and matrons of society circled around the commandant. They chatted merrily as they watched the cadets and the young women dance. She led him to a tall, thin man who was joking with the commandant. Army generals stood listening. Christ! George Natlong thought.

"Daddykins, I want you to meet someone," Elizabeth said, breaking into the conversation. The commandant, the generals, and her father fell quiet, turned and stared at the cadet. George Natlong felt like dying. Numbly he heard Elizabeth introducing him to her father and then they were shaking hands.

The commandant said, "What happened to your face, cadet?"

"Sir. I fell down, sir."

"Fell down, did you?" The commandant smiled faintly at one of the generals. "Well see that it doesn't happen again, cadet. You're a West Point man now, and we have a tradition against falling down."

"Yes sir."

The cadet turned to Elizabeth's father.

"It was a pleasure meeting you, Mr Duke." Then, to Elizabeth, "Allow me to show you the river, Miss Duke."

He held out his arm and she took it. It's getting stuffy in here, he thought as they walked away.

One of the generals who'd been chatting with Elizabeth's father turned to the commandant and asked, "This Cadet Natlong. What sort of a fellow is he?"

Her father listened.

The commandant said, "Natlong? A quiet young man. Keeps to himself. He's somewhere in the middle of his class, I believe. But, all in all, I believe he may have quite a future."

"Quite a future indeed," said the general, watching the cadet leading Elizabeth Duke from the gym.

Outside the air felt crisp. They stood on the lawn looking out over the river. They could hear the orchestra playing.

George Natlong said, "What does your old man do? He really knows the top brass, doesn't he?"

"It's terrible what our family does," she said. "I'm almost ashamed to say. We make bombs."

"Why," he said, "that's not terrible at all. Somebody on our side's got to make bombs. We'd be in a tough spot if only Germans made bombs."

"I hadn't thought about it like that."

They looked down at the river. It was dark but the moon was out and you could see a great deal. Moonlight played off the water.

"It looks just like one of those paintings from the Hudson River School, doesn't it?"

"It should. This is the Hudson River."

They both laughed and then, quite suddenly, he kissed her.

After that things happened fast. The next day he graduated from West Point, a week after that they were married, and the week after that his father-in-law, unbeknownst to George Natlong, pulled strings and the young lieutenant received orders to report to New Mexico, of all places.

He saw very little action. He was given command of a ten-man security detachment in the New Mexican desert. For weeks he and his men had nothing to do but lounge around a gray steel barrack in the middle of nowhere. He spent entire afternoons looking at cactus flowers or hiking the men across cracked alkali flats. Sometimes he felt guilty and unmanly because he'd been stationed in such a remote, peaceful place while the fighting in Europe and in the Pacific was coming to such a brutal crescendo.

Then one hot summer evening orders came for him to bring his men to a nearby desert town. The town was one of those sleepy desert places where the population always hung just below one hundred and the temperature just above. Driving into town in the cab of the troop carrier George Natlong couldn't take his eyes off the heat shimmering above the road. The red sun settled behind the faraway jagged mesas but the road still shimmered and you could look through it to the town and everything quivered.

The truck threw up a billowy plumage of dust as it bounced into town, past ragtag wooden shacks and adobe huts. The men in the back of the truck made mud when they wiped at the dust clinging to their sweaty faces. One of the men kept licking at his lips and spitting to the road from the back of the truck.

At the center of the town (which was no more than three hundred yards from the edge of town), in the square (which was really no more than a dusty swatch of desert encircled by a boarded-up hotel, a saloon, a bank, a jailhouse and a general store), the troop carrier pulled up beside an army jeep. George Natlong couldn't help thinking that everything looked like the set of a Western movie, except of course the jeep. The jeep looked out of place. His superior officer, a burly general who wore a pistol on each hip with their pearl handles facing forward like he was the Cisco Kid, jumped from the jeep. George Natlong saluted.

"A very important job," the general said. He always spoke

in clipped, hurried phrases, as if his words were perishable baked goods that must be served piping hot and devoured on the spot. "Sometime during the night something unusual might happen."

"Unusual, sir?" George Natlong asked. "Unusual in what way?"

"Can't tell you. Can only tell you that if this unusual event occurs, you will realize it immediately. Your job is to watch over this town through the night. If anything unusual happens, and if members of the civilian population become upset, reassure them. Smile, and say, 'A fuel tank caught fire out in the desert. Nothing to worry about.' Got that, lieutenant?"

"Yes, sir!"

"Carry on then." The general slid back into the jeep. "If nothing unusual happens before dawn, you and your men return to barracks." With that the jeep lurched off, across the shimmering moonlit desert, raising a column of dust.

George Natlong told his men, "Listen up!" Their faces shone in the heat in the back of the canvas-covered truck. "Sometime during the night something unusual may happen. When it does, our job will be to reassure the civilian population."

The men nodded.

"What's this unusual thing that might happen, lieutenant?" one of the men asked. It was Hodges. Hodges was all right but he asked too many questions.

"How should I know? Those are our orders. Look for anything unusual. I mean, anything the least out of the ordinary. If you spot something, and if it upsets the civilian population, smile, then say, 'A fuel tank caught fire in the desert. Nothing to worry about.' Got that? Now split up. Look this town over. I mean up and down. Hodges, you chatterbox, stay here with me."

George Natlong and Hodges stood by the truck watching the rest of the men fan out. It was getting dark. Hodges leaned against the truck's front bumper, smoking a cigarette.

"A fuel tank caught fire out in the desert, huh?" Hodges

said.

George Natlong had his back to Hodges. He was staring at the swinging doors of the saloon. Soft honky-tonk piano dinglings spilled into the square.

"You have to wonder what the hell the army's doing out here," Hodges went on, not certain the lieutenant was listening. "Some of the guys say the army's building some kind of death ray. You know, like in the comic books. I think they're making a special plane. That would explain a fuel tank fire, don't you think, lieutenant?"

George Natlong turned. "Can it. It's none of your damn business what the army's doing out there. Just do your job and never mind the rest, mister, or I'll put you on report. I've got orders to watch out for guys with questions."

"All right, all right," Hodges said. They were standing face to face in the moonlight. "I didn't mean nothing by it. I'm just curious, is all. You don't have to worry about me. In Dayton I carried the flag in the Thanksgiving Day parade. Every year. I'm just curious, is all."

George Natlong returned his attention to the saloon. Through the grimy windows he could make out several Tiffany lampshades hanging by chains from the ceiling. He could hear four or five people singing to the piano. The shadows of several dancing couples splashed against the walls of the saloon and were visible now and then through the windows.

At regular intervals the men reported back to the square. A little after midnight a boyish private from South Carolina came running back to the square yelling, "There's a pack of devils sunning themselves in the moonlight!" Hodges went off with the private to investigate. He came back laughing. The private had seen chameleons. Shortly thereafter one of the men came running to report that stars were falling from the sky, but investigation revealed a meteor shower.

A little after two in the morning, after the saloon had closed for the night and the patrons had gone down the street singing, George Natlong sleepily leaned against the truck in

111

the shadows watching the lights go out. An old man in torn prospector's clothing came stumbling through the square, past the troop carrier. In the moonlight his white whiskers resembled silk threads. A chicken flopped under his arm. The old man was very drunk and he had much difficulty walking. The chicken was a half-dead fighting cock and in the silvery light of the moon you could make out blood on its ruffled feathers.

"Wouldn't you say that's rather unusual, lieutenant?" Hodges yelled down from the cab of the truck.

George Natlong intently watched the old man stumble toward the saloon, carrying the chicken like a football, tottering from the dust onto the wooden-planked sidewalk. He braced himself against a post then fell backwards across the planks, smashing into the saloon's wooden doors. Face down on the planks, he lamely pounded at the doors. The chicken momentarily went wild in a flurry of feathers and squawks.

One of the swinging doors opened and the proprietor yelled out, "Damnit Cody, I'm closed for the night." The old man only tried to crawl past the door. The proprietor grabbed the old man by the heels of his boots and dragged him off the wooden planks into the dirt, the chicken dragging along by one of its legs.

George Natlong stepped in front of the proprietor. He smiled, then said, "A fuel tank has caught fire."

Hodges grinned beside George Natlong.

The proprietor took in the two uniforms.

"How's that?" the proprietor asked.

"In the desert," George Natlong said, trying to sound reassuring. "Nothing to worry about."

The proprietor screwed up his face.

"Uh huh," he said. He stared at the military truck behind the two army men. "Don't say?" There was a whistling sound when he spoke. He still clutched the old man by the heels of his boots. "Now if you'll 'scuse me, soldiers, I'm taking Cody here to the jailhouse to sleep it off."

He started away, but George Natlong put his hand on the proprietor's shoulder, stopping him.

With a smile he said again, "A fuel tank's caught fire in the desert. Nothing to worry about." He stared into the proprietor's eyes as if there was some hidden, yet mutually understood meaning.

The proprietor let go of the old man's boots.

"A fuel tank's caught fire, you say?" the proprietor said. He spat. "And Cody here was mixed up in it?"

George Natlong kept smiling. Hodges crossed his arms, saying nothing.

"What in blazes is the army doing out there in the desert anyhow?" whistled the proprietor. "Folks is saying things. Death rays. Flying saucers."

After a moment the barkeep turned and went back into the saloon. A bolt fell across the swinging doors and then the last of the stained-glass lights winked out.

The old man slept in the dust. The chicken briefly scratched in the dirt then roosted near the old man's head. George Natlong and Hodges went back to the truck. Overhead the stars twinkled brilliantly.

They watched the chicken fall asleep. It was nothing but a knotty pile of feathers in the middle of the road. One by one the men came back to the truck with nothing to report. One or two of them, taking a cigarette before starting off again on patrol, asked Hodges, "Why did the chicken fall down in the middle of the road?"

Hodges said, "To get some sleep."

The night passed slowly. It started to drizzle a little after four but the clouds quickly broke up and soon they could again see stars. A little before five a milk truck bounced into town. It was about an hour before sunrise and everything but the jerking milk truck was still. You could hear the clatter of the bottles inside the truck as it bounced along. George Natlong, lifting his eyebrows, sat up. Now *this* is unusual, he thought. It didn't seem right to see a milk truck out West.

The milk truck lazily rattled into the square. The headlights at last fell on the old man and the chicken. The driver stopped, got out for a look. He wore a white shirt and hat. He had a long, horsey face. He went over to where the old man slept and yelled down to him, "Is this your cock, Cody? Bet he's a good fighter, how 'bout it?"

The old man snored in the dust. George Natlong got out of the truck and walked over.

"I'll buy this here cock off you for ten dollars, Cody, how 'bout it?" The milkman reached into the pocket of his white trousers, pulling out a bill. He shoved the money into the old man's shirt pocket then scooped the rooster from the ground.

For the rest of his life George Natlong would remember those last few steps. He'd been so self-assured then, so totally in the dark. Those were the last few steps of his innocence. Always he'd remember the confident way he'd swaggered up to the milkman and the chicken. He'd walked with the swagger of a gunslinging marshal in a Western movie. He knew what he had to do. He put his hand on the milkman's shoulder. The milkman spun around, surprised. George Natlong smiled reassuringly at the exact instant it happened.

A blinding flash lit the desert. Night drained away and an unearthly light flooded in. It was a stark, white light, but you could see tiny packets of reds, blues, and yellows mixed in with the white. The men reflexively shut their eyes but still they could see red, even when they brought their hands up to cover their eyes. There was no hiding from that light. It was so intense that, covering his eyes with his hands, George Natlong thought he could see the bones in his fingers. The light receded somewhat and George Natlong lowered his hands and looked down at the old man sleeping in the dirt. Every pore, whisker and wrinkle on the old man's face was starkly lit.

The milkman blinked, looked down the road. In the receding brightness of the flash he could see some of George Natlong's men patrolling the street at the edge of town. Far on the horizon in the desert an orange and gold fireball rose from the sand. Beneath the fireball a white cloud pushed into the heavens like a column holding up the dome of the sky.

The milkman dropped the rooster. The bird flapped its tattered wings a few times then lifted its head.

114

"Cockadoodledoo!"

George Natlong turned from the mushroom cloud and saw the entire desert, as far as the eye could see, from horizon to horizon, from mesa to mesa, lit as if by the sun. Someone had thrown a lightswitch in the dark of night and had made instant noon.

As quickly as the light had flooded in, it leaked away, like the sun had been put in a trunk and the lid closed. The stars swept back across the sky. All that remained was the hot orange glow of a fireball blazing up toward the stars, high above the mushroom cloud.

Presently a hot wind blew in from the desert. It started gently, like a balmy summer breeze, but quickly it was pulling George Natlong's trouser cuffs around his ankles. In no time it was like a hurricane and the men had to double over to protect their faces from the blowing sand. The wind was rocking the milk truck and you could hear the bottles inside clattering. Then the ground began quaking. The rumbling intensified until the milk truck began bouncing on its wheels and you could hear bottles breaking. Milk streamed down the running boards, forming white puddles in the street.

"My milk!"

Around town windows were thrown open. "Get out! Earthquake!" could be heard as people jumped into the street.

A woman in haircurlers and bathrobe flitted among the startled townspeople, yelling, "I'd just got up for a glass of water. I was there at the sink when the sun came up! If I hadn't seen it with my own eyes I wouldn't believe it. It came up so fast I thought I must be dreaming. It shot up like a piece of toast. Then it dropped back down just as sudden."

"It's the army!" one of them yelled. "I tell you, they're doing something in the desert!"

They began crowding around the troop carrier. George Natlong jumped onto the bumper.

He yelled, "A fuel tank caught fire in the desert, that's all." Behind him the mushroom cloud and the fireball appeared to be rising clear to the ionosphere.

115

"A fuel tank caught fire my ass!"

They drew closer until George Natlong was obliged to pull out his .45. He fired into the air. Hodges numbly stared at the mushroom cloud.

"Lord have mercy," he said over and over, his fatigue hat in his hands. "Lord have mercy on those Japs."

George Natlong jumped from the truck.

"Can it, mister. We've work to do."

Orders came by courier at dawn. A motorcyclist, his mouth and nose obscured by a dusty red bandanna, sped into the square, wordlessly handing George Natlong a sealed messenger's pouch. The bike spun around, throwing dust, then raced back into the desert. George Natlong opened the seals, pulled out a slip of paper.

"*Prevent town newspaper from publishing account of last night's blast in desert,*" the note read.

George Natlong walked over to the newspaper office. It was a small wooden building just off the square. A truck idled out front. Two teenage boys tossed bundles into the back. Inside a man in an inky apron cleaned racks of type.

"Who's in charge here?" George Natlong asked.

The pressman looked up. He was squirting liquid from a bottle across the type and seemed surprised.

"That'd be Hank."

"Let me talk to him."

"He ain't here."

"Perhaps you can help me then."

"Perhaps I can. Perhaps I can't."

"Do you know anything about— ground tremors in the desert earlier this morning?"

"Sure," said the pressman. "Everybody's talking about it. Some say it was a quake, all right. Others— well they ain't so sure."

"I've got orders that you're not to print a word of it."

"Don't say, soldier," said the pressman. He took off his glasses, carefully wiping them on a clean spot on his shirt.

116

"Well," he went on, crossing the cramped office to the counter, "you'll have to talk to Hank. Hank's the editor."

George Natlong could hear the truck pulling away out front.

"And where the hell is Hank?"

"Over in the telegraph office. But I don't know if it'll do much good talking to him."

"Why's that?"

"The paper's already been printed. Hank wrote a nice piece about the quake. Or whatever it was. People were calling in all morning so Hank thought he'd best write a whole column about it."

The pressman threw a fresh newspaper onto the counter in front of George Natlong. On the front page, at the top, a headline screamed, "Strange Flash, Tremors Reported."

"Christ Almighty!" George Natlong folded the paper, tucked it in his jacket. "You can't publish this. I've got orders!"

"You're a little late, aren't you? The delivery trucks have gone. People are already reading this paper."

George Natlong stormed from the office. There was no sign of the truck or the two boys who'd been loading it. He went back inside.

"Where'd you say that editor was?"

"Hank? He's over at the telegraph office."

"Where's that?"

"Just across the street."

In the telegraph office a tall, balding man intently dictated a lengthy message to the telegraph operator. They were leaning over several pages of typewriting when George Natlong came in. The tall man straightened. George Natlong closed the door, saying, "I'm looking for Hank, the editor of the paper."

The tall man said, "I'm Hank. What can I do for you, lieutenant?"

"Did you publish an article about something unusual that may have happened in the desert last night?"

"That's right. I was just sending a copy of the story to the

117

wire service in Santa Fe. They're very interested."

George Natlong clenched his jaw.

"I'm afraid you can't do that."

"Why not?"

"I've orders to prevent publication of any information pertaining to last night's— event. It looks like I'm too late to stop your presses but I'm sure as hell not going to let you send that message to the Associated Press."

He held out his hand.

The telegraph operator looked at Hank.

"Are you telling me—." Hank stuttered.

"For our national security, please give me that telegraph message."

"What the hell happened out there last night?"

"A fuel tank caught fire. That's all."

"A fuel tank my ass." Hank went to the window. "I saw it with my own eyes. It was like hell on earth."

George Natlong eyed the typewritten pages, his hand still extended.

"What in God's name is the army up to out there?"

George Natlong said nothing.

"Good God! Is that what the Japs are going to get?"

Hank looked at the telegraph operator.

The operator shrugged his shoulders. "Remember Pearl Harbor, Hank," he said.

Hank slid the pages across the table to George Natlong. The young lieutenant folded them, slid them inside his fatigue jacket. He crisply spun around.

A little before noon George Natlong and his men rode the truck back to the barracks in the desert and went to sleep. George Natlong dreamed he was running through a field of white flowers, trying to escape a spreading cloud. The cloud whirled tornadolike across his dreamscape. He was running and when he'd look over his shoulder there it'd be, drawing closer. With every step the white flowers at his feet turned black and withered.

118

Late in the afternoon he was awakened by a courier. The courier's face was still covered by a bandanna and George Natlong started when he opened his eyes and saw the masked face staring down at him. He reached over to the night table for his glasses and put them on. Outside the window in the desert he could see sand blowing.

"Orders from headquarters," the courier said. He wore a leather jacket. "It's sure blowing out there, lieutenant."

George Natlong sleepily took the orders. He coughed.

"*Proceed to nearby desert hospital,*" the order read. "*Instruct hospital personnel not to report any casualties, civilian or military, to newspapers or other civilian agencies.*" George Natlong sat up in bed, cleared his throat. He ran a hand through his hair.

"Smoke, lieutenant?" the courier asked.

George Natlong took one.

"Will there be a reply, sir?"

"No," George Natlong said. The courier started to go but the lieutenant stopped him. "Wait, soldier." From his jacket pocket George Natlong pulled the typewritten pages he'd confiscated from the editor in the telegraph office. He wrote a short note explaining how he'd come by the transmission.

"Take this back right away."

One of the men had fixed some stew but George Natlong wasn't hungry. He took a jeep, rode alone into the desert. The hospital was on the road between the barracks and the town. It consisted of three sunbaked adobe houses. A clinic, really. One of the houses was half-buried in the shifting sand. Several pickup trucks and a battered white station wagon waited out front.

The air inside was stale and smelled of alcohol. A nurse sat writing at a desk. She looked up.

"May I help you, lieutenant?"

"I'd like to see the doctor."

"Is this an emergency?"

"No. Government business."

"Won't you have a seat? I'm sure the doctor will be with

you momentarily."

George Natlong sat beside an aged Indian woman. Her eyes were bandaged. On the other side of the room sat two men who looked like cattle ranchers. Cowboy types. Their faces and hands were bandaged, as if burned. One of the men held a pot between his knees and wretched into it. George Natlong turned away, gazed out the window. The sand was really blowing.

The doctor came in. George Natlong had expected someone younger. He must've been seventy years old. His face was very wrinkled. He wore a rumpled white coat and a stethoscope hung from his neck. He bobbed a pipe into a tobacco pouch.

The doctor motioned to the back room.

"Won't you please step into my examining room, lieutenant?"

They went into the back room and the doctor closed the door. It was a pleasant, book-lined room with a big desk, leather furniture and a modern examining table. The furnishings were much too plush to have been bought with the proceeds from a desert practice like this, George Natlong thought. Perhaps this old coot was one of those bleeding heart do-gooders from the city who gives up a good practice to cure the huddled masses. The sheepskin on the wall said Harvard medical school. This threw George Natlong off balance. He suddenly saw the doctor in a more respectable light. Establishment things, like the right schools, the proper families, and the army brass meant a great deal to George Natlong. Even then he was a bit of a snob.

"I have orders from army command to instruct you to—."

The doctor cut in. "You're here to tell me not to report any casualties to the newspapers."

George Natlong was left speechless.

"Why yes," he fumbled. "How'd you know?"

"I must say, I expected you to come sooner." The doctor sat at the desk, motioned for George Natlong to have a seat. The chair was solid and comfortable.

120

"Why do you say that, doc?"

"Young man, where have you been for the past twelve hours? In the morning I saw six people who'd been blinded by some kind of flash in the desert. By noon I started getting the burn cases. Mostly cattlemen and Indians. They say white ash fell from the sky all morning. Where an ash contacts the skin there is a burning sensation, followed by a red mark, then an open, oozing cut. The ash seems to burn right through. Later this afternoon I started getting nausea cases. People who can't keep anything down, and diarrhea too. These are very unusual symptoms, wouldn't you say, lieutenant?"

George Natlong didn't know what to say.

The doctor puffed on the pipe.

"Tell me, young man," he asked George Natlong, "about the explosion this morning in the army compound."

George Natlong started to reply but the doctor cut him off.

"Please don't tell me a fuel tank caught fire in the desert."

"Now wait a minute, doc. This's gone far enough. How do you keep knowing what I'm about to say?"

"There are five medical clinics in this valley," the doctor explained, puffing the pipe. "Six, if you count the one in the Indian reservation. I say counting that one because some folks don't consider Indians to be human beings. Never mind that. All day long patients have been coming into my clinic, and into the clinic in Santa Clara, and into the one outside Fairview, and into each of the other clinics, complaining of the same symptoms. Sudden blindness. Skin burns. Vomiting and diarrhea. Naturally we've consulted. Symptoms like these have never occurred around here before, lieutenant. And do you want to know something else?"

George Natlong shrugged.

"Throughout the day each clinic has been visited by an eager young lieutenant such as yourself who has told the attending physician that a fuel tank has caught fire in the desert and not to worry, but also not to report any of it to the newspapers."

Again George Natlong was taken by surprise. It'd never occurred to him that his wasn't the only security detachment in the desert. Now he realized the army'd probably assigned a security detail to each of the small desert towns near the camp.

"You don't have to worry, young man," the doctor went on. "I have no intention of going to the newspapers. But may I ask a favor of you?"

"What's that?"

"Please tell your superior officers that we desperately need medical information. I need to know the cause of the burns and the proper treatment for the sickness. It may be none of my business what's going on in the desert but the army has no right to jeopardize the lives of innocent people."

The telephone rang. The doctor said a few words into the phone then hung up.

"That was the clinic in La Cueva," he said. "A young lieutenant just came with news that an army physician will arrive shortly with information. Until then, all patients are to drink plenty of water. Well, lieutenant, you better get back to camp. You'll be getting new orders shortly and then you'll have to come back here and see me again. Maybe you can get a bite to eat before then."

George Natlong got up. It'd been a very disconcerting visit. He said goodbye to the doctor but he never did get the old coot's name.

In the waiting room the patients were doubled over. George Natlong couldn't bring himself to look at them. He reached for the door when suddenly it swung open. Two cowboys carried an old man with a scruffy white beard. He clutched a dead rooster to his chest like a doll. He was the old drunk they'd encountered last night in front of the saloon.

"We found old Cody here by the side of the road," one of the cowboys told the nurse. "Looks like he's been burnt, don't it?"

George Natlong saw bloodied burn marks on the old man's face and hands. The chicken's mouth hung open and blood dripped to the floor. It was as if the bird had been eating burning coals.

The doctor came out from his examining room. George Natlong was just leaving when the doctor hailed him.

"Looks like there's a bad wind blowing in from the desert," the doctor winked at him. "You better stay inside tonight. And drink plenty of water."

That night George Natlong drank so much water he thought his bladder might burst. Years later he would joke about it.

5

Several weeks after Nagasaki had been laid low George Natlong received orders to report to his superior officer at HQ. For weeks he'd been killing time in the desert with his men, trying not to go stir crazy, wondering what he would do with himself now that the war was over. He was overjoyed for a chance to get out of that hellhole of a barracks.

He drove a jeep to the army's field headquarters in the heart of the desert physics laboratory. It was the first time he'd set foot inside the camp where the bombs were made. Often while passing time in the desert he'd wondered what an atom bomb factory would look like. It was a disappointment. Before the war the place had been a private boarding school. The army had set up headquarters in an old weathered dormitory. Like something out of David Copperfield. Certainly not as modern as George Natlong had expected, certainly not as deadly looking.

At headquarters an armed guard escorted George Natlong into the office of General Leslie Groves.

General Groves stood, returned the salute, then moved from behind the desk to shake hands. As always Groves' face seemed somehow puffy, like he needed sleep. Even in the office the general wore his pearl-handled pistols. He resembled an overweight, over-the-hill cowboy. All this aside, he was surprisingly direct and unassuming.

"Good to see you, Lieutenant Natlong. Pull up a chair."

The general went back behind the desk, folding his hands on the desktop. He leaned forward so he could speak quietly, as if, even in his own office, he feared being overheard.

"Congratulations," Groves whispered. "Your promotion

has come through. You've made captain."

George Natlong couldn't hide his surprise.

"Why thank you, sir. I'm honored. I hardly know what to say."

"Then don't say anything."

Behind Groves, on the wall, hung a portrait of Harry Truman. It was one of the few embellishments to an otherwise plain and nondescript office. The general pushed a cigar box across the table. They were fine Havana cigars. George Natlong took one.

"It isn't such a great honor," Groves said softly. "This project has several security detachments like the one under your command, each run by a lieutenant fresh from The Point. Each lieutenant has just been promoted to captain. It's only fair. This has been an important assignment and you've all served your country well."

The general lit George Natlong's cigar.

"So you see," Groves half-whispered, "your promotion to captain isn't anything the least bit special. That's why I've requested another promotion for you. And a special commendation. By this time next week you'll be a major in the United States Army."

George Natlong choked on the smoke. It dropped to the floor, smoldering a moment or two before he could pick it up.

"A major, sir? Pardon my asking, sir, but what have I done to merit such a promotion?"

The general smiled. His eyes twinkling, he opened the top drawer of his desk, producing a stack of typewritten pages. It was the telegraph message George Natlong had confiscated from the newspaper editor on the morning of the bomb test.

"This isn't the sort of thing I wanted to see printed in the pages of *The New York Times*," Groves said. "The implications would've been immediately understood by agents of the belligerents. It was crucially important to keep word of the blast from the national press." Groves gruffly pointed at the confiscated dispatch before him. "This, son, was your masterstroke of the war."

"I don't understand, sir."

"This is the best damn description of an atomic explosion I've ever read. That bastard newsman was about to send it to the wire service in New York!"

"He told me he was sending it to Santa Fe."

"Santa Fe! Didn't you read the address on this dispatch?"

George Natlong leaned over the desk. The dispatch was addressed to the Associated Press in New York.

"We checked into this newspaper guy," Groves voice dropped back down into a whisper, his eyes sweeping the room. "Before the war he was a honcho with the wire service. Moved out here for health reasons — bad nerves. If this telegraph had gotten through they'd've been reading about our work in Tokyo. You were on the ball, son. They'll always be a place for someone like you in this man's army. Tell me—. Have you given much thought to what you'll be doing after the war?"

"No sir. Not much thought at all."

"I want you to think about joining my staff. Your record's good. West Point. Now a special commendation. I think you'd make a damn good career man. This is going to be the American Century, Natlong, and you've the chance to see it from the inside. And, believe me, you ain't seen nothing yet."

"I'm honored sir," George Natlong said. "I really don't know what to say."

"Then damnit son don't say anything. The problem today is that too many people have nothing to say but they go ahead and say it anyway. Just think it over. I'm giving you a one-month furlough. Go home and think it over."

Groves got up. Still he whispered.

"When you get back we'll talk about your future. If you decide to stay on in peacetime you'll have interesting work, all the respect and privileges of a United States Army major, and I'll see you get an office in the Pentagon. I built the Pentagon, you know. That was my job before I came here. I wanted to erect a building so strong that no bomb on earth could harm it and then I came here and created a bomb that can knock it flat. There's poetic irony somewhere in there, don't you think?"

Wearing the stripes of a major, George Natlong rode the trains home to his betrothed. On the trains he was very aware of the boys holding their mothers' hands looking up to him. In the train station in Albuquerque a little boy stopped and saluted. George Natlong saluted back crisply. He'd never forget that. It felt good to walk through the stations carrying his bag between trains. He liked the way the newspaper vendors called him "soldier," then nodded approvingly. He liked the way the girls at the coffee counters gave him free cups of coffee and smiled until they saw his wedding ring. That was always the second thing they saw, the ring, after they saw the uniform. One girl behind the counter somewhere in Nebraska smiled while she poured the coffee. "Too bad you're hitched, soldier boy," she winked at him. "You and me could've had some times together." He liked these things. There was no end to his liking them. He liked the way the soldiers walking through the stations shouldering their duffel bags snapped to and saluted him. Those major stripes sure commanded respect. George Natlong would nonchalantly return the salutes, secretly reveling when the young lieutenants and captains finally got around to looking at his face and seeing that he was invariably younger than them. That was the second thing the young lieutenants looked at, his face, after they'd seen those major stripes. George Natlong could sense the jealousy in their eyes. He could almost read their minds and hear them think, "What did that candyass do to get those stripes?"

That's when he'd feel deflated. What, after all, in the final measure, *had* he done to earn those stripes? In those days he had a vague fear that one day he'd find himself bouncing a little boy on his knee and he'd be asked, "What *did* you do to win the war, Daddy?" What could he say? What did he, Major George Armstrong Natlong, have to be so Godalmighty proud of? He'd bullied some jumpy twit into not sending a telegraph message. Very big deal! It so happens my superior officer is a secrecy nut, that's how I ended up with these stripes! he had to admit to himself.

The train ride across the American continent was long and lonely. The last stretch seemed the most unbearable of all. The passenger car was empty except for a loudmouthed captain from Pittsburgh who wouldn't shut up about a woman he'd married in Boston.

"She's from Weston. Ever hear of it? The best part of town. Her old man's got this mansion with a marble stair. Thirty two rooms. And a Rolls in the garage. Did pretty good for myself, didn't I?"

Even as the captain bragged the train pulled into Winterford's own private train depot. Henry Duke's flowers were all in bloom and the place looked like heaven. Elizabeth and Henry Duke waited on the platform, arm-in-arm with Elizabeth's little brother.

"So what," George Natlong let out as he rose with his things. "I married Delaware."

Elizabeth came to the edge of the platform. "George! I was beginning to think you'd missed the train!" Her eyes were as big and round as he'd remembered them. He took her in his arms and her hair smelled sweet.

Afterwards he shook hands with Elizabeth's father.

"I see our cadet is moving up in the world!" Henry Duke beamed with a wink, tapping the stripes on George Natlong's shoulder.

"Very big deal," George Natlong said bashfully, looking over to Inky. The boy was about fourteen years old. His name was Tod. Like his sister, his hair was jet black and his complexion dark, so much so that everyone called him Inky. He wore a New York Yankees cap. George Natlong tugged at the visor, asking, "How's it going, chief?"

The boy had the same big eyes as his sister. He looked on reverently. "Father says I can go to West Point like you! I want to play football there. Already I made fullback on the junior varsity team at school!"

"Gee Inky that's swell!" George Natlong said, wrapping his arm around Elizabeth.

She said, "Inky, get George's bag."

The boy grabbed the duffel bag. It was heavy but he managed to lift it with both hands.

"Here kid let me get that."

"That's all right, George dear," Elizabeth said. "He doesn't have far to go. I thought we'd stay here in the train depot. I've fixed it up as a guest house. Wait'll you see. It's just adorable. So snug and cozy."

George Natlong had to laugh. He could see the new calico curtains she'd hung inside the little depot.

"In that case," George Natlong smiled, "I should carry you over the threshold."

He picked her up and carried her in. They kissed. Inky followed them in with the bag.

"They're saying you saw A-bombs go off in the desert, George," Inky said. "What did you see? In school, teacher says there's a cloud shaped like a mushroom. Is that true?"

"Inky!" said Henry Duke. His hands rested on the knob of the walking stick. "George has just returned home! Don't bombard him with lots of silly questions."

"That's all right, Mr Duke," George Natlong said. "I don't mind. But I can't talk about it anyway, Inky, because it's all tip-top secret. I'm not allowed to say a word of it."

"Not anything?"

"Not a word. It's so secret I hardly know anything myself."

"Gee! Then it's true? You *did* see it go off in the desert?"

"Inky! Not another word." Henry Duke bent forward and pecked Elizabeth on her cheek. "We'll see you two at dinner, darling. Inky, come along."

George Natlong stood in the open doorway watching them go. He had his arm around Elizabeth.

"Your old man's something else," George Natlong said. "To look at him you'd never guess he made bombs. He almost sounds like he doesn't even like *talking* about bombs."

129

"Daddy's a kitten," Elizabeth said. "You have to know him before you can begin to understand him."

Elizabeth took off George Natlong's jacket.

"I've made the most wonderful plans for tonight," she was saying as she hung it up. "After dinner I thought we'd have a little Armistice Day celebration."

"Sounds swell, honey." He was happy to be with his family. He liked the sound of that word. Family. It had a warm, solid sound. He liked the feeling of being a soldier coming home from war, being met at the train by his family. It was good to have a family. Any family will do when you are coming home from war, he thought. It felt good to have a family to meet you at the train. What would it've been like if there'd been no one to meet him at the train? Might the war never end if no one meets you at the train?

A black maid came up to the open doorway, knocked on the doorjamb.

"Miss 'Lizabeth!" the maid called in. "Dinner's ready, honey!"

"Thank you Delilah. We'll be right along." Then, to George Natlong, "I thought you'd be hungry from your trip, darling. I told them to have dinner ready when you got home."

The maid remained in the doorway. She said, "To think I used to wash her bare bottom and now she got herself a fine soldier boy!"

The newlyweds had to laugh.

"Give me a minute to wash my face, will you?" George Natlong asked. She led him to a small powder room off the den, where he splashed water on his forehead. She watched in the mirror. While he pressed the towel against his face she reached around to straighten his tie. They looked at each other in the mirror.

"Don't we make a handsome couple?" She was humming.

He didn't know what to say.

"Oh I'm so happy," she said. "I wish it could stay like this forever."

He looked at her once more in the mirror.

130

"What do you say we chow down?" he said. "I'm starving!"

Inside the main house neatly uniformed servants rushed everywhere. A servant met the newlyweds at the door. The servant's hair was slicked flat against his head. He took George Natlong's hat.

They walked arm-in-arm through the mansion. "Here's a portrait of Momma," Elizabeth said as they passed a painting in the hallway. The portrait was framed in gold.

"She looks very happy."

"Momma was a happy woman. She always had everything. Daddy was hardly touched by the stock market crash."

"So that's where you got those eyes."

"Momma was much prettier than I."

They went into the dining room. Henry Duke and Inky already were seated. Henry Duke wore a tweed jacket. Inky had on a tie. They were animatedly chatting away.

"Ah here they are now," Henry Duke smiled. The mahogany table had been set with white china and crystal glasses. The crystal sparkled in the light of the chandelier.

"Well ask him Father," Inky said. The boy was smiling.

"Ask me what?" George Natlong said.

"Inky and I have a gentleman's bet," Henry Duke answered. "He says you need to be brought up to date on the baseball standings. I say he's wrong."

"It looks like a very good year for the Cubs," George Natlong winked at the boy. "Do you think just because I've been living in the desert for the past five months I've been isolated from civilization?"

"Then you know a plane crashed into the Empire State Building this summer?" Inky asked.

"It was a B-25 that hit her," George Natlong said. "Flew smack into the seventy-eighth floor. That was big news even in the desert. The cables snapped in one of the elevators and a lady dropped seventy-five floors. A Coast Guard medic who happened to be passing by pulled her out of the basement. She

131

was knocked silly and she said, 'Thank God, the Navy's here!'"

They all laughed. Servants quietly bustled around the table. One filled the glasses with clear white wine while another ladled soup into bowls, his ebony hands working the pearly white luminescence of the china bowls and the soup ladle.

"Here's something I bet you didn't know," Inky said, dipping a sterling silver spoon into his soup. "The Dodgers are thinking of signing a nigger."

"Inky!" snapped Henry Duke. "In this house we don't use that word! It's Negro, or person of color."

The servants kept bustling around the table as if they didn't hear. The one who'd been using the ladle set a bowl of soup in front of George Natlong. The soup was steaming and it made his mouth water. He couldn't wait to taste it.

"Aw that's just talk," George Natlong said. "They'd never sign a colored player. The fans wouldn't have it."

"It's been in all the papers this week," Inky said. "Some—person of color named Robinson. They say he can hit a ball."

"That's just talk. All the good players were off fighting the war. Now that the war's over there won't be any need for colored players."

Inky said, "I don't know. There's this colored person pitcher called Paige. A real old guy, about sixty years old. They say if they let him pitch out of the Negro League he'd strike out DiMaggio."

"That's just a lot of hooey," George Natlong said.

"What do you think, Samson?" Inky asked one of the servants, the one filling the glasses. "What do you think of this pitcher Paige?"

Samson held a pitcher of ice water. He looked up from filling Elizabeth's glass. "You must be speaking of Satchel Paige, Mr Inky. I went to see the colored boys play in Baltimore and that old Satchel was throwing the ball like it had the devil in it. That Satchel can throw a ball so fast they say it speeds across the plate like an aspirin in a hurry."

The servants had brought in pheasant under glass.

132

Elizabeth watched George Natlong's square, muscular jaw as he chewed. More than ever his square jaw, thick eyebrows, swept-back hair and prim officer's uniform reminded her of a nutcracker.

The wine made George Natlong talkative. Dinner went well. He was beginning to feel at home. If this wasn't his home, where was?

"This food sure is great," he said. "I really missed good food in the desert."

"The officers' mess had no good food?" Henry Duke asked.

"There wasn't an officers' mess." George Natlong finished another glass of wine. "For the sake of secrecy everybody was split up and bunked in secluded barracks in the desert. One of my men was our cook. He was very bad. You know how bad army cooking can be, don't you, Mr Duke?"

"Enough of this Mr Duke stuff. Call me Henry. You're family now, George."

"All right Henry. Henry it'll be."

"Yes you're right. Army food can be terrible." Henry Duke chewed some pheasant then added, "I guess all this secrecy surrounding the A-bomb is rather important. Isolation out in the desert and all that. We have to keep it from the Russians."

George Natlong said, "I overheard two guys say the bomb was so complicated it'll take anyone else fifty years to figure it out." George Natlong said this in a very self-important way, as if he was confiding privileged information. In fact, he'd overheard two gas station attendants talking in the town outside camp. That was how it was. You heard little pieces of talk from God knows who and you tried to piece it together.

"Even so," Henry Duke said, "this secrecy is something we must have. At this moment we're the most powerful nation on earth. It wouldn't do for anyone else to have the bomb. We don't want to wake up one morning to find New York or Boston gone, do we?"

"Is that true, Father?" Inky asked. "Are we the strongest

133

country?"

"By far and away," Henry Duke said. "We've never lost a war, have we?"

"Some day mightn't we lose a war?"

George Natlong ruffled. "Inconceivable." He was chomping on his second serving of pheasant. "This is the American Century."

"What happens next isn't my problem, young man," Henry Duke told Inky. "What happens next is the problem of your generation."

"Gosh," Inky said. He pushed his mashed potatoes around with his fork. "That's an awful lot of responsibility, Father."

Henry Duke winked at George Natlong.

My father-in-law's all right, George Natlong thought. He lifted his glass.

"I'd like to propose a toast," he said. He was a little bit lit up from the wine but his words weren't at all slurred.

"A toast to what?" Inky asked.

"To us," George Natlong proposed. "To America. The greatest country on earth. May it stay this way forever."

The four of them clinked their glasses and drank.

Elizabeth rested her head on George Natlong's shoulder. She sighed.

"When you said 'To us' I thought you were going to toast our marriage."

Henry Duke raised his glass again.

"I propose a toast to your marriage," he said, his eyes twinkling. "May the two of you have a very, very happy life together." Now his eyes were watering.

"Here here!" Inky called out. The servants had come in and were applauding the newlyweds from the doorway. Samson brought in a cake with a sparkler. Elizabeth threw her arms around George Natlong's neck and they kissed.

George Natlong felt pretty good.

"I just want to say something," he said. "I know I'm a little stiff. I'm a little bit stiff but that's okay. I want you all to know how I happy I am to be a part of your family. I've never

134

had a real family before and you're the nicest bunch of people a fellow could hope for—." He lost his train of thought then and sat there feeling foolish. Elizabeth had her arm around his neck and she drew him tighter.

"My little nutcracker," she said into his ear.

"We're lucky to have such a fine young major in the family," Henry Duke said. "I couldn't be happier for Elizabeth. She needed a nice young man like you to straighten her out."

"Father! I need no straightening out!"

The servants were laughing.

"Oh yes you do!" Henry Duke said, playing to his audience. "Every young woman needs straightening out."

George Natlong kissed her hand.

"That's all right dear," he said. "I won't have too much straightening out to do."

Elizabeth had begun to blush.

"Oh Daddykins!"

"Samson," Henry Duke beamed. "How about some brandy? The old bottle I've been saving since the end of the first world war. What better occasion? We must drink it to welcome George home from the second world war. Lord knows we might as well drink it before the third world war breaks out."

6

As Samson left for the wine cellar they heard a great commotion in the parlor. People were laughing.

"Is someone playing the radio?"

"What in the world?"

Elizabeth pushed away from the table, went into the parlor. Three couples were dancing to Glenn Miller.

"Goodness!" she said. "How'd you get in?"

"Delilah admitted us, that sweet little thing," one of the men said. He wore black and white wing-tip shoes, a red bow tie. He danced cheek to cheek with his partner and as he spoke she swung away, did a twirl under his arm then came back close. "We didn't want to disturb your dinner so we thought we'd start the party without you. Besides, I was dying to hear Mitchell's record collection again."

"Mitchell? He's back from England?" but even as the words left her mouth a man who'd been dancing with his back to Elizabeth spun around, showing his face. Elizabeth rushed to him. They embraced.

"Mitchell! Darling!"

"Liz!"

He was tall and had a boyish face and dirty blond hair. He lifted her from the floor, spun her around. "Liz, Liz, Liz, pour me a drink and make it fizz!" He set her down and they beheld each other at arm's length. "Remember we used to say that? 'Pour me a drink and make it fizz!'"

"How could I forget? That was our battle cry!"

They gazed at each other a few seconds more, drinking each other in, until Elizabeth said, "Won't you introduce me to your friend?"

136

"Aren't I a bore?" Mitchell said. "Elizabeth, I'd like you to meet Bridgette, my financée.

"How do you do?" Bridgette asked. Her accent was British.

"Your financée? Mitchell! They didn't tell me you were getting married!"

"What about you? They tell me you married a West Point chap this spring. I'm so happy for you Liz. Really I am."

Elizabeth kissed Bridgette.

"You're really a lucky girl, you know," Elizabeth told her. "Mitchell will make you very happy."

"I'm already very happy." Bridgette took hold of Mitchell's arm.

"That must be your soldier boy now."

George Natlong had come in with Inky and Henry Duke. Samson was at their heels with a tray of snifters and a bottle of cognac.

"This is no cadet," Mitchell said, shaking George Natlong's hand. "You've married a major, Liz."

"Believe it or not he was just a cadet when I met him this spring."

Elizabeth hugged George Natlong's arm, snuggling her cheek against his epaulets. She said into his ear, "Before the war Mitchell and I used to go around."

Two couples still danced cheek to cheek. One of the men was very drunk. He fairly well hung on his dance partner.

"You met those four at our wedding," Elizabeth said, nodding at the dancers. "That's Edgar and his wife, Doty." She pointed to a serious little man with a serious little face and hair slicked straight back. Doty, a full head taller, led him around the floor. "Edgar loves boats. He was an ensign in the navy when you saw him. And that's Bimmy and his wife, Natalie." She pointed to the drunk one in wing-tips and bow tie. His hair was almost as red as the tie. "He was in the Coast Guard, remember?"

She called to Bimmy, who staggered over, shook George Natlong's hand. A loud buzzing noise.

"Gets them every time," Bimmy laughed, holding up a joy buzzer. He patted George Natlong's stripes. "How're you doing, George old boy? I see the war's been good to you."

George Natlong flexed his hand.

Elizabeth whispered, "Bimmy's always been a bit of a practical jokester."

Samson doled out snifters of brandy. George Natlong started for a drink but Bimmy suddenly hooked his ankle around his foot, sending the major flying to the floor.

Bimmy laughed convulsively.

"Bimmy!"

George Natlong got up, not laughing.

"George!" Elizabeth gasped. "He's drunk."

George Natlong's jaw was clenched.

"If he wasn't drunk I'd bust him one." Then, to Bimmy, "Don't ever do that again, understand?"

"No hard feelings then?" Bimmy reached out his hand, but George Natlong declined to shake.

"I hope we didn't spoil your dinner, Papa Duke," Mitchell said, hoping to change the subject.

"Not at all," Henry Duke said. "We were just finishing up."

The music had stopped. Mitchell put on a fast record.

"Goodness gracious!" said Henry Duke. "That's jungle music."

"Don't you like Gene Krupa?"

"In my day it was necessary for the music to have what we called a 'melody,' young man. Not just a terrible thumping rhythm."

"This isn't so bad." Bimmy set down his snifter and danced with Natalie. A bouncy bump and grind.

"Well Mitchell my boy when did you get back from England?" Henry Duke asked.

"Just last night. We took a boat across and a train down from New York."

"What did you do in England?"

"Worked on sonar. Made hell for the U-boats."

138

"Now that the war's over you can come to work for the company," Henry Duke said. "Bimmy and Edgar start after the holidays."

"Well that's just swell of you, Papa Duke. But I've got an offer from this outfit called IBM. I was thinking of joining up with them."

"IBM?" Elizabeth said. "Whatever do they do?"

"They think they want to build computers and they're taking on a hell of a lot of the boys from England."

"What in heaven's name is a computer?"

"It computes things. Like a mechanical mind."

"Whatever would you use one for? It doesn't sound very practical."

"A fast computer could be used for lots of things, Liz."

"It doesn't sound like it's such a good idea. Why don't you accept Daddykin's offer?"

"I know this job with IBM is an iffy proposition, Liz, but they're offering me twenty-five thousand shares of stock. Of course it's worth peanuts but who knows?"

All this time Inky had been sitting quietly on the sofa, trying not to be too conspicuous so he wouldn't be sent to bed. Doty indiscreetly pulled him to his feet and began dancing with him. She spun the young man around the floor till he laughed loudly.

"Inky! Are you still up? What say you get to bed, young man."

"But Father," Inky said, no longer dancing or smiling. "I was having a swell time. Can't I stay up and listen?"

"Get your pajamas on and then you can come back down."

"How about you?" Mitchell asked George Natlong. "What did you do in the war?"

George Natlong was the only uniformed man in the room. The other three young men, happy the war was over, reveled in their new civilian lives, their flashy new civilian clothing.

For a moment George Natlong said nothing. At last he said, in a subdued voice, "I'm afraid I'm not at liberty to say."

As soon as he'd said it he knew it sounded very exclusive, the way an Ivy Leaguer sounds when he refuses to discuss his fraternity's secret handshake. Look who's the snob now, he thought. He hadn't meant for it to sound that way but there it was. Besides he was telling the truth. He had orders.

Mitchell wondered how to take the remark. Henry Duke leaned close, lifting his white eyebrows. "George here was working in New Mexico. On The Big One."

"Oh." Mitchell whistled through his teeth. "You don't say." He suddenly looked very interested but you could see he didn't know what to say. "You're a physicist then?"

"Hardly. I had charge of a security detail. That's all. In the desert."

Elizabeth took hold of George Natlong's arm.

"The night we met George told me his secret ambition is to be a playwright."

"I should think he has something to write about now."

Inky returned in pajamas and robe. Delilah brought him dish of peach ice cream. Inky sat quietly on the sofa. Samson meanwhile came in, Henry Duke whispered in his ear, then the servant hurried out.

Henry Duke raised his snifter into the light. "This brandy was presented to me by my father on Armistice Day. It gave him special pleasure to give it to me. Well, by jove, welcoming you boys home from your own war I finally understand how Father felt."

Samson returned with a tray. On the tray, sticking into the air like the four spires of St. Patrick's Cathedral, stood four bottles of brandy. Henry Duke handed a bottle to each of the men.

"I can only tell each of you," he said, handing a bottle to George Natlong, "that it gives me great pleasure to give these to you, that you should save them for a special occasion." There was a twinkle in the old man's eyes.

George Natlong looked at his bottle. It was fine old brandy of 1925 vintage. Already he could almost taste the fragrant brandy. He could almost see himself drinking it with a wide-eyed boy sometime in the far-flung future. He smiled.

"I suspect if there's another world war there won't be any-thing for our sons to come home to," he said to Henry Duke.

"You should know, shouldn't you?" Mitchell asked. He slapped George Natlong on his major stripes. He did it in a friendly way. They all laughed, but not uproariously. It was a nervous laughter.

George Natlong nodded his head.

"Oh isn't this just like the old days, before the war?" Elizabeth chimed in. A sad look took hold of her. "If only Tommy could be here. Then it would truly be like the old days."

"Poor Tommy," Doty said. "He'd be twenty-five this month."

"Yeah, poor old guy," Mitchell agreed. He explained to George Natlong, "B-17 gunner. Lost over the channel."

"Never found a trace of the poor boy, did they?"

"Please don't let's talk about it," Natalie said.

For a minute they said nothing. At last Elizabeth cleared her throat. "Daddykins, now that you're giving out presents, don't you have a surprise for George?"

Henry Duke lifted his eyebrows.

"I really don't know if now is the time, Elizabeth, my dar-ling."

"Now's the perfect time. The whole gang's here. What better way to welcome George into the circle?"

"Maybe you and George should talk it over first," Henry Duke suggested.

"Talk about what?" George Natlong asked.

They all were smiling at him.

"Oh very well," Henry Duke said. He reached into a jack-et pocket and produced a single key on a silver chain. He dan-gled it in front of George Natlong. They all took in his puzzled expression. George Natlong took the key. He held it by the chain.

"What's this?"

"That, my boy, is the key to the executive washroom at

141

the Duke Corporation. We're hoping you'll become our newest vice president. Of the floor wax division."

The men patted George Natlong on the back. The women were talking excitedly.

George Natlong looked at the key. Elizabeth had her arms around him, her head on his shoulder.

"Oh George," she was saying, "I've made the most wonderful plans. We'll live in Winterford's railroad depot and you'll never have to work very hard. There'll be plenty of time for you to write. On holidays we'll go on the most marvelous trips with the rest of the gang. Bimmy knows the most exquisite resorts in the Bahamas and Edgar has a yacht."

George Natlong ran a finger over the key, feeling its peaks and ridges. He swallowed hard. His neck swelled up tight inside the collar of his stiff military shirt. That's when he clenched his jaw. Elizabeth moved her head off his shoulder and watched his square jaw become even squarer.

He thrust the key back into Henry Duke's hand.

"Thank you kindly for your generosity, Mr Duke. Henry. You've been very kind to me but I'm afraid I must decline your offer."

Henry Duke's eyebrows were about as high as George Natlong had ever seen them.

"You don't need to explain a thing," Henry Duke babbled. "I understand perfectly. Mind you, the floor wax job is merely an entry-level position. I'm sure, with a word from me, a more challenging position can be found for a young man of your caliber."

"That's not it at all, sir," George Natlong explained. "General Groves wants me to join his staff. He says I've quite a future in the army."

"But the war's over," Mitchell said.

"Aren't you sick of the army?" Doty asked.

"The war ended just as I got in. I guess there wasn't enough time for me to get sick of it. I saw something in the desert, Henry. General Groves says it's going to change America. I can be part of it. He's offered me an office at the

142

Pentagon. I decided to take the general up on his offer just tonight, Henry, while you were giving us this fine brandy."

Henry Duke smiled. His eyebrows came all the way back down. He reached over and put a hand firmly on George Natlong's shoulder.

"Why, my boy, I couldn't be happier for you and my daughter. I think you're making the right decision. General Groves is right. The atom bomb will change America. You have quite an opportunity before you and if I was in your shoes I'd do the same."

"But George, dearest, the Pentagon— isn't that in Washington?" Elizabeth said, her arm no longer around him.

"I thought we'd find a nice house somewhere in the country, maybe Virginia."

"But the yacht club," Elizabeth. "I've made the most marvelous plans."

"Naturally I would've preferred discussing this with you privately, Elizabeth," George Natlong said, still clenching his jaw.

Tears welled in her eyes. She lowered her face into her hands and started to cry. The women gathered close, trying to comfort her. Doty shot George Natlong a dirty look.

Mitchell said, "Don't you think it's getting about that time, Bridgette?" He extended a hand to George Natlong. "It's been good meeting you, old boy, and I mean that sincerely. From time to time I'll have business in Washington. Maybe we can get together for lunch."

"Yes," George Natlong said. "I think I'd like that."

Natalie took Bimmy by the arm.

"Come along Bimmy. We best be going too."

"You mean the party's over? Already?"

"Come on you we're going!" Natalie tugged at his arm.

Elizabeth sank into the overstuffed sofa, burying her head in a pillow.

"Doty, dearest, everyone's leaving. Don't you think we'd best be leaving too?" Edgar asked. These were the first words out of his mouth all evening.

"Oh shut up you." Doty shot George Natlong another dirty look.

Delilah brought in everyone's coats. After the guests had gone George Natlong remained with Henry Duke, both still holding their snifters. Inky still slouched in the corner of the room. Elizabeth cried on the sofa.

Henry Duke rested a hand on George Natlong's shoulder.

"Why don't you leave me with her for a moment?" Henry Duke winked. "She'll be all right. Why don't you take Inky up to bed?"

George Natlong nodded.

"Come on, kid," he told Inky. "Show me your room."

They went out through the hall to the staircase.

"That party sure cleared out fast," Inky said as they climbed the white staircase. "You really put Elizabeth in her place tonight. I've never seen anybody stand up to her like that before, not even Father."

Back in the parlor Henry Duke sat in the sofa beside Elizabeth. He lifted her head onto his shoulder, rocked her gently. "There there." He pulled out his monogrammed hand-kerchief, wiped at the blue streaks on her cheeks. "There there."

While they sat on the sofa Delilah came in and took away Inky's ice cream dish. Samson followed, quietly carrying off the tray of snifters, which rattled as they were carried out. The servants didn't appear to notice Henry Duke and Elizabeth sitting together on the sofa but they didn't switch off the light when they left the room.

"There there," Henry Duke kept saying, wiping away the blue streaks.

"Oh Daddy," Elizabeth said when they were alone at last. "I made such wonderful plans. I only want one thing, for George to work at your company, and I'll never want anything else in the whole world again."

Sitting alone with his daughter in the quiet parlor, hearing only her sobs and the gentle tick of the grandfather clock in the hallway, Henry Duke said, "Elizabeth, my little cranberry

144

tart, there will always be one thing in this life that you can never have."

Hoping to appease Elizabeth, the next weekend George Natlong went yachting on the Chesapeake with her friends. Edgar kept a fine sloop in the bay. Much to George Natlong's surprise, quiet little Edgar turned out to be an expert sailor. He dashed about his boat wearing a white captain's hat, shouting orders, completely in his element, nothing like the mouse of a man he was on land.

It was a different story altogether with George Natlong. From the moment they weighed anchor he felt uneasy. They had fish for lunch and George Natlong spent the rest of the voyage with his head over the side of the rail, seeing to it that his lunch was returned to the bay.

That evening, back at Winterford, George Natlong wandered the dark quiet sprawling furniture museum. He moved like a drunken ghost through the endless halls and rooms, a bottle of whisky tucked under his arm. At last he stumbled into the hall which Henry Duke had transformed into a Revolutionary-era town square. Resting his back against the ancient bricks of the Golden Eagle Tavern, swigging from the bottle, George Natlong eased himself down to the cold cobblestone floor, where he slept the night away.

7

"Paul! Uncle George's coming down into the cave. He's got four army generals with him. They're wearing guns!"

The boy switched off the computer. He started for the benches, intending to hide, but Claire caught his sleeve.

"Oh no you don't," she told him. "I'm not spending the night on the hard floor behind those benches."

They heard voices and footsteps.

She pulled him up the aisle.

"Hurry!" She prodded him from the chamber into the dim hallway, into the shadows. "Against the wall!"

They pressed their backs against the cold wall. The voices and footsteps drew near.

"There's a hell of a lot we have to do," one of the voices echoed down the hall. "There won't be much time for poker."

Another voice said there was always time for poker.

The party of newcomers rounded the curve in the sloping hallway and came into view. There were five of them. Each wore green trousers, a jacket and an army general's hat. And there was something else: each wore a gun in a holster. George Natlong, a whisky bottle and glass in hand, led the way, a holster slapping his hip. The one called Hal, who the boy had met at breakfast, slugged alongside George Natlong. He also had a glass and a gun. Three more generals, each with a glass and a holstered gun, walked behind these two. They passed so close to Paul that the boy could've reached out and touched the holsters. He held his breath and closed his eyes, waiting in the shadows for them to pass, hearing the ice tinkling in their glasses.

George Natlong led the party into the computer chamber.

146

Paul took a step after them, listening. The girl caught his arm.

He whispered through cupped hands, "I want to listen."

"There's more than enough time for that," she told him. "Let's explore this cave."

She took him by the hand and led him down the dark winding hallway.

At the computer console George Natlong opened the bottle and poured himself a good one. The other generals stood beside him, admiring the computer. One of them, a heavy man with bags under his eyes, unbuckled his holster, removing the gun. He wrapped the belt of the holster around the barrel of the gun and laid it on the console.

One of the others told him to put it back on.

"But I feel so damn silly wearing it," the first one, whose name was Casey, said. "It's like we're playing cowboys and Indians."

"Put it back on," another said. "We agreed we'd wear them."

"Charlie's right. There's too much at stake."

Casey looked with uncertainty at the rolled-up holster.

"Come on Case, be a sport," George Natlong implored. "We've got to keep discipline. God knows we might have to use them before this is over. Men stationed in missile silos always carry sidearms. In case of intruder."

"Or if one of the crew goes crazy," Casey added. "Is that why we're wearing pistols? Are we afraid of each other?"

The four generals with guns strapped to their sides stared at the one who'd removed his. At last Casey picked up his holster and strapped it back on, saying nothing. Hal reached for the bottle and filled Casey's glass.

With that George Natlong asked the computer to show more of the boy's life.

8

It was this box in one corner of the living room. It was a square box, about the size of a doll house, but its top was flat and it was supported by four cylindrical legs fastened to the bottom at each corner. The grownups would sit in chairs for hours watching the box and listening to a voice that came from somewhere inside.

The memories of Peter Paul Stoken start with the box. The earliest thing he could remember was being held in the arms of one of the grownups, sitting in one of the big chairs, looking at the box. It was very curious, that box.

The box had a picture in its front, like the pictures on the wall, except it moved. It was more like a window. A wavy blue gray window on the world. Peter Paul Stoken's mother or his father would get up from the chair and turn a little clicker at the side of the box and the picture would change. The picture would get all fuzzy, the voice would go away, replaced by the most frightening hiss, then a new picture would come on and a new voice would fill the room. There was a pair of shiny sticks at the top of the box and sometimes Peter Paul Stoken's father would have to fuss with the sticks, pointing them this way or that, sometimes cursing, more often than not pounding on the side of the box before the picture would appear clearly, without fuzz or waves, and then his father would sit back down in the chair, watching and listening to the box.

Some days Peter Paul Stoken's father would have friends over to the house and they would all sit down in front of the box, yelling and screaming and drinking a frothy, bitter tasting liquid from cans. Sometimes Peter Paul Stoken would crawl around the floor, lifting a can to his mouth. He would make a face, white suds would drip from his tiny lips and the men would laugh. Then his mother would come into the room, pick up little Peter Paul Stoken and say, "What are you men doing? Letting my baby drink!" and the men would laugh some more. Peter Paul Stoken liked it when the men came over to watch the box.

Sometimes when Peter Paul Stoken was crawling around the floor, bouncing with ecstasy on his hands and knees, he would be drawn to the box. He would stand himself up in front of the box and turn the little clicker.

"Hey! Where's the picture?" one of the men would yell.

"We're missing the game!"

His father would pick him up then and carry him into the next room and set him behind the bars, where Peter Paul Stoken couldn't get out, where he would cry himself to sleep. He didn't like those bars. Sometimes, if he cried long enough, his mother would come in and lift him from behind the bars. She would lower him to the floor where he'd again crawl freely, or maybe she would carry him into another room and lie with him and sing softly to him on her big wide bed. Sometimes she would kiss him and rub his nose with hers and say, "Mama. Say Mama."

Peter Paul Stoken would laugh and bounce up and down, pushing on the bed with his feet and arching his back and maybe clapping his hands. Sometimes his mother would touch his chin with her finger and say, "You're Peter Paul Stoken. Say Peter Paul," and he would like this even more. After this had been going on for some time he would try to mimic the sound his mother made.

"Pul," he would say, and this would make his mother very happy.

She would kiss him then and beam, "Yes, you're Paul! Now say Mama! *Please!*"

Soon everyone was calling him Paul, except his father, who liked calling him Pauley. His father would sit with him in the chair in front of the box and say, "Pauley, say Dada. Make your old man happy. Say Dada."

Before long Paul learned there were names for everyone. There was Mama and Dada. The two funny looking people who always looked happy were Gramma and Grampa Pervis. The two funny looking people who always looked angry were Gramma and Grampa Stoken. Best of all there was his Uncle Jeffrey Stoken.

Uncle Jeffrey sometimes would come over to the house and take Paul for rides in the stroller, pushing him at breakneck speed down the sidewalk. Or maybe he would take Paul by the hand and say, "Come on, Paul. Let's see you walk."

Every now and then Uncle Jeffrey would race into the house and pick up Paul, even if he was behind the bars, and take him into the living room and hold him in front of the box with the moving picture.

Mama would come into the room then and say, "Jeff, what on earth are you doing? He's too young to understand the television."

"This is an important day in history," Uncle Jeff would say. "The first Catholic president! When Paul grows up he'll be able to say he saw Kennedy's inauguration."

"He won't remember a thing!" Mama would say, staring at the boy who sat transfixed before the flickering blue tube.

But always he would remember bits and pieces. He would remember that day sitting in front of the box with Uncle Jeffrey when a man called Kennedy put one hand on a book and raised his other hand into the air. But Mama was right. He couldn't understand much of it.

Some things were easier to understand. One day Uncle Jeffrey ran in and held Paul up in front of the box and there was a picture of a big cigar, standing on its end, smoking at the bottom. "T-minus ten, nine, eight, seven...." White smoke would bellow out from the bottom of the cigar. It would rise straight into the air. Uncle Jeffrey would throw Paul into the air. "This is an exciting time to be alive, Paul," Uncle Jeffrey used to tell him. "Really it is. Maybe someday you and me can take a rocket to the stars. Would you like that?"

"Yeah!" Paul would say.

150

When Paul got a little bigger he figured out how to crawl over the bars. He learned how to take the screws out of his crib and the whole thing would come crashing noisily down to the floor. Some mornings, when no one else was awake, he'd crawl over the bars and go into the living room and turn on the box in the corner. He got good at turning the clicker and fussing with the shiny sticks at the top. After awhile he could always get a good picture. The first show early in the morning was some nonsensical thing called the Farm Report. The man on the show always said things like "livestock prices yesterday were down." How dull! Then came the news (even more boring). Finally, after much waiting, Paul's favorite show would come on. He would hear the happy jingling sound, he would hear the music, and there would be old Captain Kangaroo jingling the keys to the Treasure House. What was in store for today? Would Mr Greenjeans have a new invention? Would Mr Moose drop ping-pong balls on the Captain or would Bunny Rabbit steal a nice bunch of Kangaroo's carrots? Now *there* was something to think about!

One morning, while he was waiting for Captain Kangaroo to come on, there was a picture of Kennedy giving a speech. "The energy, the faith, the devotion which we bring to this endeavor will light our country and all who serve it — and the glow from that fire can truly light the world," Kennedy was saying. Paul liked the idea of a fire that could light the world though he couldn't comprehend it. Once he'd seen a huge bonfire in Mason City after the football team had won, when everyone threw tables and chairs into the flames and screamed insanely, but the fire, even at its brightest, had lit no more than a few blocks of Mason City. He couldn't imagine a fire that could light the world.

The next Sunday, by coincidence, Grampa and Gramma Stoken and Uncle Jeffrey came over for supper and they all talked about this man called Kennedy. While he made a hole in his mashed potatoes for the gravy Paul tried to listen to the conversation.

"I think the Peace Corps is a great idea," Jeffrey said.

151

"There won't be any more wars. Why, we'll use our troops to bring food and medicine to the needy all over the world."

"Don't you believe it for a minute," Grampa Stoken said. He was dressed in his Sunday clothes and Gramma Stoken was standing behind him, holding his necktie over his shoulder so he could carve the roast beef. "There'll always be wars so long as there's commies. Like this here Castro fella down in Cuba. Almost blows us all to Kingdom Come over some missiles. As for me, I think Kennedy's a fine Catholic young man, but I don't take no stock in this Peace Corps talk. It's hogwash, like the talk you hear nowdays about flying a man to the moon. It'll never happen in my lifetime or yours, Jeff."

"I don't know, Dad," Paul's father said. "I'm kind of caught up in Kennedy's optimism. Right now we're living in the richest country in the world. I ask myself, Should we live high off the hog or should we try to help those less fortunate than us? I think Kennedy's going in the right direction myself. Like he said, we can build a fire that can light the world."

There was that phrase again. Paul pricked up his ears.

"You two are young yet," Grampa Stoken said, dismissing Paul's father and uncle with a wave of the carving knife. He laid a juicy cut of meat on a plate. "So's Kennedy, for that matter. Like I said, I think he's a fine Catholic boy — I'm not talking against him on that — but he's young, and so are you boys. When you get a little older you'll start to see things different. You'll start to see the world don't want us going around lighting fires. I saw that in Korea, for myself. One of these days we're going to light one fire too many and it'll be the death of us. Mark my words."

After supper Paul sat in front of the fireplace with Uncle Jeffrey. They were roasting chestnuts over the flames.

"How can you build a fire to light the world?" Paul asked.

"You mean like in Kennedy's speech?"

Paul nodded.

"It's not a fire that you can see," Uncle Jeffrey tried to explain, fumbling for words. "It's not a fire like the one in this fireplace. It's an invisible fire, one that warms your heart, not

152

your hearth. Grampa Stoken doesn't think that's a very practical sort of fire but don't listen to him."

But not long after that everything changed and Paul was left to wonder if his grandfather hadn't been right after all. It happened one day when Paul was out in the yard playing with one of the kids in the neighborhood. The mother of the child came out with tears in her eyes and called the boy. Paul went home then too. He found his mother crying in the living room. She was watching the box.

For several days after that the family sat together watching the box in the living room. No matter how much Mr Stoken fussed with the shiny sticks or pounded on its side he couldn't get it to play happy pictures.

There were pictures of a woman in a black dress with children walking down a broad street. Pictures of a riderless horse with boots in the stirrups pointing backwards. Pictures of a flag folded by soldiers. Pictures of a solitary flame burning in the middle of a field.

After that the family continued spending many hours watching the box in the corner of the living room but now their eyes seemed somehow glassier, as if they could not see so clearly anymore. After that Grampa and Gramma Stoken and Uncle Jeffrey still came over for supper on Sundays, and they would still talk about politics, but never again did Paul hear them talk about building a fire that could truly light the world.

Each day for Paul was a timeless page in a dreamy unending book filled with Christmas trees, drifted snow banks and billowy clouds shaped like dragons bobbing in pure blue sky. In the distance were the rolling Iowa hills, sealing in the valleys like the upturned edges of a pie. They were small hills, those Iowa rollers, but in the eyes of a young boy they embodied everything that was huge, indomitable and insurmountable in life. He wished he could one day be as big as those hills. Then, at night, out would come the stars, the winking bowl curving

153

above the pie crust. Paul thought, Those hills must have felt small when they pulled up the stars!

That winter Paul discovered snow. He rolled in it, tunneled through it. He learned to bunch it up into drippy balls and hurl them at the back of his father's neck as he trudged off to work with his overcoat, hat and briefcase. His father would drop his briefcase in the slush and give chase, throwing a few snowballs of his own, and Paul learned that life can be rosy and warm even in a frozen world.

He discovered the slippery painful joyfulness of ice. Behind his Gramma and Grampa Stoken's house a pond stretched across the frozen ground. In the summer it was like a mirror to the sky. You could see clouds in it and there was even a platform for diving but now that it was winter its surface was dulled a bit though the gray ice if anything increased its silvery hue and made it look more like a mirror. Paul would stand at the side of the frozen pond beneath layers of smooth-soled rubber boots, furry mittens and miniature eskimo parka. He'd take a tentative test of the edge, perhaps feeling it crack slightly, hearing the dry splitting sound, and then he would push off with his other foot and scuff across the slipperiness, waving his arms, wondering how it must be to fly through the air without friction, without strain, and he would look up at the clouds and wonder what it would be like to look down from the heavens into the mirror with the boy scuffing across its face.

His mother would be in the kitchen talking to Gramma Stoken, their hands wrapped around coffee mugs, and Gramma Stoken would look out the window, through the gnarled bare branches of the trees, and see the boy out on the ice and her hand would move to her mouth.

Paul's mother would spring up from the chair and bolt to the porch. "Peter Paul Stoken! Get off that ice!" Her voice rang sharply in the crisp cold air. He could see her on the porch waving him in, the steam cascading from her mouth and nose. He would say goodbye to the clouds and the pond and scuffle back to the crispy crackly edge of the ice, back into the snow, which wasn't so bad, Paul thought, but oh! how the snow must have felt dull when they first made the ice!

And the dreamy, early pages of the book of his life would fill up. He would walk from the pond through the luscious snow, imagining himself walking through vanilla cake frosting, and then he could hear the rumble of the car rolling down the road. He would look up and see Uncle Jeffrey in his green truck, its engine loud and sputtering a trail of white smoke, coming down the road, the chains on its wheels clinking and clanking. Already the window would be rolled down and Uncle Jeffrey would be waving, the words, "Hey Paul!" flying from the truck. Paul crunched through the snow to the driveway as the truck bounced in. Uncle Jeffrey opened the door. A cigarette butt flew into the snow.

"Hey Paul! How's it going?"

"Fine."

"Come for dinner tonight, did you?"

"Yes. Gramma says I can have the wishbone."

"What'll you wish for?"

"I'm not supposed to tell."

And they would go inside, the boy swinging on the uncle's arm, and they would peel off layers of clothes and set boots by the fire. And the dinner would be good, with ice cream for dessert. And afterwards Jeffrey would tell Paul they would play Candyland, and Paul would get to be Uncle Wiggily if he'd go up to Jeffrey's room for the game. Paul would scurry up the stairs, laughing happily, his hand running against the wall as he climbed. Inside Jeffrey's room there would be so many games from Jeffrey's childhood. There were games on the bookshelves, games in the closet, but where was Candyland? Were there games under the bed? He would get down on his belly and start crawling beneath the bed, finding something, something big and heavy, and he would start pulling it out but then someone caught his foot from behind and yanked him out.

"Never go under that bed again!" Uncle Jeffrey yelled, shaking the boy by his shoulders. Paul had never seen his uncle so angry. Once Paul had held a neighbor's kitten in his lap, cradling it like a baby, but the kitten one day was hit by a car and rushed to the vet, and when the kitten came back it seemed docile but when Paul had again tried cradling it like a baby it had gone off, spitting, biting and scratching, drawing a streak of blood on Paul's nose. After that he realized there were some things you could never do with that cat again because it was spooked. It was a useless and an old cat in a way. As he stood in his uncle's bedroom, with Uncle Jeffrey angrily shaking him, he realized Uncle Jeffrey too had been hit awfully hard by something. He too had his limits, he too could be provoked into going off like the cat. Whatever those limits were, could they be found in that heavy thing under the bed?

Paul's face pouted up. Tears spilled down his face. He looked down at the shadow cast under the bed by the light from the lamp on the table.

Jeffrey, his eyes a bit misty, bent on his knee, saying softly, "Aw, I'm sorry Paul. I hadn't no right to go off on you like that. Don't cry. This is a special night. There's something special on the television. Something *historic.*"

They found the game and carried it down to the dining room. The cloth had been pulled from the table and the women were cleaning the dishes in the kitchen.

"I'm Uncle Wiggily!" Paul yelled to his father, who was reading the paper in the parlor with Grampa Stoken.

They played the game in front of the television. Ed Sullivan came out from behind the curtain. He was saying something but it was hard to hear over the screams of the audience. Years later Paul would always find it difficult to describe how he felt when the curtain opened. After it was over, after the curtain closed and the commercial came on, Paul was vaguely aware of his grandfather saying, "What were those girls screaming about? Those mopheads?"

Paul's father said, "That has to be the silliest song I've ever heard. I wanna hold your hand, *oooo!*"

"Get your mouth off it, lawyer man," Jeffrey burst out. He'd turned away from the tv. "Couldn't you hear? Have you no ears? There was *something* in that music. *Something....*" he futilely searched for words. "What do you think, Paul?"

Paul's little mouth was still hanging open. The blue light of the television flickered in his eyes. He looked into his uncle's eyes and he could see that Jeffrey knew just how he felt. But when he turned to speechlessly look at his father he could see that his old man didn't understand at all, would never understand, could never understand, and neither would Grampa Stoken. From that moment on Paul would never be the same. Now that he'd seen the stars he'd never wish to be a hill again.

There was a piano in the hallway near the stairs at Gramma and Grampa Stoken's house. It was an old upright piano that someone had painted pale green. For the longest time Paul wouldn't go near the piano. He was frightened by it though he couldn't say why. Maybe it was because the piano, at its bottom, was held from the floor at each of its corners by feet with claws, though they were really carved coaster blocks. Furniture that appeared to have feet scared the hell out of Paul. Why did they used to put feet on furniture anyway? He was most frightened by the old bathtub in Gramma's powder room. It had feet with horrifyingly pointed toenails and Paul was always afraid it would come to life and chase after him. Whenever he sat on the toilet he'd talk reassuringly to the bathtub, in a friendly way, saying, "My name's Paul. Please don't chase me down the stairs. Say, they're mighty nice feet you have there, Mr Bathtub." It was an ordinary bathtub but to a boy with imagination the most ordinary things can be scary. Why did they put feet on furniture? Why of course to scare the hell out of children.

When Paul climbed the stairway he would glance at the piano's feet and maybe that is why he never got near it, except occasionally when feeling mischievous, when he would sneak up around the corner to the keyboard and push in one of its black and white teeth. A single note would rise, resonating deep in the chest of the piano. The boy would run away before the note could vanish.

157

One day Paul's mother left him at Gramma's house so she could get her hair done. Gramma entertained him by sitting at the piano with a songbook. She pounded on the keys, singing, *"Won't you come home Bill Bailey? Won't you come home? Tra la la la la la."*

Paul looked at the black dots in the songbook, the dots connected to lines and flags with everything behind bars, and then he looked at her hands bouncing up and down. There was a little sliding door in the front of the piano and when you slid it open you could watch the hammers going back and forth, making the strings tremble. In the dim light through the little door you could just make out the trembling.

"I'll do the cooking honey, I'll pay the rent, tra la la la la la."

He looked at his grandmother's lips as she sang. Sometimes she didn't seem to be singing the same song the piano was playing. She was way off in a few places and Paul looked at her with surprise and made a face.

"With nuthin' but a fine tooth comb!"

He wasn't afraid of the piano now because his grandmother was there and he knew it wouldn't act up while any adult was around, since adults have a way of not mixing with magic the way oil in a bottle of salad dressing always floats over the vinegar. The adults couldn't see that the world rested on magic, floating above it the way they did, and if they couldn't see it they believed it mustn't be there. Uncle Jeffrey told him about these things.

Halfway through the second chorus the phone rang and Gramma got up. When she came back Paul sat intently studying the keys, tapping out single notes with his right hand while singing, "Jin gle bells, jin gle bells, jin gle all the way."

"Where did you learn to do that, Paul?" his grandmother asked.

"I just hear it in my head and play it out."

Before long Jeffrey came in with a friend.

"Jeffey will you look at this!" Gramma sat on the stairs, looking down at the keyboard. Jeffrey saw the boy staring at

158

the keys, his right hand striking single notes while his left attempted crude chords. The little hands were barely wide enough to stretch over six keys but still they managed to hit the right notes. "He said he can figure it out in his head," the grandmother beamed.

Fright flashed through Jeffrey's eyes. An insane, illogical fright. Then he thought, It's just your little nephew, Paul, and the fright was over. He felt silly and baffled that a thing like this should spook him so.

He said, "Hey, Paul, stop a second."

Paul turned on the bench.

"Play this note." Jeffrey hummed a note.

Without hesitation, the boy pinged the note.

"Amazing," Jeffrey's friend said.

Jeffrey hummed another note and the boy found it just as easily.

"I think he might have perfect pitch," Jeffrey said.

The next day Paul's mother took him by the hand and walked with him to the home of the neighborhood music instructor. He was a severe-looking man with a waxed moustache. The boy hated him at first sight.

That night at supper his mother told his father, "He's the most darling man. He's been teaching piano and organ for thirty-five years now and he says he's never seen any boy Paul's age display so much natural talent. He says if we get a piano right away and start lessons immediately Paul might blossom into a prodigy. But we *must* start right now. Van Cliburn practiced every single day since he was two, you know. Dear, I think this is something we should take very seriously."

The father looked at the boy sitting at the other side of the table. He was eating peas and carrots and cut pieces of lamb chop. There was pink applesauce in there too, and pink applesauce on the boy's chin.

"What? My Pauley a musical prodigy? Nonsense. My Pauley's going to be an attorney. I can see the shingle now—.

159

What's the matter, dear? Are you mad?"

The mother was pushing her food around the plate.

"This is something I feel *very* strongly about."

"Oh all right. Rent a piano. But don't push him. And I don't want to hear any more of this prodigy business."

But push she did. It was practice, practice, practice, all the time. She got a baby grand for the living room. A metronome sat on top of the piano, among neatly arranged family photographs, cute little figurines and plants. The pendulum on the metronome slapped back and forth, tick, tock, tick, tock, and it got so that he saw it in his sleep. Then there were the music lessons. The man with the waxed moustache tried to teach the boy to read music. But there was something about the black dots behind the bars that reminded Paul of the bars of his old playpen and he couldn't see escaping from one set of bars only to land behind another. Finally he refused to practice and he'd lie down on the floor of the living room, turning himself into unbudging dead weight, when it was time to go to the music teacher's house.

The lessons lasted only a month. One day Paul's mother called the music teacher and canceled the lessons, "At least for now," she told him. She kept the piano in case the boy "outgrows his childish tantrums," as she said, but also because it looked so nice in the living room under the family photographs, the cute little figurines and the plants.

Just when it looked like Paul had been forever soured to music his Uncle Jeffrey stopped by the house with a large package. Paul ripped off the paper. It was a miniature wooden folk guitar.

"Gee," Paul said. He hefted the instrument in his hands, wrapped his palm around the neck of the guitar and pressed his soft, uncalloused fingertips against the springy tension of the strings. It felt like he was holding something he had always wanted to hold but never knew existed. Like oil over vinegar, he thought.

"It used to be my guitar, when I was a kid your age," Jeffrey said. He gazed intently at the boy, like he was trying to look into his soul. "I don't know why I didn't give it to you before. I knew you'd like it. Something told me you'd like it more than a piano."

9

Paul and Claire passed the time tripping around the vast storerooms and plush living quarters of the underground shelter when they suddenly found themselves in a very unusual and strange chamber filled with props from old Hollywood movies.

"Would you look at this!" Paul yelled. He'd come upon a marble pedestal upon which was displayed a small sled with the word "Rosebud" painted across its top.

"It's from the movie Citizen Kane."

The boy reached out and touched the sled. He was surprised to find it was very light, too light to be real.

"Say, this is balsa wood."

"What did you expect? It's a movie prop."

The boy took in the chamber. It was a strange sight. Props, costumes and assorted Hollywood memorabilia had been neatly arranged in display cases.

"How did all this stuff get down here?"

"Maybe it's like a time capsule."

"A time capsule?"

"Movies tell an awful lot about us, don't they? What worried us, what we dreamed of. Maybe this collection is meant to preserve something after—."

"Nuclear war?" Then the boy said. "Over there. Aren't those—."

A pair of sparkling ruby slippers hung on a nearby pedestal. Claire lifted the slippers, kicked off her sandals.

"Claire! What're you doing?"

She modeled the sparkling shoes. "Do I look a little like Judy Garland?"

"I don't know Claire. Maybe you shouldn't—."

Suddenly the boy's attention was drawn to a jacket. On a mannequin. A card at the foot of the mannequin read, "Jacket worn by James Dean in Rebel Without a Cause." It was an ordinary red jacket with a zippered front and an upturned collar. The boy reached up, touching the fabric. It was real.

"Why don't you try it on and see if it fits?"

"Think I should?"

Hesitating no more than an instant, he pulled the jacket from the dummy. It felt cool and snug against his chest. He lifted his hands to look at his fingers as if they'd suddenly been endowed with some potent tingling magic. Pressing his hands against his chest, he felt the smooth nap of the fabric.

"James Dean," he said. "James Dean."

He rolled the collar of the jacket high around his neck.

The girl had to grab him by the arm and pull him along.

"Come on dreamy eyes," she said. "Let's see the rest of this place."

She led him through a maze of display cases. There was the bowler hat that had crowned Charlie Chaplin's head in Modern Times. A trench coat worn by Humphrey Bogart in Casablanca. A scuba diver's mask that had kept Dustin Hoffman's face dry in The Graduate. At the very back of the chamber they came to a small door.

"What do you suppose is in there?"

"There's only one way to find out, isn't there?"

Nothing could have prepared them for what greeted them when they opened that door. Before them a wide, sweeping staircase spiraled down to a formal antebellum entrance hall.

They came disbelievingly down the staircase, pausing at the bottom.

"I'm having a *déjà vu* attack. I tell you, I was here before. Sometime long ago."

Claire laughed. Above her head a crystal chandelier drooped from a golden chain.

"This isn't *déjà vu*. You *have* seen this place before. In the movies. This was part of the soundstage for Gone With The

Wind. Scarlet O'Hara came down that very stairway."

"How'd they get all this down here?"

A mirror hung on one of the walls. The boy turned up the jacket collar as high as it would go, ruffled his hair then sneered rebelliously at his reflection.

"What's this?" Claire had found a concealed switch near the floorboards. When she flicked it light streamed in through the entrance hall's large bay windows.

"Whoa! Don't tell me there's a Southern plantation out there!"

Three doors opened off the entrance hall. The first two they tried, at either side of the hall, opened into solid stone. The third door, a large entranceway in the center of the hall, gave way and, passing through, they found themselves standing in a dank, dark cave amid a crop of stalagmites. They couldn't see the roof of the cave, it was so high, only the tips of long stone icicles which stretched down close to the rock-strewn floor. Somewhere water dripped in echoey splashes.

Behind them rose the facade of a Southern Big House, with tall white Georgian columns. It had been set into stone at the bottom of the underground complex, laid to rest. "It's Twelve Oaks!" Claire pointed above the mansion toward the unseen roof of the cave and all the stalactites. "Up there somewhere is the computer chamber. Do you think Uncle George and his friends are still up there? We must've been down here for hours and hours."

The boy didn't answer. He rubbed the back of his neck and cast low his gaze, kicking the rubble with his sneakers. The cavern and the facade of the mansion were illuminated by any number of lanterns lifted aloft by statuettes of little black men dressed in a manner that most would consider provocative.

"I haven't seen one of these in years," Paul said, going over to one of the statuettes. "They fit in with this plantation scene all right, don't they?"

"I think they're disgusting. They could've found a more tasteful way to light the cavern."

164

Claire leaned against the boy, pressing him against the cold damp rock of the wall. As she did this an entire section of the rock crumbled away. "Look out!" It was all the boy could do to throw himself on the girl as they went down. Dust boiled up from the sliding rock and he covered her face with the jacket that once had been worn by James Dean. For a moment everything was dark.

Pushing away a rock with his hand, Paul found himself face to face with the yawning eye sockets and the smiling jaw of a bone white skull. The girl screamed. She kept screaming even when he pulled her to her feet and shook her.

"Was that what I thought it was?"

"What else would it be? Looks like an Indian. A warrior maybe. Thought I saw some arrowheads thrown in with him in the dirt. Probably been down here for centuries. Maybe we should take an arrowhead for luck."

"No Paul! Don't you dare! Let's get out of here. My flesh is crawling."

"I'm sort of spooked myself."

They walked back into the Big House.

"So much for exploring. Maybe your uncle has gone to bed."

Hand in hand they climbed the grand staircase, through the neverending hallways leading past the countless ghostly quiet storerooms and apartments. They came at last to the computer chamber. The boy cautiously crept to the entranceway, peeking around the corner. It was empty, the computer screen dark. He pulled her by the hand into the chamber. Now again it was their turn to view the general's life.

10

The funeral was small and private. Sympathy cards and flowers came from all over — wreaths had even been sent by the president and the secretary of defense — but at graveside there were only his children, their families, their small circle of friends, and the minister. They looked down into the ditch as the minister sprinkled in a loose handful of dirt, so loose and dusty that some of the specks hung and whipped around in the sunny morning air before sinking into the pit.

The little girl cowered behind her mother's black skirt, peering around the pleats into the unfathomable dark hole. She saw the dirt leave the minister's hand, saw the way some of it swirled before sifting all the way down.

Elizabeth meanwhile cried into a handkerchief, leaning close to George Natlong. The dress uniform with the star on the hat and on each shoulder made him look quite a bit more imposing than he felt. He was looking at the tombstone. A cross, a name, and two dates had been carved into the stone. I guess that's all that ever matters, George Natlong found himself thinking. Thinking, He was quite a guy, did many things, changed my life, he did, from that night I met him with Elizabeth at West Point. Thinking, I can still see him as he was that night, standing with the brass next to the dance floor, shaking my hand, his flesh soft and warm but the grip firm, with that look on his face that told how much he loved Elizabeth and how much he wanted her to be happy. Thinking, Those things don't matter now. Thinking, Memories are only for the living. Thinking, Time eats away the memories, eats away the flesh of the memories leaving only the scantest skeleton of remembrance. A cross, a name, and two dates. Thinking, This man lived a full, successful life by anyone's standards but someone who passes by this spot centuries from now will see only that name, Henry Thaddeus Duke, and those dates, 1895 to 1964. Thinking, maybe that's all that matters, in the end, that you were born and died, and who gives a damn about the in-between? Thinking, And they'll also see the cross. Thinking, They'll know he was a Christian. Thinking, I wonder if they'll know he made bombs? He was a Christian bombmaker. Thinking, That's a laugh, making bombs for Jesus. Thinking, Knock it off George, this is his funeral, show some respect for the poor old bastard.

The minister closed the book and they all walked back to the limousines. George Natlong rode in the front limousine with Elizabeth and Inky. Inky's young wife, Sophia, and their little girl, Claire, sat on either side of Inky. As the short procession wound through Winterford Elizabeth kept sniffling into her handkerchief. At last she bunched the handkerchief tightly in her black-gloved hand. Her eyes red, she said, "Claire looks so lovely today with her hair combed out. And her dress is just lovely too."

"Thank you," Sophia said. "It is a lovely dress, isn't it? I found it at Laura Ashley's. Claire, honey, say thank you to Aunt Elizabeth."

"Thank you, Aunt Elizabeth." The little girl was staring at her shiny black patent leather shoes. With her thumb and forefinger she absentmindedly tweaked a button in the upholstery of the seat.

"At times like this I'm sorry George and I never had a child," Elizabeth said. "You're so fortunate, Inky."

George Natlong gazed out the window, watching the countryside. It always looks so pleasant and peaceful from a limousine, he thought. He turned and saw Inky running a hand along Claire's silky straight blonde hair. Inky, dark-eyed, dark-haired, dark-moustached Inky, and his equally dark wife — how had they had this fair, blue-eyed, blonde child? Oh cut it, he thought. Quit thinking of it. Hell, what else is there to think about when riding back from a funeral? I can't wait to have a drink with Mitchell. Yes, that's what I'll think about. That drink'll taste good.

When they got back to the mansion George Natlong headed straight for the liquor. It was hidden in a cabinet in the Chippendale parlor. The others followed him in.

"Elizabeth darling I'm so terribly sorry we couldn't be with you sooner," Mitchell's wife, Bridgette was saying. "The minute we got the cable over the wireless we turned the boat around. But we were nearly twelve hundred miles from Honolulu."

"Nonsense," Elizabeth said. "I'm just glad you and Mitchell could make it here this morning in time for—." She burst into tears, burying her face in her gloves.

"There, there," Doty said. "Sit down dear." To Bridgette she said, "It's been very hard on Elizabeth."

George Natlong brought over the glasses. He'd taken off his jacket, his sleeves were rolled up, his tie pulled down. His collar hung open.

"It's not even noon," Mitchell said.

"So what? Let's have one for old Henry."

"When you put it that way."

The men each raised a glass.

"To Henry Thaddeus Duke, 1895 to 1964, cross," toasted George Natlong. He threw the Scotch down his throat. The second drink tasted even better than the first he'd had while pouring the others at the liquor cabinet. "Whose idea was that cross anyway?"

"It was Daddy's. He wrote in his will that he wanted a cross on his stone."

Inky said, "I never knew Father had any religious sentiments."

"Daddy was a very religious man."

"He was the salt of the earth," Doty said.

"A fine man," Bimmy agreed.

"An upstanding individual," Natalie said.

"A good American," Bridgette threw in.

"A true believer," Edgar said.

168

"He made bombs," George Natlong added.

"George," Elizabeth said. "The preacher will hear you."

"He's not here," Bimmy said. "Didn't you see his car head back to town? Wise man, that preacher. He knew we'd gotten all the solace we could from religion."

"Damn straight," George Natlong said. "I said to myself, 'Damn I could use a drink.' Does anyone want another? I'm going to the cabinet now. Hell I might as well bring back the bottle."

"Could you make mine a highball?" Doty asked.

"Oh I'm sorry," George Natlong said. "Drinks for the ladies. Natalie? Bridgette? Elizabeth? Sophia?"

"A highball would be fine."

"Sounds good."

"Same here."

"Let me see if I got this. The bottle and four lady drinks."

"A highball is not a ladies drink," Doty corrected. She was leaning back in the sofa next to Elizabeth, smoking a filter-tipped cigarette.

"I always thought this highboy was positioned just right," George Natlong was saying. He was yelling across the room from the liquor cabinet. "You ever notice? When you're really crocked you can lean your back against the highboy while digging for the liquor and not fall down."

He went to the doorway and yelled for ice. Afterwards he brought a tray of glasses and bottles to the center of the room.

"So I said to myself, 'Three hundred years from now someone walking past that stone will see only his name, his dates, and that he was a soldier for Christ. They won't know what a jolly old fellow Henry was. Or that he made bombs.'"

"Stop it," Elizabeth said. "He made bombs only because it was his Christian duty to stop Germany."

"Why then did he keep making bombs after Germany was stopped?"

"Stop it will you?"

Elizabeth held her untouched drink in her lap. She touched away tears with the handkerchief.

169

"Oh will *you* stop it Elizabeth? This is where I came in. The old gang standing around the parlor, you crying on the sofa, and me feeling like a smuck. Or a schmuck, whatever it is. The only difference is now you don't have Henry's shoulder to cry on. It's a sad fact. Sad but true."

"Maybe we should go," Mitchell said.

"No, please don't. Have another," George Natlong suggested.

"Well I—."

"Go on."

"Yes go on," Doty said. "Why not? Sometimes in life it's okay to drink. Healthy even."

Little Claire Duke sat in a corner of the room. She'd kicked off her shoes, her feet on the chair. She looked into the eyes of the grownups then darted her eyes away before they had a chance to see she'd been watching. None of the grownups made eye contact with her. She made sure of it. It was a game she played. She was getting good at it. It was easier now that the grownups were drinking. Claire couldn't help noticing that their eyes were slower moving now and that they seldom looked up from the glasses filled with tinkling ice.

"That cemetery is such a peaceful place," Natalie was saying.

"Wasn't it though? So green and hilly and all those nice big shade trees. It's ever so peaceful."

"Wouldn't mind a place like that myself, when the time comes," Edgar said.

"You be quiet!" Doty commanded. "You've been planning your funeral since you've been twenty."

As they were saying this Mitchell sat down in a wing chair at the far side of the room, his drink in hand. A large potted plant sprung next to the chair. As the others spoke he leaned forward, so they wouldn't see. Slowly he lowered his drink and poured it into the pot, keeping the ice in the glass with his fingers. He lifted the glass and leaned back. Suddenly he jerked his head to the left and for a split second made eye contact with little Claire. She darted her eyes away and studied her

170

socks, pretending she hadn't seen Mitchell pour his drink into the plant. Several seconds later when she glanced at him again he was staring at her with a trace of a smile. He darted his eyes away then instantly looked back, a funny, sneaky expression on his face, as if to say, "I know that game too." Claire had to giggle.

Mitchell put the empty glass on the table.

"This room holds such memories for me," he said, patting his ribs with the palms of his hands. "Do you remember that night, twenty years ago, when I brought over my record collection? That's the night we met George. Everything springs from that time in this place. This room hasn't changed a bit. I wonder if we've changed."

"People never change," George Natlong said. "They only grow more so."

Mitchell got up, went over to the record player. It was hidden, like the liquor, in an eighteenth century cabinet.

"Is this phonograph new?" Mitchell asked. "Where's the old one? It had one of those little emblems with the dog listening to the gramophone."

"That old thing was retired years ago," Inky said. "This is a stereo. Plays something different in each speaker. Want to hear sound effects?"

"Please Inky not that," Sophia pleaded. "I can't bear to hear those train noises just now."

"Why don't you put on some nice music?"

"What's this? The only records here are Chubby Checker, Fats Domino and The Beatles."

"Henry bought those records for Claire," Sophia explained. "How he worshiped that child! They used to dance. Henry holding her in the air and spinning her around and Claire laughing so. I can still see them. She taught Henry how to Twist, you know."

Mitchell looked at Claire. The child looked on with interest as he thumbed through her record collection.

"Do you want to dance, Claire?" Mitchell asked.

Claire shook her head no.

171

"The poor darling cried all day when Father died," Inky said. He went over to Claire's chair and sat the little girl on his lap. "She's still out of sorts, aren't you, petunia?" Inky kissed the side of his daughter's head.

Mitchell put on a record.

"*A foghorn,*" said a deep voice from the speakers. This was followed by a low bellowing that rattled the glasses on the tables. Then silence.

"*A dive bomber.*" They heard the piercing whine of a plane diving from the clouds, screaming at a higher pitch every second. Then silence.

"*New Year's on Times Square.*" They heard horns. People cheering. A band playing Auld Lang Syne. Then silence.

"*A hydrogen bomb.*" The speakers roared with the sound of an explosion, gradually intensifying, building to a bone-rattling crescendo.

"*Please* shut that off!" Elizabeth said. She swallowed the rest of her drink and lowered her head to the arm of the sofa.

Mitchell lifted the needle from the spinning disk.

"So much for entertainment."

"Sounded pretty realistic," George Natlong had to admit.

Inky said, "You should hear the ocean liner and the lion. You'd swear the lion was in the room."

"Mitchell, my man, your glass is empty."

"That's all right George. We really should be going. I have some business calls to make."

"But you can't go yet! We have a surprise for you. We've been planning it for months. Or has it been years?"

"What surprise is that, George?"

"You tell him, Elizabeth. It was your idea."

"I hardly think I should be the one. Let Inky tell him. Inky is the chairman of the board of the Duke Corporation."

"Bimmy is the president of the company," Inky pointed out. "Bimmy should be the one."

"Not me. Edgar is the chief operating officer. You tell him, Edgar."

"Well I hardly think that I—."

172

"Oh go on Edgar," Doty insisted. "Don't be so shy all the time."

"Yes go on Edgar."

They all looked to Edgar.

"Well since you all think I should be the one—."

"Oh go on will you!"

"Doty, my buttercup, you're making me nervous."

"So then just spit it out, Edgar," Mitchell said. "What's the big deal?"

"The thought was—. That is to say—. The company has accrued sizable cash reserves—. But we must rely on outside suppliers for electronic components—. It looks like electronic components will play an increasingly important role in the company's future—."

"For christsakes Edgar what the devil are you driving at?"

Edgar grew red in the face. Just when it looked a blood vessel might pop he burst out, "Mitchell, old friend, we thought you'd might like to start your own electronics firm."

"Are you crazy? Of course I would. But I'd need fifty or sixty million to do the job right. If I were to scrape together all my assets, sell the stocks and the house, I wouldn't have one tenth of that."

"That's what we're getting at," Bimmy chimed in. "We thought we could help you along."

"Forget it. I don't want anybody's help. If I can't start a business on my own I don't want any part of it."

"Same old Mitchell," Elizabeth said. "Always out on a limb by yourself. Always unwilling to accept the help and goodwill of your friends."

"Damn it," Mitchell fumed. He crossed the room and gazed out a window. "Why is it I always feel so damned inferior, like a pauper, when I'm around you people? I'm a millionaire three or four times over. A self-made man. Believe it or not, there are people in this world who don't look on me as a failure. There are actually people who think I've done all right for myself."

"Cut the dramatics," George Natlong said. "Where's your

glass, Mitchell old boy? What you need is a drink."

"I don't need a damn drink."

Inky said, "You've got us all wrong, Mitchell. It's not you who needs us. It's we who need you. Weaponry manufacture is no longer a matter of smelting cannonballs from scrap iron or pouring explosives into bombshells. The future of our company rests with electronics. We need our own electronics subsidiary. Call it insurance."

"It's a marriage made in heaven," Bimmy threw in. "You have the wherewithal to start an electronics firm but not the money. We have the money but not the know how."

"I don't want your damn money and that's that."

"Get off the high horse, Mitchell," George Natlong scoffed. He was pouring himself another drink. "Get off that high horse of yours long enough to see things as they are. Sure we've got lots of money. Sure the money stinks. But the money is a fact of life."

"Dear, maybe you shouldn't be so hasty," Bridgette said. During the conversation she'd sat quietly in a chair between the two gold sofas watching the ice melt in her drink. "If it's as Inky says, that the future of his corporation depends on your help, we just can't turn our backs, now can we? These are our dearest and oldest friends."

Mitchell went to Bridgette. He stood behind her chair, his hands on her shoulders.

"You're so wonderful," he said in a quiet voice. "I imagine sometimes I must seem quite mad. But you always stick by me. What did I ever do to deserve you? By now you know how much my self-esteem means to me. It means everything. These people know I would go to the ends of the earth to help them. But I won't go so far as to take a handout. The only thing I will not do for them is receive their charity, satisfying their philanthropic yearnings. How could I look myself in the mirror every morning if I did that? Sure, I'd love my own company. But I'd have to do it on my own. I'd never be happy running a subsidiary of theirs. Don't you see that?"

"We'd be happy to be a silent partner in an independent

174

firm," Inky suggested.

"The electronics company would be all yours, Mitchell," Bimmy agreed. "You'd call the shots."

"Of course we'd expect you to sell us components at a reliable, low price."

George Natlong came over to Mitchell, gave him a drink.

"Don't be unreasonable, Mitchell," he said.

Claire sat still and quiet on Inky's lap. She saw Mitchell staring into the carpet, not looking into anyone's eyes. She watched as he absentmindedly swirled the drink in his hand, clinking the ice.

This time the fern got no drink. She saw Mitchell raise the glass to his lips and then she saw his fleshy Adam's apple bob as he swallowed. Then she saw that his eyes were closed.

"Ante up, boys," George Natlong said. "It looks like war."

He tossed five white chips onto the table. The three other officers sulking around the table threw in their chips. Four insignia-covered fair-weather jackets were draped over the backs of the four chairs. One of the five chairs was empty and the dealer skipped over the place in front of it.

The one who was dealing said, "War's in the air, all right. And there's no backing down after tonight."

When the last of the cards had been dealt the men lifted them from the table.

Elizabeth Natlong came in with a tray of sandwiches, neatly garnished, cut and stacked, and a bowl of potato chips. She set everything at the empty place on the table.

"I had Edie make these sandwiches before she turned in," she said. "They've been wrapped in the refrigerator since just nine so they're *very* fresh. When George told me the game would start late tonight I thought it would be silly to have Edie stay up."

The men didn't seem to be listening. They were looking at the cards. George Natlong chewed his cigar.

"Give me two, will ya Bob?"

Elizabeth padded off in her slippers, saying, "Now I'm going to watch Johnny Carson. I wonder who's on tonight?" but she knew she was talking to herself. None of them would answer, at least at this stage of the card game, the start.

It was always the same. At the start they always were quiet and serious, holding their cards like psalm books before their stony faces, each hoping that this night would be a lucky night, each waiting to see which of them would have his hope answered. Elizabeth knew that the men didn't play for the money (the stakes were too low and they had all been friends for years) so much as they played for the luck. She knew that the sober somberness of the first few hands quickly would evaporate in direct proportion to the bourbon that vanished from the bottles. Soon it would be apparent which way the chips were falling, the men would get smashed, the yelling and the cursing would start. Over the years the only thing that had changed was that they used to play on Sundays but some of the wives started complaining that it wasn't a proper activity for the Lord's day, so it was moved to Wednesdays. But other than that everything was the same.

And so tonight, like she did every card night, Elizabeth padded into the next room in her fuzzy slippers, relaxed in the flickering blue light of the television. Good, she thought, Johnny's still doing the monologue.

The sounds of anguish and defeat boomed in from the next room. She turned her head and saw one of the men raking chips from the center of the table. She heard the scratchy, slippery sounds of chips being pulled in. The sounds of luck, she thought. It won't be long now.

George Natlong threw his cards to the center of the table. The others did the same. The dealer began straightening and squaring the ragged pile, flipping some over, making new again the tainted and stale pile of spent luck.

"Shit," George Natlong cursed, pouring bourbon into his glass of wet melting ice. "It's going to be one of those nights, is it?" He looked at the empty chair. "I wish Casey would get here. My luck's no good without him."

"You just like to take his money," one of them said.

"Where is he anyway?"

"Beats me. Wish he'd get here."

"I think he might be involved in this Gulf of Tonkin business."

"No fooling? Is that what he's up to?"

"That's right. Asian intelligence. Looks like we'll be seeing less of him in the days ahead."

The dealer had just finished squaring and shuffling the deck, rearranging the luck and making the cards new again, and was just licking his thumb to deal the next hand, when the doorbell sounded.

"Speak of the devil. Wait a minute Bob. Let's deal Casey in this hand."

George Natlong left the table.

"Where the hell you been?" he asked the man standing on the welcome mat.

"Don't ask."

He handed his hat to George Natlong. The newcomer's rumpled uniform hung on him like loose skin. He was short, balding and (George Natlong thought) his age-lined, baggy-eyed face looked more lined than usual, especially under the eyes. He looked tired.

"What a day this's been," the newcomer said. He wearily followed George Natlong into the room where the men sat laughing, stacking and clicking their chips. They took advantage of the break to freshen their drinks and pick through the tray of sandwiches.

Charlie looked up from his rummage through the sandwich tray.

"Hey, Casey, you've finally made it!"

"Just in time to lose your money."

"I hope you brought a lot."

Casey took off his jacket, draped it over the back of the empty chair. As he sat he sniffled once, widening his nostrils, drawing up the corners of his mouth.

"Let's get these goddamn sandwiches out of the way," George Natlong said.

"Pass me a ham and cheese, will you, George?"

"How about you, Casey? Want anything before I take it away?"

"No thanks." Reaching back into his jacket, Casey brought out some nasal spray. He tilted his head, administering the spray, closing his eyes.

"You look like shit, Case."

"I've spent the day playing messenger boy for the secretary. Running my ass off. I think I'm coming down with something."

"The secretary? McNamara?"

"Who else?" Casey threw in his ante. "Mr Robert The Best and the Brightest McNamara Himself, OAG. Only After God. ALBJ. And LBJ. I thought when I was promoted to general my errand-running days were over. No more messenger boy crap. Little did I know the higher a man goes, he just runs messages to higher places. So I've been chasing after McNamara all day, waving dispatches in his face. He flinches now whenever he sees me coming. I can see it in his face. He's thinking, 'What now, more information? Just when I had it all figured out? Why don't you make life simple and go away?' I swear the man is an idiot. It's frightening. Absolutely frightening. Why the hell couldn't I've been some candyass Ivy Leaguer who met Kennedy in a Harvard washroom?"

"Then you'd only be running messages for LBJ."

Looking around the table, Casey asked, "Who's winning here?"

"We've only played one hand. Charlie won it, the bastard."

Charlie, looking over his cards, raised his eyebrows three times.

"Curt son of a bitch," Hal said to Charlie. "One hand don't mean a thing. You still have time to lose your shirt tonight, Charlie my boy."

Again Charlie fluttered his eyebrows three times. The rest of his face was expressionless.

"Do that one more time and you'll be picking this ham sandwich out of those bushy little eyebrows," Hal said.

Now Charlie batted his eyelashes.

"You guys," George Natlong said.

In the next room, in front of the television, Elizabeth thought, It's starting already.

"Only one hand?" Casey threw two cards down. "Why'd

179

you start so late?"

"We were watching LBJ's speech on television. It didn't come on till eleven thirty. Didn't want to miss it so we held off till afterwards. I'll take two, Bob."

"His speech?" Casey lowered his cards. "You mean he went on television after all? What did he say?"

"You mean you don't know?"

Casey shook his head. "The radio in my car is on the fritz. Damn motor pool cars."

"I'll drink to that," Hal said. "They always stick me with this bomb that overheats before I can get past Arlington Cemetery."

Insistently (almost too insistently, George Natlong thought), Casey said, "Well what did he say?"

"Where have you been the last two days?" Hal asked. "The Vietnamese have attacked two of our destroyers in the Gulf of Tonkin. Shot bullets two days ago and today fired twenty torpedoes at the *Maddox*. Tonight LBJ came on and said we'd retaliate by bombing North Vietnam."

Blood looked to be draining from Casey's face. The hand with the cards sank all the way to the table.

"Damnit Casey I can see your cards," Hal said.

"My God Casey you look pale. You could use a drink."

"I'll see you and raise you three," Charlie said. He tossed three chips into the middle of the table.

"I'm out," Hal said. "This hand sucks."

"Your move, Casey."

Casey stared at the middle of the table.

"Casey? You all right? Here. Take this drink."

Casey looked at the glass, at first appearing not to recognize it. Then his eyes focused, he sniffled, took the drink. His chin went up, the drink went down.

"There must be some mistake," he said.

"What's he ranting about?"

Casey glanced around the table. He thought, They don't know. They honestly don't know. They're all sitting here half drunk and they don't know.

180

"Our boats weren't attacked."

"How's that?"

"What do you mean? The Pentagon's been getting a steady stream of dispatches from Vietnam saying—."

Casey rose, kicked the floorboard along the wall. The Tiffany lamp above the table rattled.

"Goddamnit!" he gasped.

In the next room Elizabeth thought, Well here we go.

"I know all about those dispatches from Vietnam," he yelled. "That's my job. The Asian dispatches come across my desk." The others stared at him, waiting, their cards against the table.

"All right Casey," Charlie said. "So what?"

"Our ships weren't attacked?"

Casey could feel the drink coming on. His hand fell to the back of the chair. Deflated, he sat down.

"How do you like that?."

He lowered his head in his arms. His cards were flat against the table, face down. They looked at the shiny globe that was the top of his head. They could hear the television playing softly in the next room, Johnny Carson talking, an audience laughing.

Casey looked up.

"Early dispatches reported our boats had been fired upon. But all day updates have been coming in over the ticker. Turns out the early reports were wrong."

"But the North Vietnamese fired bullets at our ships yesterday in an unprovoked attack."

"It wasn't unprovoked. The South Vietnamese were shelling a nearby island with weapons we'd given them. The North Vietnamese thought it was us."

"What about the torpedoes fired at the *Maddox?*"

"There were no torpedoes. Turns out the kid reading the sonar on the *Maddox* misread waves from the wake of our other destroyer. For that we go to war."

"Do the brass know about this?"

Casey lowered his eyebrows.

"Didn't you hear me say I was carrying messages to McNamara all night? I'll tell you one thing. The goddamned Secretary of Defense knows our boats weren't attacked. That's for *sure*. And each time I gave him an update I saw him hand the message over to a courier with instructions to take it to the White House. The president must've known before he went on television at eleven thirty."

The men exchanged glances.

"What exactly did these messages say?" Hal asked. "Or aren't you privileged to say?"

"Of course I'm not privileged to say. It's goddamned classified information. Tip top secret. For the eyes of army generals and Ivy League candyasses only."

Casey hopelessly shook his head. He got up again and kicked the floorboard. The Tiffany lamp tinkled. He faced the table, his eyes closed. He rubbed the back of his neck.

"What these days isn't secret? I walk down the hall at the Pentagon and see room after room of top secrets, their doors closed. Every day thirty thousand people come to work tight lipped, ready to file away more top secrets. What the hell isn't top secret? One day after a briefing in a strange part of the Pentagon I asked an adjutant where the nearest washroom was. 'That's classified information, sir,' he told me. The goddamned washroom! What am I going to do, sell the Russians the secrets of our flush toilets?"

He poured himself a good one. It was gone in a gulp.

"What did the messages I gave to McNamara say? you ask. Am I not privileged to tell you? you ask. Of course I'm not privileged to tell you. But I'm going to tell you anyway. After all we're friends here. We've known each other for years, haven't we?"

George Natlong, tapping his cards with the tip of his finger, said, "Maybe we should change the subject."

"What a loyal son of a bitch you are, George. Anyone ever tell you?"

"Sit down Casey," Charlie said. "You've had a rough day."

Casey sat down. George Natlong reached across the table, refilled his glass.

"I'm sorry George. I didn't mean it that way."

"Forget it Case."

Casey took the glass in hand and rolled the light brown liquid over the ice.

"I must've handed McNamara a half dozen messages tonight. One report concluded that the skipper of the *Maddox* exaggerated the scope of the quote attack. One report went so far as to say the only damage sustained by our boats was a single bullet hole. I mean, we scoured both those ships up and down for evidence of attack and we could only come up with one single goddamn bullet hole. And it could've been the work of some drunk sailor shooting his pistol on some Saturday night escapade. If you ask me that's pretty slim evidence on which to march a country off to war."

"If what you say is true then tonight the president got the whole country worked up over nothing. Tomorrow the newspapers will be demanding retaliation for something that never happened."

"I can see the headlines already. I can't help thinking the American public would be better served by reading the messages that come over that ticker in my office."

"It's water over the dam now."

Casey swallowed the drink.

"Frankly I don't see what you're all worked up about, Casey," George Natlong said. "So we drop a few bombs on Vietnam. So what? It means my brother-in-law the bombmaker will eat caviar all week. I'd say LBJ is taking a gamble he can't lose. Man, we've got aircraft carriers and supersonic jets. We've got helicopters that'll destroy whole towns in a single sweep. I've seen them with my own eyes. Beautiful babies, they are. We've got our tanks and our automatic rifles. Our grenade launchers. Napalm. Heat-seeking missiles. Armor three feet deep. Not to mention The Big One. We've got a munitions industry that can crank out all the ammo we'll ever need. And we've got plenty of beef-fed young men out beating the streets with nothing better to do. North Vietnam has none of that. What'll they do? Hide in the jungle for ten years and chase our tanks with bamboo poles?" George Natlong laughed. "They'll come to terms quickly and then they'll behave themselves."

"Yes let's play," Hal agreed. He glanced at his watch. "The night's not young. It's your bid, Casey."

Casey lifted his cards, studied the chips in the middle of the table.

"I'm out. This isn't my night."

The fifth player, Bob, who until now had spoken nary a word, asked, "Where are we Charlie? Three? All right. I'll see your three and call. Let's look at those cards."

In the next room Elizabeth could hear the groans of agony. She looked in and saw Charlie raking chips from the center of the table.

"Well guess whose lucky night it is," Hal said.

Charlie said nothing. With a satisfied look on his face he stacked the red, white and blue chips.

"Forgot those chips and deal," Hal told him.

Charlie squared the deck.

"Watch him closely boys," Hal said. "No monkey business now. No dealing from the bottom." Charlie smiled, bit his lower lip.

They heard Elizabeth laughing in the next room.

"What in God's name's so funny in there?" George Natlong yelled in to her.

"Oh this Johnny Carson's *so* funny!" she yelled back. "He's got a turban on his head and he's trying to charm Ed McMahon's necktie with a penny whistle. I could watch Johnny Carson forever!"

George Natlong took a swallow from his glass. This time around he had a pretty good hand. Three kings, a two and a four. Finally, he thought, a good hand. Don't give yourself away now. The face mustn't give you away. When it came round to his turn for more cards George Natlong lowered two to the table.

"I'll take two."

He examined the new cards. A king and a ten. Here we go, he thought. Don't give yourself away now. Run up the pot. You've got the cards now it all depends on your face. Run it up.

The chips in the middle of the table began piling up. First the reds were added to the whites and then the blues were cautiously sprinkled in. This time Charlie dropped out in the second round. "You have to fold a losing hand early if you want to win consistently," he told the others with a grin when they gave him a hard time about it. The four remaining continued the business of building the pile of chips. Their faces were marvels of nonexpression. They looked neither happy nor sad, interested nor disinterested, eager nor patient. They looked like statues, except that they moved around, drank and smoked. Charlie studied the players, the way they seemed to be preoccupied with their drinks and smokes and the way they pretended to be bored with the cards. Each thinks he has a good hand, he thought.

"What the hell are you working on these days George?" Casey suddenly asked, tossing in five blue chips.

It was as though George Natlong hadn't heard the question. Finally he said, rather uncomfortably, "Since when do we talk shop on poker night?"

"Don't tell us then," Casey said.

"No offense," George Natlong said.

"It's funny," Charlie said. His tone was almost sullen. "When Casey was talking I got to thinking how I don't know what any of you do at the Pentagon. For that matter none of you probably know what I do. And here we've been playing cards every week for years."

"That's the nature of the business," George Natlong said. "Would you rather've been a traveling salesman? Then we could sit around talking about corsets and girdles."

"Of course you're right," Charlie said. "I was only thinking out loud. I just thought it was funny, that's all. Us being friends all these years and not knowing what we do for a living."

"We go to work at the Pentagon in the morning and we come home at night," George Natlong grunted. He tossed in five blue chips. The blues were starting to outnumber the reds. "Need anyone know more?"

"I'll raise that three," Hal said.

"Sometimes I wonder if anybody knows what the hell we're doing," Casey said. "Even when you shove your work under their faces, like I did with McNamara, they ignore it. It's frightening."

"Are we still on that?" George Natlong said. "How about we just play cards."

Casey threw in five blue chips.

"The pot's getting big," Charlie observed.

"I can't help it," Casey said. "I can't see one good reason why we should bomb North Vietnam."

Now the reds were being buried. George Natlong tossed five more blue chips on top. They slid slickly from the summit to the bottom of the pile.

"I fold," Hal said.

"I'm almost at my limit too," Bob said. He ran his thumb down his diminishing stack of chips. "I promised Helen twenty would be my limit." He threw in his cards.

Only George Natlong and Casey remained.

"This pot really got big fast," Hal said.

"We were in a trance," Bob said.

"What I don't get is why they even bothered to run my ass all over town tonight if they were going to ignore the dispatches anyway," Casey went on.

"Johnson and McNamara?" said Hal. "You're talking politics now, my friend, not military logic."

"That's right," Charlie agreed. "There's big political stakes in this Gulf of Tonkin thing. If the president doesn't drop a few bombs Goldwater'll say he's soft and indecisive. LBJ is an old poker player himself. He knows how to pick up a few chips on a safe bet."

"What's going on in Vietnam is just another poker game,"

Hal said.

"That's what I say," George Natlong agreed. "It's all one big poker game. We bluff, we make our bets, we pull in our chips. Sweet Baby Jesus! Did we kill both bottles already? No there's a little left in this one. Enough for one more. Yes it's all one big poker game. I'd have to agree with that. That's why, if you have a safe bet, you mustn't be afraid to throw in your chips."

With that George Natlong pushed his remaining red, white and blue chips to the center of the table. He sat all the way back in the chair, palming his cards with one hand while throwing the last of the whisky down his throat with the other. Clenching his square jaw, he smiled confidently at Casey.

"Ooo," Charlie gushed. "George's going for broke."

"Must have a good hand. The son of a bitch."

"Will you look at the size of the pot! George really ran it up."

"Someone ran it up all right."

Casey looked disinterestedly at the pot. His nose twitched. Squinting his eyes, he leaned forward, shoved the rest of his chips into the pile.

"I see you and call. Let's look at those cards George."

George Natlong slapped his thigh, let out a laugh.

"Kick the wall if you want Casey. I've got four kings."

George Natlong thumped his cards to the table.

The men sent up a yell.

In the next room Elizabeth was asleep in the recliner in front of the television. A test pattern of an Indian blazed on the screen.

George Natlong stuffed a fresh cigar between his grinning lips and stood, swaggering a bit. He reached his outstretched fingers around the massive pile of chips and began raking them in.

Casey sullenly pulled a rumpled white handkerchief from his hip pocket. He blew his nose loudly, wiped it a time or two then leaned forward and restuffed the handkerchief in his trousers.

"Not so fast George," he said.

He turned over his hand. They saw four aces and the jack of clubs.

"You lose, George."

12

The boy trembled. Finally the girl looked away from the screen.

"What's wrong, Paul?"

"The son of a bitch." He didn't take his eyes from the computer screen. "Your goddamned uncle said young people didn't have anything better to do than go to Vietnam and get shot."

"He didn't exactly say that."

"Goddamned straight that's what he said."

"What if he did? Really. I mean, it's over, isn't it?"

"My uncle Jeff came home from Vietnam in pieces." He pulled the collar of the jacket tightly around his neck.

"I don't see how you can blame Uncle George."

"Defend the son of a bitch, will you?"

Paul got up and stared down at her. He pointed at the screen.

"That son of a bitch and others like him killed my uncle."

He stormed up the aisle, out of the computer room.

"Paul!" she yelled, but he was gone. She started after him but, thinking twice, returned to the computer and switched it off, then dashed after the fading sounds of his footsteps.

Even the grandest room without people is no room at all. Without a prisoner the deepest, darkest dungeon is less than a hole in the ground. Without someone to coddle, the most lavish parlor is just four walls enclosing less than nothing. Like the song of the bird needs an appreciative ear, an empty room cries out to be filled by someone, anyone who will stomp their feet across the floor and dance up a room from less than nothing.

For several hours the grand chamber remained empty. Above, the night sky swung by, starry and blue, and the moon smiled down on the sleepy world. Near dawn, moments before the first rays of sunlight slid over the horizon, footsteps pattered down the circular hall.

George Natlong and Charlie came into the chamber, tired and bleary eyed. Charlie stretched his arms above his head, knitting his fingers, yawning.

"Had a little too much to drink last night," George Natlong confessed. His words too were tired. His words hung limply in the air like wet clothes on a line. Charlie pulled the words in one at a time, rubbing his cheek. "How about some more coffee?"

Charlie paused a moment, pulling in a word at a time, then reached for the Thermos bottle he'd set on the console. He poured out two cups. Even the coffee seemed to run tiredly into the cups.

"I haven't been up this early in years," Charlie said. "Not since my 'Nam days. We beat the sun up today, George. Wonder when the others will get the lead out and join us."

George Natlong switched on the computer.

"We haven't much time," George Natlong grumbled. "Let's pick up where we left off last night."

13

It was a scoreboard like you'd see at a football game. Except the numbers were higher. Each week during the news on television the numbers would flash. After awhile Paul would think that the scoreboard numbers had been flashed every week of his life but he knew that couldn't be true. He knew there had to have been a first night when the scoreboard read zero to zero, there had to have been a start, but Paul couldn't remember when it was.

The numbers always were flashed beside flags, like the numbers on a football scoreboard hung beside a school banner. Later, when he was older, he would always remember the numbers and the way they were flashed beside the flags but he could never remember the beginning. The farthest back he could remember was one night when he'd asked his father what the numbers meant, suddenly conscious of them, suddenly curious.

"They're the number of men who've been killed in Vietnam," his father told him.

Each week on television the numbers would flash behind an ever-calm, ever-speaking newscaster. The newscaster would read from paper stacked in front of him on a desk. He would flip a page and the numbers and the flags would flash behind him. Each week the numbers got larger, piling up like snow. After the numbers were flashed for a few seconds the newscaster would turn over the piece of paper from which he'd been reading and then the numbers and the flags would disappear.

Hearing knows before seeing reveals. Listening with eyes

closed reveals more than watching without hearing. Sitting in a chair perfectly still and listening to the grownups Paul could sit so still that they would forget he was there. Then the grownups would say things they wouldn't say when they knew he was listening. Sometimes he would sit so still with his eyes closed and the grownups would say such revealing things that he would think he must be invisible. As if he could dissolve into thin air, like the mist rising from a cup of hot tea, Paul was convinced he could fade away.

He knew he was nearing invisibility when the grownups started saying the revealing things. He would remain absolutely still for long periods of time, maybe in a chair in a corner of the room or stretched out on a sofa in the next room, enjoying the sensation of near invisibility, caught up in it like a canoe in a downstream current. Sometimes he was sure he'd blinked out of the world entirely. But everytime he opened his eyes to see if he'd disappeared there he was, plain as day, stretched out on the sofa maybe or in the chair, as real as a doll in a dollhouse, his invisibility gone.

He never knew why he wanted so much to be invisible. Maybe it was because for a boy of seven or eight invisibility seems much easier to attain than visibility, like a mountain is visible, like a bend of land is visible, like he believed a man must be visible. Visibility and noticeability out of reach for now, he worked hard at invisibility.

Sometimes he would sit so still on a chair that after the grownups had finished saying the revealing things his mother might come over and touch the back of her hand to his forehead. "Goodness, Paul, you're so quiet this afternoon! You must be coming down with something."

Even if he never attained complete and total invisibility he got one good thing out of all this. He learned a hell of a lot about his family by listening to the grownups say the revealing things. Things no one else outside the family seemed to know. One time, for instance, he was at the grocery store with Gramma Stoken and they ran into a neighbor. Gramma Stoken would brag about how well her son the lawyer was doing.

"What about Jeffrey, your other son?" the neighbor asked, gripping the handle of the shopping cart. "I hear he's quit school and has hair halfway down his back, like a girl."

"Gracious no!" Gramma Stoken said. "Where'd you hear that? Jeffey is just taking a little break from school. That's all. He's talking about going back soon. As for his hair, these young people today have fashions that're different from the ones we followed in our day. Jeffey's father and I understand that."

But the revealing things his grandmother said when Paul was sitting very still, trying to be invisible, contradicted the things she said at the store. One day he heard his grandmother tell his father, "I don't know what's got into that brother of yours! He's ruining his life! Dropped out of college and now he refuses to cut his hair! His father says he looks like a girl. Why can't he be more like you and make something of himself?"

Paul's father had asked, "What's Jeff doing with himself these days, Mom?"

"Nothing. Not a damn thing. All day long he sits around with that band of his playing guitars and drums out in the garage. You can hear it clear down to the road. Nothing we say seems to get through. If only he knew the heartache he was causing his father and me."

"Still refuses to pick an occupation, does he? Won't my baby brother ever grow up?"

Not long afterward, on another day, the grandmother had told Paul's mother, "This is the end of the line as far as Jeffrey's father and me are concerned. Do you know what that boy's done now? He's bought himself a motorcycle!"

Paul's mother had gasped. "What's he trying to do, kill himself?"

These were the days when Paul was seeing less and less of Uncle Jeffrey. For a long time he didn't even see Jeffrey's motorcycle, didn't even know what it looked like. Then one day at dusk when he was at his grandparents' house for supper

193

Paul heard the raspy whine of a motorcycle coming down the road. It seemed natural that he should hear the motorcycle before he'd see it. He thought, Hearing knows before seeing reveals.

Paul shot between the tall rows of corn behind the barn. The corn was a world all its own, thick, leafy, green, mazelike. He shot out of the corn in time to see Uncle Jeffrey, bearded, his brown hair shoulder length, riding the motorcycle at walking speed around to the back of the barn. Jeffrey had on a leather jacket. That wasn't all. Behind him on the motorcycle, arms wrapped around his ribs, rode a girl with flowing blonde hair. Her hair streamed behind in the wind like a scarf worn by a pilot in a crop duster. Paul had never seen her before.

The motorcycle came around the last corner of the barn, slowly and quietly now, the blonde hair fluttering lithely behind. A trail of dust raised by the wheels hung tentatively in the air behind her hair, bringing up the rear. They stopped behind the barn. The engine was no more than a rumbly whisper. The girl got off the bike and the engine went dead. Jeffrey put down the kickstand and got off.

For a second Paul considered yelling hello and waving (maybe he'd get Uncle Jeff to give him a ride on the motorcycle) but something made him hold his tongue. Maybe it was the laughter. Jeffrey and the girl were laughing. Paul was too far away to hear what they were laughing about, too far away even to see their lips move, but he could hear the laughter, giddy and happy, clapping the air. Something about the laughter told him it'd be best to stay in the corn, at least for now. Crouching, he stuck his head from the tall green shoots, watching Uncle Jeffrey lead the girl by the hand into the barn, through the back door. Jeffrey pulled open the door, they slipped through, the blonde whisps vanishing last, and the door closed. Now there was only the sound of crickets. Now that dusk was falling the crickets were all coming out.

The boy came cautiously out of the corn. He walked through the rough grass, toward the motorcycle, kicking up grasshoppers. The motorcycle was big and smelled of oil. The

194

engine was shiny and covered with hoses and wires. The round mirror on the handlebar reflected the crimson bands of clouds that obscured the drooping orange disc of the sun. Reaching up to the handlebars, Paul squeezed the hand brake.

He looked to the barn. It was a weathered red barn. The back door was unlocked. The hinges of the door squeaked slightly when he tried it. Inside was dark. The musty smells of the barn wafted out. For a second Paul considered yelling for Uncle Jeffrey but the muffled quiet wafting out with the musty smells seemed to gently hold his lips shut. He went inside and pulled the door closed.

At first he couldn't make out a thing. Then, from somewhere above his head (The loft, he thought instantly) he heard the rustling sounds of someone playing in the hay. Above his head the rafters creaked, like someone was jumping around up there.

The boy stood very still, his eyes closed, listening. Then he heard it. It was a woman's voice. The voice didn't seem to be speaking so much as chanting.

"...oh yes Jeff sweet Jesus Jeff oh God oh God oh yes oh yes that's it that's it oh yes yes yes dear God in Heaven oh yes..."

It seemed to be some kind of prayer. The boy thought, how nice of Uncle Jeff to pray with that girl. The rafters overhead started creaking wildly, there was a rhythmic pounding on the floor of the loft and the girl let out a hair-raising cry, the end of which sounded like it'd been muffled by a hand drawn across her mouth. Then everything was quiet.

Paul opened his eyes. It was dark. He couldn't see his hand when he held it up in front of his face. Everything was black. Suddenly he heard muffled voices and the sounds of walking from up in the loft. He heard footsteps coming down the rickety ladder. Something about those sounds he'd heard made the boy think that he shouldn't be caught by Uncle Jeffrey like this, standing in the doorway with his eyes closed, invisible or not.

Once more he heard the laughter. Both Uncle Jeffrey and

the girl were laughing.

"At least let me put my shirt on!" the girl's voice laughed.

There were more rustling sounds in the dark. The smells of damp hay filled the air as the rustling went by. The door creaked open, then creaked closed, the latch going down and catching with a metallic tinkle. In a minute the motorcycle engine coughed twice, then started.

Paul stood against the wall in the dark barn near where he knew the pitchforks were kept. His eyes closed, he listened to the motorcycle engine. He heard the tires kicking up gravel as the bike bumped around to the front of the barn and then whined off down the road, raising pitch, then dropping, then raising again. He didn't know how long he stayed in the dark barn. He could hear the crickets chirping outside in the fields. He heard two or three crickets somewhere inside the barn. It was a soothing sound. He stayed in the dark listening to the crickets until he heard the voice of his grandmother calling him to supper from the back of the porch.

One fine Saturday afternoon Gramma Stoken came over. Paul answered the door.

"Hi honey," she said, smiling down, stepping inside. Her sweater appeared disheveled, like she'd hurriedly pulled it on. An old brown hat covered her old gray hair, the hat she always wore whenever she wanted to run some errand without taking time to fix her hair. A pocketbook dangled from the crook of her elbow, her arm thrust upward through the strap. "Is your daddy here?"

"He's watching tv."

Gramma Stoken went into the living room, her steps worried, preoccupied. Paul followed her in.

"Hi Mom," Mr Stoken said, looking up from the paper. "Beautiful day, isn't it?"

"It hasn't been a very beautiful day for me or your father."

"What's wrong now?"

Gramma Stoken didn't sit. Digging in her pocketbook, she

came out with a rumpled piece of paper. It had the look of a document that had once been folded in thirds to go through the mail, had once been opened and read, had once been crumpled, only to be uncrumpled and unconvincingly straightened. Paul, standing in back of his father's chair, could see burn marks scorching one side of the document, as if it had been pulled from flames. The grandmother attempted to straighten it once more, pressing it against her chest and rubbing it with the palms of her hands. Then she handed it to the boy's father.

"It came in the mail today for Jeffrey."

"Why it looks like it's been burnt. Let me put on my glasses. Let's see here. 'The Selective Service Commission, Washington DC. Dear Mr Stoken. Please report—.' Why, Jeff's been drafted."

"He says he's not going to go!" the grandmother piped. "Says he'll go to Canada. Had a big argument with Father. They were going at it too, yelling and screaming, all morning. Jeff says he's leaving for Canada next week. Father says oh no he's not, over his dead body he's not, that no son of his is dodging the draft!"

"Slow down! Slow down Mom. Have a seat. There. Now, for one thing, Jeff certainly can't go to Canada. That would be illegal."

"That's what your father and I have been telling him all morning. But that brother of yours won't listen to reason. There's no talking to that boy anymore. Says he's going to Canada and there's nothing we can do about it. Father said, 'What's the matter with you? Do you want the Knights of Columbus to think I raised a draft dodger? A beatnik? A commie? A coward? You're going to that induction center if I have to drag you by that long hair and beard!' Yelling and screaming, screaming and yelling. Such carrying on I haven't heard since Jeffrey quit college. That boy is one big heartache. First dropping out of school, then playing guitars all day in the garage, and now this. What next? Jeffrey said he was going to burn the letter, burn it along with his draft card. He must've got the idea from those beatniks, those kooks on tv. Father got so disgusted he went down to his workshop and started pounding nails into the wall with his hammer. You know how Father gets. Then, next thing I know, I look out the kitchen window and there's Jeffrey, down by the creek, stooping down, burning something under the big elm trees. I see him walking away. The fire's still going. I ran out the door and just managed to save this letter. But Lenny—. The draft card was ashes! Just ashes. Nothing more. How's he going to explain that to the draft board when he goes in next week? I looked up then and saw him taking off on his motorcycle."

"He burned his draft card? Doesn't he know that's illegal?"

"There's just no talking to the boy. I don't know where to turn anymore. What to say. Lenny, I was hoping you'd have a word with him. You're his big brother. Maybe you can get through to him. Talk some sense into him."

"Me talk to Jeffrey? I'd stand a better chance talking to that wall with the nails in it."

"You must try, Lenny. I don't know where else to turn. Says he's leaving for Canada Wednesday morning, first thing, the day before he's due for his physical. He'll disgrace us all! What will people say? Lenny, you've just got to talk with him."

"All right, all right. I'll give it a try. So calm down. How about a nice cup of tea?"

"No, I must be going."

Gramma Stoken got up and took the letter. Once more she tried to straighten it. "I left the car running in the driveway. I told your father I was running to the store for some Rice-A-Roni. Rice-A-Roni always seems to soothe Father. He loves those San Francisco side dishes. Now don't put it off. Stop by the house tonight. Jeffrey should be home by nine or ten."

That evening Paul's father went out for about an hour. He came home about ten, fuming, untalkative. Paul concluded the talk with Jeffrey hadn't gone so well.

Hell broke loose two days later. It broke loose first (as it

198

usually does) over the telephone. Much later Paul would think, Hell has a way of knowing your phone number, of ringing you up. He was eating supper with his parents at the kitchen table. Mrs Stoken was spooning a second helping of peas onto the boy's plate when the phone rang. "I wonder who that could be," she said, putting down the dish of peas, getting up from the table. She was the kind of woman who never expected a call from hell, especially over the dinner hour.

"Hello, Jeffrey," she said into the phone. She was always very good with small talk. "How've you been? That's good. Me? I'm just fine. For awhile there I thought it was going to rain but it turned out to be a lovely day, didn't it? What can I do for you? Yes, he's here. Wait a second and I'll get him." She set the receiver on the counter and came back to the table. "Your brother wants to talk to you dear," she said to Mr Stoken.

"He does, does he?" Mr Stoken wiped his mouth with a paper napkin. "The day before yesterday he told me to jump into Clear Lake. Those were his very words. 'Why don't you jump in Clear Lake?' he said to me. Now he wants to talk, does he? I bet he wants to borrow money for his Canadian vacation. Well tough luck for him if he does. He'll get no money from me."

Mr Stoken gripped the armrest of the chair, his knuckles white, and rose. He held the receiver to his ear, his back to the table.

"Hello Jeff. What is it now?"

Then the hell broke loose.

"You what!" He was yelling.

The boy and the mother stopped eating, heir forks frozen halfway to their open mouths.

"You idiot! You've really done it this time, haven't you? Didn't I tell you it was illegal? Well I hope you're satisfied now. This is going to break Mom and Dad's hearts. This certainly will. What did those poor folks do to deserve you? Have you told them yet? Ah, I see. One phone call, huh? That's all you get, huh? And so you'd thought you'd call your big brother to get you out of this one, did you? The one you told to go jump in Clear Lake? Oh I bet you're sorry. And I suppose you want me to be the one to break the news to Mom and Dad, huh? You want me to be the one to break their hearts, huh? And then I suppose you want me to come down there and bail your ass out of jail? 'If it's not asking too much!' What's the matter, am I the only attorney you know? Aren't any of those punks you play guitar with attorneys? Aren't any of those junkies you buy your dope from attorneys? So you don't want me to jump in Clear Lake now, is that it? Now that I can be of some use. What do you expect me to do, get your ass out of the slammer so you can skip bail and run to Canada? Do you think I'm a fool, Jeff? Well let me tell you I've a good mind to let your ass rot to hell in jail. I am not hysterical! Maybe I will and maybe I won't!"

Mr Stoken slammed down the phone. He stormed from the kitchen, stomping and cursing, screaming hellfire and damnation, storming around the house like a tornado hopscotching about the countryside, a six foot tall cyclone brimming with hell broke loose.

The boy and the mother sat at the table listening to the sounds of hell breaking loose. The sounds churned first in the dining room. Then the fury drifted into the hallway, spilling into the living room, then into the study, churning around in there for several minutes, throwing paper around and slamming briefcases, then back into the hallway, up the stairs, knocking around directly overhead in the master bedroom.

"Finish eating, Paul" the mother said.

"Where's Uncle Jeff? What's happened?"

Now the sounds of hell banged down the staircase. She closed her eyes for a moment, then continued eating, her neck stiff and upright, her chewing slow, untasting, absentminded. Not wanting to get in the way of the storm she said nothing when it blew into the kitchen. Hell was dressed in a white business shirt, open at the collar, an untied tie dangling in front, hair amiss, clutching a pair of polished black shoes. Hell picked up the telephone and dialed a number.

"Hi Mom. Is Dad there? No, Mom, nothing's wrong. I'm just a little upset, is all. Mom, I really don't have time—. Will you just let me talk to Dad, please? No there's nothing wrong. Yes I'll wait."

Hell stood fuming with the receiver propped on its shoulder, waiting, saying nothing, buttoning the collar and tying the tie.

Then, "Dad, I'm afraid I have some bad news. Jeff's been arrested. Police stopped him with some friends in a van and found marijuana. Hello Dad? Dad? Are you still there? Who's this? Mom? Where'd Dad go? Yes, I can hear the pounding. When he runs out of nails tell him I've gone to Mason City for Jeff. He can meet us there. Yes he knows where we'll be. No Mom I better let Dad tell you."

Hell hung up the phone and raged out of the house, slamming the door with a bang.

"Don't play with your food, Paul," the mother told the boy.

With Mr Stoken out of the house it quieted down for a few hours. But it was only the eye of the storm passing by. The calm was like a lull in the storm, a temporary calm, a calm much too quiet, too still to be comfortable. Paul went to bed at the usual time. His mother came in and kissed his forehead, pushing back his hair, then touched the lightswitch and closed the door. From his bed, his head sideways on the pillow, he could see the shadows of his mother's feet in the bright strip of light that was the crack under the door. The shadows of the slippered feet backed up two or three steps then headed down the stairs. He heard cleaning up sounds downstairs, the sounds of pots being scrubbed and put away, the sounds of the back door being opened and a note left for the milkman, the sounds of lights being switched off, of slippers on the kitchen's linoleum floor, the soft sounds of the very end of the day. He heard her coming back up the stairs, the footsteps that were never heavy yet never light, not quite scuffling and yet not quite lifting the slippers all the way from the carpet, floating and yet somehow dragging, like tumbleweed, like a puffball from a dandelion scraping the grass, not quite airborne. The shadow slid across the beam of light under the door. The beam of light went out. Everything was quiet, still.

The boy couldn't sleep. He lay face up, his eyes open, gazing into nothing, listening into nothing. He didn't know how long he laid like that. At another time, when he was slightly younger, he might've realized he'd never felt as invisible, as inconsequential, as he did that night, lying there. He felt like the ghost of a steamboat captain must feel, walking among the living he'd once worked with and loved on the bridge of a ship, powerless to help steer the lives of those who mattered most to him. His opinions wouldn't matter. He wouldn't be asked. He was expected to sit quietly in a corner while his family tore itself to shreds. Later he'd be permitted to walk through the tattered wreckage, like the soul of a riverboat pilot drifting through the splintered wreckage of his boat after it'd been torn on the rocks. He was invisible. But now the thought didn't come to his mind. Nothing came to his mind. He lay on his back staring into the black. Then, far in the distance, he heard the whispering sounds of hell coming back.

At first the sounds were very soft, just the faintest of whispers, like the wall of a storm moving up in the distance after the eye had retreated. Listening, listening, for hearing knows before seeing reveals, he heard the sounds of tires. Then the patter of the engines. Listening knew the sounds of the motorcycle. He heard the squeaking sounds of his father's white station wagon, the sounds that always preceded his father to the house. The boy thought, It even sounds like a white station wagon, it even sounds like my father is inside. He heard something else. An engine backfire. A loose fender rattling. He said to himself, That'll be Grampa Stoken in the old green truck. He thought, It even sounds like an old green truck with Grampa inside. The sounds grew louder. He stood on his bed in his pajamas and drew back the curtain, looking down into the blackness shrouding the yard and road.

A soft yellow glow began melting in with the black. Suddenly the boy could see the silhouettes of shrubbery and garbage cans down by the road, and then he saw their shadows. The shadows began creeping around the shrubbery and the garbage cans, sweeping around like the hands of a clock, as if hiding from the oncoming headlights. A single headlight bounced by first, a shimmering yellowwhite ball, followed by two sets of two more. The blackness returned but still Paul held open the curtain. Listening, listening, he heard the sounds of wheels rolling into the driveway, of engines coughing to a stop, of doors slamming. Someone was yelling. You could hear the yelling but you couldn't make out the words.

Downstairs the front door flew open, blown wide by the fury. The boy sat in the bed, looking into the black. The strip of light beneath the door blinked on. The shadows of his mother's slippers flew by. Now even tumbleweed had wings.

Words were clapping up from downstairs like thunder, the boy's father yelling, "I had to do it I tell you! Any other attorney in town would've done the same thing!"

The sounds of shoes walking on the linoleum of the entranceway, of his mother's slippers going down the carpeted steps, her hand pulling on the banister, making it groan. The door slammed.

"Sold down the river by my own brother!" It was Jeffrey's voice.

The boy opened his bedroom door. He went to the top of the steps, leaned against the wall.

Grampa Stoken's voice sounded.

"Don't talk that way, you ungrateful junkie. Your brother did a fine job. You're out of jail, aren't you?"

"Yeah great!" Jeffrey said. "I'm out of jail for tonight and next week I get on a plane for Vietnam! Some deal! Out of the frying pan and into the fire, if you ask me! Some deal you cut, lawyerman."

"It was the only thing to do," the boy's father said. "Legally speaking, the fact that you've been drafted is the only chip in your favor. When I told Judge Pratt you were scheduled for induction next week a big smile came to his face and he said, 'Well that's just fine. A stint in the army might just straighten this boy out. I was afraid I was going to have to lock him up.' Those were his exact words. He told me he'd've given you five years, minimum. It came down to two years in the army or five in the slammer. You're in serious trouble, little brother. Caught with almost a half an ounce of marijuana! Why the police told me that's enough for almost eight or nine cigarettes! You're lucky you live in such a Christian, forgiving state as Iowa, where the penalties are light. In Texas you'd've pulled life behind bars."

"Putting that devil weed to your lips!" Grampa Stoken's voice said. "Don't you know the church teaches your body is the temple of God? You ought to be ashamed of yourself!"

From the top of the stairs the boy couldn't see any of the faces but he knew how his grandfather's face looked when he said these words. It looked bitter, unreasonable, wrinkled. The boy thought, The voice sounds like the face. He couldn't see any of them but he could see in his mind's eye the expression each wore. He'd watched the three of them quarreling countless times before. It was always the same, no matter what they quarreled about: his father and grandfather always teamed up against his uncle and each always wore a facial expression he used expressly for quarreling with the others. The grandfather's quarreling face always was bitter, unreasonable, wrinkled. The father when he quarreled always looked near the end of his rope, riled up, yet somehow at the same time confident, even big brotherly. The uncle looked confident too, but it wasn't the same sort of confidence that was worn on the face of Paul's father. The father's confidence was the confidence of a man of society, an educated confidence, a confidence that seemed to say, "I know what I'm talking about because I've read it in books." The uncle's was a confidence of conscience, a less sophisticated, wildgrown confidence, a confidence that seemed to say, "I know what I'm talking about because I feel it in my gut." The uncle waved his self-assured confidence like a matador's red cape, infuriating the father and grandfather. Often they said he was smug, even naive. So along with the look of confidence a growing look of frustration splashed across Jeffrey's face, stirred up by the name-calling, giving his quarreling expression something of the look of a deep lake in a storm, ruffled at the surface though tranquil below. He'd begun to assume the demeanor of a traveler in a foreign country who, mistakenly locked in an insane asylum, must now attempt to explain his sanity to crazy men who speak a different tongue. Finding it increasingly difficult to communicate with his family, he was beginning to wonder if he should even try. But the three of them hadn't yet reached that point, the point where they gave up altogether trying to explain themselves to each other. There were still some invisible strings binding them together.

"Well thanks for getting me out of the slammer, lawyerman. Looks like I'm going to Canada a little ahead of schedule."

"The hell you are!" Grampa Stoken spat. "You're getting on that plane and you're going to Vietnam if I have to pick you up by the scruff of your neck and throw you on that plane myself."

"Oh no I'm not!"

"Oh yes you are!"

"I don't want any part of your war. I don't even know what the hell you're fighting about."

"That don't make a damn bit of difference," Grampa Stoken yelled. "Your country calls you up and you go. Don't be so damn smug boy. Face the facts. It's these reds. We've gotta kill these reds if the world's ever going to get some peace. I was proud to go to Korea. I was proud to shoot a few reds for my country."

"Now I find out my old man's a murderer!" Jeffrey wailed. "How many Hail Marys did they make you say at confession?"

"Shooting reds isn't a sin. But it *is* a sin to disobey your country. To be so smug. A sin against God and the Holy Mother Roman Catholic Church."

"In that case my sinning days have just begun. I'm leaving for Canada first thing in the morning."

"Oh no you're not!"

"Oh yes I am!"

No one said anything for a minute. Then the voice of Paul's father said, "Before you make any more naive, childish decisions you should know that I had to use the mortgage of this house as security against your bond. If you skip bail you put me, my wife and little Pauley out on the street."

"You did *what!*" the boy heard his mother gag.

"It was the only way I could arrange the bond. I wasn't going to tell anyone but there it is."

"Well that's the topper!" Jeffrey said. In his mind's eye the boy could see the frustration splashing across Jeffrey's face. "Bringing your wife and Paul into this! You've really figured out all the angles this time, haven't you? You've really thrown me a sucker punch this time, haven't you, lawyerman?"

"Why don't you grow up!" Grampa Stoken shot back. "Or are you afraid to fight like a man? Is that what it is?"

"Haven't either of you understood a word I've said? I don't want to spend one day of my life playing soldier boy in Vietnam!"

"What kind of queer, unmanly smug talk is that?" Grampa Stoken said.

"Some queer nun learned it to me when I was a kid. Some smug drag queen named Moses said it. Don't you remember? 'Thou shalt not kill.' Or do they only teach converts to the Catholic Church dogma, not the Ten Commandments?"

The emotional storm climaxed. As if hell had blown through everywhere else now it raged through that place with the invisible strings, cutting them, like a hurricane snapping telephone lines between poles, snapping vines between jungle trees.

There was a slapping sound. Somebody's body went against a wall. Something shattered. Paul's mother cried out in a startled, brief shriek.

"I'm as Catholic as they come!" Grampa Stoken yelled. "A real churchgoing Catholic too! No one can say I'm not. And I will not have you insulting the virgin sisters of the

206

church! Whether you believe in Moses or not is your business, for he was a Jew, but no one insults a nun around me!"

After the grandfather finished yelling everything was quiet, spent, talked out. None of them, not even the grandfather, cared enough anymore to continue trying to explain. The strings had been broken. Hell had blown over. The three of them remained where they were for quite some time, not saying anything, tired and spent, not feeling anything for each other so much as remembering the feeling of the hell blowing over, the three of them standing there like bent trees, the vines that once had connected them torn away, watching a hurricane swirl out to sea, the damage done.

They started looking at each other, looking at the frozen poses they each held, the outworn expressions on their faces, the quarreling expressions, the expressions that now were as useless and outmoded as masks on the day after Halloween. It seemed as if each of them had been playing a part in a play, hypnotized, and now the spell had been broken and they woke up finding themselves in crazy roles, striking crazy poses, wearing crazy expressions.

Paul, by now in the entranceway peeking around the corner into the living room, watching each strange new expression come onto the faces of the grownups, saw the frightened look wash across his mother's face.

"Good God in heaven!" she said. "What's happening to us?"

No one said anything for several minutes. Then Grampa Stoken, in a most unusual tone, looking off into space with an odd expression, said, "You'll like it in Vietnam, boy. And Mason City won't forget your serving your country. Just wait'll you get home. There'll be a band playing at the airport to meet you. There'll be banners flying everywhere with your name on them. That's how it was when I got home from Korea. Afterwards they'll have a big parade down Main Street."

The night before Jeffrey Stoken left for Vietnam the family

gathered for supper at Gramma and Grampa Stoken's house. Paul's father and grandfather wore ties. Paul also wore a tie, one of those that you clip on. Jeffrey came to the table in a T-shirt.

Except for talk such as "Please pass the salt" the three men scarcely said anything. The women — Paul's mother and his grandmother — chattered away about the food, about whether frozen peas were better than fresh, about the latest advances in instant coffee.

Not having much to listen to, the boy studied the faces of the men. They looked and acted differently than they had just a week before.

Grampa Stoken's face was more feeble looking, more wrinkled than ever. He looked less vigorous, less capable of bitterness or unreasonableness, less alive, less like his life was ahead of him, less like he was looking forward to it with eyes afire and more like his life was behind him and he was looking back on it with cold dying remembering eyes.

Paul's father still had that look of confidence but now the confidence was tinged with something else. Doubt. Unsureness. You could almost see the doubt growing on his face, the doubt gaining confidence, as it were. He looked increasingly like a member of a jury that had found someone guilty and had condemned that someone to a harsh punishment, confident that the laws of men had been followed but not so sure that some higher law hadn't been broken.

Jeffrey's face was the strangest of all. The blue and black bruise beneath his left eye made it look even stranger. He didn't look at anyone, not even his nephew. He just sat eating, not saying anything.

After awhile Gramma Stoken got up and fetched dessert, chocolate pudding with whipped cream on top. She said, setting the pudding in front of Jeffrey, "Don't worry now. Two years will be up before you know it. When you come home you'll be a hero. You'll qualify for all sorts of veteran's benefits. And the children will look up to you with respect. That's just how it was when your father got back from Korea, isn't it,

208

Father?"

"That's right," Grampa Stoken said feebly, remembering. "There'll be a band playing at the airport when you get back. They'll be playing *Stars and Stripes Forever*. Afterwards, there'll be a big parade down Main Street."

Jeffrey looked up from his pudding. His inflamed red eye glared around the table, taking in each of the grownups in turn.

After the airplane engines started up it was hard to hear.

"I guess it's time to say goodbye," Jeffrey yelled.

"Where will you be?" Gramma Stoken asked. She clutched Jeffrey's sleeve.

"How many times have I told you? I'll be in training camp for a couple weeks. Then, who knows? I'll drop a card once I have an address. Don't worry now Ma. I'll be all right." Jeffrey hugged Gramma Stoken. The boy saw tears glistening in the grandmother's eyes.

"So long Pop," Jeffrey told Grampa Stoken, shaking hands. Grampa Stoken wore his best Sunday suit. In the lapel of his suit coat there was a small American flag pin, about the size of a thumbnail.

"When you get home there'll be a band playing right where we're standing," Grampa Stoken winked. "Wait'll you see. There'll be a big parade down Main Street for you."

"So long, lawyerman."

"Take care of yourself Jeff," Paul's father said.

Jeffrey pulled Paul aside. He bent down on one knee so that he was face to face with the boy.

"I'm going into the pit now," Jeffrey said.

"What pit, Uncle Jeff?"

"The pit we crawled out of and the pit we all return to. Stay away from the pit, Paul. As long as you can."

"I don't understand."

"Someday maybe you will. Paul, there's something I've been meaning to tell you. Something I've been putting off."

The grownups watched Jeffrey talking to the boy but they

couldn't hear what was said. They saw the boy's eyes grow big but they didn't know what was said.

The day after Jeffrey left for Vietnam the boy visited Gramma and Grampa Stoken's house. He came in the early evening, when Grampa Stoken was dozing in front of the television. Paul sat quietly on the sofa in the parlor, working hard at invisibility, while his mother and grandmother talked in the kitchen. When he was sure his absence wouldn't be noticed he crept quietly up the stairs to his uncle's old room.

The walls of the room were covered with football pennants, pop art posters, Beatles album jackets, snapshots of Jeffrey's old girlfriends and other memorabilia of the reluctant soldier's youth. Jeffrey's black electric guitar leaned against the chair in the corner of the room. The boy took several steps toward the black guitar before stopping himself. That's not why I'm here, he thought. He went to the neatly made bed, got down on his knees. Reaching under the bed he felt the heavy object that Jeffrey said would be there. His fingers tingled. He pulled the guitar case from beneath the bed.

It was a handmade leather guitar case, scuffed and scratched and caked with dust. Paul ran his hand down the top of the case, wiping away the layers of dust, uncovering the words. Buddy Holly.

The words had been stitched in large, flowing script letters across the now cracked-with-age brown leather. He unsnapped the clasps. Slowly, he lifted the lid. At that moment he thought he could hear faint whispers of music floating in on the air, wild music, joyful music, untamable music, music that could never be stilled. His skin tingled with goosebumps.

Nestled inside was a red electric guitar.

"So it's true. A Fender Stratocaster."

Wrapping his fingers around the neck, he lifted the guitar from the case. It felt good in his hands. He plucked tentatively at a string. Then another.

He didn't know how long he sat in the room with the guitar. Long after the sun had gone down he sat in the dark room. At last the door flew open and the light blinked on. Gramma Stoken came in, saw the guitar case laying open next to the bed. She flipped the lid closed and studied the words that'd been stitched into the leather. She knew the answer to her question before it was asked.

"Where'd that come from?" she said.

"Uncle Jeff said he found it the night I was born. He said if anything happens to him I'm to have it."

A stream of memories flowed through the old woman's mind. She took a step backwards, toward the door, turned and stumbled from the room. In a moment the boy heard the heavy sounds of Grampa Stoken coming up the stairs. The grandfather came in, his shadow falling across the boy on the floor.

"Why that grave-robbing son of a bitch!" Grampa Stoken snarled. He looked down wrathfully at the boy and the guitar. "So add another sin to Jeffrey's long list. How black his soul must be! That grave robbing son of a bitch!"

It would not do to call the sheriff, Grampa Stoken said. It would not do to have the whole world know that one of the Stokens was a grave-robbing son of a bitch, Grampa Stoken said. Some things are best kept hidden, Grampa Stoken said.

The electric guitar would remain a closely guarded secret. No one would say a damned thing about it, Grampa Stoken said. And little Paul would never, ever be allowed to hold it again, Grampa Stoken said.

The telegram came on a Sunday afternoon when the family was gathered at Gramma and Grampa Stoken's house for dinner. They were eating pot roast, mashed potatoes and string beans. Paul had just scooped out a trough in his potatoes for the gravy when they heard the knock on the door.

"Now who could that be?" Grampa Stoken asked, pushing back his chair. "Bet it's Cecil Burnett to borrow the damned mower again. Can't he leave us eat in peace?" He trudged across the carpet, chewing his food, and opened the door.

"Western Union," they heard someone say.

The adults looked up from the table.

Paul's father, ladling the gravy across the boy's potatoes, froze. His arm hung in midair, the gravy dripping from the ladle.

They heard the scratchy sounds of an envelope begin torn open, of paper being unfolded.

Grampa Stoken came slowly back into the dining room, the telegram down by his side. His face was pale. Everyone was frozen, looking up from the table.

"Some bad news. Jeffrey's been—. Jeffrey's been—."

Paul's father snatched the telegram away from the old man. He put on his reading glasses.

"'This is to inform you that PFC Jeffrey Hollings Stoken has been wounded in the line of duty while on patrol in Da Nang Province, South Vietnam,'" he read aloud.

"Thank God!" Gramma Stoken let out. She'd brought her hands to her mouth.

Lately whenever Gramma Stoken would see images of the fighting in Vietnam on the television she'd get up and leave the room. Just the night before, when the family had been watching Walter Cronkite at the grandparents' house, Gramma Stoken had rushed from the room when they'd broadcast pictures of a young man who'd been hit by a mortar blast.

Her emotional outburst had nettled Grampa Stoken considerably. "I have a good mind to write that Cronkite a letter giving him a piece of my mind!" the boy's grandfather had fumed from his armchair. "He should have enough sense not to show pictures that'll upset folks so!"

Gramma Stoken had stormed upstairs. Halfway up the steps she'd turned and cried over the banister, "What in God's name are we doing over in that jungle? What're our boys doing over there?"

Now, at the table, she pressed her hands thankfully to her face and again said, "Thank God! I thought it was—."

Paul's father thrust out his arm, demanding quiet. He continued reading, "'PFC Stoken has lost a leg in combat.'"

212

"Oh dear God!"

Mumbling to himself, Grampa Stoken sank into his chair at the head of the table. Gramma Stoken looked at him once, then bolted from the table and rushed from the room.

Paul's father read the rest of the telegram silently, to himself. The boy watched his father's eyes dart back and forth above the crinkled sheet of yellowed pulp. Unable to stand the thundering quiet, Paul got up and looked over his shoulder.

The telegram went on to say that whereas PFC Stoken had been grievously injured, he'd received an honorable discharge from the United States Army.

On the day Jeffrey came home the Stokens drove out to Clear Lake Airport. They waited at the edge of the runway in their best Sunday clothes, looking up into the clouds. The clouds that day were long and ivory colored, curving like elephant tusks from horizon to horizon.

The funny thing about the way a plane comes in is that you can almost always hear it before it can be seen. You would think it would be the other way around, as sight travels so much faster than hearing, but invariably, when someone watches for a plane, it's the gravelly low, buzzing sound of propellers that moves your eyes to the quadrant of the sky where beat the wings of the plane.

Hearing knows the faint buzzing sound in the sky above his head to the left. The boy's ears pricked up. His eyes swept the clouds. At last a gray speck broke through midway between two long elephant tusk clouds. Sunlight glinted off the speck.

"There it is!" Paul yelled. He pointed up at the sparkle between the clouds. "That's Jeff up there!"

The plane circled wide, its engines roaring, one wing dipped lower than the other. Its shadow skimmed across the ground, passing over the boy and his family.

Paul looked up at his parents. Forced, cheerful expressions were pasted onto their faces. If you didn't know about their hidden suffering you might have supposed they were waiting for a merry widow aunt to step off a plane from somewhere like Reno or Las Vegas. The boy knew their faces were phony. His parents had been cheerless from the moment the telegram came. They moped about the house, one moment blaming themselves for what happened to Jeffrey, the next moment exonerating themselves.

The night before, leaving his bed for a glass of water, Paul had overheard his parents talking somberly at the kitchen table. He'd stayed at the doorway, listening, no longer thirsting for water.

"I can't stop thinking it's somehow my fault Jeff's lost his leg," the boy had heard his father say in a low tone. "He didn't want to go to war. I can still see his face that day he left. The way he looked at me. It was like he was making a point of telling me it'd be my fault if anything happened to him."

"That's no way to talk," Paul heard his mother say. "How could anyone possibly think it's your fault? Jeff was doing his duty by going to Vietnam. He was obeying the law. Wasn't it your responsibility, as his big brother, to see that he obeyed the law?"

"But he lost a leg."

"It's certainly not your fault. Had you been there I'm certain you would've watched over him like a mother hen. But you weren't there. You weren't responsible for him. You're not your brother's keeper. You were here, where you should have been, watching out for me and Paul, your wife and son. You can't spend the rest of your life watching out for your brother. You're not supposed to."

"Still, this feeling—."

"No more talk of it. That's not what's needed now. You know that. What's needed now is cheerfulness. Jeffrey will be coming home and we mustn't add to the grief. We should be cheerful. The best thing you can do for your brother is radiate confidence. After all, he's still a young man with his life in front of him. He'll probably want to go back to school. Maybe he'll want to take a job right away. I bet there's plenty of places that'll jump at a chance to hire a young man just back

214

from the war. Let Jeff know you'll help him find a job. Neither of you should get bogged down in guilt, blaming each other for what happened."

"Of course you're right," the boy had heard his father sigh. "I suppose we must do our best to accentuate the positive."

So as the plane carrying Jeffrey straightened its wings and slanted down toward the runway the boy studied the preoccupied, idiotic smiles on the faces of his parents. They were watching the shadow of the plane shimmering in the heat waves off to the side of the runway. Squinting, Grampa Stoken raised a hand above his eyes and looked into the sun. "Looks like a Boeing, don't it?" he said.

Grampa Stoken had wanted a reception committee to greet Jeffrey at the airport. At the supper table on the evening the telegram had arrived the old man had told the family of his ambitious plans for Jeffrey's glorious homecoming. He would ask the high school marching band to play on the runway. He would ask the mayor of Mason City to make a welcome home speech from atop a soapbox. He would ask the boys at the VFW to organize a grand parade down Main Street beneath banners proclaiming, "Mason City Welcomes Home PFC Jeffrey Stoken."

But none of these trappings of glory had materialized. On the day of Jeffrey's homecoming the closest thing to glory on hand was the tiny American flag pin on the lapel of Grampa Stoken's good suit coat. Pinning on the flag had been the last thing the old man had done before they'd left for the airport.

All week long Grampa Stoken had been on the phone trying to get the glory together. There had been one disappointment after another. The first disappointment had come from the leader of the high school marching band, Chester Edwards. After an hour spent pleading with the bandleader on the telephone Grampa Stoken had heatedly related to the family the news that the marching band had disbanded for the summer and that no amount of pleading with "thick-headed Edwards" would secure the presence of the tubas, the slide trombones or the bass drums on the airport tarmac before the first week of October, if then.

"It don't seem right," Gramma Stoken had said, rubbing her hands on her apron. "He only has one home town to come back to. And there's only one marching band that can welcome him home."

The next disappointment had come from the mayor of Mason City. The mayor, a rather popular man named Jim Caulson, divided his time between his desk at City Hall and Caulson's Hardware downtown.

From the kitchen table Paul had heard his grandfather saying into the phone, "But I promised my boy a grand reception when he got home!"

After about an hour of this the old man had slammed down the phone.

"That son of a bitch Caulson!" he'd cussed. "Says there can't be an official reception at the airport since Jeff's coming home on a business day. Says business is too slow to risk closing his hardware store long enough to go out to Clear Lake Airport. The son of a bitch! If Jeff had been smart he would've got his leg shot off a couple days earlier so he could fly home on a Sunday!"

The final disappointment had come from the boys at the VFW. Grampa Stoken had become so riled talking to the adjutant of the local VFW post that Paul's curiosity got the better of him. The boy had crept upstairs to the phone in the hallway, softly lifting the receiver while covering the mouthpiece with his palm.

"...quite frankly," the voice of the man from the VFW had crackled over the receiver, "the boys here ain't too interested in this thing going on over in 'Nam. Believe it or not, it's a touchy issue with the boys these days. Some of us are all for shooting the commies, while others say they don't know what the hell the whole thing's about. 'Course, this is the army we're talking about, and since when is it important for anybody to know what the hell the army's up to? 'Course, myself, I'm all for shooting the commies. Why not? But some of the

216

others, they worry the kids coming back from 'Nam are gonna crowd the VA hospitals and tie up the benefits, making things worse than they already is. Like I say, it's a touchy issue with the boys. Things being the way they is, you understand, it makes no sense to go around muddying the waters by parading down Main Street beneath banners and all, now does it? That'd only alienate more of the boys. These days it's hard enough to get the boys together for a picnic, let alone a parade. But I tell you what. Maybe in a few months — if a few more kids get home from 'Nam, this is — maybe we can sponsor some sort of welcome home picnic in back of the legion hall. A low-keyed affair. The grass stays green back there almost to November, you know. That might be downright nice. Maybe by then the boys will've formed some sort of consensus about where we ought to stand on this 'Nam thing."

So because of these things the Stokens were forced to welcome their own home from Vietnam. They stood erect, almost like soldiers at attention, on the tarmac. Paul had his eyes closed. He listened to the squeal of the plane's rubber tires as they bit into the runway, listened to the tremendous hum of the wings as they sliced air, listened to the violent ripping sounds of the propellers as they whipped around, listened to the fast chunkity-chunk of the firebreathing engines.

The plane taxied down the runway, turned, then rolled up to the hanger, clipping along at a fast pace. It rolled straight toward the Stokens, looking bigger and fiercer by the moment, belching fumes from behind, shimmering in the heat waves out on the runway, roaring. A metal firebreathing bird, the boy thought. A metal firebreathing bird swooping down from the clouds with the one it had carried off into the flames of battle only two years before, a spaceage flying dinosaur returning chewed and broken the one it had carried off whole into the distant fiery nightmare only two trips around the sun ago.

Just when it seemed the plane was drawing dangerously near, just as the members of the family were considering whether there might be logic in jumping out of the way, it veered sharply around. The wash of air from the props blew into their faces, nearly carrying away the ladies' pillbox hats. The engines wound down. Soon all you could hear were the soft notes of Gramma Stoken's sobs hanging on the music of the wind.

Three men in overalls lazily rolled a portable ramp from the hanger. They talked casually of baseball while they rolled it up to the plane. This done, they turned and strolled back to the cool hanger.

The Stokens moved to the bottom of the ramp, looking up at the closed door of the plane. They heard the door seals crack.

The door opened, folding into the plane. Two bearers in drab green uniforms carried a stretcher through the door and down the ramp, swaggering slightly as they descended. They carried the stretcher past the downcast eyes of the family.

Jeffrey lie on the stretcher, his eyes closed, mumbling.

They set the stretcher down on the tarmac, before the family's gaping eyes.

"Looks like you're home at last, cowboy," the stretcher bearer in front said, looking around.

They tried not to listen to the mumbling.

"Where's the ambulance from the VA hospital, Pop?" the stretcher bearer said to Grampa Stoken.

"What ambulance?"

"Damn army. How're they planning to get this boy to the VA?"

"Got the Ford out front." Grampa Stoken pointed back over his shoulder. "Didn't stop to think there might be a stretcher involved."

"It's best if this here boy travels laying down," the front stretcher bearer said. "He ain't gonna fit in no Ford laying down, that's for sure. 'Less you want to hang him out the window, someone better go call an ambulance."

"I'll go," Paul's father said. Smiling, he looked down at the stretcher. "There must be a phone in the hanger." He walked off across the tarmac.

The others looked down at the stretcher. Jeffrey's eyes

218

were unopened. He mumbled unfathomable obscenities.

"Dear God! He's delirious!" Gramma Stoken cried.

"Don't you let that babbling worry you none, ma'am," the front stretcher bearer said. "He's just going through hell coming off the painkiller, is all. He's in good shape or they wouldn't've let him out. We brought home lots worse than this, ain't we, Roy?"

The second one nodded.

"He don't know what he's saying. He's out like a light. I bet he snaps out in time for dinner. If he starts howling about the pain, tell them to give him two aspirins. He's got to get off the painkillers. Doctor's orders. No more joy juice for this one."

Grampa Stoken said to the first stretcher bearer, "We were going to have a big welcome, with a band and everything, speeches, the works, but I guess it's just as well. We thought we'd make it a small, private thing. Just the family, you know. We wanted it this way. Nice and private, don't you see?"

The stretcher bearer looked around.

"At least this one's got a family at the other end," he said. "We left one fella in a wheelchair out near Topeka last week, left him out on the runway without a soul in the world waiting. No one gives a damn about the soldier these days. Asked him if he wanted me to push him into the terminal but he said no. Said he'd do it himself. Last we saw him he was wheeling his chair across the runway to the terminal. Kinda got to me, that one did. Hey, Gramps, got a smoke on ya?"

Grampa Stoken pulled a pack of Lucky Strikes from his inside jacket pocket. He offered one to the stretcher bearer and took one for himself.

"How about you?" he asked the second stretcher bearer, holding out the cigarettes.

"Don't mind if I do."

The first stretcher bearer lit up and walked over to the tip of the wing's shadow, blowing smoke.

Paul's father came back out of the terminal. He walked slowly through the shimmering heat waves toward the plane.

"They're sending an ambulance over from the VA," he said, walking up. "It'll be a good ten or fifteen minutes, at least."

He looked down at the stretcher and smiled.

Paul's mother smiled too.

Gramma Stoken cried softly into her handkerchief.

Smoking a cigarette, Grampa Stoken looked down and straightened the tiny American flag pin on the lapel of his jacket. He moved his hands down to his sides and stood erect, like a soldier, looking straight ahead into nothingness, the cigarette hanging forlornly from his lips, the breeze gently lifting tufts of his Vitalisized hair.

The only sounds the boy heard then were the sounds of Jeffrey's mumbling, the sounds of Gramma Stoken's sobbing, the sounds of the breeze blowing through the silently twirling propeller blades, blowing a few scraps of paper across the runway. Conspicuously missing were the sounds of a marching band, the sounds of a Main Street parade gearing up, the sounds of the grateful cheering a young man home, the sounds of speeches, the sounds of glory.

2ND MOVEMENT:
THE LITTLE COUNTRY CLUB AT THE END OF THE WORLD

1

"*I'm* out." Charlie threw down his cards. "Send the bottle my way, will you, George?"

While the generals watched the boy's life on screen they passed the time playing cards. Before they'd begun to play cards they'd scrutinized the screen in earnest for several hours. About an hour into the earnest scrutiny of the screen George Natlong got up from his chair and, without saying a word, left the chamber. A few minutes later he'd returned with four bottles of bourbon, five crystal tumblers (the old fashioned kind with round bottoms that you couldn't set down until you'd finished the drink) and a bucket of ice.

With the help of the bourbon they believed they scrutinized the screen even closer than before. They'd comment upon this or that aspect of the boy's family life as they saw it unfolding before their watery eyes. They enthusiastically endorsed the rare bourbon, calling it a boon to their concentration, agreeing that the finest of vaporous waters were an indispensable aide to the close scrutiny of anyone's life. After the first bottle had been put to use in the cause of improving their collective cognitive powers, a second and then a third were similarly employed. By the time the second empty bottle had been placed on the floor Hal boisterously suggested that a rousing game of five-card stud could only sharpen their concentration further. With that George Natlong went off roaming through the cave in search of a deck of cards.

Now they sat before the console holding cards, alternately looking up at the screenful of fate then gazing down at the hands fate had dealt. Three empty bottles littered the floor.

"Go easy with it," George Natlong told Bob. He handed

the half-empty bottle across the table. "That's the last of it."

"That's it? I thought there were storerooms stuffed to the ceiling with hooch down here."

"Those storerooms are a long walk. I don't feel like hiking all the way down through the cave to get more. At least not for a while. I don't know why I just didn't bring a whole damn case back with me."

George Natlong took in the screen. The boy and his family stood on the airport runway watching a young man being lifted into an ambulance. Behind the family a camouflaged green and brown airplane was refueling.

"It's your deal, Charlie," Hal said. "Want to shuffle the deck?"

"Yeah sure."

"Deal me out," Bob said. "If I lose any more Helen will fry me."

"What are you talking about?" Hal laughed. "What do you care about your weekly gambling allowance? This time next week the world will be in flames. Tell you what. We'll divide the world. You take Europe. Gamble it away, for all I care. So long as I can have the Middle East — including the Persian Gulf oil reserves, thank you. I've been giving this some thought. I really don't give a damn about Europe. We're all friends here. Europe might as well be yours, Bob. So what the hell do you care about your weekly gambling allowance? You're moving up in the world, my man. By this time next week you'll control the casino at Monte Carlo. You'll be wealthier than Napoleon ever dreamed. Tell you what. Why don't you bet the Eiffel Tower? That must be worth a hotten-tot's treasure chest, don't you think? This hand why don't we all bet monuments? Hal can bet the Eiffel Tower, George can bet the Statue of Liberty, and I'll wager the Dome of the Rock in Jerusalem. Next hand we'll bet cities. How's that for a hand?"

The others raised their eyebrows.

"Now hold on," Charlie threw in. "Who are you to be giving away Europe like that? You'd think you own it."

"It's all in fun," Hal chuckled. "Tell him George. Tell him it's all in fun."

George Natlong said nothing. He reached for the bourbon, refilled his glass.

While they said these things Paul crept into the underground chamber. As he entered he saw, up on the screen, images of himself, years younger, in Iowa. With great care the boy made his way down the center aisle, sliding behind a row of benches. Scarcely blinking an eye he looked on in amazement, leaning close over the back of the bench. So absorbed was he that his moonstone slipped from the jacket, striking the wooden plank.

"What was that?" Hal said.

Paul held his breath.

"What was what?"

"Thought I heard something."

Hal drew his pistol. He slowly came back the aisle, looking between the long rows of benches.

"Why don't you put that thing away before you blow your foot off?" Casey said.

"Oh go to hell," Hal shot back. He was halfway up the aisle. "Don't you think I know how to handle firearms?" He glanced under one more bench. Holstering the .45, he returned to his seat.

George Natlong threw down his cards. "Come on, guys. We're getting punchy. Let's call it a day and see what's happening back at the house."

"So long as I get some food in me I'm for anything."

"That goes for me."

George Natlong groaned from the chair. "I'm hungry myself. Tomorrow why don't we bring sandwiches?"

Behind the generals, in the rear of the great hall, the boy buried his hands deeply into the pockets of the jacket that had once been worn by James Dean. Stooping low so he wouldn't be seen he scrambled quickly up the aisle, out into the hall. He moved fast up the windowless slanted passageway to the surface, moving his feet as quickly as they would go without slapping the carpeted floor, his hands stuffed in the jacket pockets and his shoulders hunched the way he thought James Dean would hunch them if he found himself in similar circumstances. Not scuffing his feet, keeping them low to the floor, very much like ice skating, he made good time to the top. At the surface he pulled his hands from the jacket pockets and tore across the warehouse floor, not caring about the thunderous sounds of his sneakers slapping concrete.

The haphazard mountain of furniture in the middle of the warehouse now rose almost to the ceiling. The old butler had outdone himself hauling the stuff in. So startling was the sight that the boy momentarily froze at the foot of the pile to gawk up the jagged cliffs of coffee tables and ottomans. A carved hat rack tottered uneasily at the brink of the summit, hanging over the side of a china cabinet. Fearful that the slightest disturbance might touch off a calamitous avalanche he backed carefully away. Turning his head, he thought he heard the clapping talk of the generals as they came up from below. He ran full tilt to the sliding door. Drawing it back he slipped out into the twilight.

Outside the night air was damp and warm. It felt like rain coming up. Ignoring the pathway to the house he raced through the trees, breathing hard, his shirt beneath the jacket clinging to his skin. He would've taken off the jacket had it not once been worn by James Dean. Stopping to take off your jacket and to get comfortable at a time like this wouldn't be the cool thing to do. Better tough it out, he thought as he tore downhill through the darkened trees toward the lights of the house. That's the cool thing to do. Tough it out.

When he reached the lawn he bent over, his hands on his knees, his breath wild and pained. He looked back up the hill. The trees made the light atop the warehouse shimmer. Here and there in the dawning moonlight fireflies went off.

The parlor window of the house was all lit up. Through the window he saw people with drinks. The butler circulated with a tray. He saw Claire, in a pretty blue dress, languishing beside the large-screen television near the window. It looked

226

like they were showing old silent movies. Charlie Chaplin, from the looks if it.

Straightening his red jacket, pulling up the collar in his best James Dean fashion, he mussed his hair, shot one more fleeting glance up the hill, then sneered, swaggering into the house.

"If I may, I'd like to raise my glass and offer a toast to the end of the world," Mitchell called out, the alcohol giving him a surge of confidence the likes of which he hadn't felt in a long time. "So long, world. You were beautiful while you lasted."

The others froze, not joining the toast. Bimmy and Edgar, putting golf balls across the thick carpet, froze midstroke, uneasily watching Mitchell.

Mitchell gulped back the champagne, hurled the glass into the unlit fireplace.

"Mitchell!" Bridgette said. "Don't you think you've enough?"

"Not on your life. I've only just started. Where's the butler and that champagne of his? Spencer old boy! Come here with that tray. I'm afraid I'll need a new glass too, old boy."

The butler, his shoulders drooping, his eyes barely open, wheezed up to Mitchell.

"I must say you look terrible, Spencer old boy. Why don't you take a drink yourself?"

"It's all this work I have to do, sir." The butler's face was downcast and distorted by exhaustion. "I've spent the whole day moving Mrs Natlong's woodwork up from the road to the storehouse at the top of the hill. I must have moved a mountain. Then, as if that wasn't enough, I had to prepare this soiree, since I'm the only help the missus has. I'm not a young man anymore, sir." Spencer moaned, moved closer to Mitchell. "Between you and me, sir," he said softly, so as not to be overheard, "I'm thinking of giving my notice. I'm a gentleman's gentleman, you know, not a pantry maid and certainly not a bloody teamster."

Across the room Elizabeth Natlong fingered the string of

227

pearls adorning her satin gown. That whining butler, she thought, he's ruining my soiree. She'd let him go but where could she find a replacement out here, on such short notice?

It'd started out to be such a wonderful evening. She'd had Spencer prepare a fine buffet. Her dear old friends Natalie, Bimmy, Mitchell and Bridgette had shown up at the gates just in time for dinner. Bimmy as usual had found something to joke about. "That green cheese detector out by the gate tried to swallow my moonstone," he'd joked to Elizabeth as she hugged him at the door. "There must be a mouse in the machine." He'd come to the house shouldering his golf bag. "Now that I'm here I thought I'd get in a quick eighteen holes before the apocalypse." He'd looked genuinely disappointed when Elizabeth told him there was no golf course. "No links? Not even a pro shop? Say, what kind of club is this, anyway? When George starts blowing up the world remind him to save Pebble Beach."

"Bimmy!" Doty'd snapped. "That's not in good taste. This is no time for gallows humor."

"I don't blame Bimmy for wanting to lighten things up," Elizabeth countered. "God knows we need someone around here with a sense of humor."

Bimmy marched into the parlor, pulled out a putting iron. Edgar found another putter in the bag and joined in. They did it to bear the tension, Elizabeth knew. Who'd blame them? There wasn't any way around the unspeakable thing so mightn't they make the best of it? They might as well act civilized about it. They'd have a decent buffet. Elizabeth would try to be a good hostess. They oughtn't be barbarians. She'd even had Spencer clean the crystal chandelier. Oh that dreadful butler! I do wish he'd stop his moaning and groaning and complaining. And I do wish he'd stop stooping and dragging his feet so. You'd think I work him to death! Couldn't he see tonight's soiree was a difficult social situation? Had he no idea how hard it was to throw a good party in such circumstances?

In Elizabeth's mind tonight's soiree was all important. Her childhood friends had never before met the wives of the gener-

228

als. As hostess she knew she was obligated to do more than merely take everyone's mind from the unspeakable thing. She must see to it that the new acquaintances hit it off from the start. They'd spend so much time locked up together in that dreadful cave it would be awful if they all didn't hit it off.

At first everything went as well as could be expected. That isn't to say the soiree was a success. The soiree, like the state of the world, hovered on the brink of ruin. No one said a word. The wives of the four generals stood stiffly in their evening gowns, not talking to the wives of the captains of industry. The military wives anxiously awaited their husbands' return from the front down in the cave, waiting quietly like the wives of men of arms have quietly waited since the beginning of time. Bimmy and Edgar kept putting golf balls across the carpet, Bimmy now quiet and thoughtful, not talking, not even joking. Mitchell leaned against the piano silently watching the men putt. Natalie, Doty, Bridgette and Elizabeth remained quietly near the generals' wives, next to the buffet table, at first attempting small talk but soon giving up. They'd begun reading the unspoken anxiety in each other's eyes. Though they tried to be happy and gay the thing that soon might happen weighed on them.

Nobody felt like eating. They nibbled at the food. The roast beef and the deviled eggs remained largely uneaten, spread out on the table.

"Some party," Claire sighed, her words hanging disparagingly in the air.

Hoping to liven things up Elizabeth had had Spencer go for the champagne. She'd had Claire show silent movies on the large-screen tv. For awhile the wine and the movies worked. They'd all forgotten their troubles and had a laugh over Chaplin. Then Spencer offered Mitchell champagne. Mitchell at first shook his head, all the while staring icily at the magnum, saying he didn't care for any. Elizabeth saw that her old friend's willpower was weak while his troubles were strong. Just as Spencer was about to walk away Mitchell fairly well leapt at the magnum and poured himself a big one, which he gulped down as if his throat was afire. Then straightaway he'd had Spencer pour him another.

"I do wish Mitchell wouldn't drink so," Bridgette now said softly to the other women. "Before tonight he hasn't touched a drop in years. The pressure's getting a bit much for him."

"It's getting a bit much for us all, honey," Doty told her, taking a swallow of champagne. "I wish George and his soldier friends would get on with it."

Having poured himself still another champagne, Mitchell said, "Here's to us!" He raised his glass and drank. "So long as we wear a clean shirt and a nice tie anything goes. Isn't that right? It's those vodka-swilling Russians with their cheap suits and wide lapels who have it coming." He hurled the glass with a great clatter into the fireplace. The wine cascaded through the air in fine droplets.

"Mitchell! That's quite enough!"

"Obviously the gentleman has never served in the armed forces." This came from one of the general's wives, Helen, who was Bob's wife. "If he'd ever served his country he'd know these things aren't for us to discuss." The soldier's wife shifted in her gown. "Over the years our men have often gone off God knows where doing God know what for their country. I'd be a nervous wreck if I all the time sat around wondering what important decisions my Bob made for his country." The other army wives nodded in agreement. Helen gathered confidence. "In fact," she ventured on, "we should be completely in the dark. Believe me, the less we know, the better. What qualifications do we have to discuss matters of war and peace? It's best left to the experts. It's enough for me to know that competent men like my Bob are making important decisions someplace in the woodwork. A good American doesn't want to know any more than that."

"There's some truth to what she's saying, Mitchell dear," Bridgette put in. "The world today is so complicated it boggles the mind. That's why I personally prefer not thinking about it at all. I'm glad qualified men like George and the other gener-

230

als are working tirelessly behind the scenes, in the woodwork, as she says, doing the thinking for us. We're only ordinary people and there's so much going on in the world today. How can we possibly make informed, intelligent decisions? I don't think we're even qualified to be talking about this."

"That's the biggest crock of humbug I've ever heard," Mitchell gulped.

Helen shook a finger at him. "I see no reason why we should continue this discussion. My advice to you, sir, quite frankly, is to shut up. Be thankful you're an American and shut up."

Mitchell gave Helen a sharp look. "There was a time an old bulldog like you would never tell a man to shut up."

"Mitchell!"

Elizabeth Natlong's face whitened.

Mitchell went on, "There was a time in this country when a man could stand up and make himself heard, when his voice counted for something, when there was nothing under the sun to Godalmighty sacred to talk about."

"Now, now," Elizabeth sputtered, "this won't do. What do you say we all sit down and play a nice game of cribbage? I'm sure the men will return from the cave soon and they'll want to play too."

Elizabeth was about to send Spencer for the cribbage board when she heard the front door slam. "Why here they are now."

Everyone looked to the doorway.

In came a boy wearing a bright red jacket and a sneer on his face. He crossed the floor with a noticeable swagger. Claire looked up from the Chaplins and, seeing him, bit her lip.

He swaggered across the carpet toward the buffet table. Halfway there Bimmy thrust the handle of the putting iron before the boy's chest. "Hold your horses," Bimmy told him. "This is a restricted country club, young fellow." Bimmy winked at the others.

The boy sneered, but when he saw who it was blocking his way his face went blank. Bimmy! It seemed to Paul he'd

231

known Bimmy for years, decades even. Did he know too much about him? I have to act like I've never met Bimmy. That's how it has to be, he thought. You can't let them see you know who they are. You have to put on an act yourself. Act like someone else. Act like James Dean.

A smile trembled across the boy's face. Digging into the red jacket he came up with the moonstone. He held it up by its chain, bashfully running his other hand through his hair. "Ah don't go taking offense over me," he mumbled. "I belong here too. You just ask Claire and Mrs Natlong." He smiled bashfully then tucked the moonstone inside the jacket, pulling the collar around his neck, looking away from Bimmy, looking at the carpet.

Bimmy let the putting iron fall away from the boy's chest. His serious expression gave way to a good-natured grin. "Why of course you belong here," he said to the boy, twirling the putting iron. "I was only joking."

The boy nodded, avoiding eye contact. He turned to Mrs Natlong. "I hope I'm not— ah— I hope I'm not barging in on something—." He scratched the back of his head.

"Not at all, Paul," Mrs Natlong said. "Believe me, you picked the perfect moment to come."

The boy swaggered to the buffet table, lifted strands of roast beef to his mouth.

"I was beginning to wonder when you'd get here," Elizabeth Natlong went on. "Where have you been all afternoon?"

"I was out hiking the campgrounds, ma'am."

"You haven't had supper then?"

"Nope. I mean, no ma'am, I haven't."

"Well you poor dear you look starved."

Natalie, smiling like a horse, said, "This must be Claire's young man! Isn't he just a darling!"

She said this as if it was a question requiring confirmation. No reply was necessary since Claire had already moved to the boy's side. She had an arm draped across the small of his back. In her free hand she held a champagne glass.

232

"We've been drinking champagne," Claire told him, crinkling her nose. She took a sip then licked her cherry lips. "It tastes like I'm drinking stars!" The blue dress hung loosely around her. It made her look very clean-cut and innocent. Almost angelic.

She looked so good he had to look away. He watched Charlie Chaplin. An ugly woman sat at a table beside the little tramp. She batted her eyelids solicitously. Chaplin looked at the camera in such a way that you instantly saw his dislike. You always have a clear idea about what's going on in a Chaplin film, the boy thought. You always know what the little tramp is thinking. His heart is on his sleeve. How different from real life, from everyone here. In real life we always find some pretext to hide behind. Even as he thought this the boy found himself straightening the collar of the jacket that had once been worn by James Dean. I guess I do my share of hiding too, he thought. I guess I'm no different from the others.

Nuzzling the boy's ear, Claire whispered, "Were you down in the cave?"

The boy nodded, watching the screen. The little tramp wasted no time running from the woman. He hurled objects in her path. She kept coming, her arms outstretched, mouthing kisses. Chaplin raced about the room in circles, throwing every object in sight, bags of flour, chairs, an umbrella stand and more at his relentless pursuer. The woman kept falling over the objects but always she'd pick herself up and continue the chase, now latching onto the tail of the little tramp's waistcoat. It seemed to the boy that he knew the secret of Chaplin. The clue was the clothing. An apparently dignified suit, a bowler hat and a walking stick, but the waistcoat seemed ridiculously small, the pants clownishly baggy. The shoes oversized. Dignity seemed beyond his reach, unattainable. He stood like a dancer, shoulders hunched high, backward thrust hips, but he moved so clumsily, without a trace of a dancer's grace. The little tramp tries so hard to give the world the impression he's serious and important, a man to be reckoned with, but when it comes right down to it he's a buffoon. Isn't

233

that how it is with us all? Don't we try to hide the buffoon inside by wearing the clothes of kings? As the boy thought this he felt the fabric of the jacket that had once been worn by James Dean. Am I any different? The more seriously we present ourselves the more the world laughs. We make ourselves into laughingstocks. Have I guessed your riddle, little tramp? the boy thought.

"Paul," Mrs Natlong said, "wouldn't you like to meet the rest of the guests?"

She took him by his arm.

"These are two of my dearest friends," she went on, patting the boy's hand. "I'd like you to meet Bimmy and his wife, Natalie."

Bimmy lifted his golf bag. "What this country club needs is a good caddie," he said to the boy. "Someone to carry the clubs." He patted the boy's shoulders. "Now would you look at those fine shoulders! Solid as a rock! What do you think, Edgar? Have we good caddie material here?"

Edgar's facial muscles twitched. "Looks like he has all the makings of a fine caddie." Edgar tried to say it authoritively, though it came off sounding shaky, unsure.

"Unless of course you'd like us to carry the clubs for you," Bimmy said. Throwing the strap of the golf bag over his shoulder, he saluted the boy. The bag shifted and the clubs spilled noisily to the floor.

"In grade school Bimmy was the class clown," Elizabeth Natlong said softly against the boy's ear.

The boy couldn't help grinning. It was hard to believe Bimmy and Edgar were the chief executive officers of one of the world's largest corporations.

"And this is Mitchell and Bridgette," Elizabeth went on.

Mitchell sprawled in a chair by the door, a magnum clenched under an arm, his collar unbuttoned, his tie hanging loose. He didn't look at the boy. He fumbled with a gold cigarette case, taking out a smoke, lighting it with a gold-plated lighter.

"Mitchell isn't quite himself today," Elizabeth Natlong

234

said.

Paul glared at the bottle in Mitchell's arm. The only guy here with enough backbone to stand up to the generals and he's already well on the way to stone cold drunk.

"Why don't you take off that jacket?" Doty said to the boy. "It must be ninety degrees outside."

"I dunno," he mumbled, casting his eyes down to the jacket. "I guess I like it."

Claire, from behind Paul, said, "It was once worn by James Dean in one of his movies." She giggled, forgetting to hold the champagne glass evenly. A few drops spilled.

"One thing's certain," Natalie observed. "His arms are longer than James Dean's." She pointed at the boy's forearms, protruding two or three inches from the cuffs of the jacket.

The boy took in his bare forearms. The jacket was a little small. Funny he hadn't noticed before. He'd been so caught up in wearing James Dean's coat he hadn't realized he'd outgrown his idol.

"This James Dean must've been a runt," Bimmy said.

"No he wasn't!" the boy returned. "I'd give anything to be half as cool as him."

The women laughed.

Elizabeth Natlong chirped, "When we were growing up every boy wanted to look and act just like Gary Cooper."

"But they didn't get to wear his clothes," Doty said. She'd come over to feel the nap of the jacket. "Where on earth did you find this old thing? It must be twenty years old."

"Same place I found these shoes." Claire lifted the hem of her dress and turned, showing off the sparkling red shoes. "Don't you recognize them? They're Dorothy's ruby slippers. From The Wizard of Oz. Aren't they boss?"

"Wherever did you find them, child?" Doty bent close to examine the ruby slippers.

"Who gave you those slippers, my little pretty?" Bimmy shrieked shrilly.

"Oh Bimmy you're such a card!" Elizabeth Natlong laughed.

"We found the shoes and the coat in the cave. In the Hollywood Room," Claire said.

"The Hollywood Room?"

"It's like a museum," Claire explained, bubbly from the champagne. "Filled with junk from old Hollywood movies."

"There's a museum in the cave?"

"Oh yes. There's even one of Charlie Chaplin's bowler hats! Imagine!"

"Is that a fact?" Bimmy said, interested. "I'd like to wear that around camp, if I may."

"You'd be amazed at what else is down there. Enough food to last us all many lifetimes. Not to mention luxurious private apartments, a gymnasium, a swimming pool, a sauna. There's even a computer that can look back into the past, like looking out a window."

"Now you're not making sense," Elizabeth said. "How can any machine look into the past? Only God in heaven can look into our pasts."

"That must be what they said about cloudtops before they invented airplanes," Claire said. "Yesterday Paul and I looked back to when I was a little girl in Winterford. We saw Mother and Father on the screen. It was so real it brought tears to me eyes. We even saw Grampa Duke. He was just like I remembered, smiling and happy and ever so handsome and young looking."

The girl felt the boy's elbow in her ribs. He wore a tight-lipped expression.

"You've seen pictures of Daddy and Inky?" Elizabeth started. Then, "I'd rather we not talk about this anymore. Spencer! Didn't I ask you to please bring the cribbage board?"

The whole time they'd been talking Spencer had been wheezing sorrowfully around the room with the tray and a fresh magnum of champagne. Now the butler set the tray on the closest table and left the room. The boy watched Spencer's hunched, stiff back dissolve into the darkness of the hallway.

Just then they heard the sounds of men coming into the house.

236

The boy stiffened.

"Ah here they are now!" Mitchell said, raising his bottle. "Hail the brave warriors returning from another day of unequaled combat on the fields of glory!"

2

The five generals lumbered into the room like tired dinosaurs, heavy on their feet and showing the strain of one campaign too many. The brass stars on their shoulders shined brightly, the insignia on their chests gleamed a rainbow but these baubles couldn't make their uniforms any less rumpled nor could they make the faces of the generals any less worn. The .45s in the holsters at their sides seemed almost too big and heavy for such tired old men to pull out and fire.

George Natlong was the first into the room. He came in stone-faced and quiet, his hands on his gut. When he saw the boy the fire in his eyes rekindled.

"Hail the conquering war heroes!" Mitchell went on, slouching in the chair with the bottle.

George Natlong ignored the salutation. He crossed the room, his hands stiff at his sides. Passing the boy, he sneered.

The boy sneered back.

An aching sense of desperation welled up inside George Natlong. The obsessive megalomania that stirred in him the desire to force his will upon the world now focused completely on the boy. Without first conquering this boy he'd never conquer the world. His face contorted with rage, he brought back his hand and smashed it against the boy's cheek, driving him to the floor. He stood over the boy, his face trembling with rage.

"For the last time, what have you done with the upgrade?"

George Natlong strained to lift the pistol from the holster but he found Elizabeth's hands clamped firmly around his wrist. "Have you lost your mind, George!" His arm was

238

frozen. They stood locked in combat, frustrated soldier and wealthy wife, one dressed in officer's uniform, the other in satin gown and pearls, staring into each other's eyes as if they could see the opposing forces in their souls, the one straining to be a soldier, the other holding him back. Here in a nutshell was the story of their marriage. Here was the same spoiled little girl and her nutcracker, still feuding it out after all these years.

"Get a hold of yourself, George," Charlie said. "Now's not the time for this."

He pulled him back and held him.

Claire and Bimmy helped up the boy. His lip was bloodied.

"You'll be sorry you did that!" he sneered at George Natlong, touching his jaw.

"Looks like you'll have a fat lip," Bimmy said softly, giving the boy a handkerchief.

"This 'boy' as you call him is a spy, a saboteur!" George Natlong told the guests. They began to laugh at this, asking if he had taken leave of his senses, but suddenly George Natlong groaned, slumped forward.

"George, is something wrong?"

"It's my stomach." George Natlong straightened somewhat, his eyes closed, his jaw slackened. "I'm all right." He struggled to master himself. If you can't conquer yourself you can't conquer this boy, he thought. He turned to Elizabeth. "For thirty-two years of marriage you've lorded your wealth over me. But you will do so no longer. You will now toe the line."

"Why George," Doty gasped, "in all my years I've never heard you talk that way to Elizabeth. You'd think she was one of your foot soldiers to command."

Elizabeth Natlong needed no defending. "Toe the line! Who do you think I am? I'll have you know *I'm* a Duke, a family whose members have dined with kings and hunted with presidents, and we toe the line for no one but Almighty God Himself, and sometimes even He must be defied!"

"You are no longer a Duke, my dear," George Natlong said. "Your father gave you to me. You're my wife. That's who you are. And that's why you'll do what I say."

For a moment the two stood measuring the steel in each other's eyes, feeling the sting in each other's words, gauging the lifelong tensions of the little girl's struggle with her nutcracker.

Presently Elizabeth's gaze crumbled. She began to sob.

"If Daddy had known you'd talk to me like that I'm sure he'd never have given me to you," she sobbed. Natalie and Doty had their arms around her.

"Nonsense," George Natlong said crisply. "Your father told me there would be times when I'd have to put you in your place."

"Daddy would never have told you anything like that," Elizabeth sobbed. "Daddy always saw to it I got whatever I wanted."

"That's not true. Old Henry told me there'd always be one thing he wouldn't let you have, no matter how much you kicked and screamed and carried on. He wouldn't let you have it, if only for discipline's sake."

Elizabeth Natlong, sniffling, tried to remember long ago.

The boy, hatred burning in his eyes, looked on from beside the buffet table. The handkerchief pressed against his lip, his rib cage huffing and puffing, he bent forward, his upper extremities drawn close against his body. Hunched up like that in the red jacket he looked compressed, set to explode.

He watched Hal moving down the buffet table, piling a plate with food. The general stopped at the salad bowl, his back close to the boy, sniffing the croutons. Paul shifted his eyes, studying the handle of Hal's automatic in its holster, only inches away. The holster was unbuckled. The boy felt the urge to grab the gun and unload most of the clip into George Natlong's aching stomach. The murderous revenge tempting the boy played out fully and vividly in his mind. In his thoughts he saw himself grabbing the gun, pushing Hal aside and wrapping his finger around the cold trigger. He imagined how the gun would feel in his hand, heavy and cold, how he'd point it with both hands at George Natlong and squeeze off shot after shot. He imagined the surprise in George Natlong's face as he slumped to the floor. Serve the bastard right, he thought. Teach him to slap me around.

The boy pursed his lips, tasting the warm saltiness of blood. He remained absolutely still, tensed, ready to spring, hunched up, tasting a copperish taste, like pennies, the handkerchief pressed against his chin. His eyes darted about the room. No one was watching. His eyes flashed to the gun. It hung like an apparition, floating within easy reach, bobbing ever so slightly from Hal's round hip, begging to be used. Use me, it seemed to say, pick me up and use me. His heart racing, the boy flexed his hand, preparing to strike.

It was then that the butler tramped into the room, wearing overcoat and bowler, suitcase in hand and walking stick under elbow. The boy started, taking his eyes from the gun. The others, including Hal, turned. Paul's eyes flashed back to the holster, seeing the weapon recede, vanishing as Hal turned, receding like a moon orbiting behind a planet. Reflexively the boy moved his hand, starting for the gun, but checked himself so that the outstretched fingers had a chance to travel no more than an inch or two. He closed his hand and drew a deep sigh, trembling. I guess I'm no killer, he thought. Now that the heat of the moment had passed he saw it was a pretty dumb plan after all. He was glad the butler had come in when he did. James Dean would never've contemplated something as dumb as that, he thought.

"Spencer! Where the devil are you going man?"

"I've come to take my leave," the butler said, his once polished voice feeble and broken. "You may forward my mail."

The broken-down butler hobbled for the door, pain in every step, his eyes wincing.

"Now hold on!" George Natlong called after him. "You can't run out. There's the matter of your contract."

"My contract mentions nothing of transporting heavy woodwork," the butler returned. "And it specifically precludes the preparation of food. As well, I am to have one free night every week, plus Sundays. Every day since your household has arrived here I've found myself carting furniture like a pack mule, cooking meals like a common pantry maid and I've hadn't a day off in weeks. Sir, I am a butler, as my father and his father before him were butlers, and the proud tradition of my family trade demands I take leave of your household if I'm not relieved of these most ignoble and unsavory duties."

"I take that to mean you'll hit the road if you have to move one more stick of Elizabeth's furniture," George Natlong said.

"That is correct, sir." Spencer's gray moustache twitched.

"You're perfectly within your rights to feel that way," George Natlong told him. "I don't blame you for wanting to clear out. But where would you go, and how would you get there?"

"My sister is employed as a nanny in Boston. I thought perhaps I'd make my way there. As for the transport: there's a small shop several miles down the road. The other day Mrs Natlong and I came upon it and stopped for directions. It's manned by some very interesting fellows who claim to be the last of an all-but-extinct Indian tribe called the Mingos. They make their livelihood from the sale of trinkets and artifacts from their lost civilization. It struck me as sad to see them reduced to liquidating their past so. Under the circumstances I thought they might be happy to enter upon an arrangement whereby they would deliver my person to the nearest town in exchange for payment, as I noticed they maintain a rather decrepit yet none-the-less workable pickup truck."

"That's not what I meant. Man where've you been? The world is slated for destruction tomorrow. How could you consider going anywhere?"

Spencer managed a smile. "Sir, since I've been a child there's scarcely been a day when one group or another hasn't called for the destruction of the world in the morrow, much like the weatherman forecasts snow or sleet. If I'd remained indoors with every report of inclement weather I dare say I

242

might never in my life have ventured outdoors. It's the same with these everpresent predictions of impending armageddon. Personally, I've always thought these predictions to be greatly exaggerated. You say the world will be destroyed tomorrow, and that may very well be true, but I understandably must think of my livelihood and my well-being. If over the years I'd allowed myself to take seriously every report of apocalypse I would have long ago emptied my savings of funds like there was no tomorrow, leaving myself destitute in old age. Likewise, if over the years I'd bent the rules of my profession to squeeze an eternity's worth of labor into a single day, as Mrs Natlong would have me do with her woodwork, I would've long ago broken down my health and reduced myself to penury."

"I see," George Natlong said. "Perhaps then you'd consider staying if I gave you the rest of the night off and threw in tomorrow for good measure?"

"And Mrs Natlong's woodwork?"

"I promise you won't have to move another stick."

"And the cooking, sir?"

"Forget it. We'll get by, I'm sure. So no more talk of going."

Spencer removed his bowler. His moustache twitched. "Very well, sir, I shall stay. And if it is agreeable with you, sir, I shall now repair to my chamber for a good's night rest."

The butler nodded appreciatively, then turned.

No sooner had he left than the boy bolted from the room.

"Hey! Come back here!" the general commanded. "I'm not through with you!"

"Let him go, George," Charlie said. "We can talk more freely with him gone."

They heard the front door slam.

Elizabeth Natlong cried to her husband, "Now see the jumble you've made of things! First you strike and chase off your niece's boyfriend and then you doom Daddy's woodwork to the elements at the side of the road. Without Spencer's help how in the world do you expect me to move all that furniture to safety? What's come over you, George? Why deny me the only two things on earth I care about?"

Now that the boy was gone George Natlong felt his senses returning. It was hard for him to think straight while fighting the urge to ring that punk's neck. Perhaps I have overreacted, he thought. Perhaps I should throw Elizabeth a bone. Wiping his sweaty palms on the seat of his pants he turned from the empty doorway, facing his teary wife.

"There will always be one thing you cannot have," he said. "Take your pick. Chose between the furniture or a boyfriend for Claire. One or the other. But not both. What'll it be?"

Elizabeth brought a hand to her mouth. "How could you give me such a choice? You know I couldn't possibly sacrifice Daddy's woodwork." She moved her eyes furiously as if searching for words. "What would you have me tell the boy? That he's no longer welcome?"

"You can't make him go!" Claire cried. "He's got a moon-stone."

"She's right about that, George."

"That moonstone was given to him," George Natlong countered. "It can be taken away. By force, if necessary."

"You can't make him go!" the girl repeated, her arms stiff at her sides. "I won't let you! I won't let you!" She stormed from the room and tore upstairs, her feet pounding the steps.

"I hope you're happy." Elizabeth turned to each of the guests. "I'm sorry you had to witness this. You came expecting a good time and the evening's in shambles. Thanks to George there's no one to prepare desert or even wash the dishes."

"Don't fret, honey." Natalie patted Elizabeth's shoulder. "We'll all pitch in and wash the dishes, won't we girls? Why, I suppose we can even cook the meals. It'll be fun, just like when we were girls away at summer camp. We can even help you move some furniture."

Natalie and Elizabeth turned for the kitchen. The other women, even the generals' wives, followed.

"That's taking charge, George old boy," Mitchell said

244

when they'd gone. He'd already retrieved the champagne bottle Spencer had left on the table.

Straightening his tie, George Natlong said, "I'm sorry if there's been any unpleasantness." He brought both hands to his gut and moaned.

"George, you better take it easy," Charlie said, guiding him to a seat. "If you let things get to you you're sunk."

The boy came quickly into the underground chamber, his eyes angry and intent, his teeth clenched, his hands balled into fists and stuffed into the pockets of the red jacket. He stood quietly for some seconds before the blinking console, watching the colorful lights, unsure. One of his shaky hands went to his mouth and he felt the swollen lip. With a fast, catlike sweep of the hand he switched on the computer.

The giant screen flickered once or twice, like a television set that had been switched on. What about the general? he asked the machine. Was there more to know?

3

The first intimation George Natlong had that the world was changing came to him one morning on his way to work at the Pentagon. He was surprised to see large groups of young people walking along the gentle slope at the side of the road. It was an unusually chilly morning, even for October, and he wondered what could bring them out on such a raw day. He'd nearly reached the Pentagon when traffic slowed to a crawl, then to a dead stop. "What the devil's going on?" He poked his head from the window. Up ahead hundreds of young people blocked the road. They chanted and held hands as they blocked traffic.

"What the—."

Horns sounded. George Natlong got out of his car, craned his neck for a better look. The place swarmed with young people.

An army lieutenant, loaded down with briefcases and thick reports, came huffing up the side of the road, his breath steaming from his mouth.

"What in deuce's name's going on?" George Natlong barked at the lieutenant.

"War protesters, general," the lieutenant replied. "They've blocked the roads leading to the parking lots, sir. No use trying to get through, least not till the MPs can haul them off."

The lieutenant tried to salute, though it was impossible due to his burden, then he started off across the lawn for the Pentagon. It was a long walk for a chilly morning.

"Damn!" the general yelled. He hit his horn. "I've got important meetings to attend! Clear this road!" He waved an arm, but couldn't be heard over the sounds of the horns and the chanting.

He threw the stub of his cigar to the street, stamping it. "Blazes!" He pulled the car to the side of the road. "What's wrong with these idiots? Don't they realize there's a war on?" He gathered up his newspapers and abandoned the car, following the lieutenant across the wide lawn.

Ahead, dwarfed by the imposing walls of the Pentagon, protesters fired up the mob with bullhorns. Everywhere banners waved. Here and there, sprinkled in the crowd, you could see North Vietnamese flags. The closer you got the clearer you could hear the chanting.

"No more war! No more war! No more war!"

Up ahead a knot of young men burned draft cards. The occasion was filmed by an eager television crew. A marine colonel, like George Natlong on his way to work, indignantly came up to the young men and they had words. A scruffy looking hippie girl sneaked up behind the colonel and stuck wildflowers into his epaulets, evoking laughter.

"You lazy beatniks!" the colonel yelled.

They circled round him, sticking flowers under his hat, in his shoes, between the buttons of his jacket.

"Stand away I say!" the colonel yelled, spinning around, flapping arms, brushing off flowers. "Stand away!"

George Natlong charged through the crowd.

"Release this man!" he commanded. "Let him pass!"

A half dozen MPs charged up, pushing the protesters aside. Held at bay by the MPs, the protesters tossed daisies at George Natlong's feet.

The two officers saw no point in holding ground. They fell back across the lawn with all the dispatch of infantrymen crossing a battlefield. They'd almost made it to the safety of the Pentagon when a wild-eyed priest stepped from the chanting crowd, bucket in hand, hurling its contents. In the corner of his eye George Natlong saw the bright red blob expanding and then it hit. He found himself splattered head to toe with blood. A cheer went up from the crowd.

The drenched officers lost no time pushing their way into

the building.

Outside the chants grew louder.

"No more war! No more war!"

Inside the lobby George Natlong looked down at his uniform. Blood dripped everywhere. From his decorations. Down his khaki slacks. From his hands. Lifting a hand, he watched the blood drip to the marble floor.

"Those dirty rotten no good sons of bitches!" he cursed, feeling the stickiness of his fingertips. His newspapers had been ruined with blood.

It was then that he looked at the marine colonel. Blood dripped from his nose and splotched his cheeks in measlelike dots.

They looked at each other.

It was then that they saw in each other's eyes that the world was changing.

4

"Enough! No more!" The boy held his forearm before his eyes, blocking the screen. He could hear the protesters chanting. "I don't want to see any more."

The screen blanked out. The boy lowered his forearm.

"There's still more I must tell you about George Natlong," the computer said.

"I don't want to see any more. I know who he is, what he is."

"Very well."

From the pocket of the red jacket the boy pulled a cassette tape. He loaded it into a tape player on the console.

"What are you doing?"

"You'll see."

Before long the stalactite-ceilinged cavern resounded with the clap of electric guitars, and the lights along the console flashed in time with the music. Paul insisted it be cranked up, all the way, to ear-splitting levels. Only at this volume did the cavern ring with the echoing thunder the boy liked so much. He danced rapturously before the flashing console, snapping his fingers and swinging his hips.

He instructed the computer to make a copy of the tape. This done, the boy commanded the computer to synthesize the sounds of violins, horns, tuba and bass drum which, lickity-split, they mixed in with the guitars.

When the boy heard the playback he slapped his knee and declared they had a Top 40 hit on their hands. So absorbed was he that he almost didn't hear the sounds of hurried footsteps. Only at the very last possible instant, when the footsteps clapped outside the chamber in the hallway, did he look up

249

with a start, remembering where he was. He barely had enough time to fling himself over the first row of benches. Only then, with his head tucked low, did he realize he'd neglected to shut off the machine. His heart raced. *The generals will know immediately.*

He uneasily peeked over the back of the bench. It was only Elizabeth Natlong. She wore a frilly pink bathrobe that shivered in the breeze as she came down the aisle. Her eyes were red and she kneaded a Kleenex at her breast.

She marched despondently to the front of the great chamber, red-eyed and mumbling inaudible worries. Reaching the console, she took in the endless rows of knobs, gauges and blinking lights.

"Oh I'll never work this thing myself," she whimpered, stamping a foot like a child.

"Why don't you give me a try?" the computer said, startling her.

"Who said that?"

"You're standing in front of him."

"Is that you, machine?"

"Call me a machine if you like, I don't mind. In reality I'm Epimetheus, Greek god of hindsight."

"You *are* a smart machine, aren't you?" Elizabeth sniffled, dabbed her eyes with the Kleenex.

"You must be Elizabeth Duke Natlong, wife of George and daughter of the late Henry Duke. At last we meet."

"How do you know so much about me?"

"We Greek gods get around, you know. Since there's nobody left to worship us these days we have plenty of time to pry into the affairs of mere mortals such as yourself."

Elizabeth began sobbing into the handkerchief.

"My niece told me you were showing George pictures from the past. Pictures of people who are no longer with us. I keep thinking, if only I could see my father the way I used to see him, the way I remember him, when he used to hold me in his arms when I was just a girl, it would help me so much to be strong, to make the right decisions. Is it asking too much?

250

To see a picture of my father?"

The screen above the console began shimmering, sparkling silver and gold, and from all this shimmering emerged the larger-than-life image of Henry Duke, sitting in one of his favorite wing chairs back at Winterford. In his arms he comforted his little girl, who was crying, having just thrown a fit.

"Now now, my little apple dumpling," Henry Duke consoled young Elizabeth, stroking her silky black hair. His face was every bit as kind and warm and caring as the grown-up Elizabeth, watching with the Kleenex clenched to her mouth, remembered. She broke down and cried as abandonly as the little girl in his arms. The overpowering emotions that had driven her down to the cave in the middle of the night poured fully into her tears. "Daddy! Daddy!" she cried, holding her hands up to the screen. "George expects me to chose between the only two things in the world that mean anything to me. The only two things that mean anything!"

"There, there, my little pumpkin pie," Henry Duke consoled the child in his arms. A wry smile played upon his lips. He said softly, "There will always be one thing you cannot have."

"But Daddy! Daddy!" grown-up Elizabeth cried, her face awash with tears. "How can I chose between you and Claire? It's not fair Daddy! It's just not fair!"

Saying this, she'd begun climbing clumsily onto the console, climbing as if she believed she merely had to walk through the screen to once again enjoy the shelter of her father's arms.

Paul saw all this from behind the first row of benches. He came quietly up behind her, placing a hand on her shoulder, holding her from climbing further. Tears streamed down her cheeks and splashed on the sleeve of the red jacket.

"Ah now don't go climbing up there ma'am," he said bashfully, unsure of himself. "You'll fall and bust something. Pull yourself together, ma'am."

He switched off the computer. The screen went blank. Elizabeth continued sobbing, though she'd stopped trying to

251

boost her leg onto the console.

"It don't pay to look so closely at the past, ma'am," the boy said softly. "We can get lost in the past too easily. We'd end up living in it when it's here we should be doing our living."

The woman lowered her eyes from the darkened screen.

"Paul. What brings you down here at this hour?"

"I couldn't sleep so I went out for a walk under the trees," he lied. "At the bottom of the hill near the house I heard someone crying and I followed the sound, followed it all the way down here. You sure were sobbing up a storm, ma'am. I could hear you nearly all the way back to the house."

"Aren't you a dear sweet boy," she said, wiping her cheeks. She brought the Kleenex away from her eyes. Now she looked at the boy with what could only be called a queer expression.

"Are you all right, Mrs Natlong? Should I run for help?"

"No, no," Elizabeth said, straightening her robe with her hands, trying not to look at the boy but unable to stop herself from flashing that queer expression. "I'm all right. Really I am. I'm sure sometimes I must look like an old fool but I'm all right, really I am. There's no point waking everyone in the house over me."

She cast her eyes then to the back of the chamber, up to all the stalactites, remembering where she was.

"I suppose we should leave here before George comes. He'd be furious if he found us here."

The boy let his hand fall from her shoulder and together they started back to the surface, but not before Elizabeth cast a final glance at the dark computer screen.

All the way up the slanted corridor that led from the underground installation Elizabeth Natlong kept giving the boy that queer look. She looked him over as if sizing him up to say something but when she saw he'd detected her stare she'd look quickly away. She kept working the phantom string of pearls. The two of them came up into the warehouse and approached the gigantic pile of furniture. The closer they got

252

to the dark mountain of woodwork the more furiously she kneaded the invisible string of pearls.

She said then, with a hint of desperation, "I'm afraid it's going to rain! Daddy's precious antiques will be ruined. Unless—."

She looked at the boy.

"My dear sweet boy," she said, squeezing his shoulder. Her breath caught. "How would you like to do me a tremendous favor in the morning?"

He looked coolly at the hand on his shoulder.

She asked him to move the rest of the woodwork up from the road. It was really more of a command than a request. He got the feeling she never really had learned to ask for anything in her life. She asked it as if there was never any question he would do it, like she would ask one of her servants to do something. The boy remained quiet the whole time she told him what to do. She must've mistook his silence for acquiescence, since she took her hand from his shoulder and, pointing to the forklift parked near the door, said, "This is what Spencer used to move the woodwork. Now you must promise me not to drive it too fast on the way up from the road less the woodwork fall off and be damaged. I don't want to see a single scratch."

The boy sized up the yellow forklift.

They walked down through the darkened trees to the house. The whole way Elizabeth kept saying he must be especially careful with her woodwork and how important it was he do the job right. He mustn't be careless, she kept repeating, but neither should he take too much time moving it into the warehouse. It had to be moved quickly, she emphasized, the faster the better, but again, she cautioned, it mustn't be moved too fast.

As she said these things the boy remained quiet. Walking along he saw through the breaks in the trees clouds coming up under the stars. He thought it would be nice to have a smoke. He hadn't smoked in ages, since he'd left home. When daybreak comes, he thought, he'd shanghai the forklift and drive down the road for a ways, till he came to that Indian trading post he'd heard Spencer talking about. Maybe those Injuns would sell him some tabacci.

The house was dark and still. They went in and started up the steps to their rooms. Elizabeth said quietly, "Now be sure to get a good night's rest. You'll need every ounce of your strength in the morning." At the top of the darkened staircase the boy whispered goodnight to Mrs Natlong, then slipped into his room.

All this time Claire had been turning sleeplessly in bed. She sat up when she heard the boy come in. In the dim light she just barely made out the figure of him standing with his ear pressed to the door. She could see his mussed hair outlined against the white paint of the door and she thought she could also make out his red jacket though the room was darkened to the point where it's difficult to make out colors. For the better part of a minute he kept absolutely still, as if listening for something in the hallway. Then he slowly opened the door and slipped back out into the darkened hall as quietly as he'd come.

"Paul?" she said into the darkness, but already the door was closed and he was gone.

She rolled from bed and threw on the dress she'd folded over the arm of the chair by the window.

The boy had already reached the bottom of the steps and was feeling his way across the dark hallway for the door, trying not to bump into the heavy furniture Elizabeth Natlong had arranged at every turn, when he heard the door opening upstairs. Spinning around, he detected the ghostlike figure of the girl gliding down the steps. Outside the house a single electric light burned on the porch and the light shone through the windows on either side of the door, softly lighting parts of the stairway. As she came down the steps the girl passed through the sections of light and her blue dress looked neon purple. The boy started to whisper, "What're you doing—," but before he could finish she came up and pressed herself against him.

She drove him back against the wall.

"Not here," she said, taking his hand. She led him into the den, wasted no time. Beneath her, the wide-eyed boy watched her ghostlike movements with an odd sense of detachment, like it was happening to someone else. He felt like a ride at Disneyland. In the wash of the electric light coming through the windows he saw her face.

The windows were brightening. It no longer felt like night, no longer felt like the same day. Outside he could hear the first tweets of early birds.

He looked at the girl.

"The night went on forever," she said weakly. "I was lost in it. Waiting for you to come." Then, "You mustn't do another thing. Promise me. Last night Uncle George told Aunt Liz he was going to make you leave. If you act real nice maybe he'll have a change of heart."

"You saw him slap me around. Damn near busted my lip open. I'll show him. I swear I will. I decided I'd use that machine to cut a demo tape. Now I'm going to put as many miles between me and those screwball generals as I can. Someday they'll turn on the radio and they'll hear a Top 40 hit I made with the help of their precious computer."

She laughed. "Don't you understand? When Peter and Linda get back with that computer part Uncle George keeps screaming about, they're going to press the button. They're going to drop the big one. Comprende? They'll be no one left to listen to your silly tape. They'll be no more radio and no more Top 40 hits."

His face went blank as her blunt words sank in.

"No more radio?"

He rose to his feet, pushing back the sleeves of the red jacket, pushing them all the way to his elbows. Looking down at Claire he erupted, "Maybe I'm no hero. But there's got to be somebody who can stop them. There's got to be at least one hero out there. I'll find a hero and bring him back. I swear I will."

He started away.

"Be quiet. They'll hear."

"I don't give a damn. Let 'em hear! And don't you tell me what to do. And me thinking I had a thing for you. You're just like your aunt, you know that? I'll never have a rich girl again. Think they own the world. All the time tryna tell a guy how to live his life."

He stormed from the parlor. Claire heard the front door open. Straightening her dress she started after him, but stopped. She waited at the door and in the growing light of dawn watched him rushing up the wooded hill toward the warehouse.

By the time he reached the top of the hill the sun already was sitting big on the horizon, winking between the wavy green tops of the trees. The boy charged into the warehouse, mumbling to himself, gesticulating wildly with his hands as if talking to someone and trying to make a point, mussing his hair with his fingers as he mumbled. "No more radio! We'll see about that!"

A chest of drawers still lay on the tangs of the forklift. He charged up and violently kicked the chest onto the concrete floor, causing a great clatter.

"Oh do be careful with the woodwork!" he mimicked Elizabeth. "Do make sure not to scratch anything!" He kicked the chest over and over on the concrete. "Goddamn furniture! Hope I never see another stick of goddamn furniture as long as I live!"

In no time he'd started the forklift and was driving hunch shouldered across the warehouse for the open doorway.

"Those goddamn generals! We'll just see! Put me out, will they? Who do they think they are, anyway?"

5

The Natlongs and their guests, the welcomed and the not-so-welcomed, weren't alone at Camp Moonstone. Outside the gates of camp, hiding in the thick woods close to the sky-high pile of furniture at the side of the road, two scruffy-looking men kept an unending vigil of misery. You probably wouldn't guess from their rugged attire the high station in life they occupied. You probably wouldn't guess from their unshaven scruffiness that one was United States Congressman Thomas P. Marcus, while the other was his congressional aide, Clarence Jones.

Congressman Marcus was one of those ambitious young lawmakers who never lost an opportunity to launch a flashy investigation. He'd learned that such investigations, risky as they may be, always made good press. Several years earlier the young congressman had made network television by visiting the South American campsite of bizarre religious extremists-in-exile from California. When the crazed leader of the group had opened up with machine guns on the congressman's party, wounding the congressman superficially in the shoulder yet killing his top aide and a newspaper reporter, then bade his followers to poison themselves with cyanide-laced Koolaid mixed like witches' brew in a bathtub, Congressman Marcus became front page news. The jungle became littered with the bodies of nine hundred dead religious fanatics, a congressional aide and a newsman had been senselessly executed, but the congressman himself found his star rising. With his arm bandaged and in a sling he'd cut a heroic figure on the Today Show.

The congressman's staff had made lavish preparations for

his excursion to the wilds of Camp Moonstone. They'd outfit-
ted Marcus and his aide with outdoorsy clothing from
Abercrombie & Fitch, clothiers of famous explorers from
Perry to Hillary. They'd supplied both men with lightweight
survival gear, including down sleeping bags and a camouflaged
tent, and laid in an impressive supply of dehydrated food and
canned water. No detail, they thought, had been overlooked.
In a similarly well-planned fashion they'd painstakingly
arranged for Marcus' and Jones' transport to the gates of
Camp Moonstone. The two had been dropped off some distance down the deserted road in the dead of night. A congressional staff member had driven them to the spot in an
unmarked government car with headlights doused, then had
departed in a similarly clandestine manner, leaving Marcus
and Jones to fend for themselves.

It was only after their ride had disappeared into the night
and the two had hiked the last mile to the gates of Camp
Moonstone that they realized an important detail had after all
been overlooked. They had neglected to pack a can opener,
without which they found themselves unable to open their
impressive supply of canned water, which meant they were
unable to eat their impressive supply of dehydrated food.

So they were starving. Great events sometimes turn on
comparatively small affairs, and the oversight made in
Washington concerning a small implement of machined steel
proved to have a crushing impact on the congressman's latest
swashbuckling investigation. He was becoming too weak to
investigate. After two days and as many nights without food
or water our young congressman would have gladly traded his
public office, his seat on the House Ways and Means
Committee, even his Franking privileges, for a common church
key can opener. But alas! There is always one thing we cannot
have.

This particular morning finds our dedicated public servants in bad shape. Picture, if you will, this forlorn scene of
investigatory American democracy at work. At the center of
the makeshift campsite, everywhere littered with dented but as

yet unopened cans of water, a hastily pitched two-man tent sagged after a long night of the tossing and the turning of its restless occupants. And what a night! The whispers of the crickets were punctuated at regular intervals by the slaps of mosquitoes being exterminated, the murmur of the pine trees sometimes mixed with the whistling buzz saw of deep snoring. With dawn the snoring sputtered and stopped and the men awoke in their sagging tent feeling completely and totally miserable, not only hungry and thirsty but also cold and unrested. No one sleeps well on an empty stomach and the gentle deep full sound of the wind moving through the trees above and around the tent only reminded them of the hollow emptiness of their biting hunger.

The congressman, picked by *Time* magazine as House Freshman Worth Watching in 1972, normally had that calculatedly groomed, spit-and-polished JFK look preferred by the young pols of his generation. Today he looked all the world like an Arkansas pig farmer struggling back to life from a three-day drunk. Behold the modern leader of men. Take *Time*'s advice and watch closely as he lamely rubs his dirt-streaked, unshaven face. See his black hair hang limply in greasy strands before his red eyes as he crawls on hands and knees from his sleeping bag in the tent to the pine-needle-and-twig forest floor, where he commences in weak fury to beat an already dented can of water with a rock. Futile labor. The can had been designed as a survival ration for World War III. It was sealed in a shatter-resistant plastic so sturdy that it wouldn't break if hit by a nuclear missle.

"Goddamn!" the congressman cursed, desperately beating the can with a rock the size of his head. "If I ever get my hands on the idiot who covered these survival rations in unbreakable plastic he'll wish he was this can!"

Jones, the congressman's aide, was of robust health with an intelligent, open face. He moaned as he lumbered stiffly from his sleeping bag, stooping, rubbing his back.

"Do you have to bang that can?" he said to the congressman, his voice raspy with early morning irritation. He looked

259

with contempt at the forest floor and the tall evergreen trees. "I was dreaming of hot food."

"What the hell would you have me do?" the congressman snarled back. His hair hung down in front of his face like a yak's. "Do nothing? Is that what you want? You want us to try eating that dehydrated food without water again?"

Yesterday, in the throes of hunger, they'd torn open one of the packets of dehydrated beef stroganoff and had tossed down some of the dried chips. It only made matters worse. The little compressed squares not only had the consistency of balsa wood and like sponges sucked off what moisture remained in their mouths, it was much too salty and had to be spat out.

"Honestly, Jones, if I'd known you'd turn out to be such a bellyacher I would've left you in Washington. I always thought you'd hold up much better than this in a crisis. That's why I brought you along. Of all my aides I thought you could tough it out if the need arose. I see I was wrong."

"Don't hand me that jazz. I know why I was selected for this field trip. Be truthful now. It's because of my black ass, isn't it? The others didn't want to end up like poor Henderson down in South America with a bullet up his nose. Let's face facts, congressman. There wasn't exactly a line forming to join you here. I know my black skin makes me a little more— shall we say, expendable."

"That's nonsense, Jones, and you know it." Marcus said this through gritted teeth, as he'd resumed banging the can against the rock. "And that'll be all about poor Henderson. Don't you think I feel bad enough?"

"I honestly don't know what you feel, congressman. I can only tell you what I feel. I feel cold and hungry and weak and every joint in my body aches from lying on the ground all night and sitting on the ground all day. Here I am, the top of my class at Yale, Phi Beta goddamn Kappa, an overachiever, and I'm sleeping on the ground like my great great grandfather, the slave. In just two days I've wiped out one hundred years of family progress."

260

"Now don't start up on your great grandfather the slave. I had about all I could take of that yesterday."

"The trouble with you ambitious white men is that you have absolutely no sensitivity. I should've listened to Mama and gone into banking. I could be snug in my own little house somewhere in Connecticut. I've had enough of these trees and this primitive lifestyle and I'll tell you something else. I'm going to do something about it."

Jones stalked away from the campsite, through the trees toward the road.

"Just where do you think you're going?"

"If we must stay here we might as well make this place livable." Already Jones had disappeared into the trees.

A few minutes later he returned with an overstuffed easychair, which he set down beside the tent.

Marcus looked up from the can. "Where'd you get that?"

"Where else? From that mountain of furniture at the side of the road. We can use a couple of wing chairs and a coffee table. Hell, I think I even spotted a poster bed."

"Put that chair back!" Marcus commanded. "You want them to suspect our presence?"

"Are you kidding? Someone's got enough furniture by the road to fill Buckingham Palace, and then some. Who's going to miss a few pieces?"

"I said put it back."

"I don't give a damn what you say. You obviously have very little regard for the safety and comfort of your staff. And I'll tell you something else, Mr Congressman. At the very first sign of trouble around here — and by that I mean guns — I'm heading for the hills. I'll be damned if I'm going to end up like Henderson."

Jones set about lugging the better part of an antebellum living room suite from the road. He hauled piece after piece through the thick woods to the campsite, neatly arranging around the cold fire circle a small sofa, two armchairs, an embroidered footstool and a hand-carved end table. Upon the end table he set a lamp.

261

"You're making a terrible mistake," Marcus told him.

Jones was straightening the lampshade.

"You don't have to sit in a chair if you don't want."

Jones returned to the pile of furniture, intending to hunt for a coffee table or maybe a china cabinet in which to store gear, when suddenly he was startled to hear the sounds of the forklift coming down the path. For the last two days he had nothing better to do while Marcus beat the cans than to lie in the shade of the trees watching the bent, gray old fellow transport pieces of furniture by forklift from the pile to an unknown destination within the compound. Now he found himself caught in the open. No time to make it back to the trees. In a flash he bolted with more energy than he thought he possessed deep into the tangle of woodwork. His imagination ran wild. He imagined the heartstopping scene which might follow. He'd be caught hiding like a frightened rabbit in the woodwork. He'd be hauled unceremoniously into the compound, where he'd be summarily tried and executed before a grim military tribunal. He vividly saw himself cowering before the firing squad, a death mask strapped over his eyes. He saw himself crumpling to the dust in a bloody mass. Damn that crazy-ass congressman! How'd he let himself get talked into this?

Peering rigidly around the legs of a dinette set, Jones saw the barbed wire-topped gate swing open, then close. He could hear the forklift coming. He whimpered. The forklift sounds drew nearer and he began praying to the congressman's slain aide.

"Henderson, if you can hear me," he prayed softly, his face breaking out in a cold sweat, "if you're up there Henderson, put in a good word for me, will you? I'm too young to die. I don't want to die."

The forklift drew near the pile, kicking up specks of gravel. Jones made up his mind to fight. He thought he could probably take the old guy. He'd take him by surprise. He'd leap up from the woodwork and hit the little fellow upside the head with a chair. Then he'd beat it into the trees. The congress-

262

man's investigation would be shot to hell but it was better the investigation be shot to hell than his own skin.

Jones wrapped his sweaty hands around a straight-back chair. He prepared to swing it, waiting for the precise moment when the forklift came into view. From behind a walnut dining table he saw a flash of yellow as the front end of the forklift rolled into sight. Then he saw a flash of red.

It was all he could do to stop himself from swinging the chair. The old man wasn't on the forklift. It was a boy. No more than seventeen or eighteen. His hair was mussed and he wore a tight-fitting red jacket with sleeves slightly too short. The collar of the red jacket was pulled high around his neck. The way he hunched his shoulders as he gripped the little wheel made it look like he thought he was driving a race car instead of a sluggish bouncing forklift. The boy appeared to be in an agitated state, for as he drove by the pile of furniture and continued down the road Jones heard him mumble, in an angered, brooding tone, "No more radio! Who do they think they are? We'll see. We'll just see what happens."

So surprised was he by this sight that Jones released his grip on the chair. He hastily tumbled from the woodwork onto the road, calling after the boy, "Yo! Stop! Hey there! Hold up!"

The boy stopped the forklift and turned.

"Who're you?" the boy asked.

"I might ask the same of you. Let's just say I'm a friend who's been hiding in the woodwork."

"Was that you I saw running into the trees a day or two ago?" The boy squinted his eyes and looked the stranger over. "No. It was a white man I saw."

"Maybe you saw my boss."

"There's more of you?" The boy peered into the shadowy recesses of the mammoth pile of furniture. Then, "What're you doing out here, hiding in Mrs Natlong's furniture?"

"Let's just say we're having a look-see. What're you doing here?"

"I'm trying to get some help. I thought I was alone out

here."

The boy pointed at the closed gates of the camp. "Back there," he said with renewed excitement. "Those generals are planning something bad. You dig? I need to find a hero. I heard there was an Indian trading post down the road and I was going to get some smokes and ask them if they knew where I could find a hero. Unless— are you a hero?"

"Me? That's a laugh. I'm no hero. My only interest is self-preservation." Jones gazed down the gravel road. "You say you're looking for a hero?"

"Know one?"

"Do I ever."

Jones motioned with his hands for the boy to follow. He led the way into the trees. Walking along, the boy heard the dull sounds of pounding. They emerged from the woods into a small clearing. A disheveled man sat forward in an easy chair, weakly pounding a rock against a can at his feet. He slowly lifted the rock, moaning as he did, then sent it crashing to the dented can.

"Here he is," Jones said with a flourish of his arm. "A hero for our time."

The boy took in the careful way Mrs Natlong's furniture had been arranged around the fire circle. The living room suite looked absurd in the middle of the woods, with the greens and browns of the trees all around, the soft spots of yellow sun-light playing down through the treetops and the gnats flitting in and out of the columns of sunlight. It looked like a very comfortable living room, very light and airy and restful.

"Hey, Disraeli!" Jones called to Marcus. "We've compa-ny!"

Marcus looked up from the battered can, squinting through the greasy strands of hair hanging lifelessly before his eyes.

"What?" he said.

"This boy says there's an Indian trading post a little way down the road. Maybe we can scare up a can opener or some water."

264

Marcus got up, came forward.

"I thought you said he was a hero," the boy said to Jones.

"But he *is*," Jones said. "Before you stands a genuine American hero. He just needs a little cleaning up."

The congressman held out his hand. His mouth hung open, his tongue appeared slightly swollen.

"I'm Congressman Ray Marcus," he said to the boy, forcing a smile. "You may recall I was *Time* magazine's Freshman Congressman Worth Watching in 1972."

"Well you're not much to look at now," the boy said. He shook the congressman's hand. It felt weak and clammy, like there was nothing behind it.

"I don't know, mister," the boy told Jones. "You said a hero."

"He'll look better after he's had a shave," Jones said. "Even heroes sometimes have bad days. Who were you expecting? Superman or the Green Lantern?"

"I don't know." The boy dejectedly scratched his head. His hand traveled down his neck, making sure the collar of the jacket was pulled up as high as it would go. The two men couldn't help noticing how genuinely disappointed he looked. "I guess heroes are in short supply these days. If this is the best we can do, we better get going."

The dying are like the living in one way. The dying too have rituals. Rituals are always the last thing to die.

So these then are the rituals of the dying. Each morning when the sun peeks above the black hills and slants down into the doorway of the cluttered shack the three old Indians arise. One slowly draws a bucket of water from the well then bears the bucket to a shady place just inside the shack. One methodically stretches strips of meat on a board then places it on the porch in the warming rays of the sun to dry. The oldest Indian, in remembrance of the dead, stands in the morning sun mumbling a few all-but-forgotten words, scratches up a fistful of dust from the sunbaked yard, shakes it into the wind.

Everyday these rituals are done as they always have been

done. Then the three old Indians repair to the porch of their shack to drink rotgut and to wait for the sun to set.

And there was one more ritual of the dying which the rest of the world was in too much of a hurry to note. Once a year the three old Indians would paint their faces with colors they made from clay, dress up in war bonnets which they made from eagle feathers and sinew, and slip into ceremonial beaded costumes of blue and red with the white bone vests. Then they would string their bows. At dusk they would walk somberly into the deepest part of the woods to a place they were the last three men on earth to know about and visit, the sacred ground where their ancestors had been laid to rest, a secret place where they would dance and sing and beat tom-toms and smoke aromatic tobaccos in pipes until the sun once again rose, at which time they would douse the torches and walk quietly back through the woods to the shack and unstring their bows. They hadn't set foot at the sacred burial place for almost twelve months now. They were such old men and it was a difficult and dangerous trip. They were dying out and were in no rush to go to The Final Place, which is what they called the sacred ground. They were happy enough spending time rocking on the porch and remembering the days when they had been young.

Every once in a blue moon, when they were rocking on the porch, strangers would venture down the primitive road to take photos of the last of the Mingos, and the Indians would somberly relate the lore of their vanishing tribe and attempt to sell trinkets. They used the money from the sale of the trinkets to buy provisions in the nearest town, some eighty miles away. Because of the shack's great isolation such visits from outsiders were rare and so they'd have to wait six months or more before they had enough money to go to town. But when they did they really raised hell.

They naturally were glad this particular morning when they heard someone coming down the road. Already they'd performed their daily rituals and were rocking on the porch when they heard the sounds of wheels kicking up the gravel. In

266

anticipation they leaned forward in their rocking chairs waiting to see who it was. They hoped for a carload of tourists from back East or, better yet, Europe, as these were the kind of people who spent the most on trinkets. Once they sold an ordinary pinecone for seventy dollars to a tourist from Italy who had come with his fat wife.

Imagine their surprise and consternation when, before their tumbledown shack, a yellow forklift driven by a highly excited boy in a red jacket jerked to a sudden stop, raising a cloud of dust. Two men, one white and the other black, rode on the tangs of the forklift, visibly relieved now that their rough ride was over.

Jones and Marcus rolled from the tangs of the forklift. Beating road dust from their jeans and plaid shirts they came shakily across the yard for the porch, the boy at their heels.

The old Indians exchanged glances. They struck their poses, raising their heads high so that their weathered and lined red faces, set off by the large hook noses, resembled as near as possible the heads of cigar store Indians. They pulled themselves up in their rocking chairs so that they sat very stiff and erect. They had learned from experience that tourists expected Indians to look and act and talk a certain way and over the years they'd found it profitable to play along.

Jones and Marcus stumbled dizzily to the porch. The oldest of the Indians, who sat in the middle rocking chair, a half-breed whose real name was Schwartz though for the purpose of tourists he went by the name of Running Deer, held up an open hand and, with the appropriate amount of resonance and gravity that tourists demand of Indians, intoned, "How. Me Running Deer."

Running Deer looked skyward. Sweeping his hand in a wide arc above his head, he said, "Many moon go by since the great feathered bird in sky has brought visitors to hear the sad tale of the last of the Mingos. You have come—."

Here Running Deer's well-rehearsed spiel was cut short. Marcus and Jones caught sight of the water bucket and they fairly well leapt at it, entering the shack unbidden, falling to their knees on the cool planked floor and lapping at the bucket like dogs.

Running Deer rose from his chair and followed the two men inside, where he continued his spiel.

"You have come many mile to hear our sad tale. And sad it is, for the Mingo have reached the end of our trail of tears. Among our fallen fathers is the great brave warrior Tahgahjute, known by pale face as Logan." At this juncture Running Deer reached into a pile of trinkets on a table by the open doorway, holding up a plaque made of wood. On the plaque was painted a picture of an Indian chief in a feathered war bonnet, beneath which words had been etched. Pointing at the words on the plaque, Running Deer cast his eyes down to the men who greedily lapped water from the bucket, saying, "Logan heap famous. Logan help white man but white man turn against Logan and slaughter his kin. Logan heap angry. Him go on war path. Many braves killed. Many pale face killed. Do you remember from your days at school Logan's famous lament? He say," —here Running Deer read from the plaque— "'I appeal to any white man to say if ever he entered Logan's cabin hungry and he gave him not meat—.'"

Again Running Deer was interrupted. The boy with the red jacket bounced into the cabin, followed by the two remaining old Indians. "We don't got time for this right now, Injun Joe," the boy spat, his face lit with urgency. "This is a real emergency." He turned halfabout and pointed over his shoulder. "Back there, down the road a piece, these crazy generals are planning to hit the war path. You dig? They've got a secret camp, hidden deep in the trees, and they've got a computer down there and they're going to push the button and drop the big one. You know what I'm saying? Kaboom! Someone's got to stop them. They ain't all that tough, believe me. So why don't you get your strongest braves together and we'll saddle up. We'll ride in together. It's time to hit the old war patharooni. You dig?"

The three old Indians looked at each other.

Running Deer kept pointing at the plaque. He went on,

"So Logan lamented, '...I appeal to any white man to say if ever he came cold and naked, and he clothed him not—.'"

The boy grabbed hold of Running Deer's arm.

"Are you crazy or something?" he let loose. "Didn't you hear me? They're about to kick off World War III back in those woods. Five US Army generals. You have to believe me. You just have to. They're led by a crazy man. His name's General George Armstrong—."

"Custer?" Running Deer said, his interest sparked.

"No! Natlong. General George Armstrong Natlong. I bet he thinks he's Custer. He thinks he's Cæsar. He's flipped out. Wants to rule the world. The government's built a gigantioso compound out there. You must've seen the bulldozers and things coming through when they built it."

The three old Indians exchanged glances.

"There were bulldozers," one of the Indians said. "Many years ago. We thought someone was building a vacation home."

"It's no vacation home," the boy said. "They call it Camp Moonstone. It's a secret government complex. They've got a cave where they plan to ride out a nuclear war. That's where the computer is, deep down underground with the rest of their supplies."

Searching for something, anything to incite the old Indians to action, the boy added hurriedly, with the desperate tone of one who is grasping at straws, "And that's not all. At the very bottom of this cave they've dug up old bones. Old Injun bones, from the looks of it. I saw them myself. When they were digging their shelter they must've broke into a graveyard 'cause there's bones and feathers and arrowheads scattered all around. I saw them myself."

The old Indians started.

"The Final Place!" one of them gasped. "Could the white men have broken through when they were digging? Could our sacred ground once again be desecrated by white flesh? How else could this boy know of The Final Place?"

"I'm not lying!" the boy pleaded. "You've got to believe

me. Those generals are desecrating your sacred ground. If you ask me, it's time to saddle up your braves and hit the old war path-arooni. There's only five of them and I'm sure you can take them. You could say I've known them all their lives and I think they'd back down if anyone stood up to them."

The two men kneeling at the water bucket coughed and sat up in the warm wedge of sunlight pouring in through the doorway. Jones wiped at his mouth with his forearm. At that moment the light from the doorway suddenly went dark, like a cloud had passed before the sun.

Five army generals, dressed in decorated khaki uniforms, each with a holstered automatic pistol strapped to his belt, stood wordlessly in the doorway, looking as neat and groomed as only military men can look so early in the morning, though they also looked a little ruffled around the edges, razzled, red eyed and a little shook, a little edgy.

George Natlong tried to force a smile. For an instant the smile went dead. His jaw sagged a bit. An almost undetectable twinge came to his eyes. His hand moved ever-so-slightly to his gut, above the holster, before he checked himself and brought the hand back down.

These slight movement didn't go unnoticed. Jones, seeing the general's hand move toward the holster, imagining the worst, let out a groan. Slowly he rose and moved backward toward the rear of the cluttered shack, his eyes on the general's hand.

"Why, there you are, Paul," George Natlong tried to say pleasantly to the boy. "We've been looking for you. You've no idea how concerned we've been. Breakfast is ready. Won't you join us?"

Charlie and Hal, straight faced and somber, stepped through the doorway and grabbed the boy by his arms, lifting him from the floor. They turned and whisked him out.

"Hey! Where you taking me?" The boy flailed his legs, to no avail. "Get your fat hands off me! I said let go!" As he was being borne across the porch he twisted his neck around so that the collar of the red jacket pressed flat against his cheek.

270

"Remember what I told you!" he yelled back into the shack.

Those remaining heard a girgling noise, as the boy had been gagged.

"You must forgive my nephew," George Natlong politely said to the Indians. He forced a smile. "The poor boy isn't quite right in his head. Result of a childhood accident. He doesn't have much sense left to him but his imagination was left very much intact. He has a very active imagination. What was it he was telling you? The doctor likes us to keep a record of his imaginings, as they may provide insights into his therapy."

Running Deer, still clutching the wooden plaque, said, "He told us many things, that boy. He said five army men were planning to make war from a camp in the woods."

George Natlong began to laugh. He clutched at his sides and laughed heartily. Casey and Bob also laughed.

"That's a rich one!" George Natlong chuckled, tears forming in his eyes. "What an imagination that boy has! We're army men, that much is true. But as is well known, no one wants peace more than us. A military man's job is to keep the peace."

"What then are you doing out here in the middle of nowhere with those cannons strapped to your sides?" Marcus asked. He still kneeled beside the water bucket.

George Natlong brought his hand down and opened the holster, extracting the .45. Jones gagged and dove to the floor behind a pile of Indian artifacts, covering his head with his hands.

The general said. "Just because we have guns doesn't mean we plan to use them, now does it?"

George Natlong slipped the gun back into the holster. He looked at the one who was slowly rising to his feet from the water-soaked floor beside the bucket.

"Say, don't I know you?"

Marcus said nothing.

Snapping his fingers, Casey said, "Aren't you, what's his name, Tom Marcus, the congressman?"

"Congressman?"

George Natlong's face whitened.

"Sure, that's who he is," Casey went on, "Congressman Tom Marcus. I've seen him on the Today Show. You know, George, the gallivanting Congressman Thomas P. Marcus. The one with those flashy investigations. Don't you remember? He's the one who went to South America when those religious nuts drank cyanide from a bathtub." Casey abruptly quit talking.

George Natlong brought his hand to his gut. His jaw slackened.

"A congressman, huh?" The words felt dry and crackly as they left George Natlong's throat. He was very stiff and erect, his face pale. "And what would our gallivanting congressman be doing, as you say, out here in the middle of nowhere? And him?" He nodded back at Jones. "Is he one of your aides?"

"Him?" Marcus said coolly. "He's my nephew."

"That's right, Uncle Tom," they heard from the back of the shack.

"My nephew and myself, like you and your nephew, have come to this out-of-the-way place to get some fresh air. I'm sure you know what I mean. The air back in Washington is so— stale and dirty. Perfectly putrid. I'm sure we understand each other."

"Perfectly," George Natlong said.

He turned, holding himself very stiff and upright, and burst past Casey and Bob, leaving the shack.

The two remaining officers exchanged awkward glances with the Indians. Then they followed George Natlong out. Marcus went to the door. Already one of the generals had climbed into the forklift and was turning the machine around, starting back.

The three little old Indians looked at each other.

One little Indian shuffled across the floor, lifting from a shelf three jars of paint mixed from clay. They were the colors of the earth. Another little Indian determinedly took the war

272

bonnets from the pegs on the wall, the war bonnets stitched together from eagle feathers and sinew.

Jones rubbed the butt of his hand across the rear window, clearing a swatch in the grease. Nimbly he came away and whispered to Marcus, "There's a pickup truck out back. It's not much but maybe it'll get us out of here."

"I have no intention of leaving," Marcus said softly. "I didn't subject myself to all this horseshit to turn back now. I think these old men may be able to get us into the compound."

Running Deer was stringing his bow.

"Now just one minute, King o' Sobby," Jones shuddered. "If you think I'm going to crawl into some hole in the ground after these crazy-ass Indians you have another thing coming."

When he was thrown into the backseat of the Natlongs' silver Cadillac the boy expected the worst. But the worst never happened. The whole way back to the camp George Natlong never took his eyes from the road, didn't even glance at the boy through the mirror.

After they'd passed the mountain of furniture Casey got out of the car and opened the gate. They drove the boy to the house, wordlessly marching him up the stairs to his room. All the way up the steps the boy watched George Natlong. The general seemed subdued, out of it, almost wooden. His eyes looked glassy.

He remained in the doorway, his hand on the knob. He said tersely to the boy, "You are confined to quarters." Then he closed the door and the boy heard it being locked from the outside.

Once George Natlong had locked the door he excused himself from the others and hurried off down the hall, to the bathroom, where he closed the door and vomited blood. When he looked up into the mirror blood dripped from his nose, lips and chin.

3RD MOVEMENT:
THE WOULD-BE CULT HERO

The boy pressed his cheek against the windowsill in the locked room, and gazed out over the camp. The room was a full story off the ground and he could see well over the trees. He leaned his elbows against the windowsill, cupping his head in his hands. Before long he heard the front door slam. Below he saw four generals leaving the house. Another minute, and the fifth general came out. Though he was looking down from above and could see only the khaki uniform, the epaulets sparkling with stars and the officer's hat he could tell the last one out was George Natlong. The roundness of the shoulders and the disjointed, self-important, toysoldierlike stride gave him away. George Natlong hurried up the path behind the others, calling after them, joining them under the trees. Then all five of them were walking up the hill together.

Soon they'll know, the boy thought. Soon they'll find out the last there is to know. How long before they find out?

After the generals had disappeared into the trees the boy moved away from the window. He laid down on the bed and closed his eyes.

He thought of the things they were sure to find out, all the things they were sure to see on the computer screen in the next few hours. He had to laugh. Once they got a look at his bedroom walls back in Iowa they'd know everything. They'll know the most important thing about me. And once they know the most important thing the rest will fall quickly into place, like one of those little wooden Chinese boxes slides open once you hit the crucial hidden panel.

He thought of the walls of his room back in Iowa. The

277

walls were the giveaway. Once they saw those walls, covered with all those pictures of Buddy Holly, they'd know everything. Now that he thought about it, it was pretty silly, all right, but it was the most important thing he believed. It might seem silly to the generals but what did he care? Lots of things those generals believed in he thought totally ridiculous. Why should he care if the generals laughed at the most important thing he believed?

The most important thing was this: he believed in another life he had been Buddy Holly.

He couldn't pin down the exact moment he came to suspect this. Such suspicions overcome you slowly, like the rising of the sun. Like the rising of the sun over time he sensed something lurking on the horizon until finally it dawned on him, and when it finally did dawn on him there was no overlooking it.

It began dawning on him one day in the eleventh grade, on his birthday, the third day of February. A girl in biology class, someone he'd scarcely before noticed, came up to him before class and mentioned out of the blue she'd heard his band. By this time the boy and three of his friends played regularly at a local firehall, every Saturday night.

"I saw your band last weekend," the girl told him. Her name was Candy and she had a sweet face that always managed a mischievous smile. Candy was a slender girl though she had strong biceps. Once in study hall she'd beaten four boys in arm wrestling, gnashing her teeth as she fought, flushing red, causing loud routing yells from everyone watching.

"Yeah?" Paul had said. "Why didn't I see you there? You could've come up and said hello."

"I know. It's just you looked like you were having fun."

The boy tried to read her expression. She was a nice girl.

"Well what did you think of the band? Or aren't you going to say?"

"I especially liked your voice. Maybe I shouldn't say this. Don't let it get to your head or anything." She touched his hand. "You sound a lot like John Lennon."

The boy looked surprised.

"Really? You think so?"

The girl looked away. The teacher had come into the room.

"Hey. Isn't today your birthday?" Candy said. "You know this is the day Buddy Holly crashed outside town, don't you? Did you ever think maybe in another life you were Buddy Holly?"

"No, not really. Maybe when I was a kid but not any more."

"There's plenty of people who believe that sort of thing. My grandmother used to say never kill a bad pig on the day a sow's expecting litter 'cause the mean spirit in the slaughtered hog will fly into the firstborn."

The boy looked at her searchingly.

"Really, Paul," Candy said, "you ought to look into it."

The more he thought about it the more he came to believe it was a completely reasonable supposition. He had been born the same year, the same day, almost to the same minute, the same exact instant Holly had died. This he knew because that day after school he found himself in the Clear Lake library gathering facts. At first he was so sensitive and secretive about his suspicions that he leafed through the books and the yellow dusty old newspapers while hiding out in the back of the library behind the history shelves, where he had observed few people ever browsed, keeping an ear open for intruders and nosy librarians as he prowled like a cat burglar snapping bubble gum through the words and paragraphs, hiding what he read behind a *National Geographic* in case anyone came near. With wide eyes he softly yet electrifiedly moved his lips, reading aloud as he greedily drank in the words, "Buddy Holly died tragically at the age of twenty-one in a plane crash outside Mason City, Iowa, in the early morning hours of February 3, 1959."

"Gosh," he said aloud, looking up, snapping a bubble.

Later that evening he'd gone home and asked his mom

when it was he'd been born. She was copying a recipe from a tv cooking show.

"1959."

"I mean what time of day?"

"Early in the morning."

"How early? Exactly."

"Oh believe me it was early. Too early."

"How early? This's important, Mom."

She looked away from the tv.

"Really, Paul. Can't you see I'm busy?"

"This's important. A guy needs to know these things. When *exactly* was it."

"About one in the morning."

"One o'clock, huh? That's early in the morning, isn't it? Wouldn't you say?"

Yet in his own critical mind there remained a shadow of a doubt. Had he been born minutes before or minutes after Holly died? He told himself this was the single most crucial question. If he'd been born only minutes before the plane had crashed all this reincarnation stuff would be just bs. Anyone knows you can't lay claim to having been someone else in another life if that someone else hadn't kicked off yet when you were born. How could he know for sure?

This point troubled him no end. He worked it over every-whichway in his brain. That night as he was lying in bed in the dark unable to sleep for thinking he found himself remembering a certain mysterious guitar. He remembered as though in a dream the time long ago he'd come upon the battered red electric guitar under his Uncle Jeff's bed. What was he doing? He'd been fishing for some game under the bed and had pulled out the handtooled leather guitar case all done up with the scripted words, "Buddy Holly." Or was it just a dream? Holding the guitar he had felt something deep inside, a magic feeling, but it was then Uncle Jeffrey had come in, exploding, throwing a Godalmighty fit, demanding the boy never lay hands on his things again.

Or was it just a dream? In a way it felt like a dream,

280

remote and troubling, one of those dreams you'd rather forget.

No, it had happened. He knew because there was the other time, when Jeff was away in Vietnam, when he'd come upon the guitar again. This time he had even read the word Stratocaster, had plucked the untuned strings, once again feeling something, way down inside, and then Gramma Stoken had come into the room and had damn near burst a vessel when she saw it.

"That no good grave robbing devil!" hadn't Grampa cursed? Hadn't he forbid him to ever set eyes on that mysterious guitar again?

These pieces of the puzzle that was his early life were not dreams. The things he had seen as a child and the vague shameful whisperings of the adults coalesced in his mind till he sat suddenly up in bed electrified by realization.

His Uncle Jeff had stolen Buddy Holly's guitar.

Everything he'd seen of the strange guitar and everything he remembered of the grownups' furious reaction to it made perfect sense. If he was right about the mysterious guitar, perhaps Jeffrey Stoken would be the only person on earth who could tell the boy the one thing on earth he wanted to know. Had be been born before or after the plane carrying Buddy Holly had crashed?

He'd have to ask Jeffrey. But that was altogether another problem. He hadn't seen his uncle for over a year. The family didn't talk much about Jeffrey anymore and no one seemed to have a clear idea where he was living. After Jeffrey came home from Vietnam with his leg shot off things were never the same. He'd let himself go. His hair and beard grew wild and shaggy about his face. In those early days, when Jeffrey would sit alone in his room for days not talking only staring into space with eyes that looked like they'd seen the devil, Grampa Stoken had had the priest over to the house and both of them had told the young man he'd better get a grip on himself and realize he had his whole life in front of him. It was true he had government disability money coming to him but the priest pointed out it was neither the American way nor the Christian thing to do to be taking money from the government. He should consider using the money as a temporary means of bettering himself, the priest said, to pay for some vocational training or maybe some physical rehabilitation so that he might one day find gainful employment and become a contributing member of society. The priest ticked off examples of all kinds of legless and even armless men and women who had gone on to do good things. Jeffrey sat wordlessly in his room in his chair taking all this in, his eyes the only moving feature in his dark and brooding face, when suddenly he'd exploded, swinging his cane at both the priest and his father, ordering them to get out. He screamed he planned to live forever on the government disability money, for the rest of his life, that his country had taken his leg for no good reason and he intended to milk his country for every goddamn stinking penny he could get, though it would never be enough. He said a few other things in front of the priest that greatly embarrassed Grandma and Grampa Stoken and for which they uttered their sincerest apologies to the clergyman at the door. Not long after that Jeffrey had left the family home for good, using the disability money to rent a room somewhere in town. With the disability money he also bought a motorcycle, a big Harley. Soon the family heard talk that Jeffrey had been seen racing like a wildman through the streets of Mason City at all hours on the Harley, not wearing a helmet, his great head of hair blowing everywhichway. He wore Bermuda shorts whenever he rode and the stump of his leg stuck out like a 4 x 4 on a lumber truck, almost as if he wanted the whole world to see. When he rode his bike he'd strap a single crutch behind his back with a piece of clothesline. He looked like a cross between Dickens' Tiny Tim and a Hell's Angel. He was nothing but a heartache.

It was all Grampa and Gramma Stoken could do to hide their grief. Then talk started coming back about Jeffrey getting involved in drunken fracases downtown, of his spending all his disability money on drink, of his keeping company with characters of unsavory nature. At first the police looked the other way, feeling sympathy for the disabled vet, running him back to his squalid flophouse after his violent drunken rampages. Next thing word came back from someone Grampa Stoken knew at the American Legion that the chief of police himself had had words with Jeffrey, that the chief had told the young man that if he was looking for a run-on in his town, disabled vet or no, he would get it, despite the chief's desire to protect the young man's folks, who were good and decent people who deserved better from their kin. Finally one night after a particularly drunken and ribald marathon climaxing in a Chinese restaurant downtown where Jeffrey had plastered the owner, Lu Duk, with a bowl of chop suey noodles, he had been thrown in the drunk tank for the night and it was all Paul's father could do to get the charges dropped and to keep it out of the paper. It did little good. Soon afterwards Jeffrey started getting thrown in the drunk tank on a regular basis. His name became a running feature in the back pages of the paper, in those single paragraph crime reports of low-life goings on and senseless barroom altercations. Over the years whenever anyone mentioned to Grampa Stoken that they'd seen in the paper where Jeffrey'd been involved in something or another downtown the old man's head, which by this time had developed a noticeable tremor, would begin to quiver and quake energetically. Grampa Stoken would look down and spit on the ground and say with a wave of his hand, "Why should I care? He ain't no son of mine." Jeffrey'd fallen completely from grace. No one in the family spoke of him. Nothing but heartache. It was as if they were trying to distance themselves from the heartache, as if they believed if they could put enough distance between themselves and the heartache it would be like none of it had happened.

It was because of this distancing that the boy had no clear idea where his uncle lived. For long stretches of time it appeared Jeffrey would leave the area, going God only knows where, for he would drop completely from sight. Then Paul would hear talk from his friends in school that Jeffrey had been seen again in town, that he was living in dissipation in some dilapidated building downtown.

The more he thought about these stories the greater was his desire to seek out his uncle, to ask him about the fabled plane crash and the mysterious red guitar he had seen only on those two brief moments of his boyhood. But he couldn't begin guessing where to look (this was one of those intervals when Jeffrey had dropped from sight). He guessed he'd have to sit tight. Jeffrey was one of those people who came looking for you, not the other way around.

That was how it'd been the last time he'd seen his uncle. On Paul's sixteenth birthday Jeffrey had come to the house, saying he had a present for his nephew, but the boy's father had chased him away. Paul and a few friends had just blown out the candles on the cake when they heard the terrific roar of the motorcycle rolling up to the front porch. The boys went to the window. They saw Jeffrey on the bike, putting down the kickstand. He cut the great sputtering engine.

Mr Stoken went to the door.

"What do you suppose he wants?" Mrs Stoken quietly asked her husband.

"We'll know in a minute, won't we? Stay in the house with the boys."

"Dear, why don't you ask him in?" Mrs Stoken suggested, catching the door. "Remember, Lenny, he *is* your brother."

"I certainly need no reminding."

"Ask him—."

"I said get in the house, Marge," Mr Stoken said, annoyed.

He closed the door and went out.

From the window the boys watched Mr Stoken go up to the motorcycle. Jeffrey swung his crutch off his back. He lowered it to the walk to get off his bike but Mr Stoken kicked the rubber tip of the crutch from the ground. Again Jeffrey tried to set down the crutch but Mr Stoken kicked it away.

"Hit the road," they heard Mr Stoken say through the glass. "You're not welcome here. I'm raising a family inside."

"Is that's what's going on in there? I thought it looked pretty sinister."

284

Jeffrey propped the crutch across the handlebars. He looked at his brother.

"What's it gonna take?"

"You know damn well what it's going to take," Mr Stoken shot back. He said it with the anger only one brother can feel toward another. "Did you ever stop to think of the heartache you've brought Mom and Dad? If you want things to change it's up to you. It's up to you to straighten out. Just look at you. You smell like a brewery! You want into my house? Huh!"

Jeffrey half smiled, half sneered. He shook his head.

"You still like to lay down the law, don't you, lawyer-man?"

He swung the crutch around to his back.

"Well that's all right. It's all right by me. I didn't want to come into your Godalmighty castle anyway. You just give this to my buddyroo, will you?"

Reaching into the pocket of his leather jacket he fished out a small package, which he tossed to Mr Stoken. This done, he jumped once on the kickstart with his remaining leg, gripping the handlebars. The bike roared up. After gunning the engine loudly a time or two he took off across the lawn, flinging dirt, carving deep ruts in the neat grass.

"Get that blasted thing off my lawn!" Mr Stoken yelled.

Listening to the engine roar out of earshot one of the boys said, "God, I wish I had an uncle like that."

Mr Stoken came into the house with the little package, grudgingly handing it to the boy. "Your crazy uncle said to give this to you. For his sake it better not be anything illegal." The package was wrapped in paper from the Sunday comics, neatly tied with a piece of red shoelace. The boy tore off the paper and shoelace and found a hand-held electronic calculator. There was a note.

"Hey, buddyroo," read the neat, nun-trained handwriting, "I saw on the calendararooni this was your Big 16. Mucho congrats! I hear you're quite a student, a straight A student they tell me." (This was true — at the time the boy was pulling

285

in good grades.) "Keep up the good work. This calculator should help you add things up. In my day we used slide rules but they tell me they don't make them anymore. I must be a relic of the past. Your unc, Jeff."

Reading the note over the boy's shoulder Mrs Stoken had said, her voice charged with feeling, "It's almost as if he knew you wouldn't let him into the house."

Mr Stoken looked suspiciously at the calculator.

"I bet he bought it with that government disability money," he said.

The boy didn't care. He treasured it.

And that was the last he'd seen Jeffrey. On the night he put two and two together and came up with the realization that his uncle had stolen Buddy Holly's guitar he got out of bed and touched the keys of the calculator. 2 + 2 = 4. Clear. 0. 99999999. ÷ 3 = 33333333. = 11111111. = 3703703.6. = 1234567.8. Clear. 0. 2 + 2 = 4.

He wished his vague suspicions could be added up as easily as the little numbers in the window of the calculator. He wished the lose ends of his life could be tied together as neatly as Jeffrey had tied up the present with the red shoelace. He wanted, needed, desired to know the whole story, not just a few facts, fractions of the truth. Without Jeffrey's help, he feared, he might never know the whole story. But Jeffrey was nowhere in sight.

Over the next few days the undeniable fact that he had been born the night Buddy Holly died kept blinking in his mind like the numbers in an overloaded calculator. So what if he didn't know the whole truth? he told himself. He began believing a few broad brushstrokes of fact were enough to deduce the fine painting of truth. He reasoned he didn't have to see all the pieces of a pie to know if the pie had been round.

In his mind the simple fact he had been born the same night Buddy Holly died became all the proof he needed, became all-important to him, grew much larger than life, mythical in proportion. What after all is a myth but a story meant to explain something we don't completely understand, a story meant to divine the truth when all the facts aren't available?

He all but made up his mind. In another life he had been Buddy Holly.

Late at night he lay in bed imagining the fire and lightning things that must happen when someone dies and someone is born. He imagined what it must've been like going down in that little plane in the blinding snow, imagined the impact of the crash driving out the spark of life, blowing the eternal spark across the snowy fields, flying high and free in the prairie night, carried on the wings of angels a tolerably short distance to the hospital, where the errant spark blew in from the fields to the maternity ward where he'd been born, where the spark had found new kindling in which to smolder and catch fire, the place where a new mouth sent up its first crying song of life. All these things he imagined and saw very clearly in his mind. Like young Einstein visualizing a wild bronco ride on the back of a photon speeding at the slick velocity of light, he imagined his indestructible soul carried on the bent wings of angels from a broken body to the new.

Then came the day when these unspoken thoughts were burning bright in him and he asked Grandma Stoken in an offhand way about reincarnation. Did she believe in it? She was ironing clothes and had not even bothered to put down the hot iron as she told him, "Catholics don't believe in that. It's sinful to believe in it. Such beliefs might be all right for those Hindus who let cows run all over India when everyone's starving to death, but those Hindus won't get into heaven anyway." She said Catholics didn't believe that reincarnation talk for a minute. She said the fact of the matter is that our souls go to heaven, or hell, or purgatory, or limbo, or various other obscure antechambers to eternity. "It's forbidden to think otherwise," she said.

But this confident admonishment had only reinforced the boy's secret thoughts, since a young mind is driven to seek out and explore forbidden territory. If a soul can jump from a fellow's carcass and fly clean to heaven, he wondered, what was to stop it from flying into another carcass. Did souls ever get sidetracked?

He thought about these things till he nearly drove himself crazy. Then one day he impulsively took himself to the record store in town. He shuffled through the stacks looking for something but the girl there said rock 'n' roll was dead. She tried to sell him a disco record but the boy only looked sad. Disco, he said, didn't do anything for him.

"It doesn't *move* me," he said with such sad eyes. "It doesn't have anything to *say* to me."

So disconcerted did he look as he turned to walk away, so utterly lost, that the girl felt sorry for him.

"Hey!" she called after him. "Wait a minute."

She was rummaging through a bin behind the counter where they kept records played on the store's stereo.

"The manager's a bit wacky," she said softly, flipping through the jackets. "He's an oldies freak. Plays 50's rock 'n' rock when he's alone. Let's see. Chuck Berry. Little Richard. Dion! Good God! Does anyone listen to Dion anymore? Here we go. Buddy Holly."

From the back of the pile she pulled a worn and tattered record jacket. She held it out to the boy. He came near, taking it.

"How much?"

"That's the manager's record," she said quietly. She looked over her shoulder into the back room, where the manager busily sorted merchandise. "It's not for sale. But, for you, five dollars."

He slipped her a five-spot and she rung it up. All the while he clutched the old record in both hands, as if afraid it might slip away if he didn't hold on tight. He studied the record jacket with wide, reverent eyes. You would've thought it was one of the lost tablets Moses had brought down from Sinai.

When he turned to go she stopped him again.

"Don't I know you?" she asked.

It turned out they went to the same high school. They'd

288

gone to different grade schools and when they came up to high school had been thrown in together, though they didn't share any classes and didn't have the same friends. She told him her name was Jodie. She was the daughter of the president of the bank in town, she said, and her father made her take the job at the record store to help pay for college.

"So you're going away to school?" he said. "What'll be your major?"

She said she didn't know what she'd study, only that she wanted to go away to school, someplace far from Mason City, Paris maybe, or Boston. "Who wants to stay here?"

And what about him? she wanted to know. Wasn't his father an attorney in town?

She crinkled up her nose. "Law seems so exciting. I suppose that's what you want to get into?"

"Hell no." He felt suddenly awkward. "That's not for me."

"I know just what you mean about today's music," she said. "It doesn't move me either. I've often thought the exact same thing myself but until now it's never found expression."

"Found expression," the boy mumbled. "Yeah, I know what you mean. Disco really sucks."

"Hey, you're kind of cute," she told him.

He flushed. "Yeah, I know."

"You do, do you?"

"I mean, I try to be cute. Well, that's not what I mean, either. You know, you're kind of cute yourself."

She laughed at him.

"I have an idea," she said. She rifled through a large book beside the cash register. "Maybe there's more in the catalog. They call it the backlist."

He was in luck. In the back of the catalog they found a few more Buddy Holly records. He ordered them all. Then he thanked her and said he'd see her later maybe, in school.

Leaving the store with the record he thought he heard her giggling. He didn't think much of it.

These were the charmed days when around every corner

289

he found life, full and promising. There was always something new at every turn. Later it would be different but now everything seemed fresh and new and charged with life. Peddling his ten-speed home over the wide country roads with the record packed away in his Boy Scout backpack he smelt traces of spring in the cold February air. Breathing the air deeply made his head feel light and he thought thoughts and felt sensations he hadn't considered or experienced since playing little league ball as a kid. He remembered when he'd been a kid how he used to think he could bound so high he'd never come down, if only he truly believed he could. He often felt his thoughts were the only thing holding him down.

When he got home he came in through the kitchen with the record in hand. The floor had been scrubbed and everything smelled of Pinesol. Mrs Stoken had minutes before returned home from shopping. Bags were all over the still-damp floor.

"Where were you five minutes ago, Paul?" Mrs Stoken said. "I could've used your help carrying the groceries in."

He looked at all the bags. Lately his mom had been buying large quantities of things the family couldn't possibly use, not in a million years. She brought home entire bags filled with tubes of toothpaste. Paper towels by the hundreds of rolls. Cartons of Coca Cola. Carloads of canned goods. She hoarded these things in the garage on shelves she'd had Mr Stoken build, and when the shelves were lined three deep in paper towels or toilet paper or toothpaste or whatnot everything would overflow onto the floor. The boy didn't like it because he practiced guitar in the garage and he feared his band would get crowded out by canned peas. Mrs Stoken defended buying such outrageous quantities by saying it was cheaper to buy in bulk, when things were on sale, but sometimes it seemed to the boy that his mother was expecting a nuclear holocaust and was stocking up.

Today the bags on the floor again were filled mostly with paper towels. Must've been twenty rolls of paper towels.

"What're we gonna do with all these paper towels," he

asked.

"We'll use them up. Paper towels go fast."

"Why do you have to buy so much stuff? Last week you came home with *thirty rolls* of toilet paper. Thirty rolls! Those clerks at the store must think we got the shits or something."

"Don't use that language, mister."

He went to his room and slid the record from the jacket. It was badly scratched and dusty. The years had been hard. He wiped off the dust but that could do nothing for the scratches. Setting the needle on the groove, he feared he wouldn't hear the music for the popping noises. In a moment he stood transfixed between the speakers. He heard none of the static left by the years, only the music.

In the music he heard the sound of America dreaming. A confident and daring sound, with a hint of vulnerability, shyness, childlike hoping and longing. The vibrant sound, the bouncy sound, the electric sound — vivacious, bounding, electrified America. Ripping. Raging. Ringing. Surging with energy. Peddling pop prophecy.

Do you want to know how it's going to be? You're going to give your love to me. And if you don't, I'll just sit myself down and cry to the end of time, that's all. I'll just cry to the end of time.

Somewhere in those dusty old record grooves he heard the sounds of America dreaming, the soft rustling sound of mild-mannered Clark Kent, that wimp of wimps, pulling off the eyeglasses, saying woozily to Lois Lane, 'Tell Perry I'm not feeling so well, Louis. I think I must be coming down with something,' then, ducking into the nearest supply room for a quick change into the Man of Steel, that 'Look! Up in the sky! It's a bird! It's a plane!' whistling overhead sound of American rapid eye movement, the sound of Clark Kent coming down with a bad case of greatness.

He heard the sound of America dreaming, a sound from a time when a people had still been young and trusting, a teenage America crying, waiting and hoping under the eyes of old pop Eisenhower. Sure, kids, you can conquer the world tonight, just be home by nine. He heard the heartbeat sound of the young coming of age, a smiley young nation stepping into the spotlight of Amateur Hour to measure itself against the great nation-states of the ages.

America dreaming sounded pleasantly happy, like a well-tuned V8 engine, only there was that tiger in the tank, that high-octane roar, that saber-toothed Stratocaster bite, barely kept tame by the whip and chair bop harmonies of The Crickets and the smoking cracking gunfire of the rat-a-tat-tat big beat drums. America dreaming sounded like a cross between Mozart and a Thompson submachine gun.

The boy listened carefully and wondrously to the sounds of America dreaming, as a shipwrecked castaway might hang on every crackling syllable delivered by crystal radio. He listened with a sense of irony, a gnawing sadness, like he was an urbane alien on a distant planet picking up radio signals broadcast through space and time from a dead civilization, sadly pondering the ill wind that had blown on these remarkably naive people. Still there was no denying it. He considered the spellbinding implications. At one time, long ago, at one place, now far away, for one brief shining moment, there had been a people called Americans who dreamed of better days.

Could these starry-eyed teenagers have grown up? Did they deport Superman for un-American activities? Is there in some lonely wastes of frozen Arctic tundra an icy cavern where a bitter, broken-spirited, cynical middle-aged man in blue tights sits crying into his red cape till the end of time? These were questions that listening to the sound of America dreaming made him wonder.

Listening like an outsider, Paul gazed down at his feet, seeing the backside of the record jacket. Buddy Holly's photograph smiled up.

He lifted the record jacket from the floor and took it over to the mirror. He compared his face to the face on the cover. Now into his parents' room he dashed, rooting furiously through the bureau there. Beneath his father's handkerchiefs he found what he was looking for. A paint-splattered pair of hornrimmed eyeglasses. It's been a long time since the old man's worn these. Since he painted the house all those summers ago. The lenses were speckled with green and white house paint. He brought the glasses back into his room and closed the door. In front of the mirror he put on the glasses, then held up the photo.

"I'll be." His eyes darted from the mirror to the photo. Then back again. "There *is* a resemblance!"

So what if Buddy Holly's hair had been black and wavy while his was straighter and lighter? So what if Holly's face was longer and leaner than his, that he had freckles when Holly had none. Forget Holly had a long, straight nose while his was wider and more upturned. Never mind his own eyes were big and oval, while Holly's had been thin and narrow. And never mind those drips of paint on the hornrims. Forget these slights and he looked *exactly* like Buddy Holly.

He wanted a dream. What's so wrong about that? He wanted to have a dream he could believe in with all his might, as if believing was all he had to do to make it come true.

In another life he had been Buddy Holly. Anyone could see that.

With his pocketknife he cut the picture of Buddy Holly from the record jacket. He taped it to the corner of the mirror on his bureau. In another week he'd covered every inch of the mirror with Buddy Holly photographs. He spent more time than he should in libraries around town, digging up photos from old magazines and books, hiding out from the librarians as he ripped out anything and everything having to do with Buddy Holly and The Crickets. He was fanatic about it. In two weeks he had the walls of the room covered. In three, the ceiling.

If any doubt remained in his mind that he had once been Buddy Holly the doubt vanished as he covered up the last corner of his ceiling. It was as though by covering the last of the walls and ceiling he had covered up the last traces of doubt in his mind.

Lying in bed at night in the darkness of his room, surrounded by all those dim likenesses of Buddy Holly, the radio softly playing beside his bed on the night table, he would get to thinking. Big thoughts. In another life I was a famous cult hero, he'd think. This time around I'll be a cult hero too. My records will sell by the tens of millions and girls will follow me around wherever I go.

He thought himself fortunate to know his true calling so early in life. It was good for a young man to know what he was about early in life so he could apply himself earnestly to his chosen profession. It gave him a jump on the competition, he thought, an edge on all those other cult-heroes-in-the-making out there. Then he got to thinking. How does one become a cult hero? How does one become a king like Elvis? If you wanted to be king of England everyone knew the rules. First you have to be prince. You had to be born into it, or else you had to launch an intrigue, bumping off the royal family, locking them in the tower, and then you could install yourself on thrown. But how are the great American cult heroes crowned? Can anyone apply for the job? Was it just a matter of being in the right place at the right time? No. He suspected you just didn't accidentally stumble into such a high and exalted station in life as cult hero. There must be a certain amount of intrigue, preparation and planning involved. He thought there must be books written on the subject. They wrote books on just about everything. Something like Machiavelli's *The Prince*, only geared for rockers. Tomorrow he'd go to the library and look in the card catalog under, *Cult Hero, How to Become A*. Or maybe he'd find it under, *Inspiring Your Generation for Fun and Profit*. Yes, I certainly better study up on this cult hero business, he told himself. The sooner the better. Like his old man was always saying, education provides a leg up.

So the next day he skipped his morning classes to go to the library. He found absolutely nothing in the card catalog. The librarian finally came up and asked if she could help. He felt embarrassed talking about the nature of his research.

"I guess I'm looking for— something on success," he said softly to the stern-faced librarian.

"Success?" She pulled out the S drawer. "We have an entire wall of success books. What kind of success were you interested in? Success in real estate? Success on Wall Street? You were thinking of becoming a Wall Street broker?"

"Well that's not exactly what I had in mind," he said, blushing. "You got anything on Bob Dylan?"

Fate or luck again was with him. The librarian took him back among the shelves and handed over a biography on folksinger Dylan. He looked significantly at the paperback, as if some great mysterious power had set the book in his hands, not a knobby-kneed librarian wearing bifocals.

To the school cafeteria he went, for already the lunch bell had rung. He studied the biography even as he walked through the halls, ignoring the cries of students changing classes and the slamming of lockers. In the lunchroom he got a good start on the book. He sat at a table, drinking now and then from a carton of chocolate milk.

Looking up, he saw the girl from the record store come into the room. She came in with a big brute of a football player. Jodie said something to the brute, leaving him. She had a very upright posture and her long hair lifted from her back in delicate strands as she came across the floor. She came up to the boy's table and sat down.

"So here you are," she said to Paul. With her hands she gathered together her hair and let it drop loosely down her shoulder.

The boy looked up from his book. He pretended he hadn't been watching her come across the floor.

"This came in yesterday. I thought I'd bring it to you myself."

From her backpack came a box of Buddy Holly records.

"Great!"

"It's a six-record set. It cost *forty* dollars. Don't worry, I have a discount at the store."

"Thanks a lot, Jodie. You can't know how much this means to me. You just can't."

He looked at her.

"I have a job at the firehall Saturday night. I'll get you the money first thing Monday."

"If you need more records let me know."

As they talked another girl came up to the table. This one had a lunch bag and a cartoon of white milk. She froze when she saw Jodie. Then she saw the smiling, hornrim-framed face of Buddy Holly painted onto the record box.

"Hi Candy," Jodie said, looking up from the table. "Will you sit down?"

"No thanks," Candy said. She looked away from the box of records. She smiled slightly and shook her head. "There was something I wanted to tell Paul but it can wait."

She looked at the boy, at the way he held the records between himself and Jodie.

"How are things at the record store, Jodie?" Candy said.

"Fine," Jodie said.

"I didn't know you and Paul knew each other."

"We met at the store a few weeks ago," Jodie said.

"And how's Roger?" Candy said.

Jodie turned, glanced over her shoulder. The big brute she'd come in with stood in the cafeteria doorway with friends. Jocks. To show off their overdeveloped chests and powerful biceps they wore tightfitting jerseys. They laughed loudly and slapped each other in the jocular way of high school athletes. Every so often the one named Roger looked full-faced at the table where Jodie sat with Paul.

"Roger? Oh he's just fine," Jodie said to Candy.

"Well I must get going," Candy said. "Your band's playing this Saturday at the firehall, isn't it, Paul?"

"Yes."

"See you then," Candy smiled. She walked away with her lunch bag.

After she'd left Jodie said, "Did I chase away your friend?"

296

"Her?"

"You must like her."

"Her old man drives a truck. An eighteen-wheeler. He lets me drive it. I dig the sound of the gears."

"What's that you're reading?"

She lifted the book from the table.

"Dylan?"

She looked through the book.

"You like Dylan?" she asked.

"He's all right. He grew up just north of here." He pointed over his shoulder. "Up in Hibbing, Minnesota."

"Wasn't his name Zimmerman?"

"Yeah. Robert Zimmerman. He was just an ordinary boy."

"Why do you suppose he changed his name?"

"You don't think he could've made it if people knew he was plain folks, do you? An ordinary man's got to have something to hide behind in life. A shield. A myth."

"Is that why you're reading about him? You want a myth of your own?" She giggled at him. "I'll always remember you as that tongue-tied boy who came into the store for Buddy Holly."

He bristled.

"I don't need a myth. When you're for real like me you don't need a myth. Like Superman doesn't need that shield on his suit. It just looks nice, that big red S on his chest. But he doesn't need it. He's strong without it. It just looks nice. See what I mean?"

Jodie said, "I hear people talking about your band."

"Why don't you come hear us?"

She shook her head.

"Candy said she'd come," the boy said.

"I bet you'd like every girl in school chasing after you."

He smiled.

"Why don't you come?"

"Daddy'd never let me," she said. "He's so strict. He only lets me out for work and for dance classes on Saturdays."

"It's him, isn't it?"

He was looking out across the room beyond Jodie, at the brute standing in the doorway. He was alone in the doorway now, staring uneasily across the tables, at Jodie's back. He looked a little lost. All around him kids passed with lunch trays, whooping, enjoying lunch.

"Roger's very nice," Jodie said. "You wouldn't guess it from looking at all those muscles but he's very sensitive. Soft on the inside. He's got these secret feelings. Sometimes he tries to tell them to me but they're so swamped in the softness of him he can't get them out. Sometimes I wonder how he ever became captain of the football team."

Paul shrugged. "He's dumb. That's how. I can't understand you girls."

She fought back laughter. Her eyes really beamed.

"Don't. Roger's so sweet. He's really a hush puppy."

"I believe it."

"You're not like that inside, are you?" she said. "You've got something hard in there, haven't you?"

"You shouldn't be talking with me. You belong with someone like Roger. Go to him. He looks like he's about to have a hemorrhage."

The boy in the doorway had begun pacing, glaring out over the lunch tables, looking like he was deciding what to do.

"I'm not his."

"But he's yours, isn't he?" Paul said. "If you want him. You're so damned pretty that—." His voice trailed off.

"That what?"

"Never mind."

"Tell me."

"No."

"Please."

"Forget it."

"Maybe you'll tell me someday," she said.

She gathered up her things and smiled at Paul.

"I'll be seeing you around," she said. "I hope you enjoy the records."

298

Then she left.

Enjoy the records he did. That night he listened to them closely, hanging on every note and phrase. He listened to all six albums, one after the other, four and a half hours of listening, listening, listening. He listened to every damn song Buddy Holly was known to have recorded. Everything had been pressed onto those six vinyl discs. The boy marveled that a lifetime could be compressed into such narrow groves.

In those magical grooves, running through every song, beating with every note, he heard a golden sound, a heartbeat sound. Sometimes he sang along, picking up his electric guitar and playing with the record, stretching his voice, singing like Buddy Holly.

"For godsakes, Paul!" his father would yell, pounding the door so that it rattled its frame. "It's eleven o'clock at night. Shut off that stereo!"

In a breathless flash everything fell quiet. The boy stood dazed in the middle of the room, surrounded by all those grinning pictures of Buddy Holly, the stereo silenced, the guitar muzzled for the night, his head spinning.

He burned to hear the heartbeat sound. All he heard was the sound of his own heart. Racing.

Some nights he had to hear a good song before he slept. He'd turn on the small radio in the clock on his night table. He could get away with listening to the radio because it was small and did not rattle the walls and ceiling like his stereo rattled things.

Nothing good on the radio.

Quietly he brought the extension in from the hallway, closing the door but for a tiny crack, for the cord. Sitting on the floor, leaning against the door, he dialed the radio station.

"KIZN."

"Hey how about something good for a change?"

"How's that? I can hardly hear you, kid."

Bad connection. Crackling.

299

"Something with the heartbeat in it."

"Speak up kid. I can't hear you."

"Can't talk louder. My folks are in bed."

"What'll it be?"

"A good song, mister. How about Elvis Presley's Devil in Disguise? You know, a *good* song. With the heartbeat running through it. Ticket to Ride by The Beatles. How about I Feel Fine?"

"Those're pretty old songs, kid."

"Please mister. I'm here by myself, with nothing to do but stare out the window. I'm pressing my face flat against the screen and I got a waffle pattern imprinted on my cheek. I got to hear a song. A good song. You know how it is?"

The DJ hung up.

Paul shut off the lights, went to the window. The radio played softly on the night table. Still nothing good. Outside, on the other side of the screen, the night air was windy and cool. The wind blew through the screen and brushed softly past his face. In the darkness of the room he could just make out the many faces of Buddy Holly.

What the hell kind of behavior was this for an American boy? he asked himself. Could it be this kind of thing is going on in homes, good homes, all across America? Someone in Congress ought to hold hearings. Eminent scholars should write papers. Thoughtful television documentaries should be produced. Why wasn't this boy earnestly preparing himself to run the churning machinery of America? Why wasn't he earnestly preparing himself to become a physician or an attorney, an engineer or a farmer, a scientist or a soldier? Why didn't he give a damn?

It was just as well. True, America needed people to run machinery. America needed leaders. America needed brains. That part about the brains is especially true. But more important. The world needed a heart. Desperately needed a heart.

In the darkness by an open window an American boy stood listening to his heartbeat. A song came up from somewhere deep inside. Driven by the beating rhythm of his heart.

The tune hung on his lips. He hummed softly, looking out into the dark night, half believing all he need do was sing out loudly and clearly enough and a whole world would sing along, that he could hum a lullaby to a troubled planet.

What's so wrong with that?

Night after night the boy kept listening to vintage rock 'n' roll records and reading books about his favorite cult heroes. From his friend Terry Turner, who played bass in his band, he borrowed a set of headphones, which enabled him to sit listening to loud music at all hours of the day and night. From the library came books on The Beatles, Elvis, Sam Cooke and Chuck Berry.

Of all the recording artists in his Pantheon of Heroes only the Beatles came close to the elevated stature held by Buddy Holly. It seemed to him that the Beatles had picked up where Buddy Holly had left off. He listened to his Beatles records endlessly, forwards and backwards, and every note, every word became as precious to him as diamonds, especially those lyrics hardest to understand, such as, *"Crabalocker fishwife pornographic priestess boy you been a naughty girl you let your knickers down."* He was also similarly taken when his ears absorbed such lines as, *"Semolina pilchard climbing up the Eiffel Tower. Elementary penguin singing Hare Krishna man you should have seen them kicking Edgar Allen Poe."* The more twisted and meaningless the lyric the more he came to be convinced some hidden meaning lay in there somewhere, and he would go so far as to play the record backwards, only creating a bigger jumble of things.

The poor boy lay awake nights trying to untangle the meaning of this poetry, something Cervantes himself wouldn't have been able to do had he been rolled out of his grave and raised from the dead solely for this purpose. Complicating things, in his mind he was uncertain as to whether Paul McCartney was actually dead. A Day in the Life told the story of a terrible wreck, but was it Paul who blew his mind out in a car? At the end of Strawberry Fields Forever he heard John chant, "I buried Paul." Or was he saying something else? Cranberry sauce? Countless times he played Revolution 9 backwards, an act which nearly destroyed his record needle while scrambling his deranged brains even further. The words "Number 9" played backwards sounded all the world like "Turn me on, dead man." Then there were all the clues on the record jackets, which he scrutinized no end. McCartney standing backwards on the Sgt. Pepper album. McCartney wearing a patch with the initials OPD (Officially Pronounced Dead?). McCartney walking barefoot across the street on the Abbey Road album. What did it all mean? In the boy's highly impressionable state these clues fell together so that he became absolutely convinced McCartney had fallen victim to a terrible accident, yet this unsettled him even more, for no matter how much the plastic surgeons had worked over McCartney there must certainly be scars left over from such a terrible ordeal, though this did nothing to explain the fact that the poor man still had the face of a choir boy at age thirty-five.

Despite these many troubling mysteries of pop culture, he nonetheless was hopeful the songwriters from Liverpool would one day get back together, that they'd be coming in and out of style. In these mad, frenzied states, convinced as he was that it was only a matter of time before the Beatles' sound came back, he happily told himself there remained whole avenues left unexplored by his heroes, tremendous pieces of unsung music in the vein of I Want to Hold Your Hand or You've Got to Hide Your Love Away, songs left unmined by the musicians in too great a rush to get on to other things. Every good Beatles' song held out the promise to him of an entire symphony left unfinished. He wanted to pick up where they left off. Sometimes he'd race to his guitar to finish their unfinished symphonies, to sing their unsung songs, for already he was beginning to believe he had the abilities needed to improve upon the masters. In these moments he conceived composing a modern fugue for electric guitar based on Yesterday, or perhaps a symphony orchestral arrangement inspired by Day Tripper, and he might have worked out these arrangements had not his thoughts been constantly burning with bigger and better ideas.

He emerged from these all-night sessions completely exhausted, his head empty and spinning, his eyes red. It was all he could do to drag himself down to the bus stop, put himself on the bus, then stumble into his first period class to pass out on his desk. Sometimes, half dazed, he'd talk about the things occupying his mind with the driver of the bus. He was an old hippie of about thirty whose name was Rick. He said he'd been to Woodstock.

On the way to school the two of them would often talk over their opinions as to who had been the better Beatle, John or Paul. One morning as they discussed this topic one of McCartney's songs came on the little red transistor radio Rick kept swinging by a piece of ribbon from the bus's wide rearview mirror. "Someone's knockin' at the door-hor," the radio let out. Pointing to the little red radio, swinging all the while like a pendulum at the end of its ribbon as the bus bounced along, the driver predicted he'd probably be humming that stupid song all day long. Further, he predicted it'd probably go on to become a hit. The discjockeys, he said, were sure to play it into the ground until everyone wished they'd never heard the damned thing, since whenever one of McCartney's tunes finds its way into your brain it's like bubble gum in your hair only it's inside your head and you keep whistling and humming it and working it over in your head till it gets to be like worn out bubble gum and you wish it would go away. This is what made McCartney so good, the driver posited, his uncanny ability to make you like his work so much that you become sick of it. The boy countered by saying this was precisely what made Paul second fiddle to John. McCartney's songs were too sweet and lacked substance. A McCartney tune without Lennon's hard edge is like one of those hollow chocolate bunnies you get at Easter, the boy said. You bite into it and there's nothing there. Like an Almond Joy without the nuts. Something's missing. The boy maintained John was the better Beatle because he had something to say.

"Without Lennon, McCartney would've been just another bubble gum singer, not the world's most successful songwriter."

"Ah, but without McCartney," the bus driver argued, "Lennon would've been just another toothless philosopher out on the street." It was quite a debate. Maybe John and Paul had needed each other, they concluded.

About this time one of the farmboys who'd climbed into the bus a few miles down the road at a solitary highway crossing said Lennon and McCartney couldn't hold a candle to Jeff Beck. Rick looked disdainfully back at the farmboy through the rearview mirror. He laughed derisively. "You obviously have your head shoved up your ass," Rick told the farmboy. The farmboy was a real country cracker with a crew cut and an Iowa tuxedo — bib overalls. "Beck isn't even in the same league as Lennon and McCartney. You kids today have no conception. No conception at all. Just because somebody plays a fast guitar you think he's good. That's why your generation has no good songs of its own. You're a songless generation. Lots of fast notes but no songs. Just a lot of noise. That's why this radio spews shit." He switched off the little red radio. McCartney's song had ended and some tuneless shitkicker band had come on.

"What was it like to be a teenager in the sixties?" Paul reverently said to the driver. The bus had come to a railroad spur next to the mill creek and Rick had stopped to open the doors. He looked both ways down the track.

"It was real, man, it was real. Nothing like today. There was a future. Young people had fire in them."

Paul dreamily asked the driver if he thought there'd ever be another group as successful as the Beatles. He was looking out the window, his fingers drumming gently against the glass.

"Hell yeah," Rick prophesized. He was taking the rumbling bus for a fast ride down the long straightaway approaching the school. "You better believe it. They'll be a group bigger than The Beatles. Just like The Beatles were bigger than Elvis. I heard the rumor on the street. The rumor is rock 'n' roll ain't

304

dead. Somewhere out there practicing is a band that'll update the sound of the Beatles as cleanly as the Beatles updated Elvis." He pointed at the little red radio dangling from the mirror. "One of these days we'll turn on the radio and we'll hear a new sound. In one little moment we'll know. You'll swear up and down you've heard it before. But it'll sound fresh and new, zinging with energy. Young people will be the first to realize the importance of it. They'll scream and shout and wonder out loud how they ever got along without it. Watch out when that happens, when someone teaches a song-less generation how to sing. It'll be the background music for the movie of your generation. You'll welcome it into your songless little hearts."

In the boy's suggestive state these ideas were as powerful as tonic.

"What'll it sound like, Rick? What'll the new sound *sound* like?"

"You think I'd be driving this goddamn bus if I knew that? I'll tell you one thing. You'll know it when you hear it."

The boy, in short, became so immersed in his listening to records, forwards and backwards, and reading books about cult heroes, that he spent whole nights from dusk to dawn and days from sunup to sundown thinking only of rock 'n' roll music till finally, from so little sleep and his listening to loud music, his brain fogged over and he lost all touch with reality. His imagination filled with everything he'd heard and read, American myths and legends of leather-jacketed punks with switchblades, passionate encounters with nymphomaniac groupies, guitar duels, Superman and the Silver Surfer, motor-cycles, T-shirts and Levi jeans, The Justice League of America and Superman's Fortress of Solitude at the north pole, number one top 40 hits, rumors of the conclusion of the golden age of rock 'n' roll, blue suede shoes, drive-in movies, teenage dreams of love and glory, Rock 'n' Roll Heaven and glorious ham-burger stands in the sky, any number of American myths — his imagination became so filled to the brim with these things that he came to think of these pop culture fantasies as true.

305

They became the realest thing in the world to him.

In his deluded mind he pictured Rock 'n' Roll Heaven as an actual all-night diner of sparkling chromium steel and red patent leather bar stools, where James Dean, Buddy Holly, Elvis and all the other greats could sit out the long black night of eternity sipping Coca Colas, playing a juke box of golden hits and acting cool. Real cool. Cool till the end of time.

At last, his brain fried beyond repair, he conceived the strangest idea ever to come to a boy from Mason City, Iowa. It now seemed to him the most natural thing in the world that he should become a cult hero, to take up his guitar and roam the world. He felt certain fate was about to carry him away from his lonely teenage existence in Mason City, much like those silvery waves of fate swell up and carry the Silver Surfer to the farthest reaches of the galaxy in those comic books the boy often studied while blowing bubble gum. He too would catch the waves of fate, riding the crest of a wave to where he wanted to be. He'd look for a particularly good wave and when he caught it he'd ride it the hell out of Mason City all the way to the top of radio, all the way to Rock 'n' Roll Heaven. He even went so far as to imagine himself sitting in the booth by the jukebox in Rock 'n' Roll Heaven, playing gin rummy beside Janis Joplin and Jimi Hendrix, now and then snapping his fingers at James Dean, coolly demanding Dean fetch him over a Coke, occasionally trading witticisms with Jack Kerouac, who washed dishes in the back, sometimes coolly looking out the front window to see if Elvis had made progress with Marilyn Monroe in the backseat of the '55 Chevrolet out in the starlit parking lot beneath the flashing neon Rock 'n' Roll Heaven sign. He'd be one of them, there at Rock 'n' Roll Heaven, and everyone there would treat him with respect and courtesy. Not like he was treated here in Mason City. He wouldn't be just another lonely kid.

Caught up and carried away by the strange pleasures these thoughts gave him, he moved to put his plan into action. As it was after two o'clock in the morning when these unheard of ideas came to him he had to be quiet so as not to wake his parents before he got a chance to ride the waves of fate. He dressed quickly, in the darkness of his room pulling on his ankle-high black sneakers, watched over by all those dim faces of Buddy Holly staring down like stars from the walls and ceiling. He went to his door and crept out into the hallway. The light in his parents' room was still on. He crept to their open door. Peeking around the corner, he saw the old man in bed with a book in his lap. Mr Stoken was at that middle ground between waking and sleeping. His eyes would close and his head would begin drooping to his shoulder when suddenly he'd straighten up and recast his dreamy gaze away from dreamland to the book. The boy dared not risk sneaking past the doorway, not yet anyway, for he'd wake up the old man, sure. But he *had* to get out of the house. For a moment he stood wondering what to do. At last he tiptoed back to his room and softly closed the door. He went over to the window and took out the screen. It was a split-level house and the window was no more than ten feet or so above the dark ground. He figured he'd easily make the jump though he knew he'd never be able to climb back in the same way. He could always let himself in the back door with his key once he'd started the wheels of fame and fortune rolling. By then the old man would be asleep, for sure.

In a moment he'd slipped off the cool windowsill and felt himself falling effortlessly through the slick coolness of the American night. It felt like he was falling forever. He hit the dark lawn painlessly, as if in slow motion. Looking back up over his shoulder at the yawning dark window, seeing the draperies his mother had made blowing through the open window in the moonlight, he had a strange feeling of regret. He couldn't help thinking he was leaving something behind.

Then he was running. He ran wildly, like he was trying to escape something having to do with the open window and the curtains blowing in the moonlight. He ran as though in slow motion, bounding across the fields, half convinced his next giant leap would set him free of the earth's pull and send him rising to the stars. He ran wild and free and invincible.

The knotted ground of the open fields soon gave way to slopes running downhill and here the boy cut loose, bounding from one sloping ridge to the next, coming down into the trees. He smelled the wood smoke rising from the dark houses below. Not a light burned. They had all gone to bed, leaving the world to a boy with mad plans.

At his friend Terry's house he came up under the trees and with a penny from his pocket he knocked on Terry's window. He was all out of breath and sweaty. The window abruptly slid open. Paul climbed in.

Terry lit a lamp. He was sitting on his bed in his underwear, scratching his head.

"Paul. Goddamn. It's three in the morning, man." He got up to put on his pants.

Paul eased himself down from the windowsill. He paced excitedly across the floor, his eyes lit with madness.

"What's eating you?"

"Hey, you know what I was wondering on the way over?" Paul said exuberantly.

"What's that?"

"About Superman."

"What about him."

"Why does he hide behind Clark Kent?"

Terry coughed, clearing his throat.

"Is this why you woke me at three in the morning?"

"I'm serious now," Paul said. He kept pacing, gesturing wildly with his hands as he talked. "It seems to me if you got to the bottom of this Superman and Clark Kent business you'd understand a hell of a lot about most folks. I mean, why is it old Clark doesn't want anybody to know deep down he's really a man of steel? What's he got to be ashamed of? Is it a crime to have x-ray vision? Did you ever notice the sneaky way he'll up and leave a room to go change into that blue suit of his? Real sneaky like. Most people never question the sneakiness of it. It only goes to prove my point. Folks accept it as perfectly normal behavior. Didn't you ever wonder about that?"

"Can't say I have."

308

"It just had me thinking, that's all." Paul's face was sweaty from his run and his excitement. "Most folks act all the time like Clark Kent, keeping the best part of themselves out of sight. Well not me, Terry."

Before this Paul hadn't said a word to anyone of his secret ambitions. Now things came spilling out. He told Terry the two of them were going to the top of radio together, that their band would be the biggest thing to hit the airwaves since the Beatles, that everywhere they went they'd be chased by hordes of screaming girls.

These were remarkable things to hear when you've just been awakened in the dark of night. Terry looked at his friend as if he was crazy. There was almost an alarmed look on his face as he listened to Paul, though, it must be said, he raised an eyebrow at some of the more fanciful things, such as the hordes of screaming girls.

"I'll tell you how it'll be," Paul raved on, his voice growing loud and excited, his eyes glowing with the madness of a prophet's. "There will come a band to teach a songless generation how to sing. It'll mark the conclusion of the golden age of rock 'n' roll. It'll be our band. Don't ask me how I know. All I can say is, though it may now seem a little crazy to you, it's in the cards."

"Shh," Terry said. "You'll wake Mama." He went over to the door and listened. He said from the door. "Are you off your nut? You talk about these things like they're foregone conclusions."

Paul's eyes widened. He spun around and fell loosely into the chair by the bed, smacking his head with the palm of his hand.

"That'll be our name! The Four Gone Conclusions!"

Unable to agree on a name, the four musicians in their band had been playing without an identity.

Terry came over from the door.

"The Conclusions," he said thoughtfully, sounding out the name.

"The Conclusions," Paul said.

They smiled at each other. They shook hands. In those days they were all the time shaking hands. Whenever they thought they'd done something right they shook hands.

"Not everyone can be famous. Not like Elvis and the Beatles were famous."

"I don't know," Paul said. "Tonight I was thinking maybe everybody has something special inside. A Super Hero. They just never learn to use the Super Hero in them to take them where they want to go. They never learn to spot and ride the waves of fate, like the Silver Surfer does in those Fantastic Four comic books. We'll teach ourselves to live and love with all our might."

"Speaking of love," Terry put in, "I noticed you talking with that girl the other day at lunch."

"Jodie?"

"Is that her name? Doesn't she spend an awful lot of time with the captain of the football team?"

Paul shrugged.

"You're too much. That jock was standing there while you made time with his girl."

"I wasn't making time. And she's not his girl."

"Well that's just what it looked like to me."

"Too bad."

"You're too much, man. One of these days someone's going to break your little fingers and then how'll you play guitar?"

"With my toes. I can pick with my tongue."

They laughed. The Jodie business was really quite funny.

"She's pretty cute, huh?"

"Who?"

"Who do you think?"

Paul smiled.

"Yeah, she looked all right. But I thought you were hanging out with Candy."

"She's all right too."

"Yeah, they're all all right."

"You can say that again."

"Okay. They're all all right."

Paul skipped from one crazy yet alluring subject to the next. He told Terry of the sound he'd been hearing in the dark of night, a new sound, and how he'd like to arrange old-time vocal harmonies around it.

"Say," Paul said, "do you still have that big old upright bass?"

"It's in the basement, in the closet."

"Bring it along to practice tomorrow."

"That old thing?"

"You can play it, can't you?"

"Sure. I can play any bass you set in my hands. But nobody plays those big dinosaurs anymore. Electric bass, that's what everybody uses."

"Not us. I bet we can get some wild sounds out of that thing. The Crickets used an upright bass." Then, off on another tangent. "Man, did you ever notice the shirts Buddy Holly used to wear?"

Terry shook his head.

"What about his shirts?"

"They were very futuristic looking shirts," Paul explained. "His shirts had a real space age look to them. Zippers running at strange angles down the front and Star Trek collars."

"Are you saying futuristic-looking shirts are the key to our success?"

"No no no, not at all. That was *his* style. I think we should take the opposite tack. We'll wear plain white T shirts. Like Marlon Brando in Streetcar Named Desire."

"What named desire?"

"Man, you need to study up on American history," Paul told him. "I mean, we should mix the new with the old. Somewhere back there maybe we'll find a hopeful future. We'll look around and find a style and a sound as sleek and powerful as a '58 Corvette."

"The Conclusions," Terry said. "It has a good sound."

He yawned. His face dulled.

"Yeah maybe we should call it a night."

The next day, a mild and sunny Saturday, Mrs Stoken was surprised to find her son and three other boys dressed in white T-shirts and faded blue jeans. The white cotton T-shirts were a strange sight in this age of perma-pressed color. And what about those Levi's? Didn't these boys realize blue jeans were out of style, that the college boys back East had finally come to their senses and were once again wearing nice slacks?

The Four Gone Conclusions were getting ready to play. In the middle of the oil-stained garage floor Terry leaned against an ancient upright bass, his long-fingered left hand deftly breezing up and down the fretless sounding board while his right hand slapped the thick strings, plucking out melodious scales of low notes, to the rhythm of which he bounced his lanky frame and moved his lips. Behind Terry another T-shirted boy, Doug, who worked part-time as a garage mechanic, presided over a set of drums, furiously twirling two drumsticks, warming his hands to rhythms only he could hear. Paul and a light-haired boy known only to Mrs Stoken as Ace were tuning up their electric guitars, smoking cigarettes and talking excitedly. Behind them towered a wall of buzzing amplifiers.

Mrs Stoken came in loaded down with a fresh supply of paper towels and canned goods.

"It's such a nice day," she said, coming in. "I'm surprised you boys aren't outdoors." Casting a glance at the blue jeans and the white cotton T-shirts, she said, "Don't you realize those clothes are out of fashion? And that music you boys play— what good is it?"

The boys laughed. Paul tapped his sneaker three times against the concrete floor. A wild Chuck Berry riff howled from the amplifiers. Mrs Stoken hurried from the garage with her hands pressed against her ears.

It might have been laughable had it not been so sad and pathetic, this obsessive identification with America's bygone decades, America's golden years. Those who saw our would-be cult hero and his three friends on the streets of Mason City

312

had to wonder what they were up to. They acted like foreigners from another land. The boys expressed amazement at all sorts of things most Americans took for granted. American music. American clothes. American food. American cars. The American style, they got to calling it. So long as it was American the four boys ate it up. And if they came across a vintage piece of authentic culture dating "all the way back" to the fifties or early sixties they went crazy for it.

In early spring when old Milt Stewart ran a James Dean film festival down at the Bijou he didn't know what to make of the four boys dressed in the white T-shirts and blue jeans. Show after show they sat in the back row with their feet propped up on the seats studying James Dean's every move. The old man puzzled over the intense way the boys studied the screen. When James Dean had his quiet moments, when he would smile bashfully or scratch his head, the four boys in the back row did the same. When Dean exploded in those electrifying moments that used to distress parents so, the four boys would light up with amazement, spellbound by the spectacle of pent-up emotion released. Then, when Dean brooded, he seemed to brood for them. Night after night, after the curtain had come down on the last show, Milt Stewart watched from behind the candy counter as the four boys silently swaggered from the theater, their hands buried deep in the pockets of their jeans, their collars turned up, almost touching the lobes of their ears. They looked like four James Deans swaggering out into the loamy-scented night air of Mason City, Iowa.

It was about this time that Doug, the drummer, came across the '53 Plymouth convertible. He bought it from an old woman who had it stored under a blanket in her garage since the day her son went off to Korea and never came back. She didn't know what she had. She kept apologizing for the car as she showed it. It was nothing like the cars they make today, she kept saying, "but it's good solid reliable transportation." It was a beautiful car. She asked two hundred dollars. She said she hoped she wasn't asking too much. Doug went nuts. That morning he emptied his savings account and generally made such a fuss over the old car that the woman had to wonder if he wasn't nuts.

Later that same day The Four Gone Conclusions piled out of the convertible downtown. Storming into the record store wearing sunglasses, they ordered old records by Elvis Presley, the Everly Brothers, Jan and Dean, and Chuck Berry. Jodie wrote up the order while a Captain and Tenille record played in the background. The four boys suddenly dropped to the floor gasping for breath, yelling they'd suffocate if the record wasn't removed. The manager came out and said he'd remove them from the store if they didn't knock it off. They got up and leaned heavily against the check-out counter, rubbing their necks, faking pain, apologizing. Paul explained that the music of Captain and Tenille always brought out "the jungle impulses" in them.

Jodie had to laugh.

Things might have been laughable had not The Conclusions suddenly found themselves taken seriously.

Before long they started attracting crowds at the firehall. They started playing full houses.

Kids decked out in blue jeans and white T-shirts started filling the parking lot of the firehall an hour or more before each show. They cheered when The Four Gone Conclusions cruised up in that slick convertible with that outrageous upright bass sticking from the backseat. As the weeks went by kids started coming to the firehall in their own repainted fifties roadsters.

When the adults of Mason City started asking their kids about the T-shirts and the blue jeans with the cuffs rolled up around the ankles and the old cars and the ankle-high sneakers and the popping of the bubble gum they were told all the kids were doing it. It was the latest thing. The American style, the kids called it.

314

Their parents couldn't comprehend why they'd suddenly taken notice of things that'd been around for years, for decades. It was as if the young people one day woke up amazed to find themselves living in the USA. Where the hell did they think they'd been living all this time? the men joked at the barber shops.

They shrugged it off to the fickleness of youth.

Before long the adults started hearing the kids rave about some sound they said they'd heard. A new sound, the kids said. At the dinner tables the kids talked so exuberantly about this new sound that the parents had to wonder how their children had gotten along without it. Where on God's green earth had they heard this amazing new sound? the parents wanted to know. At the firehall just outside town, the kids said. All the kids went out to hear it, they said. Every Saturday night they went to hear a band called The Conclusions.

"The Conclusions?" the parents laughed. "What a silly name. The conclusion to what?"

"The conclusion to the golden age of rock 'n' roll," the kids smirked back. "What else?"

The parents didn't know what to think of any of this. So they shrugged it off.

One Saturday night early in May Mr and Mrs Stoken were on their way to dinner when, driving past the firehall, Mr Stoken had to slam on the brakes to avoid plowing through a mob of young people. The kids formed an uneven line running from the big firehouse doors all the way to the road, stopping traffic. Kids slouched against cars, or lay across the hoods of cars parked in the shoulder of the road while others tossed Frisbees. Still more streamed across the road to fall in line.

"Well what do you make of that?" Mr Stoken said, driving slowly past the firehall. Kids were streaming all around his car. "You'd think they'd have better things to do with their time on a Saturday night. I wonder if their parents know where they are."

Then, after a moment, "By the way, where's Pauley tonight?"

"Oh he and the boys are off playing their guitars somewhere," Mrs Stoken said.

The kids began getting out of hand. The chief of police finally came out to the firehall to say whatever it was that was going on had to be stopped on account of the traffic being blocked. The fire chief took the chief of police aside and pointed into the swarm of young people. He pointed out each one of the filthy little brats was worth two dollars a head when they got in the door. These damn kids were the best thing that ever happened to the firehall and it'd be craziness to stop it now. At this rate, the fire chief went on, by Christmas they'd be able to buy that new pumper truck everybody'd been wanting. Besides, wasn't it better the kids were coming to the firehall, where they at least had some adult supervision, instead of going God-only-knows-where-else?

The chief of police looked uneasily into the mob of young people. He said he didn't know. He said he never knew about young people.

The fire chief slyly pointed out that, at this rate, what with all the money the firehall was taking in, come August the Fraternal Order of Police's Annual Gala Committee might get to rent the firehall for just about next to nothing.

Two policemen began directing traffic out front.

In those dreamy days of June that lead so much like a pleasant slow song into summer, the kids of Mason City were in need of something new. School was over and the corn had been planted. Now there was only the long wait for classes to begin again in the fall and the much longer wait for the corn to grow. A big chunk of eternity had been dropped in their laps and they were itching for something new. Word began getting around about a certain new band. People said you really had to hear it. Those who went to hear it kept going back for more.

Kids who went to hear the sound walked around for the rest of the week humming one or two of the tunes they'd heard. After they'd been to see the band two or three times they'd be seen around town wearing white T-shirts and black ankle highs.

If you had a girl she'd tell you she wanted to go see the band everyone was talking about, The Conclusions. If you were bold enough to say, "What's so special about these Conclusions?" she'd look at you like you were a Neanderthal.

You heard people say there was something special about this band. But when they were pressed they couldn't say what exactly that something was. Only that this band *had* it. Some said it was their songs that were special but others said no, it was the way they played. Wild. Abandoned. Crackling with nervous energy.

You heard all kinds of talk going around, some of it pretty crazy. Talk had it one of the kids in the band, the one who wrote their songs, had been born the exact day Buddy Holly's plane had gone down outside Clear Lake. Some of the kids thought he might be Buddy Holly reincarnated. Some said he even believed it himself.

It got to be you couldn't go anywhere without hearing talk like this. It got your curiosity up. Not only that, such excited talk made you secretly glad. It made you hopeful this wouldn't be such a long drag of a hot summer after all.

Soon you went out to the firehall to judge for yourself. When you got to the firehall you saw the sign out front reading, "Tonight: The Conclusions," you saw all the kids waiting to get in and you felt inexplicably excited. It felt like something was up. You said to yourself you hoped these guys were as good as everyone said. Then, as you fell in line, you found yourself hoping this band would really be special. Somehow you knew it would. You knew they couldn't let you down on such a long endless night as this.

In all of Mason City there was only one person who felt a sense of dread when he heard the first excited talk of a new band. He wasn't surprised by the news, only morbidly fearful. For years he'd been watching and waiting for just such news. Over the years as he watched and waited it by and by had become the worst fear of his life. Sometimes he told himself maybe the thing he most feared would never happen but deep down inside he knew it would only be a matter of time now since his worst fears always had a way of coming true. So when he at last heard the excited talk of the new band he braced himself. His spider senses were tingling. There's no use turning white with fear, he told himself. What's the good in that? Hadn't he after all always known deep down inside it would only be a matter of time?

He went to the firehall that Saturday night, bringing along his deep sense of foreboding. When he saw the mob of kids outside, and as his eyes swept across the sign out front, "Tonight: The Conclusions," he knew he must begin preparing himself for the very worst. So it was starting already. So soon. So little time. At last. He drew a deep breath.

He asked one of the kids for the names of the band members.

He tried to hide his anger when he heard the names but from the look the kid gave him he irrationally believed his eyes must've given everything away.

He had to curse.

There's nothing to do now but watch and wait, he told himself.

So with the burning eyes of a madman he watched the kids streaming into the firehall.

One night during a break between sets The Conclusions were just stepping outside for air when Paul's eyes landed on a solitary figure perched on a motorcycle at the far end of the parking lot. The man on the bike sat looking on through the dark visor of a helmet.

Paul tried to divine the face behind the visor but in a moment the bike came alive, spun around and roared away.

Paul watched the red taillight streak away to the road. It

was a loud bike, a Harley, from the deep low growl of it.

"What's the matter with you?" Terry said. "You look like you've seen a spook."

"Nothing," Paul mumbled. "Thought I recognized someone, that's all."

Looking back on things, the sighting of the spectral motorcyclist was the turning point. After that Paul couldn't shake the feeling he was being watched. After that he felt something hanging over him. A day didn't go by without feeling eyes all around him. He felt spooked.

The others couldn't help noticing something had come over him. He was all the time looking over his shoulder, half expecting someone or something to any second drop from nowhere.

As far as the other three band members were concerned things couldn't be better. They told each other there was nothing to this cult hero business. Their following *was* growing. They were sure it'd only be a matter of time before they'd go all the way to the top. They began recording their better songs with the intent of mailing the tapes to bigwigs in the recording industry. They had only the vaguest ideas how to go about finding the bigwigs but they felt confident when the time came they could probably flush out one or two of them. Until then, to further spread their fame, they made plans to compete in a rock band contest sponsored by a local radio station. The contest was held late every June at the Surf Ballroom in Clear Lake. The Surf had been the place Buddy Holly had played on the night he died, the last place the music played. Local legend had it one day a great band would naturally be discovered at the Surf, that this place which had been the end of the road for one great musician should rightfully be the starting point of another. Paul said it was important The Conclusions win this year's contest.

The four drove out to Clear Lake in the Plymouth. Wearing sunglasses, they sat across the dusty street in the convertible surveying the old ballroom. It was a blistered, tumble down, vacant-looking supperhall of a place, low to the sky, hugging the black earth like a pill bug. A faded sign creaked in the wind. They could just make out the faded script letters. Surf Ballroom.

For several minutes they sat in the Plymouth wordlessly taking in the desolation of the place before Paul broke the silence by saying he found much significance in the dilapidated ballroom's name. "The name surely refers to the waves of fate," he said, arching his eyebrows significantly. The name couldn't possibly refer to the ocean's surf, he went on, noting, "the closest stinking ocean is fifteen hundred miles from Clear Lake." In ominous tones he said the old ballroom was obviously at the very center of something he called a cosmic vortex. Terry looked suspiciously at the old building and asked what he meant. He replied that he knew such vortexes actually existed, that around them turned "fateful events of great cosmic mystery and importance, the same way water swirls in a toilet before it drops down the tubes," he tried to explain. He said he'd heard Mr Spock talking about one on Star Trek. This made them laugh and say he was talking through his ass. He got angry. It was nothing to laugh about, he said. "The waves of fate splash hard around this place." The surf referred to in the ballroom's name, he said, like the ocean's surf, was capable of picking you up and carrying you great distances at great speeds, but that it could also dash you onto the rocks, like it destroyed poor old Buddy Holly. It was nothing to laugh about, the waves of fate, and he said it so seriously the others stopped laughing. Wait and see, he said. "If we hang around this place I just know a big wave will come rolling our way."

This year they'd take the Surf Ballroom by storm, they agreed. Thereafter every spare minute was dedicated to practicing new songs. More dedicated and serious young men you'd never see. They were probably a little too dedicated. So dedicated and serious were they in the weeks leading up to the contest at the Surf they had no time for school. So busy were they studying James Dean, the Beatles and the Beach Boys they had no energy remaining for geometry, the history of the

320

Napoleonic wars, the subtleties of English grammar and composition.

Paul's fourth quarter report card summed it up. Five Fs, a D in driver's ed, and an incomplete in gym. He thought it was funny, particularly the D in driver's ed, which he'd earned by backing the driver's ed car through a plate glass window into the school lobby. They'd had a good laugh over that.

Of course, Paul was discreet and prudent enough to realize his father wouldn't see the humor. So when the notices and letters began arriving from school he made it his practice to meet the mailman at the door and confiscate the letters. This had been going on for about three weeks, since school let out. No use getting the old man riled up, he told himself as he tossed the letters away. Don't want things to sour. He looked at himself as an enterprising young man with enough business sense to realize many small jobs such as these must sometimes be performed once one set oneself on the road to the bigger job of becoming a cult hero.

He decided it'd be best for all concerned if he kept his report card secret until his band hit the big time, which, from the looks of things, would be any day now. Unfortunately, fate had other ideas. Fate, as is fate's devilish habit, picked the worst possible moment to raise the submerged to the surface, to bring things into the open. The day the waves of fate began rolling happened to be the very day in late June our would-be cult hero planned to take the Surf Ballroom by storm.

It'd been a bad day in suburbia for Mr Stoken. At breakfast he'd been reading his usual paper while he ate his usual bowl of raisin bran at his usual place at the table out on the veranda where they usually ate breakfast in the summertime, trying not to listen to the usual patter of his wife, wondering when his son would get a decent haircut, when he'd chomped on a raisin and the pain of a toothache flashed across his face.

At the time of his toothache his wife had been talking about the new burglar alarm she'd had installed in the house. Several homes on the block lately had been burglarized and

Mrs Stoken said she couldn't believe what things were coming to. A body used to be able to leave the front door hanging open and no one would walk in, she said. The thought of a complete stranger getting into her house and touching her things with their fingers sent absolute shivers up her spine, she said.

The Stokens had been feathering the nest a little lately, buying new furniture and original artists' prints from galleries in Chicago. When news of the burglaries spread around the neighborhood Mrs Stoken had gone right out and purchased the best alarm system she could find. Every door and window had been wired so that the slightest tremor sent off a screeching assortment of bells and alarms you could hear halfway to the Mississippi. Yet lately, when you opened the front door with your key, the sirens would go off, the police would come with guns drawn and the neighborhood would be in an uproar until the blasted thing was shut off.

That morning at breakfast Mrs Stoken was going on about how the security contractor had better show up soon to work out the bugs. She didn't feel secure knowing the alarms weren't functioning properly. A body wasn't safe these days without a good alarm system, she said, adding that she'd read in the paper just the other day about a family in Wisconsin who'd been victimized by burglars.

"It was horrible," she was saying, "they tied up the man and made him watch while they did all sorts of atrocious and unspeakable things to his wife and children." She bunched up the neck of her robe and shuddered.

To all this Mr Stoken said nothing. Over the years he'd learned to tune out his wife so he could read the paper. At last he folded it over and glanced across the table at his son. Paul dreamily leaned against the table playing with his cereal as he stared out the glass windows of the veranda at the willow trees outside. Mr Stoken had no idea what dreams danced in his son's head. He only noticed the hair.

"Don't you think it's time to get a trim, Pauley?" he said, and that's when it happened. He shoveled a spoonful of raisin bran into his mouth and let go a holler.

"Damn!" he gasped. He said it so loudly and so suddenly his wife and son started. It made the boy realize how quiet and lifeless breakfast had been up till that moment.

"What's wrong, dear?" Mrs Stoken said.

"My tooth!" her husband moaned, his hand at his jaw.

"Oh dear! Well it's probably a toothache," Mrs Stoken said.

"Well of course it's a toothache! It's not a sprained ankle!"

"I better call the dentist," Mrs Stoken said.

Because of the toothache Mr Stoken had been unable to go to court that morning. He'd spent the better part of the day in the dentist's chair, where he'd been given bad news. To save the tooth he had to undergo root canal therapy. That was the kind of day it was.

By midafternoon he'd left the dentist's office with a temporary filling and his cheek puffed with cotton. He drove home, wanting only to relax in his favorite chair, hoping only to escape from the drilling and the pain.

Too bad. At about three in the afternoon, an hour or two earlier than he normally got home, he came up the walk to his front door, briefcase in hand. The mailman was coming across the lawn. Mr Stoken stopped for the mail.

"How are you today?" the mailman asked, coming up with his satchelful of letters.

"Jush terruble," Mr Stoken said slowly through the cotton. "Toothache." He brought a hand to his cheek. "Bit into a raisin dish morning at breakfasht. Thought I'd been shtruck by lightning. Dentisht shays I need root canal work. Opened up my tooth and the nerve was dead."

The mailman made a sympathetic face.

"Too bad," he said. "'Course, that's the way it is with teeth. You know what they say: Ignore them and they'll just go away. Me, I lost mine years ago. They all started falling out one summer I went to Reno. It must've been the desert air. Everytime I'd turn around there'd be one of my teeth on the floor. Had the dentist yank out the rest of the damn things and now I don't got a real tooth in my head, you know. I got me a set of choppers and I've never been happier."

The mailman flashed his dentures.

Mr Stoken looked uneasily at the pearly white teeth. He'd brought up the subject of his toothache because he'd wanted sympathy. The thought of losing them all only made him feel worse. He was getting on and he didn't need reminding. In two more years he'd be forty. Where had all the time gone? Gray templed, his eyes weary, he saw himself moaning and groaning and aching every step of the way up the front walk of his old age.

"Never been happier," the mailman winked again. He handed over the mail and went his way.

Mr Stoken took himself slowly to the welcome mat and fumbled with his keys. He pushed open the door and the burglar alarm sounded.

"Ah Chrisht!"

Paul came down from his room to investigate the alarm. He was surprised to find the front door hanging open. At first he thought his mother's worst fear had been realized, burglars had invaded, but then he saw his old man in the den, beating the hidden alarm control panel, fuming, "Damn thing! Why won't anything work these days!"

The boy went to close the door. He saw the mailman sauntering away from the house. He closed the door and leaned against it. Don't jump to conclusions, he thought.

He looked into the den. His eyes caught the stack of letters under the old man's arm. Mr Stoken continued beating the alarm panel. At last the alarm went dead.

Then the doorbell rang.

"What now!"

Mr Stoken stalked angrily into the hallway, surprised to see his son.

"What's the matter with you?" Mr Stoken barked. "Why don't you see who's at the door?"

The boy only held his ground, frozen, staring at the stack

324

of letters in the old man's hands.

"What's the matter with everyone today?" Mr Stoken fumed.

Again the doorbell rang.

Mr Stoken threw open the door.

The burglar alarm came back to life. It was really clanging.

"Cheesus Chrisht!" Mr Stoken pressed a hand against his ear. "I'm going to need a trainload of aspirin!" He turned to his son. "Don't shtand there like a department shtore dummy! Kill that damn alarm!"

The boy took off for the den. The alarm went dead.

A policeman stood at the door. He looked suspiciously at the cotton hanging from Mr Stoken's mouth.

"We got a report of a silent alarm going off," the cop said.

"Silent!" Mr Stoken said.

"Do you live here sir?"

"Of courshe I live here." Mr Stoken tried to smile. Cotton dangled from his mouth. "Dis ish my houshe." He grimaced, took the cotton from his mouth. "Forgive me, officer. As I was saying, this is my house. I just this minute returned from the dentist's office. Would you believe, he opened up my tooth and found the nerve dead! Anyway, I was just getting home and I must have set off the alarm by accident. We've been having trouble with it lately."

"Well I can see this isn't your day, is it?" the cop said. He took out his ticket book. "Unfortunately, sir, I have to write out a citation."

"A citation? A citation for what?"

"This is the third time this week we've been out to this address on a false alarm, sir. I told your wife the next time she'd be fined. The law says the third time we come out on a false alarm you get slapped with a twenty-five dollar fine."

"Twenty-five dollars!" Mr Stoken choked.

"I hate to fine you, sir," the cop said, writing out the ticket, "but it's the law. We have to find a way to discourage these false alarms."

"But twenty-five dollars! This burglar alarm is robbing me of a fortune! It's cheaper having burglars!"

"My advice to you sir is to shut off your alarm until you can get a repairman in to look at it. The fines get stiffer, you know. Next time we come out it's fifty dollars." He handed the ticket book to Mr Stoken to sign. "That's the law." Mr Stoken set the mail on the table by the door.

Paul pounced on the mail. Where is it? he thought, rifling through the letters. A renewal notice from *Time* magazine. A package of coupons. Bills. A letter from Mr Stoken's broker. Come on, come on, where is it? There! He caught sight of the letterhead. Mason City High School.

Just as he was about to spirit away the troublesome letter Mr Stoken said goodbye to the cop and closed the door. He slammed his hand down on the stack of letters.

"And what do you think you're doing?" Mr Stoken said to his son. "Get your hands away! A man comes home, he reads his mail!"

The boy backed warily away from the letters.

"You'd think there was something in here you don't want me to see."

Paul turned to hurry away.

"Wait one minute, mister," Mr Stoken said. "What's this? A letter from school?"

The boy's back was to his father. He closed his eyes.

The sounds of an envelope being torn open. He heard a gasp. For a second he was afraid the old man would fall down.

"Four hundred dollars for a plate glass window!" Mr Stoken stammered. "And these grades! Five Fs and a D in driver's ed! There must be some mistake! It says here you scored a two hundred and nine out of a possible fourteen hundred on your college board examination! What the hell is going on? Pauley, Pauley, what's the explanation?"

The boy, his back still to his father, couldn't help smiling. He'd forgotten about the college boards fiasco. After one particularly inspiring night of loud musical abandon he'd stumbled into school to find himself scheduled to take his college

326

boards. He'd filled out the answer sheet randomly, putting dots in spaces where they looked good. So he'd managed a two o nine. Actually, it was pretty good considering he hadn't even read the questions. They must've given him one hundred seventy-five points for signing his name.

"Oh don't worry about that," the would-be cult hero said. He turned to face his father. Now that things were finally in the open he felt better. The cringing had left his face. "Don't worry about that," he said again, waving it off. "That's just school."

"Just school!"

Disbelief lit Mr Stoken's eyes.

"Are you out of your mind? Have you no idea what you've done? No college would accept anyone with scores like these. To get into Harvard or Yale we'll have to get this expunged from your record. You'll have to take the test again and score at least a twelve hundred."

"I'm quitting school."

"Quitting school? Are you mad?"

The boy said nothing.

"I said are you mad?"

Mr Stoken held up the day's mail. He slapped at the envelopes.

"You see these?" he said, slapping the envelopes. "Know what they are? Bills. Ever see one? Here we have a bill for the house, a bill for the car. Do you want some sound advice? One word and one word only, Pauley. Bills. I hate to be the one to break it to you, Charlie, but that's what life's about. Bills. How will you pay your bills if you don't go to a good school?"

"I'm not building my life around bills."

"Is that right? Is that right? Well let me tell you something mister. As long as you're living under my roof and as long as I'm footing the bills around here you'll do things my way. Understand? And that means school." Mr Stoken touched his forehead, worked his jaw. "I can see we're overdue for a little talk. Only, good God in heaven, I have such a blessed headache I don't want to talk about this now! I hate to have to

327

do it but these grades leave me no choice. You're grounded. Now get to your room and I want you to think things over. Later we'll talk. I can tell you right now, it looks like summer school for you, mister."

The boy didn't move.

"I don't believe my eyes!" Mr Stoken said. "I told you to go to your room and there you're still standing! Is something now wrong with my English? Everything else is failing — my teeth, my burglar alarm, my son — why not my English?"

"I'm not a kid anymore," Paul said. He was getting angry. "I'm seventeen years old. You just can't send me to my room anymore. I've got places to go."

"Damn right you've got places to go. Your room."

The boy held his ground.

"Look, Pauley, I'm not in the mood."

"I've got someplace I have to be. There's a contest this afternoon. A big contest. I'm not sitting around here."

"Like fun you're not. You're grounded, buddy. Up those stairs."

The boy's face glazed over at the thought of the curtains blowing through his open bedroom window in the blue moon-light.

He glared at the old man, then pounced up the steps.

"Grounded am I!" Paul huffed when he reached his room. All those pictures of Buddy Holly stared down at him. "We'll see!"

He threw open the window and would've jumped out there and then if the old man hadn't been standing in the front doorway, poking around the defective burglar alarm wiring with a screwdriver.

Before long he saw the waves of fate rolling down the street in the unlikely guise of Doug's old Plymouth convertible. The white top was down and he could see Terry's upright bass sticking out over the trunk. The Chrysler rolled up in front of the house, purring loudly, its muffler about shot. Terry, Doug and Ace jumped over the sides of the convertible and crossed

328

the lawn.

"Hey Mr S," Terry said, coming up to the front door. "Tell Paul to come on. We're late."

Mr Stoken lowered the screwdriver. His face solemn, he said, "Sorry, boys, but Paul's not going anywhere today. He's been grounded."

"Grounded! You're joking!"

"I'm not joking." Raising the screwdriver, he looked back at the wiring.

Terry's heart sank. He was thinking of all the untold hordes of screaming girls he'd miss.

"But we need to be at the Surf Ballroom in Clear Lake in half an hour," Terry told him. "There's a contest."

"Well you'll just have to play without Paul."

"Play without Paul? No way! You've just got to let him out, Mr S."

"Sorry Terry. He's been grounded, at least till the end of the week. And I'd say if your grades were anything like his you boys should by all rights be grounded too."

The three boys exchanged smiles.

"What's this bit about the white T-shirts lately?" Mr Stoken asked, looking the boys over. "You'd think it was 1955."

"They're real cool," Terry said, pulling at his cotton T-shirt.

"Yeah, like everybody's into them," Ace said.

Mr Stoken harumphed, "Well I've been into them for years." He opened his collar, revealing his white undershirt.

"Wow, Mr S, you *are* a cool dude," Terry said.

"Fruit of the Loom," Mr Stoken winked.

They made a fuss over Mr Stoken's undershirt. Ace asked if he could put it on. While the old man was occupied with this talk Terry happened to glance at Paul's bedroom window. A guitar case appeared on the windowsill. A hand reached out from the window, lowering the case to within a foot or so of the neatly trimmed hedges, dropping the instrument ever so gently into the hedge. A black-sneakered foot wiggled from the window, joined by another, followed by a pair of kicking legs in blue jeans, all proceeding the bottom edges of a white T-shirt.

Terry's heart rose. Once again he could hear those hordes of screaming girls. Paul's butt hung halfway out the window, his legs kicking air. From the looks of things he was stuck on a nail. And any second Mr Stoken might turn and catch him trying to escape.

Terry focused his attention on Mr Stoken's puffed cheek. "What's that I see in your mouth, Mr S?" he asked, looking with curiosity into Mr Stoken's mouth. "That cotton I see there?"

"Why yes it is," Mr Stoken said. He opened his mouth, pointing at the temporary filling. Behind him, Paul freed himself and eased down from the window. "Was at the dentist's today. Bit into a raisin this morning at breakfast and let me tell you I thought I'd been shot in the mouth. The dentist looked at the tooth and, would you believe, the nerve was dead. Completely dead. I'd been walking around town with no nerve in that tooth. Now I'm a candidate for a root canal. Let that be a lesson for you boys. Take care of your teeth."

While he said these things Paul bounded spiritedly across the lawn. Near the sidewalk the fugitive would-be cult hero almost tripped, but no matter. In a moment he'd scrambled into the idling Plymouth, joining the upright bass in the backseat.

The three boys said sudden goodbyes to Mr Stoken. They bowed out, backing hastily from the door, smiling, nodding their heads goodbye. They turned and ran across the lawn to the Plymouth.

Paul lie brooding on the musty backseat, his guitar case by his side, his head resting stiffly against the workings of the folded-down top.

"Come on let's get this crate the hell out of here."

Doug wrestled the transmission into gear. They lurched away. "Whoee!" he crowed. "Did you see that! The greatest escape ever! Thought I'd shit when you got stuck in the window!"

Paul lifted his head, saw the house receding. He could make out the old man leaning in the open doorway, the screwdriver in hand.

"What was that about?" Ace turned and asked. He was in the front seat, beside Doug.

"Fucking old man with his rotting teeth got home early and found my fucking grades."

"Oooooo," Terry groaned. He was in the back, between Paul and the upright bass. "Shit hit the fan?"

Ace handed out cold beers.

"We picked up a case on the way over," he said to Paul. "Been celebrating all afternoon."

"What's there to celebrate?"

"Doug here knocked up his chick." Ace patted Doug on the shoulder.

"Did what?"

Paul saw Doug's eyes in the rearview mirror. He looked a little drunk.

"Yep, I knocked up Tina," Doug was saying. He kept grinning. "Must've been that rubber I used twice. Must've put it back on inside out."

"You dumb shit. What're you gonna do now?"

Doug shrugged.

"Thought I'd get fucked up," he said. He smiled as though he hadn't a care in the world. He slouched behind the wheel, a bottle of sudsy beer in one hand, a cigarette in the other. "Thought I'd just ease myself on down the road," he laughed, lifting the bottle for a swig.

"Don't get too smashed to play drums."

"Ah Christ you don't have to worry about that. The more I drink the harder I chop the skins."

Terry opened a brown shopping bag that'd been resting on the seat. "I bought us something special to wear at the Surf." From the bag came four white T-shirts. Printed across the front of each was the oversized red and yellow crest of Superman. He tossed one of the shirts to Paul.

331

With a reverent sweep of his hand the boy caressed the big red letter S.

He peeled off his ordinary white T-shirt, pulled on the new one. He felt indestructible. They were rolling along a straight stretch of shady country lane banked on both sides by tall oaks. Bunching his old white T-shirt into a ball, he yelled, "No more Clark Kents!" then hurled the hapless shirt skyward from the speeding convertible. The shirt rocketed up fifteen or so feet and snagged a branch, wrapping around once before hanging lifeless above the road.

Clear Lake was a resort town, a favorite vacation spot of Midwestern boaters and anglers drawn back once each year like salmon to the blue green waters of the lake. By this time in late June the place was jumping with boats buzzing out on the lake and still more boats hitched to station wagons. Winnebagos crowded both sides of the wide dusty streets. Everywhere men walked about clutching fishing poles and tackle boxes. After a long lonely winter of Midwest desolation Clear Lake felt like heaven to them. The guest houses were filling up with long skinny grain dealers and their long skinny wives, the hash houses were spooning out long skinny spaghetti while the bait houses shoveled out long skinny worms. And always in the background you heard the buzzsaw ripping of boats out on the lake.

Into this watery version of the American dream rumbled the old Plymouth, through the streets filling up with vacation homes, past men lugging fishing poles between parked cars. When the four long skinny boys riding in the Plymouth caught sight of the Surf Ballroom they couldn't believe their eyes. The sidewalk beneath the marquee overflowed into the street with kids decked out in white T-shirts, sneakers and horn-rimmed Buddy Holly glasses.

"Would you look at that," Ace gasped as they rumbled down the street. "They're waiting on us."

Sure enough, the Plymouth rolled into sight and a cheer went up from the crowd. Kids ran into the street.

332

"Dig this!" Terry sang happily, bouncing in his seat, elbowing Paul's ribs. "You really put your finger on something boy," he said under his breath. "Look at all those kids wearing Buddy Holly glasses. Hundreds of them."

Paul fitted his sunglasses over his eyes, trying to look cool. Terry, Doug and Ace pulled on their shades too.

The crowd came rushing up, at first running alongside the Plymouth, soon swarming so thick around the car that the street was made impassable. Doug tried to wave them out of the way. But suddenly, as he rose to do so, to their left, a girl let out a scream.

Everyone went quiet when they heard that first scream. A girl in the crowd appeared to have lost her senses. She pointed into the car, her eyes wild and manic, one hand pressed against her head, another hand reaching past the shoulders of those before her, trying to touch one of The Conclusions. Another girl began screaming. Suddenly it was a free for all. Girls pressed close around the car, crawling over the hood and the trunk, screaming, tearing at the boys.

Hanging tightly to his guitar case, Paul tried to beat a path through the girls. He stood poised on the trunk, swatting his hands and ducking, ready to jump at first opportunity, but a tide of screaming girls descended upon him, engulfing him.

Ace started across the back of the seat to help but found himself in the same predicament. Girls everywhere. He couldn't bring himself to fight them off.

"Cool out! Cool out! There's plenty to go around."

Terry offered no resistance. "This is all right by me," he smiled, leaning his head way back as they carried him from the car.

The sudden riot caught sleepy Clear Lake by surprise. Men with fishing poles came running, half expecting to see someone's head lopped off in a traffic accident. Horns blew and men climbed from their Winnebagos to see what was happening. The wailing horns and the snarled traffic brought out more people, including the town's deputy sheriff, who came running from the lunchroom on the square wiping his mouth with a paper napkin, looking up the street at the confusion in front of the Surf before running to the phone in the hardware store to report a riot.

Dozens of high school-aged boys wearing white T-shirts, jeans, black ankle-highs and Buddy Holly hornrims circled the car enthusiastically watching the girls, cheering them on. In the street a Winnebago driver futilely tried to get the screaming girls to see reason by yelling that they were blocking traffic and that their fool screaming was sure to be scaring the fish out on the lake, but the girls acted like they didn't care about the fish.

Several of the fishermen tried to break it up. This incited the by-now considerable crowd of high school boys. The strongest among them charged up and tore the rattled Conclusions from the hysterical girls, yelling for everyone to clear out of the way so the band could be escorted into the ballroom.

This was about the time the cops showed up, blowing whistles and announcing over bullhorns for all to disperse. The warning fell on deaf ears. Enraged, the sheriff sent a deputy into the ballroom to close the place down, but the owner came out yelling the order was impossible.

"These damn kids'll tear the place apart if this show don't go on," the owner of the ballroom pleaded with the sheriff. The owner was an elderly man with a bald head. Sweat beaded atop his head and he kept wiping at it with a tattered white handkerchief. "This is just like one of those horror movies you see on tv," he kept saying. "The little boogers came out of nowhere and took the place over. They really believe that darned Buddy Holly kid ain't dead. They think he's playing in this band that just rolled up."

The sheriff gawked at the kids. They swarmed around the four boys in the Superman T-shirts, who by now were making their way slowly into the ballroom on the shoulders of the football players, followed by the big upright bass, shouldered above the mob by four or five beefy jocks. Short of calling out the National Guard, there didn't seem to be anything the sher-

334

iff could do.

The Conclusions were borne into the Surf, led by two boys in Mason City High letterman jackets who hefted Paul on their shoulders. From his perch Paul saw it was a very roomy high-ceilinged place, more like a hanger than a ballroom. Ceiling fans slowly whirled. You could barely see past the crowd to the stage, where a band played a song by The Who. They took turns pretending to smash their guitars against the stage and amplifiers. They couldn't afford to actually trash their equipment like The Who so they swung their guitars with mock brutality over their shoulders like they were swinging pretend axes at pretend trees, stopping two or three inches short of doing any real damage. A very bad act.

Kids packed the dance floor. As The Conclusions were brought into the hall heads began turning. Paul's breath caught. Just about everyone wore Buddy Holly hornrims. You'd've thought it was a 3-D movie.

The jocks bore The Conclusions with much bravado into the crowd, sweeping across the dance floor. A great hush swept the old ballroom. Everything went dead except the terrible band playing onstage, which was probably the one thing that should've gone dead.

Kids began chanting, "Not fade away! Not fade away!"

The jocks boosted The Conclusions onto the stage. Frenzied girls tried to follow them onto the platform but the jocks held them off.

Mistaking the wild burst of enthusiasm, the band on stage kept pretending to smash their equipment. Ace grabbed the microphone. Puffing up his chest to better show off the emblem on his T-shirt, he said in a deep voice, "This is a job for Supermen!" The Who imitators finally were hooted off stage. Ace and Paul pulled their guitars from the cases and plugged into the wall of amps next to the drums. The kids took in the Superman crests on their T-shirts.

Gripping a red lipstick, one of the boys on the dance floor drew a crude Superman crest across his own white T-shirt. When the others saw what he'd done they all wanted to bor-

335

row the lipstick. "What about me?" a girl yelled, wanting a shield of her own. A boy hugged her tightly. "Hey what gives!" He peeled himself away and they saw he'd smeared so much lipstick onto his shirt that the red S had transferred onto hers, though backwards. Kids hooted approval. The girl hugged another guy, transferring the S to him. Like that, they passed around the S.

Terry hunkered over the upright bass, putting it in tune, while Doug rearranged the drums, a pack of Marlboros rolled up in his sleeve. Suddenly they moved close to the microphones, breaking into a fast tune.

"Not fade away!" the diehards kept chanting. Others picked up the chant, shouting down the band. They had to stop playing. Terry and Ace came over to Paul.

"What do you guys think?"

"Looks like we'll be playing Not Fade Away."

Paul said it was a good sign. He surveyed the ballroom significantly, his eyes catching the chanting faces.

"Didn't I tell you guys this place was at the center   of some kind of cosmic vortex?"

Leaning over the drumset, he told Doug to lay down a beat for Not Fade Away. Doug managed to kick it off. Only when the drums sounded did the crowd begin to settle down.

Of the few dozen songs left behind by Charles Hardin Holley of Lubbock, Texas, none is more difficult to play than Not Fade Away. There is a spirit and a simplicity to the song that over the years no one has been able to recapture. It is as if when Holly died a flame at the very heart of the song was snuffed out with him.

As Doug belted out the beat on the drums all the kids fell silent. Paul, Ace and Terry brought their instruments near the drumset, listening to the beat. Kids pressed close around, sharing the heat.

The electric guitars came alive. The big upright bass sung out low and sweet. Now the backing vocals.

Kids found their heels tapping. They swayed, bounced

336

their heads to the beat.

Paul knew they played the song badly. The run-on he'd had with the old man had taken the edge from his concentration. Worse, Doug's rhythm was off. All that beer had taken its toll. He kept missing the beat. His tongue hung out and every few beats he missed the snare altogether.

The song might've fallen apart there and then if Terry hadn't been playing so well. Terry, alone among the four boys, was concentrating. He leaned close up against the big bass, slapping the strings with his right hand while he worked the expansive sounding board with his left. Bent backed, bouncing at the knees, his lips sounded the notes as he played.

Listening, listening, Paul pulled his guitar close and played. He picked up Terry's bass line and both of them cut loose. With a snap of his wrist, without missing a beat, Terry spun the great bass all the way around. He dropped the bass and fell atop it, riding the rugged beast in circles on the stage, madly pulling the strings. Kids crowded the stage, whistling and yelling, their sweaty T-shirts clinging to their backs, kicking up their heels. The song ended, a great cheer went up.

Before the cheering could die, at the rear of the stage, emerging from behind the curtain, came a wild figure of a man, the lines of age just beginning to crack his brow and cheeks. His hair fell brown and long, dangling to his shoulders, the first streaks of gray barely visible. Beneath his lined cheeks hung an untrimmed beard. His eyes, deep blue and clear. Fiery oceans. Almost mad. But they were not the most striking thing about him. The most striking thing about him was that he was missing a leg. His right leg. The right leg of his jeans was pinned to his thigh.

A lage burlap sack, a gunnysack, hung from his free shoulder by a thick strap. His only boot, his left boot, was caked in mud, as was the tip of his crutch. He came forward, the dried black mud flaking off, trailing dots and dashes across the worn floorboards creaking beneath him.

The apearance of such an ancient wild character at their rock contest caused a stir to go up, followed by a sudden hush,

337

until at last the house fell quiet and it was possible to hear the shuffling sound of the newcomer's boot dragging across those floorboards, punctuated by the single, slow thud of the crutch. All eyes rested on him as he hobbled slowly to the front of the stage.

The one-legged man looked wondrously out into the ballroom, not at the silent staring kids cramming the floor, but through them, like they weren't there. The craziest grin lit his face. He surveyed the ceiling fans whirling overhead, the four corners of the ballroom. His eyes landed on something none of the others could see, a spot near the center of the stage, five or six feet in front of the drums. Several kids crowding the stage had to jump out of his way, since he moved like he didn't see them, like they were the ghosts and the invisible thing that drew him was the only thing he could see. When he reached the spot on the stage he turned, facing the dance floor. Looking down, he carefully placed the tip of the crutch and then his only foot at precise spots, like you would fit your feet in footprints at Hollywood's walk of stars. You could hear the boats buzzing out on the lake in the still summer air.

Only then did he notice the kids. Jeffrey Stoken looked slowly out across the ballroom, taking in all the white T-shirts and the Buddy Holly hornrims. He grinned and shook his head. His hand came off the handle of the crutch and ran through his long hair.

"Man," he grinned, shaking his head, "you punks have no idea." He said it slowly, taking his time, his voice filling the hall. They watched him slip the strap of the gunnysack from his shoulder. Sweeping the burlap bag away, he held a guitar. An electric guitar. Fender Stratocaster. Candy apple red. A deep scar ran down the face of the Strat. A gash or two cut into its neck.

Despite the deep scratches the old guitar looked remarkably preserved. Over the decades someone obviously had sat up through the long lonely nights caring for it. The red paint had been lovingly polished. Buffed. It gleamed in the stage lights. The worn fretboard had been scrupulously cleaned. The

338

wood there glowed with a soft patina that could only have been brought out after years of touching and playing. Through the dark decades someone had cared.

From his jacket pocket came a pick. He cast his eyes about for an amplifier hookup.

Paul pulled the cord from his own guitar. He coiled it up, threw it over to Jeffrey, who caught it with a swoop of his hand and plugged in.

Buttressing himself with the crutch, he proceeded to play Not Fade Away as if old Buddy Holly himself was singing into his ear. He played it slowly and with much feeling. The slow and steady way Jeffrey moved with that guitar put the kids in mind of old crackly records they'd heard. Conjured in their minds were images of fifties teenagers dancing close to the slow, sweet tunes that every once in a while you still hear crackling over the radio.

Mixed in with the slow and the sweet sound was something else. A raw edge. An exposed nerve. The wailing sound of something defiant. The roar of an injured lion. Something that moaned the sadness of the years. Something fearlessly proclaiming it would never lay down and die. Something of steel mixed in with that slow sweet sound.

It came alive for him. He played it with what could only be called reverent, religious devotion, like another man might moan a prayer, as if pursuing the heart of that song was his only salvation. He played it with all the careful devotion of a monk whose mission in life had been to keep the song alive through the American dark ages.

When Jeffrey came to the end of the tune you couldn't hear a sound. Suddenly a shaggy-looking kid pointed to the Strat, yelling, "Look at those gashes."

Kids started coming out of their trance, looking at the guitar in the arms of the one-legged man. A few more boys pressed close around Jeffrey, prying for a look. One laid his hands on the Strat's scarred face. Jeffrey smashed him a good broadside with the crutch.

"Ouch damnit!"

339

"Keep your sticky hands off punk!" Written on Jeffrey's face was all the fiery zeal of a mad saint protecting sacred relics from the touch of infidels. "All of you get back!" he growled, waving the crutch high. The boys crowding Jeffrey fell back. Jeffrey pulled the plug on the Strat, covered it with the gunnysack. Holding the burlap bag close, he broke past the kids and made for the wings, racing through a side door opening to an alleyway. Paul had to jump to see over the heads of those in front, catching a glimpse of Jeffrey climbing onto his motorcycle.

Paul made it as far as the curb before Terry yanked on his sleeve, pointing down the alleyway. Paul saw his father's station wagon pulling up out front. The old man struggled out, and God he looked pissed.

Back home Mr Stoken had been tinkering with the burglar alarm until the repairman showed up and took over. Fiddling with the wiring a minute or two, he announced he'd found the problem, a loose nut, which he tightened. But when he activated the system to test the repair the alarm had gone off. Within five minutes a police car rolled into the driveway. A cop got out and summarily wrote out a fifty dollar fine. Mr Stoken was angry, but he managed to contain his rage, at least until the repairman, mystifiedly snooping around, found one of the bedroom windows hanging open. The boy's bedroom window. That did it. Mr Stoken chomped down hard on his bad tooth and let out a roar the likes of which hadn't been heard in that neighborhood since the glaciers melted. The bottled rage of a bad day came pouring out. Remembering Terry had said something about some contest at the old ballroom in Clear Lake, Mr Stoken had jumped into the station wagon. God, was that place still standing?

Standing it was. When he pulled up in front of the blistered ballroom and got out of the car his eyes swept across the outrageous marine motif, taking in the shabby blue paint splintering on the sun-cracked wood, allowing himself a moment to remember this was the place where he had met his wife. That was way back in '57. Damn, it was still standing.

He caught sight of the kids streaming out the side door into the alleyway. They were making a big fuss over something. Had he once been such a scrawny kid? Scrawny as that? Impossible! These kids today. They were missing out on something. Beef, from the looks of them. Well no, something besides beef. It was nothing like growing up in the fifties. Something sure was missing.

He saw his son in the alleyway, standing beside Terry, that guitar strapped to his back.

"Peter Paul Stoken!" he yelled, rushing from the car into the alleyway.

The boy shrank.

"Peter Paul Stoken!"

He heard the roar of the motorcycle. Jeffrey swatted kids away as he rolled through the throng. At last he broke free and revved the Harley, lifting the front wheel from the pavement. He was heading down the alleyway, straight for the boy.

Paul felt caught between two lives, two ways of living. He stole one more glance at the old man, no more than twenty paces away, and closing fast.

Do we ever really get a choice? The boy stepped from the curb in front of the motorcycle and raised a hand. The bike slowed. He jumped on.

"Hang on tight buddyroo."

Mr Stoken at first did not recognize the motorcyclist. He saw only his son defiantly jumping on the bike.

"Wait one minute—," he started to yell so proper and lawyerlylike at the biker. Then he saw those eyes, set like mirrors in that face that looked so much like his own. He saw the scraggly beard and the tip of the crutch protruding behind the biker's shoulder.

"Jeff—," Mr Stoken gasped, falling back in surprise.

His hesitation lasted only an instant. The surprise in his face gave way to anger. As the bike roared past he stretched for the boy's arm.

341

Jeffrey leaned away, twisting his wrist to change gears. That hog really squealed. The boy held fast, Jeffrey's burlap bag and its hidden treasure pressed to his chest. He saw the old man's fingers brush up against the sleeve of his T-shirt. That moment lasted forever.

Then they were gone.

Mr Stoken spun around as the bike roared into the street.

"Goddamn you Jeff come back with my son!"

The bike was just rounding the corner at Main. Mr Stoken jumped into the station wagon and took off after them.

Hearing knows before seeing reveals. Hearing knows the sound of the old man leaning on the horn, sending up infuriated blasts. The boy looked over his shoulder, saw the white station wagon weaving through traffic not far behind.

"He's gaining!" Paul yelled over the fury of the engine and the wind.

Jeffrey didn't have to answer. They flew across a set of railroad tracks, spun down a side street. He rode that bike like he'd played that guitar, stretching for the limit. He rode that bike like he'd been running all his life, his hands gripped to the handlebars, this just another short mile in the endless running. They whipped past slow lumbering trucks, swooping low to the road, Jeffrey stretching out the stub of his leg for balance, Paul closing his eyes and holding his breath, murmuring prayers.

Across a church parking lot they stormed, then off the pavement altogether into a little league ballfield, where kids were having a game. Jeffrey let it rip across the infield, barreled out past the grandstands then up a hill into the farmland outside town. The hill was rough and bumpy with gopher holes and it was all the boy could do to hold on.

At the top of the hill Jeffrey put his foot down in the grass and stopped. They looked back down the hill. The white station wagon had stopped at the bottom, near the ballfield, overheated, white steam pouring around the hood. Mr Stoken was a speck beside the open door of the tiny car, surrounded by kids in baseball hats. You could hear the faint wailing of the horn, coming in and out with the warm dry breeze.

Jeffrey smiled, wiped the dust from his cracked lips with the back of his hand.

"What's the matter, lawyerman?" Then, to the boy, "Hey—. Where to?"

Paul gazed at the gunnysack strapped to his uncle's shoulder.

"You know where."

"Do I, old buddyroo?"

The boy looked east, away from town, across the fields. In the distance he made out Clear Lake Airport. A small plane swung in low for a landing, slanting down from the sky above the rolling fields, the sun glinting on its wings. He raised his arm and pointed across the fields to the airstrip.

Jeffrey rubbed his whisker stubble, brought his hand down, gripping the handlebars.

"Have it your way then."

They spun around, the bike's back tire biting loose dirt, speeding off, racing across the fields toward the distant airport. They took a straight line, going point to point, ignoring the boundaries of farms and fields, creeks and roads lying between themselves and the gray runways, plowing through cornfields, bending and breaking stalks, ripping over fallow land, chasing startled prairie dogs that bolted out in front of them before veering away into their holes. Everywhere farmers ran tractors on the quilt-patched hills, and the air smelled of hewn hay, dung and ripening corn.

The bike broke over a hill. They saw a small white farmhouse set like a jewel in the folds of the rolling land below. An old woman slopped pigs in the side yard. When the bike roared past she scarcely took notice, only casually looking up from the slop, as if deranged bikers regularly rode past her pigsty. Near the airport the land flattened and the rolling countryside fell away behind them. Here the boy tapped his uncle's shoulder, correcting their course. He felt Jeffrey's shoulder muscles tighten.

They came to an old road overlooking the field. Jeffrey slowed the bike and put his foot down on the roadbed, gazing down a gentle slope. He shook his head. Paul pointed intently down the slope.

"Okay buddyroo we'll ride straight into the mouth of the pit, just you and me."

They lurched on, riding slowly across the slope, cutting through high grass, swerving between trees, breaking into a field. An endless long wire fence came into view. Jeffrey cut loose at the fence, gunning the engine, standing on his remaining leg. The bike roared along, taking a wide arc around a tall oak, circling back till they came again to the fence. Jeffrey cut the engine. He leaned the bike against the fence and the boy hopped off.

"Some kids at school say here's the spot the plane ended up," the boy said wondrously, pointing to a portion of the fence near the tall oak. But when he turned he saw his uncle, now off the bike and hobbled over his crutch, mesmerized by another stretch of fence, farther down, a section overgrown with weeds. He knew then the others in the past who had visited this place with him had been wrong.

Jeffrey staggered uneasily before the fence, bringing that gunnysack self-consciously around in his arms, looking into the tall grass.

Kneeling at a precise spot, he gingerly laid the sack in the deep weeds several feet from the fence. He touched the fence then, touching the barbed wire. As he did this the boy was drawn to the gunnysack in the weeds. Loosening the drawstring, he opened the sack. Yellow sunlight poured in and he saw the head of a guitar. The painted words. Fender Stratocaster.

"It's true. You found his guitar."

Jeffrey gazed through the fence at a plane that had just lifted off from the airport.

"It's got to stop, buddyroo," he said quietly. "You see that don't you? That band of yours. You've got to stop playing. While there's time. You've got to break up, while you can.

344

You've no idea what you're playing with."

The boy sat in the tall grass, the electric guitar in his lap, touching with delicate brushes of his fingertips the deep scars in the lustrous red enamel. It was an old-fashioned electric guitar, solid, and heavy as a machine gun.

"About this guitar. I put two and two together, Jeff. I know how you got it."

Jeffrey stared through the fence, at the other side.

"You have to tell me something, Jeff. The night I was born—. The night you found this guitar—. When the plane crashed—. What time of night was it? Exactly, I mean."

Jeffrey spat through the wire. "What the hell difference does it make?"

"All the difference in the world. You saw the kids at the Surf. They think I'm Buddy Holly reincarnated."

Leaning heavily on his crutch, Jeffrey came slowly to the boy, looking warily at the guitar in his hands.

"If they do it's because you put that crazy idea in their heads. I don't want to hear any more of that Buddy Holly reincarnation shit, you hear? You got the whole damn town worked up. It's getting out of hand. It's got to stop, you hear me?"

"It's not just talk."

Jeffrey's face reddened.

"Come off it!" Both hands tightened around the crutch. "Do you have any idea how many third-rate punks just barely able to strum a guitar think they're Buddy Holly reborn? Each thinking they're destined to rewrite Peggy Sue. What makes you think you're any different?"

"You know damn well what makes me different. I was born the night Buddy died, not ten miles from here. I measured it out myself, in the old man's car."

"Don't act so dumb, Paul. That's just coincidence."

"That's not all. There's one more thing. This."

He held up the red electric guitar, his arms stiff.

"You think it's just coincidence this guitar's in my hands now? If Beethoven came back, in another life I mean, don't you think fate would bring him together with his piano? If Buddy Holly came back, don't you think sooner or later he'd have to run into his guitar? Or else he'd go through life with a terribly mysterious feeling that something was missing. That's how I felt, until a few moments ago, when I laid my hands on this Strat."

Anyone else would have found amusement in the boy's reasoning. But Jeffrey took a step back.

"It proves nothing," he lashed out. "That guitar is just a prop from the play of someone else's life. That's all. It has no magical powers of its own." He said this like he was trying to listen to his own words, trying to convince himself. "That Strat's not going to play Not Fade Away all by itself. It's like that stupid Superman T-shirt you're wearing. You're confusing Buddy Holly with his guitar. Superman with his cape. The real Superman didn't need a cape to be strong. He could bend steel rails without that funny blue suit. That cape's only a prop and if you or I could put it on we're still not going to be able to leap tall buildings in a single bound."

The boy drew in his breath.

"This *is* his guitar."

He looked with renewed worshipfulness at the old Strat. His uncle smiled ever so slightly then, bashfully.

"I was just a stupid kid. Younger than you are now."

The boy brought his hand up to the worn fretboard.

"I have to know something, Jeff." The boy scraped his fingernails against the strings. "About me. I guessed I was born the exact instant that plane crashed."

Jeffrey began to shake. He looked like he was holding onto that crutch with every atom of his strength. He looked hard into the boy's eyes. A long moment went by like that.

"You were born before the crash. Several hours before the crash."

Paul saw his uncle shake.

"I don't believe you."

"That's the way it happened, damnit!" Jeffrey lifted the crutch, swinging it down hard into the grass. "I should know.

346

I was at the hospital. I was hanging around the waiting room with the folks. I decided to go for a ride. I left the hospital and ended up witnessing the crash. By then you'd already been born, several hours before."

"You're lying! I can see it! Look at you! I'll tell you how it happened. On your way back from the Surf you found this guitar. Then you went to the hospital, didn't you? And when you got there they told you I'd just been born. Isn't that the way it happened?"

They were eye to eye, both of them shaking, the boy from anger, his uncle with fright. Shaking his head, Jeffrey looked down at the guitar in the boy's hands.

"You can't hide the truth," the boy cried. "Sooner or later it works its way into the open, whether you want it or not."

"No—. No—."

Jeffrey took a step back.

"You found this guitar in the wreckage then you went to the hospital, didn't you?"

"No—. I swear."

"And that's not all, is it? Way down inside you think the same as those kids back at the Surf. You think I'm Buddy Holly reincarnated too, don't you?"

"I do not!"

Jeffrey reached for the guitar. They struggled over it but the boy, benefiting from two sound legs, managed to pull it away. Jeffrey tumbled backwards against the fence. He slumped, clutching the wire.

"I saw a generation die on this fence," he sobbed. The wind was blowing pretty well and you could hear it whistling through. "I saw the heart of America torn from the sky. Thrown lifeless against this rotten tangle of wire and wood posts. And you think you want to play guitar, do you?"

Turning, still clinging to the fence, he looked at the boy.

"So young I once was," he muttered, "so much like you. Whole and unbroken. Straight backed and proud shouldered. Defiant. Thinking I'd never grow old. Then I met this fence."

347

It'd been snowing all night, he told the boy. He was taking the back roads into Mason City when he'd seen the streak of light. He remembers the rest of it like it happened in slow motion. Stopping the truck to get out. Through the blowing snow he saw a faint glow. Now he was running down a slope, between trees, feeling superhuman, taking giant strides through the luminescent falling snow, feeling indestructible, almost unbound by gravity, running through the drifts until he came to the fence. "I guess I was like all Americans back then," he said. "Thinking nothing in life could faze me." Then, the instant he reached the fence, he was forced to grow up.

He said he'd seen all four of them. Only minutes before they had been alive. Now they hung in the wire of the fence.

"Wreckage burning all over the place. I looked down at my sneakers. That's when I saw them. Half buried in the snow. Right about where you're standing now. Those eyeglasses. Hornrims. My hands were trembling even as I bent to pick them up. I could see the lenses were broken out, and my hands shook so that what was left of the glass crumbled free of the frames and shimmered into the blowing snow. Through those jagged shattered lenses I could see their bodies slung so cruelly across the fence and I just wanted to scream. I dropped those glasses into the snow. I wanted to run but my world was falling apart and I didn't know where I could go that it wouldn't be the same. More than just those hornrims had been shattered, more than just those four killed. A dream had been shattered. An entire generation brought down. This here's no ordinary fence, buddyroo. The heart of my generation stopped beating here. No more teenage America. We were all about to come of age. Before that night at this fence I didn't know how cruel life could be.

"That night I'd seen my world fall from the sky. I half expected the frozen ground to give way beneath my feet.

"It was like those stories you read of people who, out for a pleasant walk, suddenly feel the earth giving way beneath them. They begin to run, but already it's too late, because the pit's opening too fast. They feel it crumbling beneath their feet. That's what I thought. A pit had opened up beneath those poor guys. They'd been sucked down into the blackest pit.

"In one single instant I no longer felt indestructible or immortal or even young. A shadow had fallen over me. I was looking into the pit. I realized then into that pit we all must fall, sooner or later. The trick must be to stay out of it for as long as you can. That's what life's all about, what Buddy's music had always been about. Man was he ever full of life. If you could have seen him that night at the Surf. Some people are just a little more alive than others. They stand out in a crowd. The moment they come into a room everybody *feels* someone special just walked in. That's how he was. How he danced when he played! None of us thinking it could end. Man it all seems like a faraway dream. Bet he couldn't believe it when that plane started going down. Some folks, like Buddy, they get thrown forcefully into the pit since they'd never go on their own. Some fools jump in willfully. Others spend years at the edge of the pit, waiting for the ground to crumble beneath their easychairs as they watch tv.

"Well not me. I made up my mind there and then I'd stay out of the pit as long as I could. I'd always keep my eyes open, always keep running. I'd never let the ground open beneath *my* feet.

"Then I saw the guitar. In the snow. In a leather case. The words Buddy Holly in the leather.

"I was numbed all over, inside and out. I must've put my hands to my ears. I could still see and hear old Buddy Holly singing Not Fade Away back at the Surf, and now there was only the terribly lonely and empty blowing of the wind. Those broken bodies. That crunched plane with the windows bashed out. The musicless falling of the snow. Before I knew what happened that guitar was under my arm and I was running as fast as I could. Somehow I thought if I didn't pick it up and run with it something that should live would die. All that was left was for me to run, run from the opening pit, run before the ground crumbled beneath my feet, with that guitar you're holding, with one eye over my shoulder, and I've been running like that ever since, seventeen years now."

He said he'd been foolish enough to stop running only once, long enough to get his leg blown off in Vietnam.

"You saw lots of action?"

"Yeah, action. Saw plenty of action. Mostly the action of assholes running to keep from getting shot off. They'd send us out into the jungle on search and destroy missions. I had almost a year of that shit. You'd be marching through the swamp neck deep in slime with your rifle over your head, praying someone in the trees up ahead didn't have a bead on you. You'd imagine what the one who'd kill you must be like. Where he came from, whether he had a family, stuff like that. You had to wonder if somewhere out in those trees wasn't the man who had your number. We called him Charlie. That was the first four months or so. The next four months of your tour you didn't worry so much about dying. You put it out of your mind. If it happens, it happens, you tell yourself. You just keep pushing through the slime. The last four months, the last months of your tour, you started counting off the days till you went home and you got edgy. You got to calling him Sir Charles. You imagined Sir Charles around every bend, down every foot of jungle trail. You got to hate him, hate the way he taunted you, stalked you. You wished he'd get it over with. Sometimes, at night out on the trail, you'd see him smiling at you in your dreams and you'd wake up screaming and they'd have to gag you until you came around.

"In the morning they'd send you out to evacuate and destroy another village. It'd be a village thought to be helping the guerrillas. That was my job. Village destroyer third class. You'd evacuate and burn five or six a week. It was a neverending job, village burning. Before long you'd realize why that was. Just about every village was helping the guerrillas. That's when it hit home. You were the enemy of these people, not the guerrillas. You weren't the good guy, the guy with the white hat riding in to stick out his neck for the underdog. No. You were the bully, the brown shirt, the one who had it coming.

350

"I don't know what I thought I was doing over there. *My* heart certainly wasn't in it. I was thinking I'd play the game. You know, try to stay alive. Wear the uniform, carry the gun. But I told myself that didn't make me a soldier. There must've been a million other guys thinking the same.

"One day it all caught up. They'd ship these young lieutenants fresh in from West Point. They'd only be twenty-one years old, younger than some of the guys they're supposedly commanding, with no more combat experience than what they'd seen on the late show. Many of the guys in the squad were serving their last months, counting off the days till they go home, and when some gung-ho jerk fresh from officers' school shows up with plans to win the war with your skin that smart ass is just begging to be fragged."

"Fragged?"

"It's a lovely business. One day this pretty boy officer ships in. This one really had cement between the ears. He had some idea we were going to march down this road into a dense jungle and I guess you could say the men vetoed him. God what a persistent little fuck he was. You could smell an ambush down that road. There were practically neon signs advertising it. This being the kid's first command he couldn't take being disobeyed. He got red in the face. He stood there with his hands gripped into fists at his side, stamping his foot. One or two of the guys came up and told him it wasn't such a good idea, going down that road, but he was too dense to understand the nature of their warning. He only got redder in the face and started waving his pistol around, yelling we'd follow him, all right. The men looked at each other. There was something real ugly about that look. I watched them all pick up their gear, agreeing to go along with him for a little walk. That put me on warning. They'd given in too quick. I told myself to get ready to run. That's when it happened. From behind. I saw one of our men lob a fragmentation grenade right alongside our little Custer. I don't know why I did it. That stupid little shit meant nothing to me. But there it was, in the grass next to the kid, and he didn't even see it. I had time to run. But I didn't. I pushed that fuckhead lieutenant out of the way and gave the grenade a good kick.

"When I woke up I was lying in the deep grass. Snipers firing over me. I could hear the sizzle of bullets. Sounds like mosquitoes.

"I knew I was hurt bad. My uniform and rifle were red with blood. I thought I was dying.

"I couldn't take my eyes off the rifle. It seemed like the most absurd thing imaginable. What am I doing with this thing? I asked myself. I'm not a soldier. I'm not a trained killer. And this uniform. How did I come to put it on? What am I doing in this jungle?

"I felt the ground giving way beneath me. It was the pit, as deep and cold and terrible as I remembered it from that night of the plane crash. I can't describe the terror I felt. I realized I'd been walking all along on the edge of the pit. I'd stopped running, stopped looking over my shoulder, like I'd promised myself I'd always do, and now I was paying the price for not learning the lesson the first time. The pit had been creeping up behind me ever since I got to 'Nam and now I was about to slide over the edge.

"Only when you're staring into oblivion do you begin to appreciate life. It's all we have, buddyroo. A little piece of warmth and light in cold eternity. Each moment of life is more precious than all the world's diamonds. I'd been dumb enough to trade it all for a rifle and a uniform.

"More than anything then I wanted to live. More than anything. You can't imagine. I let go of the rifle and held on to the grass, held on with every atom of my strength to keep from sliding into that pit. I made up my mind if I could hold on I'd never stop running again. Never.

"Listen, Buddyroo: one day there'll come a time in your own life when somebody'll ask you to go somewhere. I can't tell you who, and I can't tell you when. It might be another American who'll ask you to go, maybe even, maybe even someone in your own family. I can't even tell you where they'll ask you to go. All I can say is, it'll be someplace your better judgment tells you to stay the hell out. They might ask you pleasantly, or they might order you to go. It's all the same. Don't hesitate. Stay out of that pit for as long as you can. Turn and run."

Paul was looking at the stub where his uncle's leg had been. He swallowed hard.

"You mean another American did that to you?"

Jeffrey smiled.

"Well that's the funny part, buddyroo. The guy in our squad who tossed the grenade— his name was Charlie."

"Shit."

"That's what Vietnam was about, buddyroo. Americans at war with Americans. It wasn't important that you came from the same country as another guy. If that guy stood in the way of your going home that guy was your enemy. I can't help thinking that countries and nations are old-fashioned things. We no longer need them. I can't help thinking something better's evolving. It's just a ways down the pike, that's all. We just got to hold on till we get there. Just the other day I was thinking we're the ancients. We're the first to have motorcycles and electric guitars. The first representatives of a new world, a new way of living. It might not come into being for hundreds of years, this new world we're inventing, thousands of years maybe, but I know something better's coming. We can't live forever on the edge of oblivion, with darkness so close."

He said he couldn't help thinking this was just another dark age we were passing through. He'd had lots of time for thinking about it, he said, after he got home from 'Nam. He knew there was only one thing to be done. Never again did he stop running, never again did he let that Stratocaster out of his sight. There was something he had to keep alive. He never stopped polishing that old Strat, never stopped caring. A night did not go by when he didn't take it up and play Not Fade Away. He resolved to keep the music alive through the dark ages, however long it would take. It became his great mission in life. Like those medieval monks who preserved civilization through the long dark centuries, he took it upon himself to

353

preserve America's heartbeat sound. It was his way of seeking atonement for what he'd done that terrible night back in '59. Someday, he told the boy, people would be glad for everything he'd done.

Over the years he watched, waited and listened. Like a mad hermit he watched, waited and listened for a sign. He waited until one day not five months ago, when he'd been sitting in a bar in Emory, when he'd heard talk of a new band. It was a new sound, he heard someone say. When he'd heard them say one of the kids in the band had been born the night Buddy Holly died he'd damn near choked on his beer.

That was the night he'd gone out to the firehall in Mason City to see for himself. He saw the mobs of kids, the tangle of traffic. A new generation of kids, unaware of the dangers of dancing bravely.

Jeffrey gazed at the fence. Paul, the guitar. One was caught up in the fall, the other, the rise.

"You've got to quit that band of yours, buddyroo. I'll be watching. Laying for you."

Paul took in his uncle's wild intent eyes, the tangled beard and long, unkempt hair. For the first time he allowed himself to wonder if the things he'd heard about Jeffrey might be true.

Just then a small plane, taking off from the airport, appeared above the horizon and, banking sharply, flew over the fence, not too far above them. Jeffrey started to say something but the roar of the plane drowned him out. He lifted his head and gazed up as it soared over. He shot a strange look at the boy. It sure was a busy spot for air traffic.

"The scars on that guitar should be stars that guide you away from the sufferings of others," Jeffrey told the boy after the plane had passed. They watched it fly off. "I don't want my nephew's bones picked out of a crash at a godforsaken place like this. I swear I'll lay for you boy. I'll ruin everything."

"Just try! Next time you show up I'll give *you* a little guitar lesson. Then we'll see."

"And what makes you so damn sure of yourself?"

354

The boy crossed his arm over the Strat. He said he'd already explained what made him so damn sure. He was Buddy Holly reincarnated.

Jeffrey sat shaking his head, moving his lips like he wanted to say something but had run out of words, out of patience.

"Didn't I tell you to cut that reincarnation shit?"

"Why should I?"

"Because, buddyroo, you're shortchanging someone."

"Who?" the boy shot back. "My old man, who wants me to go to law school?"

"You'd be shortchanging someone very special named Paul from Mason City, Iowa. He's got a life of his own. I bet it could be an important one in its own right. Don't cheat him of it."

The boy had to admit Jeffrey had something there. Even though it was pretty pleasant to be the reincarnation of someone great, the grandest thing of all must be to be great in your own right. But he couldn't let on to Jeffrey that he saw his point. A fellow can't let on he has doubts.

By now the sun was setting. You could look up at the darkening sky and practically see forever. The first stars were coming out. Already a little sliver of a moon was on the rise, clear on the other side of the world from the setting sun.

Jeffrey said he guessed he'd best get the boy home before the lawyerman set the cops on him. All the way back to Mason City they didn't have a word. Jeffrey didn't even ask for the Strat. The boy held it in his lap, on the tail of the Harley, his own electric strapped to his back. He had Jeffrey stop several blocks from the house so the old man wouldn't hear the engine. When he got off the bike he handed over the Strat.

"Here. You keep it safe until the dark age is over."

Jeffrey took it, held it against his hip.

"Get out of here before I grab it away and play That'll Be the Day," the boy told him.

"Don't think I could bear that. Been waiting a long time

now."

The bike idled, sputtered.

"Think about what I told you, buddyroo."

He patted the boy's shoulder, gave a thumb's up.

Paul watched from the road until the red taillight disappeared around the curve. Straightaway he crossed the highway and ran down to Terry's house but the light was out. No doubt the guys were celebrating. Now what? He couldn't go home. The old man would have his skin, for sure.

He walked around the dark fields a bit, looking at the moon and the stars, but there's only so long you can look at them when you've got things on your mind. He wondered what time it was. He thought of visiting some girls he knew but he decided it was probably too late for that, that their fathers wouldn't think well of it.

Whatever hour it was, the old man's probably sitting up waiting, he thought. Well to hell with him.

He sat down in the tall grass to think things over. As night came on the air was cooling fast and it was damp sitting there. He swung his electric around and plunked at it with a bare thumb, listening to the dead notes. After a minute or two he stopped, not much into it.

He felt like a kid, skulking around in the weeds. He ought to march into the house and tell the old man to get off his back, that he was going to play guitar and that was that.

Across the fields he heard the whine of trucks. The cool night air carried sounds a long way over the fields. You couldn't tell how far away the trucks were. Sometimes you thought you were hearing clear across Iowa to the Mississippi. Nights like this the road called to you. Well, Paul thought, if the old man gives me a hard time I can always hit the road. The idea seemed romantic and exciting. To live like the old-time wandering bluesmen, taking up the guitar and roaming the nation's interstates, going wherever the road took you. Wouldn't that be living!

Wasn't it best to get it over with, to face the music? There was always the road. Straightaway he felt better. Besides, he

356

figured he couldn't sit out in the grass forever.

From the front lawn he could see the light burning in the living room. He went in through the front door and started for the stairs. The folks were in the living room. They looked up when he came in. You could tell they'd been talking, since the talk still hung thick in the air.

Paul stopped short of the steps. Gathering himself, he turned, going into the parlor. His mom, in her robe, sat in one of the upholstered chairs. The old man had kicked off his shoes and was leaning back on the sofa, his stocking feet propped up on the coffee table. A tumbler of whisky and ice rested on a coaster on the table by his feet. In his hand, pressed up against his cheek, a filter-tipped Newport burned. He looked hard at the boy.

They were perfectly quiet as he came in, that electric guitar slung loosely across his shoulder. They saw the Superman emblem on his T-shirt, the tail of which hung sloppily from his jeans. His mother, sitting off to the side, could see where his back jeans pocket had been ripped by his fast getaway through the bedroom window. She had to smile but, sensing the intent, angry glare on her son's face, she knew enough to cover her lips with the back of her hand and look to the side.

The boy stalked to the coffee table, opposite his father. He looked down at the table, beside the old man's feet. A stack of report cards were spread out near his mom's cut crystal figurines of cats rubbing themselves up against gate posts and doorways and other things like that. The report cards at the bottom of the stack were the old ones, filled mostly with As and some Bs. The one at the top was the latest. Those Fs really stuck out.

"I don't care what you say," the boy choked out. "It's my life and I'll do what I want."

He expected the old man to start in yelling. But it didn't happen that way.

Mr Stoken had a bemused look on his face.

"When I was your age they called boys like you rebels.

357

You know, I was a little rebellious myself." Mr Stoken said this quietly, his friendly tone taking the boy by surprise. "Why, I once stood up to the most powerful man alive. Eisenhower. Didn't I ever tell you?"

The boy suspiciously shook his head.

Back in '56 President Eisenhower had come to town to meet the party faithful and to grin before the local tv cameras. By then Hollywood had arrived on the Potomac: the era of television demanded something be done with the old soldier's face. Whenever Eisenhower went on these political excursions the Republicans would select a local kid to apply Ike's pancake makeup. Back then Mr Stoken had been eighteen years old. He was chairman of the Cerro Gordo Young Republicans, and the job of smoothing over Ike's wrinkles fell to him.

Everything had gone wrong that day. The presidential party was supposed to fly into Clear Lake Airport, where there would be a welcoming party and speeches, then Ike and his aides would be driven in the airport limousine to the hotel in Mason City, where there would be supper and more speeches. It was a very big day for Mason City. Ike. President of the United States. War hero. Ike was coming to town. You'd have thought it was Santa Claus, the way everybody fussed and ran around. Banners hung all over. Clarence Kelly over at the barber shop had a red-letter week. Everybody dressed like they were going to a burial. Out at the airport they spent four days getting ready, wrapping red, white and blue crepe paper all over everything, all over the ramp they'd roll up to the plane, all over the little terminal, all over everything. They built a platform for the welcoming speeches and wrapped that in red, white and blue bunting too. Then there was the high school marching band. They wrapped the instruments in the stuff. And the airport limousine — they spent two days cleaning it out, waxing and polishing. They even pulled out the backseat and stuck in a new one all because the old one had a little quarter-sized rip in it. They made old Cyril Wiggins, who drove the limousine, get a shave and a haircut, and they made him buy a new brown suit. Nothing was overlooked. Sam Marshall over at the rug shop even chipped in a long red rug to roll out.

Well if something can go wrong it will. The plane carrying the presidential party was forty minutes late. Everybody stood around the hot runway, the band, the mayor, everybody, pulling at their collars, fussing with their girdles, looking at their watches.

They'd made old Cyril wait in the limousine the whole time and since it was such a hot day he naturally began thinking of wetting his whistle. He must have had his flask along, since he got pretty drunk sitting there waiting.

The plane finally touched down, they rolled up the ramp, but someone got it caught in the crepe paper and ripped half of it off. Sam Marshall tried to roll out the red carpet but the plane had taxied closer than expected and he couldn't roll it out all the way. He urgently yelled for his men to give the carpet a tug to take up the slack, but while they were pulling on the thing the plane's hatch opened and Ike himself stepped out. They were still working on the carpet, trying to pull out the lumps and get it to lay straight, when Ike and his men stepped down. Eisenhower hardly even set his heel on it.

Old Cyril Wiggins was never one for speechifying, and while the band played and the speakers spoke he stayed in the limousine pulling on the flask. By the time the speeches were over he was pretty well crocked.

All this happened before America's loss of innocence, back when we used to drive our presidents around in any old car, without bulletproof glass, without bomb shielding. This was just a few years after Harry Truman used to go for those brisk morning walks down Pennsylvania Avenue, just a few years before Jack Kennedy rode through Dallas in a convertible.

Eisenhower and his men were at last led through the crowd to the waiting limousine. Old Cyril saluted in the rearview mirror. He slurred that Ike shouldn't worry, that he'd drive that old bucket of bolts "fit to make Ulysses S. Grant himself proud." He yelled out the window for everyone to clear the hell out of the way less he run them over, for, GOD-DAMNIT, he had old bloody Eisenhower himself in the car. With that he slammed on the gas, greatly alarming the Secret Service agents, who lost no time jumping over the seat and wrestling Cyril away from the wheel.

The result of this was that everything was tremendously behind schedule. Since they wanted to catch the tv cameras in time for the six o'clock news, the president's handlers told him he'd have to get made up before dinner. Missing dinner always made Ike cranky. Often he complained there wasn't any point in being a successful man if you couldn't eat, play golf and go on vacation when you wanted.

Mr Stoken was waiting in the back room at the hotel with the pancake makeup when the presidential party arrived. In a moment the place was swarming with dour-faced Secret Service men in dark suits. A few seconds later, the retinue of White House aides swept in. The speechwriters, looking bored. The aides, looking important. A military adjutant, carrying a small black briefcase that was handcuffed to his wrist, looking like he wanted to slip into the room unnoticed and blend into the woodwork. Another aide came in, this one carrying the presidential seal for the podium in the dining hall, that bald eagle clutching an olive branch in one talon and a bunch of arrows in the other. Out in the hall, above the incessant shuffling of feet, they heard someone say, "This way, Mr President."

Everyone stiffened, just a bit, and their breath caught. All eyes were on the doorway.

In came Eisenhower. He was in one of his fit-to-be-tied moods. His eyes were fiery, his head held low. To sweeten his mood, his aides were practically spinning cartwheels around him.

"That man driving that limousine was inebriated!" Eisenhower steamed. "Who was he?"

"An employee of the airport, Mr President," an aide answered. "Hoover's men are running a complete check on him now. You'll have his file on your desk in the morning."

360

"Well whoever he is I want him fired."

"Yes, Mr President."

The handlers led Eisenhower to the chair in front of the makeup mirror. Someone laid a white apron under his chin.

"To think the leader of the free world got into a car driven by a drunkard!" Eisenhower fumed on. "Unbelievable! What kind of security is that? We'd never tolerate it in the military. Let me tell you one day some kook's going to get too close to a president and then we'll all be sorry. Maybe then Americans will wake up to what this world's about."

"Yes, Mr President."

Eisenhower snapped his fingers.

"Well, where's the boy with the makeup?"

They pushed the boy front and center.

Years later Mr Stoken could still clearly describe that face to his son.

He said what you remembered most were those wrinkles. There were surprisingly few of them for a man of his years but the ones that were there were cut bold and deep, deep as the English Channel. You realized here was a face that had been sculpted by the great events of the twentieth century. The stars and bars on that face weren't earned by the common trials of common men. Those lines were sketched by the heroics of a modern warrior and an American president who served at the zenith of his country's power, and if you looked carefully enough you saw that his face read like a history book of his time, a testament to his trials. If that face could only talk! That deep line there, above the left cheek, under the eye — that was creased in by years of grimacing at the back pain he'd sustained when he'd gamely tried to tackle Jim Thorpe in a West Point football match. The hairline above had been completely outflanked by the time he'd finished learning from MacArthur. The deepest trenches, below there in the cheeks, had been dug in preparation for D-Day. The crow's-feet around the eyes were bought by sending wave after wave of men to scramble like ants up the beaches of Normandy. Through it all, the once-smooth forehead kept crinkling, even as Berlin fell. Then there was the presidency of the United States. It takes a toll on the face. Photographs before and after reveal a startling buildup of wrinklage. Clearly you do not grow younger in the Oval Office. All that heart trouble. Nixon waiting anxiously in the wings. Could any man rest easy? Then there were the top-secret national security problems. You don't talk about them, not even to your wife, but still they show up on your face. As a rule, the more top secret and sensitive, the greater the wrinklage. Secrets; weighty decisions reached in the woodwork; plots and intrigues never seeing the light of day — these too were things that took their tool on that face. Why, for every Francis Gary Powers there must have been thousands more just like him whose names will never reach our ears. And there were wrinkles on Eisenhower's face for things most Americans have no business knowing.

Mr Stoken said he brought his hands up to that face, ready to apply the pancake makeup like he'd been practicing all week to do, but his fingers began to shake uncontrollably. He couldn't bring himself to touch those wrinkles. There sat the most powerful man in the world, right in front of him, and he couldn't stop shaking. He dropped his hands and stepped back.

Eisenhower saw the boy's hands.

"What's the matter, son?"

"The man driving the limousine—," Mr Stoken had choked out, his voice all aflutter. "You don't have to investigate him. I can tell you who he is, Mr President. That's old Cyril Wiggins. Cyril, he might take a drink now and then, but if he does, it's only because that flask of his is all he's got. That flask, and his job driving that limousine —that's all he's got. His wife died in a fire a couple of years back. Ever since we've all kind of looked out for him around here. You can't have him fired, Mr President. Old Cyril, he's not been very lucky in life, not like you. He's never had a parade in his honor, never heard people cheering him on. But he's a good man, if that means anything. He's a good man just the same. Honest he is. And if he were to lose that job he'd have nothing. Don't you see? You'd be destroying him just because he made one stupid mistake—."

Eisenhower leaned forward in the chair. He thrust out a hand, stopping the boy in midsentence.

Everyone in the room had stopped breathing.

"I'm just afraid for him, that's all," the boy sputtered. "Here you are, the most powerful man on earth—." Someone was poking him hard in the ribs from behind, trying to get him to shut up.

All eyes were riveted on the president's granite face, wondering which way things would go.

Then it happened. That famous grin. It broke across Eisenhower's face. Reaching down, he took hold of the boy's trembling hands. His hands felt all solid. Like stone.

"Now let me tell you something son," he said. "There have been times in my life when I've had more fear in me than I thought any one man should ever have to hold. But I never showed it. Never. There was something I had to do and I did it. I trusted somewhere would come the strength to do what had to be done. That's because I was an American and, thank God Almighty, there's pioneering iron in our blood. We Americans have a difficult role in the world today, and that role is bound to become more difficult, for the pioneer's road is never an easy road, but we can never shrink from our responsibilities, never show our fear. We are the pioneers of a bold new future, clearing the way for broad humanity. And I can think of no better people suited for the job than ourselves. We must always remember that we have iron in our blood. Pioneering iron. That's why I'm glad to hear you speak out on behalf of this— this Mr Wiggins. It shows the iron in your blood, and I like that. Between you and me, let's agree to give Mr Wiggins another chance." Eisenhower nodded at an aide. "But this trembling of the hands. Let's see no more of that tommyrot. You have to fix my face for the cameras."

Years later, as Mr Stoken told this story to his son, there was more than a hint of reverence in his eyes as he told how he fixed Ike's face. He described in detail the soft fleshy texture of those cheeks, the lines on that forehead, the strong jaw. Paul couldn't help thinking how oddly American it was. In another country they'd pickle and seal such a man in a glass vacuum bottle so people could see for themselves he wasn't just myth, that he was once real flesh and blood. In America we don't pickle our heroes after they've had their day. We don't set them out in display cases. No, we run them for president and we let our young people touch their faces and apply the pancake makeup so they can tell their kids about it someday, so their kids can tell their kids, so the memory never completely fades, so distant generations will know their fathers were real, with real hands that trembled, with real faces worn by troubles, just like them.

"Since that day I've never forgotten what Eisenhower told me," Mr Stoken said to his son. "It's okay to be afraid, but never show it. All my life, when things got tough, I told myself to be more like Eisenhower. Gentle on the outside, yet tough as granite on the inside. He had hidden strengths. Always try to be like Eisenhower, son, try to be like Eisenhower."

The boy felt patronized. This advice sounded ridiculous. He had no inclination to model himself after a World War II general, and he told his father as much. He said he had other heroes, heroes that had never spilled a drop of blood.

"Like whom?"

The boy pointed at the emblem on his shirt.

"Superman, for one. He never kills nobody. Then there's Spiderman, and the Silver Surfer."

"They're not real. They're all comic book characters. Made up. You know that, Pauley."

"You have your heroes and I have mine." The boy said it was funny this business of hidden strengths had been brought up. He wondered aloud why it was that Superman hides behind Clark Kent. "Why do you suppose he doesn't he go to work at the Daily Planet dressed as Superman?"

"Honestly, Paul," Mrs Stoken said. "Sometimes I don't know how you think up these things."

"I'm serious, Mom. Don't you find it all peculiar that

364

Superman, the strongest man on earth, has to change into his costume in a dingy broom closet? Haven't you ever stopped to wonder about it? What's he got to hide? Is he ashamed of those muscles or something? Even more peculiar is the way most Americans never think twice about it. Like it's the most natural thing in the world for a fellow to step into a broom closet and assume a hidden identity. There's something absolutely sinister about this Clark Kent business, if you ask me. I just can't stop thinking about it. Everywhere I go these days I've been asking people why they think it is Superman doesn't come to work at the Daily Planet dressed as Superman."

Mr Stoken played along.

"For one thing I'd bet he'd look pretty silly hanging around the water cooler in those blue tights and red cape."

"I'm serious, Dad. I think there's something real strange about this Clark Kent business, and if the Russians or somebody ever were to get to the bottom of it they'd find out an awful lot about the psyche of Americans. Why does Superman sneak around pretending to be some wimp named Clark Kent? They never explained that in the comic books."

"Sure they did," Mrs Stoken said. She rolled her eyes up and off to the side, remembering. She had a terrific memory for trivia like this. She could recite the names of all five little Peppers. "When I was a little girl they explained it in the comic books this way: they said the Kents — they were the old man and the woman who came across Superman as a baby in that rocket out in a field and raised him — the Kents told him he must hide his great strength or people would be afraid of him, but that one day the time would come when he must use his strength to help people. Until then, they told him to hide his strength away so he could live among them."

The boy repeated her words like they held much hidden meaning.

"So he could live among them? Is that why you want me to live a normal life, to go to school like everybody else and forget about playing guitar and becoming a cult hero? So I can

365

live among normal people?"

Mr Stoken said the boy had to admit there weren't very many cult heroes living in the neighborhood. But he said that wasn't the only reason why he was concerned about the boy's low grades. Far from it. He said education was all-important in today's world. A body couldn't get by without it, he said. They wanted their son to have every possible advantage because, he said, they loved him.

The boy said it was a lie. They didn't give a hang about him, he said, and if they did they wouldn't always be giving him such a hard time.

Mr Stoken rose from the sofa, a little wobbly, stepped over the coffee table and embraced his son. Paul stood uncomfortably in his father's arms, not knowing what to do. He could smell the whisky on the old man's breath. He wished he'd let go.

The old man told the boy never to think they didn't love him, as they loved him more than he could know. He said he and Mrs Stoken probably were a lot like most Americans. They found it hard to express their true feelings, but they were there, beneath the surface, just the same. The boy should never doubt it. If sometimes they did things he didn't understand it was just the twisted way the true feelings had of coming out.

"Let go of me!" the boy finally put out, breaking away. "You're suffocating me!"

He stood by the curtains, his back turned.

Mrs Stoken implored her son to be reasonable. She came up behind him and laid her cheek on his shoulder. She said he didn't have to study law, not if his heart wasn't in it. She fielded a piercing glare from her husband. She told the boy he could go away to music school, to some conservatory back East.

"That's not to dissuade you from thinking about jurisprudence," Mr Stoken put in. "There's plenty of people who don't know what they want in life going to law school. Believe me, son, if you don't know what you're doing in life it can't hurt to be making a hundred and twenty-five thousand dollars a year while you're wondering."

The boy said money wasn't important to him.

"Now just a minute son," Mr Stoken said. He pulled up his belt. "There's nothing wrong with money."

"It's all I hear from you. Money and school. Money and school!"

The boy paced back and forth, rubbing the back of his neck.

"Honey what else is there?" Mrs Stoken said. "Someday you'll find a nice girl and settle down in a home of your own."

"What else is there is right!"

"Now, Pauley, what your mother says has some sense," Mr Stoken choked. "I can see, if your heart's really not into it, your not having to study law." Those were hard words for Mr Stoken to say. He'd always kept alive the secret hope that his son would give up rock 'n' roll and go on to become the chief justice of the Supreme Court.

"Who can say?" Mr Stoken wondered. "Maybe one day we'll have our own Stravinsky or Gershwin in the family."

"Dad," the boy said, dismissing the suggestion with a wave, "the most successful composers in the world weren't Stravinsky or Gershwin. They're John Lennon and Paul McCartney."

"Lennon and McCartney? Did they write for Broadway?"

"They're the Beatles, Dad." The boy threw up his hands and shook his head. "Oh what's the use?"

"So go to school and learn to compose like this Lennon and McCartney."

"You can't learn to do that in any school. Lennon and McCartney never even bothered learning to read music!"

"Well how did they compose?"

"Better than anyone else, that's how. They had imagination."

"School isn't going to hurt your imagination any."

"I haven't time for school. Do you realize Lennon and McCartney had written some great songs by the time they were my age, when they were just kids? And here I am, seventeen years old, and what do I have to show for my years?"

"Maybe these Beatles had special talent," Mr Stoken allowed.

"It's nice of you to come around to that point of view," the boy steamed. "More than ten years after Ed Sullivan, the queen of England and the rest of the world recognized the Beatles had special talent, it's magnanimous of you to come around. Did you ever stop to think I might want to be on the Ed Sullivan Show myself, that I'd like to be knighted by the queen?"

"But, honey, Ed Sullivan's dead," Mrs Stoken said.

The boy looked shook.

"And, ahem, as for the knight part— forget it," said Mr Stoken. He drank from his glass. "Americans aren't allowed titles. There's no royalty over here. That's why I say, Prince Charming, you better go to school."

"Don't call me Prince Charming."

"I'm sorry, Pauley, it's only because I don't—."

"And don't call me Pauley. God how I hate that!"

"It's only because I hate to see you deluding yourself."

"I hate to see you deluding yourselves! Can't you see how much I hate it here?" the boy finally lashed out. "Living like this!" He held out his arms at all the living room furniture.

"What's wrong with the way we live?" Mrs Stoken asked. "Do you mean the slipcovers? We can get new slipcovers if you don't like these." She said it just so happened she'd been thinking about new slipcovers for the sofa and the chairs herself, and she pulled a sample of swatches from behind the curtain to show the boy. "Now this is a lovely pattern but it's so dear I'd almost hate to sit on it. We'd have to get plastic slipcovers to put over the new slipcovers."

The boy pulled at his hair.

"No, Mom, I'm not talking about slipcovers." He pushed the swatches away. "There's something else missing, something that can't be pasted out on a swatch board. Life. There's no life here! Sometimes when I'm eating breakfast and Dad's reading the paper and you're talking away about some special coupon offer you got in the mail I just want to scream. I just want to haul off and scream just to make sure I'm still alive and it's all I can do to fight it. We sit together at the table dead still not saying anything. Everything is as quiet and still as that sofa over there. Sooner or later everything here will be covered in plastic slipcovers. Well not me. I don't want to wake up one morning covered in plastic."

"Now Paul don't be ridiculous."

"I'm not being ridiculous. Near as I can find words, it's like that bad tooth Dad's been bellyaching about to everyone who'll listen."

Mr Stoken had managed to put the tooth out of his head, as it were. Now they saw his tongue roving over his molar, under cover of his cheek, darting around like a mouse under a rug.

"When Dad said they opened the tooth and found a dead nerve do you know what came into my mind? I pictured the inside of the tooth as a living room, with slipcovers and sofas and chairs and everything, and there was the poor nerve, lying dead in one of the armchairs, slumped over, no more than a skeleton."

"How do you think of these things, Paul?" his mother asked.

"He certainly doesn't get it from my side of the family," Mr Stoken said. He was taking a few more painkillers from the bottle on the table. "Now that uncle of yours. What's his name? Osgood or something. The crank who wanted to bring outdoor ice hockey to Florida."

"Uncle Osgood was just a little ahead of his time, is all."

"I'll say. About ten thousand years ahead of the next ice age, he was."

The boy paced back and forth.

"I imagined Dad going around with that dead nerve in his tooth, with all that living room furniture sliding around in there, inside the tooth, and the dentist opened it up and found the nerve lying dead on the sofa—."

"I assure you son," Mr Stoken laughed, "it was nothing

369

like that."

"Don't you see I'm talking symbolically, Dad? If a man can go around without knowing the nerve in his tooth's dead what's to keep him from knowing when the brain in his head has shriveled up and died, or when the spark has gone out of his life? I don't want somebody to open up my life and find the spark's gone out. I can't live like this. Don't you see? Someone's gone and squeezed all the life out of us. Somehow it's all been reduced to money. Money and school."

"As people get older and more successful they want to reward themselves with a few creature comforts. I see nothing wrong with that."

"Come on Dad. Isn't this taking it to the extreme?"

The boy charged to the closet near the kitchen. He threw open the door and a wall of paper towels fell out, followed by a cascade of canned peas. Everything rolled all over the floor.

"It's the same out in the kitchen, and down in the basement and out in the garage. Everywhere, cans stacked sky high, and more paper towels than you'll need to wipe up a supertanker spill. It's got to stop, Mom. Don't you see it's got to stop?"

"Things are less expensive when you buy in bulk," Mrs Stoken said. "You have no idea how much money I've saved by buying these things." Already she was down on her knees, gathering up the cans.

"Mom it's like this. One of the guys in the band, Doug—his old man got laid off at the brick factory and I know they've been having rough times. How do you think he feels when you come in all loaded down with cans? You've got enough food stacked in the garage to feed the Fifth Army, when some of the friends I bring over don't know how they'll eat next week."

Mrs Stoken looked genuinely concerned.

"I didn't know Mr Lowery wasn't working. Why didn't you tell me? You could have given Doug some food to take home."

She started handing cans to the boy. He looked disbelievingly at them.

"Ah Mom they don't want handouts!" He dropped the cans.

"Now why'd you do that? I'll only have to pick them up again."

"Ah Mom forget about the cans for a minute will you? Will you look at me and forget about the cans?" He rubbed a hand through his hair, his face inflamed. "What's the use? You haven't heard a thing I've said, have you? Sometimes it's like you're both on automatic pilot. Set it and forget it."

Mr Stoken said he's heard about all he was going to hear. He leveled his most piercing stare at the boy. "How do you intend supporting yourself without a college degree?"

The boy said he'd already given it some thought, that he'd been thinking of reviving the calling of bluesman.

"Now Pauley don't be ridiculous!" Mr Stoken chortled. "People just don't go around singing for their supper anymore."

Paul said that showed how much he knew. "Bluesmen were just poor black boys but man they traveled about everywhere like rich men, like kings, making the road their home, living off the land, going from one shantytown to the next, where people would fight for the honor and privilege of putting them up for the night."

Mr Stoken held his head in his hands and rolled his eyes skyward. It was all he could do to contain himself. Laughing, he told the boy he could never hope to be a bluesman.

"And why not?" Paul fumed.

"For one thing, you're not a poor black boy."

The boy appeared shaken. He looked every bit as disconcerted as when his mother had pointed out Ed Sullivan was dead. It seemed like all the cards were stacked against him.

Angered, he choked out, "Well that's what I'm gonna do!"

He said he'd always been told the color of a man's skin wasn't important, that it was the strength of a man's character that counted, that a body could do whatever he set his mind to. Wasn't that true? he asked his father.

Mr Stoken was stuck for words. "Well, in principle, yes.

There's nothing to stop any man from becoming a doctor or a lawyer or even president of the United States. But what you're talking about here is insane, son."

Well that was too bad, the boy said, because he had a good mind to hit the road and become a bluesman, whether his parents approved or not.

Mrs Stoken clamped her arms around him. She said she'd never let him go. She couldn't sleep nights knowing her baby was out there tramping the interstates with a guitar. She'd put bars on his bedroom window if that's what she had to do.

"Oh no you won't!" the boy shot back, breaking free. "I'm not one of your china vases that you can lock up and wire to the burglar alarm!"

Mr Stoken said of course they couldn't lock him up. Good as the idea might sound. He said his only hope sprang from the fact they'd raised him to know the difference between right and wrong, and when the time came they'd have to trust he'd do the right thing.

"Jeffrey put this idiotic idea into your head, didn't he?" Mr Stoken came out with at last. It'd begun to dawn on him that his son was seriously thinking of becoming an itinerant bluesman. "The nerve of that bum telling my son to hit the road! Doesn't he have any sense of responsibility?"

"Uncle Jeff has nothing to do with it," the boy answered. "It just so happens he tried to talk me out of it."

"Yeah I bet!" Mr Stoken raged. Now he was the one pacing. "Wait'll I see Jeffrey. I'll give that good-for-nothing little brother of mine a piece of my mind."

He never got the chance. That night Jeffrey was seen drinking in a bar outside town. He sat off to himself in a dark corner, mumbling like a madman into his whisky and beer, and when the barmaid brought refills she heard him mumbling, "Haven't I paid enough? Why bring him into it? Why bring him into it?" He grew more agitated as the night ground on, mumbling louder with every round of drinks, till everyone in the place could hear. He became belligerent, yelling when

372

the barmaid wasn't quick to refill his glasses, pounding the table with a crutch, declaring he was a veteran of a foreign war trying to get through the darkest night of his life and such a man deserved a drink. The owner came over and asked if he didn't think he'd already had enough. Those sitting at the bar and in the booths looked over, expecting trouble, but it didn't happen that way. Jeffrey looked up, unsteadily. He smiled. He had to agree. He'd undoubtedly had enough, he said. Quite more than enough actually. To settle the bill he handed over all his money — eighty some crumpled dollars, though he owed less than ten. The owner tried to return the excess, but Jeffrey refused, saying it was his style to tip extravagantly. He rose unsteadily from the table, gathering his things, bracing himself with the crutch, taking a large burlap bag resting in the chair beside him and sliding its strap over his shoulder so that the bag hung behind him. Then, looking up, brushing a wild shock of hair from his face, he saw every eye in the place on him. "I guess you're wondering what brings a man to these circumstances," he wheezed, looking in turn at the ones at the bar and those scattered around in the booths. "It's what comes of fighting for you, my friends. It's what comes of fighting for you."

Straightening himself, leveling his chin, he turned for the door, moving slowly across the floorboards. They heard a motorcycle starting up out front. Someone asked who he was. Someone said he was just another one of those poor fools who'd got his leg shot off in Vietnam. Next thing someone at the bar said it wasn't right for the barkeep to put him out. The poor fellow wasn't hurting anyone sitting off to himself mumbling. Maybe they should have put up with it, he said. It was the least they could do for a guy who needed a quiet place, someone else said. One of the women got up from the bar and said she didn't care what the others thought, she was going to bring that poor man back in and sit with him until he sobered up. No man had any business on the road in such a condition, she said. She asked the barmaid to make some coffee, then went out.

She told the police she'd gone only seconds too late. She managed a glimpse of him riding off on a motorcycle onto the darkened highway. She stood for a moment under the neon sign listening to the bike accelerate, following the red taillight as it glided over the surface of the road. Then came the shower of white sparks shooting out behind the taillight, which itself took on wild spinning gyrations, intensifying, so that at last the looping taillight and the sparks shooting out behind looked very much like a shooting star rocketing over the roadbed. Everything went dark then, and ghostly quiet.

The strange thing about it, she said, was how long it took the sound to come up. After what seemed like an eternity spent holding her breath she heard the screech of rubber and the tearing of metal. Funny, she said, she didn't have to hear the sound of the crash to know for sure. When she'd seen that spark going out across the road somehow she'd known someone had died.

Late that night the police came to Grandma and Grandpa Stoken's house. The old folks came to the door in their robes and slippers. When they were told their son had been killed in a road accident they were very upset, but as the deputy talked on about the motorcycle wiping out in gravel Grandma Stoken calmed herself, then brought a hand to her mouth.

"You mean Jeffey?" she said. "My little Jeffey's dead?"

Grandpa Stoken rubbed his rough hand across his lips, snorting, "Ah that boy ain't no son of mine. He was coming to this long ago." His head tremored from his nervous tick.

The deputy seemed surprised. He said they'd recovered a few things from the wreck and they'd need someone to sign the papers. Naturally they thought the deceased's closest known kin would want to take possession of his belongings. He held up a large burlap bag.

"Looks like your son played guitar," he said, opening the bag. He pulled out a red electric guitar. Grandma and Grampa froze. "The boys at the station tell me it's a good one too. A

Stratocaster, it's called. Practically an antique, they say. Worth a little something. One thing for sure, your boy did value it."

He noted the burlap bag had hardly been scratched by the crash. "You know, the way he took that fall made you think his only concern was looking out for this guitar. Everything else was pretty well tore up. But not this. It was in his arms."

The deputy pointed at the face of the guitar, at several deep scratches. Gashes, really. They didn't appear to be recent marks, he observed, since you could see they had been polished over. Had this guitar ever been in another crash? the deputy asked the old people in an offhand way. Grampa Stoken's head trembled, his jaw hanging open. He was looking fearfully at the gashes on the guitar. Grandma Stoken's eyes widened. She snatched the guitar away from the deputy, and the burlap bag too.

"The boy's dead," she said. "Can't we let it rest there?"

She slid the guitar into the gunnysack and held it by its neck, out away from her, not getting too close.

From his pocket the deputy produced a mangled wallet. It was one of those oversized biker's wallets on a chain, ripped to shreds and empty of money. "The only thing in it was this." The deputy picked out an identification card. It was a 1955 membership card to *Boys' Life* magazine. Grandma Stoken took it. She held it up into the light.

"This card entitles the bearer to full privileges in the official Life Saver's Club," she read aloud slowly. "The undersigned pledges always to be prepared to save lives...." Her voice caught when she saw the faded ink of her son's signature.

The deputy took out an envelope stuffed with cash. He laid it in her hands. Before the accident the deceased had overpaid his bar tab, he explained, and the proprietor of the bar where the deceased had been drinking felt badly. The rest of the money — a little over two hundred dollars — had been collected from the other patrons in the bar. They wanted the money passed on to whoever cared for him. For flowers for the grave or whatever.

375

And ah yes, one more thing, the deputy said. Maybe the most important. The deceased had happened to mention something to the waitress about being a veteran of a foreign war. Well the deputy said he'd taken the liberty of calling the records office at the veteran's administration in Des Moines and had learned Jeffrey Stoken had some war medals coming. A Congressional Medal of Honor, a Distinguished Service Cross, and a Purple Heart. They were the most important medals his country could bestow but, for some reason, he'd never claimed them.

"Your boy was a war hero," the deputy said. "Right here in Mason City we had a hero living among us and we never knew it."

The deputy said this being the case, the Stokens should expect a thorough investigation into the circumstances surrounding the hero's death. Although foul play wasn't suspected, the deceased had apparently been upset shortly before his accident, and the mayor's office wanted to make certain the hometown hero hadn't been maltreated by anyone.

Late that night, well before dawn, Grandma and Grandpa Stoken drove into town to the flophouse where Jeffrey had had a room. They got the landlord out of bed to open the door. They practically tore Jeffrey's room apart looking for something, though the landlord hadn't a clue what they'd been searching for, or whether they'd found anything.

In the morning it was all in the paper about Jeffrey's tragic end. One of the reporters working for the paper called to Washington DC, to the Pentagon, to find out what exactly Jeffrey had done to earn his medals. "While on routine patrol PFC Jeffrey Stoken risked life and limb, far above the call of duty, to save his lieutenant officer and fellow soldiers from an incoming enemy grenade," Jeffrey's citation read. It went on to say this act of uncommon valor cost Private Stoken his leg. The grateful lieutenant he'd saved, who since had risen to command rank in the United States Army, highly recommended the Medal of Honor.

All this, on the front page of the paper. There was also a photo of Jeffrey, except it was from the 1959 high school yearbook, when he'd been about fifteen or sixteen, before his hair had gone long, before he'd grown that shaggy beard, before that wild look had completely possessed his eyes, before he'd ever set foot in Vietnam. He looked like an innocent boy and it was hard to picture him as a hero performing manly acts of glory on the field of honor.

All that day visitors came calling at Jeffrey's parents' house. Grandma and Grandpa Stoken received them in the parlor. The two old folks sat in their Sunday best on either side of a card table they'd arranged in the middle of the room. An old hand-tinted photo of Jeffrey leaned up against a bouquet of wildflowers. Here again you'd be hard pressed to imagine a war hero, as it was a picture of a chipper boy of eight or nine in a Cub Scout uniform. His cheeks were tinted rosy pink.

"One Christmas we all went out looking for a tree together," Grandma Stoken said to one of the callers. "Jeffrey brought his little sled along and we all took turns going down the hills. My the fun we had together."

Grandpa Stoken dug out a black star poster left over from World War II. He hung it in the front window. It's what you did when a World War II hero died, he said. He wondered aloud why they never bothered distributing updated versions for dead Vietnam heroes. He said bitterly if a man was going to sacrifice a son for his country the least they could do was give him a lousy poster with a little stinking star on it. But mostly he sat beside the table saying nothing, his head quivering, watching the tv which all the while blazed in the corner. Not only did he have a nervous tick in the neck, his memory was fading and he had a hard time keeping up with conversation. From time to time he would look up and break into whatever was being said, offering some incongruous remark or another. At one point, as Grandma Stoken was remembering to some cousins how handsome Jeffrey looked at his first communion, Grampa Stoken looked up from the tv and said as far as he was concerned this country had gone to hell when they'd taken Bonanza off the air, and things had only gone from bad to worse now that Gunsmoke was gone too. He said, with much disbelief, he'd heard Lawrence Welk might also get the ax.

"At times like this, if I could only see Hoss and Little Joe riding tall in the saddle into the Ponderosa I would know things was all right with the world," he whistled.

The sheriff and a deputy came to see Paul at his parents' house. The sheriff was a large man who forced himself to smile a lot. He said he'd heard the boy had been with the war hero on the day he died. What had they'd talked about? Had his uncle seemed upset about anything? The boy replied that if the sheriff really cared to find out about Jeff he should ask his jailer.

"Why do you say that, son?" the sheriff said, forcing one of his smiles.

"Because I hear you used to throw the war hero into the drunk tank twice a week."

The smile slipped from the sheriff's face.

It seemed like the whole town turned out for Jeffrey's funeral. At the cemetery Terry Turner came solemnly to the edge of the large gathering. Craning his neck, he caught sight of the Stokens, standing beside the open grave. At the fore stood Mr Stoken, decked out in his best dark court suit, trying to look as respectable and bedrock solid as always, yet coming off shaken and uncertain. He seemed a half a bubble off plumb. Beside him, Mrs Stoken cried into a hanky. Beside her, Grampa Stoken, his head all atremble under an American Legionnaire's cap, an Old Glory pin in his lapel, and next to him, Grandma Stoken, her face ashen, downlooking. At the very end of the line stood Paul, his hands in his pockets, a black carnation in his lapel, his foot tapping out the beat to some rhythm in his head. Terry cut through the crowd, coming to stand beside Paul.

The monsignor himself said a few words. He said birth was a mystery and death was a mystery. He said life itself was a mystery, and most of them shook their heads to that. Yes it was all one big mystery as far as he was concerned, and he said that was because the Lord, He works in mysterious ways.

He said a body needn't look any further than that casket holding the lifeless body of Jeffrey to see the mysteriousness of God at work. He said it was a complete mystery to him why such a fine young man, such an outstanding pillar of his community as Jeffrey Stoken, would be called away at such an early age. He said it seemed like only yesterday he'd given little Jeffrey his first communion. He said he remembered when little Jeffrey used to come to church every week on the hand of his parents and his brother. Of course, Jeffrey had stopped going to church as soon as he was old enough to smoke cigarettes, back in '57 or '58, but listening to the monsignor talk you'd have thought he was a churchgoer up to the very end.

He painted Jeffrey as a war hero, a kind of modern-day crusader. He said today's young people could take a lesson from his sacrifices. "Jeffrey saw his duty to God and country and he performed it, though it cost him much. He lost a leg, but I can imagine how he must have felt repaid when he came home from Vietnam and saw just how much gratitude and appreciation we had for him in our eyes." They all nodded to that. The monsignor waxed over something about Jeffrey having had some difficult days there at the end, and about how the community had done its best to give him guidance in his hour of need. He went on like that, making everyone feel less guilty about the way they'd treated him all those years, till everybody started feeling better about themselves. The way the monsignor went on about the fine way Mason City had treated Jeffrey you'd have thought he'd held the post of mayor or at least had been the town banker. You'd have scarcely guessed he'd been the crazy-eyed town misfit.

At last the monsignor said the outside world could never

know half of just how well they had treated their hometown hero. They all said amen to that, and then the monsignor drove a small wooden cross into the loose dirt by the headstone. He drove the cross in with his heel and an altar boy had to steady him so he wouldn't trip over his cassock.

Then Grampa Stoken asked the commander of the local American Legion post if he cared to say a few words. This fellow had a mottled complexion and a pot belly. Like Grampa Stoken, he wore a legionnaire's cap, while in his hands a small American flag fluttered in the soft breeze. Behind him stood a contingent of legionnaires, mostly of World War II vintage (though some rickety Great War survivors were sprinkled in) and they listened attentively and nodded their heads as their commander spoke.

He said he couldn't agree with the monsignor more, that His Eminence had hit it right on the button when he'd said today's young people could take a lesson from what had happened to Jeffrey. He said Jeffrey's life exemplified what this country was all about. "A young man who never questioned authority, who knew his duty to his country and never forgot it."

He went on to paint Jeffrey in the same heroic colors used by the monsignor, so that by the time he was through you could've sworn he was talking about Audie Murphy, single-handedly knocking out dozens of tanks on the French plains, or Teddy Roosevelt, leading his charge up San Juan Hill.

He'd communicated with Washington, he said, and had learned of the daring exploits committed by Jeffrey on the field of glory and honor. He said at the time Jeffrey's detachment was bravely engaged in holding off an entire company of godless red insurgents, whom he described as Neanderthal-like tribesmen who "didn't give a lick for the time-honored conventions and rules of manly warfare.

"One of the enemy got lucky," he choked out, "landing a grenade beside Jeffrey's commanding officer, and PFC Stoken gallantly placed himself between the enemy grenade and his comrade-in-arms." While he told this story the womenfolk

380

cringed. That's why, the post commander concluded, he had no patience for spineless anti-war protesters, "not when there are such fine upstanding true blue specimens of American manhood as Jeffrey Stoken here." He patted the side of the casket. Anyway, he said this magnificent ceremony — the flags, the honor guard, the turnout of mourning townsmen — all this should make it plain to every young person what they too could look forward to if they too would answer the call of their country.

He said he and his brother legionnaires would always be happy to stick up for their beloved brothers in their final hour of earthy need, and if anybody else wanted an honor guard at their burial all he had to do was call the post. With that he plunged the small stars and stripes into the earth, beside the wooden cross at the head of the grave.

Just when it seemed the circumstances of Jeffrey's life had been so completely and irreparably distorted, misrepresented and twisted that they might never be straightened, and as everyone stared down at the open grave, a pair of feet kicked the flag and the cross from the dirt. Terry saw with alarm that the feet belonged to Paul.

"It's all lies!" Paul lashed out, tears streaming down his cheeks. "Another American threw the grenade that took Jeffrey's leg. My uncle was fragged! He didn't believe in war and he didn't believe in fighting or killing. You all made him go to Vietnam. You all as good as fragged him yourselves!"

"Peter Paul Stoken!" Mr Stoken gasped. "Now you listen here!"

"No, you listen. You and others like you destroyed Jeffrey with your double-talk."

The boy pointed at the monsignor. "You wouldn't give my uncle the time of day when he was alive!

"And you legionnaires—" he pointed at the post commander. "You wouldn't even meet Jeff at the airport when he got back from Vietnam.

"You all ought to be ashamed of yourselves. Lying to yourselves about the way you treated Jeff." Bending, he scooped the cross and the flag from the dust and held them up. "You people aren't here today to bury Jeff. You're here to bury your own guilt. You come and put these empty symbols on his grave now that he's dead when you should have felt them in your hearts when he was alive. Why do you place on graves the symbols of things that have died in your hearts? Like that eternal flame your generation put on John Kennedy's grave. You let the flame go out in your hearts. It would've been better to let one little corner of Arlington Cemetery remain in the dark if you would've kept even the tiniest of flames burning in your hearts."

The boy let the cross and the flag drop into the dust.

"You let the flame go out of your hearts. My uncle Jeff, he was a keeper of the flame. I see that now. And now that he's gone, I just don't know who can keep the flame alive. I just don't know."

They watched him wipe his cheek. Terry came up and rested a hand on his shoulder, whispering, "Why don't we cut out?"

But the boy saw his grandparents leaving the grave. He ran after his grandmother, saying to her, "Jeff had a guitar with him the night he wiped out. A very old electric guitar. What happened to it? I've got to know."

"That devil guitar!" she muttered into the air. "I know where he got it. Stole it from the dead and the curse was on him from the day he did. Well no more. The night his punishment caught up with him we had to search his room for that case it came in. Thank God I remembered seeing it all those years back. It had the name of that boy on it, and Jeffrey didn't care one bit about the shame it would bring his family if it was found. Well no one's going to get to that guitar now."

"What have you done?"

"It's what we're gonna do!" Grampa Stoken answered, his head shaking. "So help me after this damn burial's out of the way I'm gonna bust that devil guitar into a hundred million pieces with my ax. No one's gonna play that guitar again. I'm sending it back to the flames of hell, to the devil, where it belongs. Because after I bust it up I'm gonna burn it!"

The boy stepped back. His eyes caught Terry's.

"Come on!"

The two of them ran into a stand of trees, leaving the cross and the flag lying beside each other in the dust at the grave.

Running full speed it didn't take the boys long to reach his grandparents' house. Terry stood lookout while Paul ran inside. The boy scrambled up the stairs, going first to his uncle's childhood bedroom, looking under the bed.

No dice.

"Hurryup!" he heard Terry yelling from down below in the yard. "I think I see them coming!"

To his grandparents' room he charged, checking the closet smelling of mothballs and old fur, then under their old poster bed, almost frantic. Still no guitar.

"Paul! It *is* them! They're coming!"

The boy hurried to the open window. Below, in the sun-parched yard, Terry pointed down the road. A string of cars appeared. They mustn't have even waited to stick him in the ground.

"Damn!" Paul had his hands on the sill, his head stuck between the sheer curtains that wisped around in the breeze. He was still breathing hard from the run.

"You better hurry!"

"I don't know where else to look!"

"He said he'd burn it, didn't he?" Then, "Look! There's smoke coming from the chimney. In June? Check downstairs, quick! The furnace!"

Paul swept back the curtain and leaned halfway out the window. Black smoke poured from the chimney. Why hadn't they seen it when they were running through the grass to the house?

The line of cars drew near the driveway. About twenty or thirty cars. Each had its headlights on, and one of those little purple burial flags on its antenna. The car up front, the boy saw, was his father's station wagon, followed by his grandparents' Buick.

"Shit!"

Terry flattened himself against the azalea bushes.

Paul bounded away from the window and bolted down the creaky steps, flying through the old house with all the spirit of a wild bird, hearing through the open windows the sounds of the cars filing into the gravelly driveway outside, passing the formless shapes of tables and sofas and chairs and refrigerator, down into the dank damp basement smelling of potatoes and mildew and earth and the scent of coal smoke. The black coal burner glowed full out. Its heavy cast iron door hung open so that you could see the orange conflagration raging within while black smoke curled from the top of the opening, fouling the air. It was hot as deuces down there. A single yellowbulb burned overhead in the rotting wooden rafters and as the boy stepped before the furnace sweat glistened down his face and he could see it splattering onto the compacted dirt floor.

"Come on man! Shake a leg!" Terry pleaded through the cracks in the wood of the basement door.

A row of splintery rotting wood shelves hung on the far walls. The boy moved his hands furiously in and around the shelves, past the dusty boxes, the cobwebs, the rattling ancient elixir bottles and Mason jars filled with rusty nails and screws and whatnots, past a mousetrap that nearly caught his finger when it went off with a loud snap, but nothing. No guitar.

"Oh please. Please."

He stuck his head into the coal bin. His heart skipped a beat. There it was! The gunnysack and, beside it, an old ax. He felt light as a feather.

"Found it!" he yelled, but not before he heard car doors slam.

"Hurry!"

Paul picked up the ax, flung it across the floor.

Opening the gunnysack, he slid out the guitar, his eyes afire. Still in one piece.

"Oh I do believe in magic!"

384

"Come on, Paul!"

He slid the Strat back into the sack. It wasn't until then that he saw it. Leaning against the coal shute, off to one side. Handtooled. Leather. A guitar case. Inscribed: Buddy Holly.

It only took a few seconds more to pack the guitar into its rightful case, and then a few more to fasten down the clamps, and when he tightened his hand around the leather handle he felt instantly better. More than that. For a second or two he even dared to feel superhuman, unstoppable, but all that changed when he reached the bulkhead door. It was locked! His breath left him. Terry pulled frantically from the outside, Paul pushed from the inside, but it was only good for a lot of noise.

"It's locked!"

Terry kept pulling but it was no good. Paul slid his excited hand along the splintery doorframe until he came to a padlock.

"It's padlocked!"

He pulled futilely on the lock, with all his strength. Through the cracks in the old wood he could see Terry's silhouette. He saw him looking towards the driveway.

Paul reached for the ax on the dirt floor.

"Stand back!" he yelled. "I'm gonna bust out!"

He hauled back as far as he could and let go a hard smash against the wood door. There was a crash, but hardly any damage, and the axhead ended up wedged tightly between two wood planks. He pulled wildly at the ax.

"Forget it!" Terry moaned. "Here they all come into the house!"

"Please!" the boy prayed, trying to free the ax. It was boiling hot down there but he was cold with fear. "Don't let it die here, in the hands of these people. You can't let it die!"

Abandoning the ax, he bolted past the hot blazing furnace, tripping up the steps to the kitchen. Almost at the back door he stopped, listening. There was a loud scraping sound, drawing close. He moved to the window and saw his father dragging an ice chest up the back walk. Pop bottles rattled inside and the old man groaned as he struggled with the chest.

"Damn!"

The boy watched the old man struggle up the steps to the back porch, pulling the ungainly chest up one step at a time, his face all sweaty and red.

Now Paul was running through the house, listening to each rattly thud of the ice chest as the old man banged up the steps. He went to the front door, but heard a key turning in the lock, and the voices of his grandparents and others on the front porch stamping their feet on the mat before coming in.

The boy heard the old man opening the back door, groaning from the strain of his load. Backstepping, clutching the guitar case close to his chest, feeling the grain of the leather with his fingers, he came up against the banister. Turning, he tore up the stairs, just as the front door opened.

Into Jeffrey's room he flew, throwing the screen from the window. It overlooked the side of the house away from the road. Terry stood anxiously down below, looking around the corner at the arriving guests. He looked surprised when Paul whistled from the upstairs window.

"I'll have to jump!"

"You better drop it down to me first." Terry, his face upturned and anxious, pointed at the guitar case.

"No. I got it."

Paul surveyed the drop. It was a good twelve or thirteen feet, but into soft grass.

"I must be going up in the world. I keep jumping from higher windows."

Behind him he heard what sounded like his grandmother's feet coming spiritedly up the steps. He knew it didn't matter. In another few seconds he'd be gone. It'd be a long time before he saw this place again, he suspected. Sitting on the windowsill he had to turn for one last look. He swept his eyes across Jeffrey's old room. After all these years they'd still kept his old college pennants tacked to the wall. And a Beatles poster, up over the bed.

"For christsakes *come on!*"

386

Paul tossed his black carnation onto the bed.

"You did more than you had to," he said, as if his uncle was watching from the bed. "Above and beyond the call of duty."

The footsteps drew near the room. But it didn't matter. The next second he was falling through air, holding tight to the handtooled leather guitar case. The ground rushed up and he felt the stinging in his ankles. He crashed down onto his knees, his feet out to both sides. Somehow he'd managed to cushion the guitar in his arms.

"You all right?"

"Yeah. Let's get the hell out of here."

Grandma Stoken came into the room and saw the black carnation on the bed. She picked it up, sniffing. The window hung open, curtains blowing, the screen on the floor like it had been blown out. She went to the window. The two boys were running through the tall grass into the trees.

Run they did, through the trees, over roads and fields high with corn, splashing across murmuring creeks, not stopping till they put at least two miles between themselves and that old house. When at last they stopped in the middle of a thicket and doubled over in exhaustion, Terry looked up and examined the guitar case at Paul's side.

"Well I'll be," he said, seeing the inscription in the leather. "It *is* Buddy Holly's guitar."

"Jeffrey happened across it the night of the crash."

"I only come across pennies, mostly tails side up — so I leave 'em — an occasional butane lighter, which is always out of fuel. Why don't I ever come across things like this?"

"Something tells me Jeff didn't think it was all that much good luck. Seems to be a streak of bad luck surrounding it."

Paul opened the case. Without words he took the red Strat from the burlap gunnysack, returned the unshrouded Strat to the case and snapped it closed. Now he slid the voluminous burlap bag up around the leather case, pulling the drawstring tight.

"There. Don't tell me that's not better. The lettering on that case makes it a little too conspicuous for its own good."

"I'll say! But suppose you're right about this guitar being bad luck. First Holly goes, then your uncle. Who's next? Maybe your grandmother was right when she called it the devil's instrument." He warily studied the gunnysack.

"Don't be ridiculous." Then, "I didn't know you're superstitious."

"I'm not superstitious. But I can't help thinking about all the trouble that guitar's raised around here."

In the distance they could hear the sounds of trucks rolling over the road. The road, with its wide open whine, gently recommended itself to Paul's frenzied senses.

"Now what?"

"There's no turning back. You heard my gramps. He'll trash this guitar."

He said they'd probably ship him off to private school in the bargain. They'd have to hit the road and live like oldtime bluemen, and the sooner the better.

"Hit the road? With what?"

"Why Doug's Plymouth, I guess. We'll head east."

"In that old thing? It wouldn't make the Mississippi."

"Then we'll just have to hitch."

"Hitchhike?" Terry looked hesitantly over his shoulder. "Well—. I don't know."

"What do you mean you don't know? What's the alternative?" He said as far as he could see if they ever wanted The Conclusions to hit the big time it was now or never.

"Look," he said to Terry, "my mind's made up. I'm going back to the folks' house to get some things together while they're still out. You do the same. Then give Doug and Ace a call and tell them to pack. I'd call myself but I don't want to stick around the house any longer than I have to. I'll meet you guys in an hour at that old burned-out church outside town. Know where I mean? And do you still have those demo tapes we made?"

388

"Yeah, I got 'em. Too bad we never mixed them. They sound pretty rough. Like a vacuum cleaner's running in the background."

"Don't worry about that now. Just bring them along. Who knows who we'll run into. And throw some work clothes into your pack and bring along your upright bass—."

"You expect to hitchhike with an upright bass? Who'd pick us up?"

"Well all right then bring your electric bass. Though it doesn't seem right. Bluesmen traveling around with electric guitars. Who ever heard of it? When we're out in hobo jungles we'll have nowhere to plug in."

Paul hightailed it home, where he lost no time stripping off his dress clothes in favor of a T-shirt with a Superman emblem, faded blues jeans and sneakers. He rifled through his chest of drawers, taking all the socks and underwear he could stuff into his daypack, as he reasoned you could never have too much of these when you're out on the road, in desolate places where laundromats might not always be at hand. You didn't want to get caught short in the underwear department. He made sure to bring along his Big Muff and his phase shifter, for use with his Strat. What competent latter-day bluesman would travel without them? From the darkest corner of his closet came his box of valuables. Inside, a roll of currency, almost one hundred and twenty dollars, savings from his share of the firehall gigs. They'd been doing all right there at the end. Now it was over. It felt over. You can feel when things are wide open and you can feel when they're over and that's how things felt now. Over. They could have their Mason City. He counted the money, snapping the red rubber band around the roll.

He'd already started to return the box to the closet when he got an idea. He returned the box to his bed, laid its lid partly off to the side. Now he found a California road map, dropping it haphazardly to the floor near the open box. There. That'd make them think he'd gone west.

Before he left his room he stole one last look at all those

389

pictures of Buddy Holly pasted to the walls and ceiling. Sure were a lot of Buddy Holly's up there. Other than that he never looked back. Everything felt wide open when he left the house and set his foot to the street.

The street carried him to the burned-out church outside town. It was in a desolate and overgrown state. No one seemed to know exactly when, but it must have burned decades ago. The stained-glass windows had been broken out by vandals so that now only a few jagged fragments of colored glass remained to crown the window frames. Tree limbs and vines poked through the empty sashes. When you stood in that burned-out shell of a church you couldn't help feeling terribly lonely and abandoned. Overhead the roof had fallen through in places so that you could look up and see the clouds and birds flying by. Weeds had overgrown the place. Torn and scorched pews where people once had knelt now laid toppled over. What was left of the altar was rotting, and green with moss. The forest was reclaiming its own on the altar of God. What god had these people prayed to anyway? the boy wondered. From the looks of things they should have been praying to the forest, for it was going to win in the long run.

He wished he'd told the guys to meet him someplace else. The old ruins were enough to give anyone the creeps. He sat on the concrete slab by the broken altar. Birds awhistled out in the brush and every so often a few of them dashed through one of the windows and swooped around into the church before darting abruptly skyward, disappearing through one of the yawning tears in the roof. This place must be jumping with bats at night, he thought, reeling in his neck. It wasn't the sort of thing to think about when you wanted to relax.

He sure wished the others would quick hurryup and get there. It was just too damn quiet. He considered taking the Strat from the case and playing Not Fade Away right there on the crumbling concrete slab. At least it would kill time. No. Better not. Someone might come along and then he'd have to get away in a hurry. He laid down and closed his eyes, resting his cheek on the cool slab, holding the guitar case tightly in his arms. He hadn't been sleeping too well lately and he could use whatever shuteye he could get. Once or twice it felt like he was drifting away and then he fell into a dream. It was the same dream he'd been having since the night Jeffrey died. He started, gripping fast to the guitar like a man adrift in the sea holds fast to whatever floats. Opening his eyes he sat up, rubbing his head. Man! what a dream. No use sleeping. No use at all if you can't stop dreaming that. Now he really felt spooked. Why the hell didn't they come?

It seemed like he'd been waiting a long time in the ruins before he heard foot falls. Up he sprang, to the crumbling back wall, to gaze out through the tangle of vines.

Terry hiked down the road. Alone. Emptyhanded. Without a pack or his electric bass. At the curve in the road he came off the gravel, wading into the high summer weeds. Grasshoppers jumped all around. He gave a yell. Paul waved.

Terry came up.

"Doug and Ace can't make it."

"What do you mean they can't make it?"

"All this is happening so fast. You can't expect people to drop everything and hit the road on the spur of the moment. I talked it over with Doug and he says he's thinking of getting married."

"Married?"

"He's knocked up his chick. Remember? Says he can't just cut and run."

"And Ace?"

"He's got that summer job piloting boats over at Clear Lake."

"Boats! Is that all he can think about? A few measly bucks running boats?"

"He's got to put something away for school."

"Well that's just great. I guess it's just you and me then, isn't it?"

Paul spilled his mad plan. He said the two of them would travel the country together, like old-time bluesmen. They'd try to find an old-time blues club in Chicago.

"Maybe we'll go see John Lennon in New York. Man, once he hears us he'll *know*."

Terry shook his head.

"Paul," he said suddenly, "I can't go either."

Paul looked as if he didn't take him seriously. His eyes traveled to Terry's empty hands.

"So that's why you didn't bring your guitar!"

Paul turned abruptly, stormed back into the ruins.

"So that's how it is with you guys!"

Terry was at his heels.

"I have Mama to think about."

They'd come to the concrete slab. Paul busied himself by sliding his pack onto his shoulder, all in a huff.

"Listen to me, Paul," Terry pretty near yelled, taking a firm hold of his shoulder. Paul looked down at the hand. "Do you honestly think I could go off and hit the road, just like that? It'd break her heart."

"Is that all you can think about? Your Mama?"

Anger erupted on Terry's face.

"For your information—."

He reached into his back pocket for a folded sheet of paper.

"This came in the mail today. I've been accepted to college in the fall. It means lots of work this summer. That's why I can't go."

Paul snatched it away. His eyes swept across it.

"I'm going to be an engineer."

Paul dropped his hand.

"Why that's great. I'm glad for you. Really I am." He handed back the paper.

Paul bent to pick up the guitar case. He brought it close, looking at it.

"Then you're still going through with it?"

"Someone has to keep the faith."

He drew the case close up under his arm. Beneath the canvas he felt with a sweep of his fingers the upraised handtooled lettering. Buddy Holly.

392

He looked at Terry.

"I must be crazy! Thinking I'm good enough to carry this guitar!"

"You're not crazy. I used to be so envious because you could play the guitar so much better than me. I can hold my own against any of these small-town beerhall players. But you. It's always been different with you. I guess it's always been just a matter of time before you blew this place."

They didn't say anything for most of a minute. A breeze came up. It made an awfully lonesome sound coming through the ruins.

"Well then I best be going," Paul said. "Hey. We sure had them jumping at the firehouse."

"Yeah. We really made those cats jump."

"Don't think any of them will forget The Conclusions anytime soon."

"No."

"Well. I guess this is it then. Be getting dark soon."

"Wait a minute. Almost forgot—."

He gave Paul the demo tape.

"Now if you hook up with anyone in the recording industry don't hesitate to give me a call, you hear?"

"Yeah. I hear you."

Reaching back, Paul stuck the tape way down in the pack, beside the Big Muff and the phase shifter.

"And there's one more thing. The girl who works at the record store. Jodie. You know, the banker's daughter? The one who's going steady with the football team. She's been calling around for you. Before I left the house she called and made me promise to pass along a message. She says she wants to see you. Downtown. In front of her father's bank."

"Wonder what she wants."

"I think she likes you."

"No fooling?"

Paul gripped the guitar. His head turned toward the road.

Terry cast his eyes at his own plain white T-shirt. He looked up. Paul was gone. Terry took himself out of the ruins to the weeds swaying in the wind by the side of the road. A solitary figure ran down the road toward town, lugging a gunnysack. A stiff breeze came up. For a moment he considered following his friend but his feet did not move. Regretfully, he looked down into the weeds.

The road carried Paul into town. He hurried along the alleyway behind the First National Bank then came up through a colonnade to the Main Street side, peeking from behind a column. Jodie stood only a few feet away, in front of the bank. Beside her father. Her old man wore a three-piece suit. He kept looking at his wristwatch.

"Honestly, Jodie," her father said, "I don't know what you expect me to do."

"He just can't fit in around this awful place," the girl was saying. "Just be nice to him Daddy. That's all you have to do."

"I don't understand your interest in this Stoken boy. What about Roger?"

"But Roger's so dumb!" Paul laughed softly to himself.

"Roger's just— Roger!" Jodie said. "But Paul's—. He's got—." She crinkled up her nose in that way girl's have. "Something—. Ooo I can't expect you to even begin to understand."

"Really, Jodie."

Paul wouldn't have minded saying goodbye to her. No. You have to be willing to sacrifice everything. Jodie sure looked good. Everything. With his cheek he touched the cool concrete column. No. Leave it.

He felt the road pulling him on. Gently recommending itself. First one backward step, then another. Soon he was running down the alley behind the First National Bank, leaving Main Street behind.

And the road carried him to the edge of town. Romantic notions of hitchhiking billowed in his brain. He half imagined all he need do was stick out his thumb and every trucker on the road would race to the shoulder for the honor of picking him up. He resolved to turn down any ride that didn't take him all the way into Chicago. But one after another the trucks plowed by, roaring deafeningly. When they went by there was a frightening wash of air that threatened to tug you into the road. None of them stopped.

After what seemed like hours a car pulled off some distance ahead. Paul grabbed his things and scrambled down the road. The car pulled away, then stopped, then pulled away again, so that the boy was made to run some distance before the car finally sped off. He saw the kids in the front seat laugh, shoot the finger.

"Well fuck you guys too!"

Traffic flowed by. A Ford sedan finally pulled off. A middle-aged woman rolled down the window and asked the way to Cedar Rapids. The boy pointed down the road. He started to say he was going that way himself but she sped off.

Now great thunderheads rumbled above. Everything got dark. The rain came and he got a thorough soaking. He wished he'd brought along a raincoat or an umbrella. The traffic kept whizzing by, sending up great waves of splashes. He rummaged around in his pack for something to pull over his head but there was nothing but underwear. He pulled a pair of Fruit of the Looms over his hair so that the elastic waistband came down around his eyebrows. He supposed he looked ridiculous but he didn't care. Just then a truck bounced into a water-filled pothole, and next thing he was drenched in muddy brown slime.

"Son of a bitch!"

He started hiking down the side of the road in a great huff, kicking up loose gravel, the underwear capping his head. To hell with it. He'd walk to Chicago, if that's what he had to do.

And the road carried him on like that, muttering obscenities and hunch-shouldered, for what must have been the better part of a mile. The world and everyone in it seemed dark and unfriendly. As he huffed along a green car pulled over and the window came down. An elderly couple looked out.

"Where you going?" asked the old man behind the wheel. His hair was smoke white, the same shade as his wife's, and they both had kindly, concerned faces.

"Chicago."

"We can take you as far as Interstate 80. Will that be all right?"

"Are you kidding?" Already he'd lunged for the door, tossed his things onto the backseat.

It was a big old cushy boat of a car. Now this is traveling in style, Paul thought, settling back.

"When we saw you walking down the side of the road you reminded us so much of our own grandson, Jack," the old woman said.

"Say, what's that on your head, son?" the old man asked, looking in the mirror.

They turned out to be a retired couple from Minneapolis on their way to St Louis, where they had family. Once it got dark they got off the road at a Howard Johnson's and they all went in. Paul pulled a sandwich and a chocolate milk from the stainless steel display case. The old man made a big deal about paying for it. "Now that'll be our treat," the old man said. He led them over to a table by the doorway and they sat down and watched the people coming in. The old man and his wife didn't have much to say. They'd been together so long they'd even begun to look like each other. They were all right.

Afterwards they drove on. Somewhere on the boundless interstate the old woman asked the boy to play something on his guitar. Paul took out the Strat, played That's All Right Mama. The strings sounded faint and tinny without an amplifier but the old woman sang along and clapped her hands. At Interstate 80 they pulled over. The woman offered the boy her plastic rainhat. It was one of those ladies' fold-up jobs with flowers all over. The boy said thanks anyway, but such a thing wouldn't look becoming on a bluesman. Besides, it wasn't raining anymore. He waved goodbye to them when they pulled off, and they waved back. He couldn't help thinking he'd see them again sometime, somewhere. That's how it is with people

396

you meet on the road. You always think you'll run into them again though you never do. What you see again is the same friendliness in some other stranger down the road.

By now it was well into night and the boy thought he'd sleep. Someplace undercover. The clouds rolled dark and menacing in the night and he wouldn't have been surprised if there was another thunderstorm.

A shopping mall loomed just off the highway, the stores closed. The parking lot, abandoned. Not a soul in sight. In the parking lot he spotted a Goodwill box, one of those tin boxes with a slanted roof and a wide chute. There'd be no harm in spending the night in the box, far as he could see.

Cartons of musty old shirts and broken shoes hung from the chute. Inside, it was pretty near stuffed to the top. Stacking the old clothes on the pavement, before long he'd cleared away enough to slide his pack and guitar down the chute, then followed them in.

It was dark in there. Dark, but comfortable. Below, the old clothes made a good mattress. Above, the tin roof was still intact. There was only a single rust hole, in the back wall, through which the light from the parking lot shone through. He lost no time plugging that with an old hat he found. Then it was all dark and quiet.

He settled back on the bunched up clothes, feeling pretty good about things. Now wasn't this living! If only Terry, Doug and Ace could see him now.

Resting on his back, elbows spread out on either side of his head, waiting for a sleepy feeling, he heard the faintest of sounds. The chute opened an inch or two. At first he thought nothing of it, thinking it was only the wind. Then he made out an object protruding from the chute. He lit his Bic. A firehose nozzle. "What the?" Slowly, cautiously, he tilted open the chute. Looking out, he saw a firehose snaking away from the box across the great ocean of parking lot to the mall beyond. Under the lights he saw a cop running alongside the hose, undoubtedly to turn on the water. Paul grabbed at the old hat blocking the hole in the back of the box. A black and white

397

police cruiser sat a short distance behind the box.

"Son of a bitch!"

It was all he could do to get out of there, groping in the dark for the guitar and his pack, expecting the hose momentarily to come alive, when the idea came to him. He quick grabbed the nozzle and yanked the hose all the way in, shoving it out the rust hole in the back.

Scrambling out the chute with his things, keeping low, he hurried to the rear of the box, grabbing hold of the firehose, hauling it to the police cruiser. The somber tones of a dispatcher drifted in over the police radio. He rolled the window securely up around the hoze, then closed the door.

Now he was the one snickering across the parking lot. In a moment he heard the violent blast of water dousing the inside of the cruiser. He lit out past the dark edge of the parking lot into the dense brush, straight for the highway. Through thicket and bog he breathlessly stumbled, then up over a fence, emerging finally on a dark stretch of interstate. Cars and trucks whizzed by, headlights beaming. He stuck out his thumb, though he was just about out of wind. Every set of approaching headlights made his heart race. One of those pairs of headlights might be the cops and he'd never know it till they were right on top of him.

Not far up ahead a pair of headlights slowed. For a second he thought of bolting back into the brush. It could be a ride.

Hearing knows the sounds of a diesel. The moan of big tires. The rattle of chains. A truck! He stuck out his thumb just as the rig rumbled up and stopped, snorting. It was the finest thing he'd ever seen. Feeling light as a feather he jumped up the running board and climbed in. The boy never said a word to that trucker and he didn't look him in the eye till he climbed out miles down the road, but that one look would last a lifetime. It was one ride he'd never forget.

He found himself at a dark underpass in the middle of nowhere. It was the darkest part of the night and there was hardly any traffic. The air smelled of water. During those interminably long stretches when there were no cars or trucks within earshot he could make out the sounds of water. And millions and gadzillions of crickets. It was the lonesomest sound he'd ever heard. Then he'd hear something coming on the road, at first sounding weaker than the buzzing of a fly, finally thundering back the sounds of the night, before fading once again into the sounds of the river and crickets.

Paul leaned up against one of those concrete pillars beneath the overpass, the back of his head pressed against the cool hardness of concrete. When he heard a car he'd go to the side of the road and level his thumb. After a while there were no cars for a very long time and he slumped down and rested his back against the pillar. Well that cop got a taste of his own medicine when he got back to his cruiser, that was for sure. He broke out laughing and the laughter echoed off the walls of the underpass and came back sounding rubbery and abrupt. The air felt cold and damp and he wished he'd thought to bring a jacket. Pulling his arms close in at his sides, he covered his chest with his pack.

He had no idea how long he rested like that, since the night slips by so unevenly when you're alone. He never closed his eyes but there were spots in there where he wasn't fully awake either, more like in a trance. One minute he'd be looking out across the dark road into the night, hearing the lullaby sounds of the crickets and the deep soothing rush of water, then he'd see a car or maybe a truck flash by, not realizing at first what he'd seen before stirring himself.

Like that the night passed. Before dawn birds began chirping. In the east the sky between the stars took on the most delicate shades of purple. Birds called up a storm. After it got bright the first thing the boy made out was the sparkling dew covering everything, including himself. He moved his arms and watched the dew sparkle, dreamlike and magical on the hair of his forearm. Then, through the mist to the east, he saw the mighty Mississippi, rolling slowly onward. The riverbank wasn't three hundred feet away! Iowa, almost behind!

Down the embankment sparkling with dew he ran, to the riverside where he wondrously looked through the still mist to the Illinois side. A great bridge had been built across the river but it did nothing to detract from the wildness of the Mississippi. It just about knocked you out to see the mist taking on shapes out across the brown water. As far as you could see tall reeds and graceful trees lined the banks of the river. Then, splash!, a catfish would break water someplace in the mist. It was worth a king's fortune to see.

Beside the murmuring river he dropped to his knees and splashed water on his face, the back of his neck. Man did it feel good. He took a taste. Very tangy. Very muddy. He had to spit it out. God only knew what they're dumping upstream these days.

Once he'd washed up and had a change of underwear he went back to the underpass. He hadn't any real sleep but he felt good. At this rate he'd be in Chicago by nightfall, playing those Windy City blueshalls he'd read so much about. Traffic was light and the first few cars buzzed by. Just when he was starting to fret he might never get out of there, here comes an old farm truck, slowing. His first ride of the day! He climbed in feeling light as a feather. The driver was a chuckle-headed farmhand who said he could take him as far as Rock Island. Everything felt so upbeat and exciting as they started across the bridge and over the Mississippi he abandoned all caution and took out the Strat. Soon wild Chuck Berry riffs drifted from the old truck.

The farmhand looked on in amazement. He said, "Why that there's just about the best picking I've ever heard." He looked at the handtooled leather guitar case on the seat.

"Buddy Holly," the simpleton read slowly, sounding out the name. "That's a nice sounding name, isn't it? Holly. Buddy Holly. Say, is that who you are?"

Paul stopped playing. He looked with much surprise at the simpleton.

"Yeah. That's who I am."

And the road carried him on, past the billboards, past neverending stretches of sooty railroad track, past roadside restau-

400

rants and truck weigh stations, past broken-down cars with white handkerchiefs tied like flags of surrender to their antennae, past overheated cars abandoned still steaming under the bright midday sun. He hadn't eaten since the sandwich the old folks bought for him back at the Howard Johnson's but he didn't care. Every mile that brought him closer to Chicago brought him closer to his dreams. From his wallet he'd bring out a tattered newspaper clipping and reverently reread the story about all the renovated blues clubs that had recently reopened on the South Side. Each mile marker that zoomed by meant one less mile between himself and his fortune. Every curve filled his imagination with countless hopeful imaginings.

From the Mississippi it took four rides to reach the city. The chuckle-head in the farm truck; an insurance salesman from Dayton, Ohio, driving a rented car; and two eighteen-wheelers. The last leg of the ride, in a big Kenworth.

At last, deep in the city, the truck rolled to a stop before a small building. Paul's heart sank. One of those fancy glass-enclosed menu cases hung outside by the door and you could make out the words "Quiche Lorraine" and "Soup du le jour." It sure was hard to imagine Blind Lemon Jefferson or Robert Johnson spooning out soup du le jour. The outside brick walls had been sandblasted and painted over a somber Georgetown brown. Fancy red and white striped awnings slung across shiny yellow brass poles overhung the freshly swept walk. Little shrubberies planted neatly in oversized wooden pots stood guard on both sides of the new mahogany door. None of it seemed right.

"They call this a blues club?" He compared the address to that in the newspaper clipping.

The boy hopped from the cab, gave the driver a wave, then crossed the street. The door was ajar and he went in. Inside he made out the faint tinkling of coins being stacked and counted. It was coming from the office, all the way up front, near a small stage. The door to the office was open and you could see a shadow playing on the floor.

"Hello?"

He came a step closer.

There was the furious sound of coins being raked into a bag, followed by the sounds of a heavy steel door closing, like the door to a safe. A head appeared in the doorway.

"We're closed," yelled the head in the doorway. "Won't open till nine."

He came out, wiping his hands on his pants. God was he fat. He kind of oozed into the room, up to the bar. Without looking at the boy he took down a glass and poured himself a drink.

"Kid, there's lots I've got to do before the doors open tonight."

He drank deeply, smacking his lips, then looked at the empty tumbler. After he drank his voice got huskier.

"So why don't you close the door when you go."

"Don't you know who I am?" the boy asked.

The fat man set down the glass.

"Let me guess. You're Clark Kent."

The boy brought a hand to the crest on his Superman's shirt.

"No, I'm the Great White Hope. I've come to play this guitar at your blues emporium." He lifted the gunnysack.

"Now I've heard it all. What makes you think I'd even let you sweep my floor? Now beat it!"

"But I'm the real thing. The keeper of the flame. And, mister, I can prove it."

The boy looked around, making sure they were alone. He drew back the burlap. The fat man saw the lettering cut into the leather. He came closer, touching the scripted scroll lettering. Buddy Holly.

The boy unsnapped the case, taking out the Strat.

"Would I have this if I wasn't for real?"

"You mean to tell me you've found—." He laughed. "Now I *have* heard everything." He pointed at the door. "Now, if you'll excuse me, I've work to do."

"But I'm serious, mister, I'm from Mason City, Iowa. My uncle was a witness to the crash. He pulled it from the wreck."

402

The fat man took the Strat from the boy, held it into the light. Something about the wood caught his imagination, reached into his soul and changed his outlook.

"You know, I remember reading it was missing. But never in my wildest dreams did I think Buddy Holly's guitar would walk through *my* door! This is a horse of a different color. Why didn't you say you'd brought Buddy Holly's lost guitar? This is a find!"

The boy pulled the Strat away, strapping it behind his back.

"I'm hungry," he said, looking around. "Do you have food?"

"Food? Of course I have food. You think I'd have a stomach like this if I didn't have food? I make the best cheesesteak in Chicago. You sit right down and I'll see if I can't find us something to eat. And then we'll talk all about this uncle of yours."

He hurried to the door and turned the lock. Presently Paul heard pots and pans rattling, cupboards slamming. The boy took a look around. Above the door to the fat man's private office an ancient yellowed photograph of a black man in raggedy clothing stared down at the empty tables.

The succulent aroma of the steak soon hit his nose and made his mouth water. It'd sure been a long time since he'd sat down to a good meal. Since before Jeffrey died. Since before they'd won the contest at the Surf. Man I sure caught a wave of fate coming out of that place, he thought. His head still spun from the road. It was all still moving like it always is when you first get off the road.

The fat man carried a tray from the kitchen. A cheesesteak and a thick malted.

"Soup's on!"

They sat down at a table by the bar. The boy wolfed his food.

"My my you certainly are hungry aren't you?" the fat man asked.

Paul ate as the fat man blithely spoke of his past. He said

he'd started in Philadelphia back in the fifties, when he'd been about Paul age. In Philly he'd learned how to make cheesesteaks and had met Dick Clark. That was his first big break in the business, he said. Got a job spinning records on American Bandstand.

"Then you kow some bigshots in the recording industry?" the boy said hopefully.

"Sure. I've known them all."

He said it got to be where he was all the time quarreling with Dick Clark. He couldn't get Clark to take payola. Before long the job with American Bandstand turned sour. "Still I can't complain. Made my bundle. Clearasil money. To this day every time I see a kid with zits I smile to myself. There's a buck to be made in everything." He laughed heartily.

After he left American Bandstand he fell in with the folk music scene in Greenwich Village. It was the early sixties and he'd owned one of those smoky little coffee houses that were all the rage. He laughed that he had an uncanny instinct for making loot while the going was good and getting out before the bubble burst. Before the coffee house went bust, in the mid-sixties, he'd gotten involved with a few heavy metal bands. He hinted he'd had a hand in Woodstock. He hunched up on one of his hams and from his back pocket pulled his wallet, from which he produced a wrinkled photo of himself posing in love beads, flashing a peace sign. He said he'd sold peace symbols, even though, he said, "There's no money in peace. Found that out too late in life." When the bottom dropped out of the peace movement there'd been years of drifting. For the last few years he'd run a disco somewhere in New York. After he'd sucked all the juice he could from disco he'd begun looking around for fresh meat. Something a man of his talents could really sink his teeth into.

"The blues," he said softly, almost at a whisper. "The blues. Let me tell you something boy. *The blues is coming back.*"

He said he made it his business to keep an eye open for lucrative opportunities. One day he'd been reading the trades

404

when he'd come across a small news item announcing the sale of a famous old-time blues club in Chicago. That very night he'd hopped on a plane. By noon the next day he'd bought the club for back taxes and had hatched plans to milk it for all it was worth.

"That's my talent and I have no apologies. I find something worth exploiting and I waste no time exploiting it."

"How do you mean?" The boy was just sipping the last of the malted through the straw.

"Take that guitar strapped to your back," the fat man said, his eyes narrowing. "It'd fetch a pretty penny. There are plenty of guitarists who'd love to have Buddy Holly's sound. I bet that old Stratocaster has a sound like no other on earth. Am I right? Now I myself know people who would pay handsomely for it."

"Except it's not for sale."

"Don't be a fool," the fat man said. He reached across the table for the guitar.

The boy moved away, pushing the chair over backwards. Suddenly he felt disoriented. Pressing his knuckles against the table, he swayed.

"Is something wrong, my boy?"

"Funny—. I feel—. A little dizzy."

"'The time has come ,' the walrus said, 'to talk of many things,'" the fat man recited gleefully. "'Of shoes — and ships — and sealing-wax — Of cabbages and kings.'"

"What?" Paul said. The fat man's voice drifted in and out. It sounded like he was talking from the other side of a long tunnel. The boy's vision began to blur and distort, like he was looking at the fat man's Cheshire smile through a funhouse mirror. It was suddenly all he could do to hold on to the table.

The fat man held up a little bottle. A prescription bottle.

"You've never failed me yet!" He kissed it, then set it on the table. He laughed, his belly rolling. "Strap yourself in boy. You're about to go for the ride of your life."

Paul glared at the empty glass.

"The malted?"

405

"You guessed it."

"How could you stoop so low?"

"My boy, I've stooped lower."

Laughing mirthfully, the fat man dragged himself to the boy's backpack. He rummaged around but, finding only the underwear and a few other trifles, threw it contemptuously to the floor. Now he brought the case over to the table and opened it. Not missing a step, he bent to take the Strat from the boy's back.

"You can't have it!" Paul moaned, feeling the fat man's hands on his arm.

"And what will you do if I take it? Call the police?" The fat man couldn't stop laughing. He pulled the Strat from the boy's back.

Paul dizzily reached up.

"Why?" he asked. "I only wanted to play guitar in your club."

The fat man grabbed the boy by his Superman T-shirt, pulling it taut.

"Listen punk. If you play my place it's because I tell you to. Got it? You'll take what I give you and you'll like it. And if you don't play my place it's because I say I don't want you to. Got that? And if I dope you up and toss you to the dogs in the street it's because I want it that way. And you'll like that too. Got that?"

He let go of the boy and happily resumed the business of packing away the guitar. He hummed. At last he turned, scooped up our would-be cult hero and hefted him over his round shoulder. He stuffed the guitar case under the opulent flesh of his arm and sauntered lazily past the tables into the back room, humming all the way.

Rocking on the fat man's shoulder, Paul opened his eyes in time to catch a last glimpse of the club. In his daze he thought he saw the blues club as it must have been long ago, before the formica and the glitter, when the floors and tables had still been of wood. He thought he saw and heard a skeleton blues-

406

man wailing away up front on the soapbox stage, a dusty guitar on his knee, a gold pick shining yellow in his bony white fingers. Now skeleton couples appeared, swirling dreamlike and graceful as sailboats in each other's arms out on the floor. Holding up his own hand he was surprised to see only the bone, white as chalk, and none of the flesh. It was then he realized all of us are like those silent twirling skeleton dancers losing themselves forever to that old-time blues beat. There is something immortal about us all.

It was all our would-be cult hero could do to keep his eyes open and look out through the dreamlike haze. He saw, as in a dream, the fat man carrying him into the back room. He saw the fat man open an old-fashioned safe and place the guitar inside. "I'll be back, my precious," he said to the Strat. The boy heard him close the heavy steel door and give the ratchety combination a twirl.

He dragged the boy out the back way, clumsily pulling him into a van. Then they were driving, driving, the road carrying them on, outside town, driving until the fat man's screeching laughter echoed through the van like crashing thunder. At last the boy felt the van stop. The door opened and Paul felt himself being lifted from the hard gritty floor.

"I'll get you fat man!" the boy moaned. "If it's the last thing I do I'll get my Strat back. I swear I'll get it back."

"You will, will you?" the fat man laughed.

With that he tossed the boy and then his pack out over the guardrail, watched them roll down the embankment quite a distance from the interstate. It was really quite surprising how far the boy rolled.

Still laughing, the fat man grunted as he climbed back into his van. He had to wipe tears from his eyes in order to see the road as he drove away, so hard was he laughing.

Our would-be cult hero spent a night he'd never forget in a culvert by the highway. Fireworks went off in his head all night. There was a stretch when he irrationally feared he was about to become a victim of spontaneous human combustion. He felt himself getting warm all over and he couldn't keep his mind off those stories he'd read in newspapers like *Midnight* and the *National Enquirer* of people who'd suddenly burst into flames, disintegrating where they sat, leaving a pile of ash. It was a terrible thing to worry about. After awhile his fear of spontaneous human combustion eased and he looked up and saw that it was night. Stars shone a million different crystalline colors, ever so subtly shaded and delicate. By daybreak he was pretty much himself again, though it felt like the Civil War had been fought in his head. After the sun had risen well over the horizon he sat up. His backpack lay nearby on the culvert, the underwear spilled out all the way up the embankment.

He gathered up the underwear. What now? He wanted to go back for the Strat but he was afraid. Afraid or not, he couldn't see abandoning Buddy Holly's guitar.

With a heavy heart and his pack stuffed full of damp underwear he treaded up the last of the grassy embankment to the side of the road. Things sure had a way of turning out different than you expected. Rubbing the hair on the back of his head, he sat down on the guardrail to think things over. It only went to show what happens when a fellow trusts someone. Well wasn't it his own fault? He'd gotten too cocky, taking the Strat from its case when he was on the road and showing it to people and now he'd paid for it. He began to see the advantage of keeping things hidden away. Maybe some things are best left hidden. Maybe there's something to be said for old Clark Kent after all.

Wasn't that pretty much how it'd always be with that cursed Stratocaster? Wouldn't there always be be someone like that fat asshole trying to take it? It was really too hot to hold. What good was it? You could never play it on stage, out in the open. It was good for nothing but trouble.

For the longest time he sat on the guardrail with his chin in his hands trying to decide what to do. Out on the interstate cars whizzed by but he paid them no mind. That fat asshole sure had all the angles figures. He couldn't go to the cops.

408

The signs along the shoulder of the road said he was back on Interstate 80. A few miles outside Chicago, one sign said. If he wanted to head east, maybe on to New York, all he had to do was stay on this side of the road and hitch the hell out of there. But if he wanted the Strat he'd have to cross the road.

Rising from the guardrail, he hesitantly put out his thumb, then reeled it back in. He couldn't bring himself to do it. He couldn't abandon it. Wasn't he the keeper of the flame? He couldn't stand the thought of the fat man pawing over it with those greedy little sweaty hands, selling it to the highest bidder. Not after Jeffrey had sat up all those dark nights polishing and shining it. How could he let Jeffrey down like that?

Suddenly he heard someone calling. A little ways down the road. A Volkswagen had pulled off and it sat there chugging. A woman waved.

"Do you want a ride or don't you?" she yelled.

The car was heading east, away from Chicago. He hesitated, looking back toward town.

"Hey you! You want a ride or not?"

The next instant Paul found himself running to the waiting car. It was as if the road carried him on, step by step, till he reached the Volkswagen and saw the girl in the backseat.

The girl sometimes feared she would never meet the right boy. She'd just about resigned herself to oldmaidhood, as she was practically *eighteen years old* and had yet to fall in love. Oh there had been boys all right, lots of boys, but she'd never been knocked out by any of them and it made her sad to think about it.

Until she saw him. She'd been riding in the backseat, the man and the woman up front, listening to the man's unending stories of his childhood.

"Then, when I was about twelve, Aunt Tilly got this garden tractor, you know the kind you ride—."

That's when she saw him. She sat up in the backseat and shrieked for them to stop. He was standing on the roadside wearing a light blue T-shirt with a Superman emblem printed across the chest. A vexed look on his face. With one hand he rubbed the hair on the back of his head while the other tentatively hoisted a thumb to traffic.

"He's adorable!" the girl in the backseat raved as they came up. "Stop! Stop!"

Paul ran up to the bug and saw the girl in the backseat. He got in and settled uneasily beside her.

Her hair was blonde and cut close to her scalp. A crew cut. She had pretty, big eyes, blue-green, that rolled around fast. After the bug had pulled away she turned and looked full-faced at the boy. She took in his mussed hair and his dirt-streaked Superman T-shirt. She laughed gayly, then stopped herself, pressing the back of her hand against her thin lips.

"What's so funny?"

"Nothing."

She smiled mysteriously, unfathomably. She leaned up against the front seat, her cheek pressed against the headrest, now looking straight ahead and inscrutably down the unwinding interstate.

And the road carried them on, eastward, past farms and neverending stretches of flat plain, here planted in red beets, there green soy, everywhere golden wheat, then sudden yellow explosions of sunflowers standing at attention millions to the acre in the morning sun. Funny you never thought there'd be so many sunflowers on earth. After about an hour they came to a roadside diner and they stopped for coffee. The girl got out of the backseat and stretched like a nimble dancer. Paul watched her over the roof of the car. Funny he hadn't known this girl existed an hour ago and now she was just about all he could think about. He followed her in. Inside, the man and the woman who were traveling with the girl went to the counter to order. Paul and the girl took a table by the front window. You could look out and see the interstate slashing through the patchworked flat plain.

"Where I come from there's hills," the boy said, staring

dreamily out the window. "The roundest green hills."

The girl was looking at him over the menu. Her eye shadow was green. The boy turned from the window, catching her stare.

"Do you always make eyes at boys you don't know?"

She laughed, kicked his shin beneath the table.

"Oh I'm sorry. You must think I'm the rudest. I'm Claire."

The boy introduced himself.

She stretched out a hand and they shook.

"And them?" He pointed at the ones by the counter. The man was enthusiastically sharing a story from his childhood with the woman.

"They're friends of the family. She's super smart. Linda's the smartest person I've ever met. And do you know what? She's a feminist. She tells me all about Susan B. Anthony and the suffragettes." She smiled.

"And him?"

"He's a jerk. Works for my uncle. Wish we could ditch him."

Looking rather impish, she bent close, hunching her shoulders, saying softly, in a confidential tone, "He's really madly in love with her. Can't say I blame him. If I was a man I'd be in love with Linda too." A dreamy look came across her face. It was really a very animated face. It lit up in a hundred different ways when she spoke.

"And her? Does she love him?"

"Are you mad? She can't stand him. Can't you see how bored she looks with his stories? Men are blind."

"What happened to you?" the boy asked.

"It's cool." She self-consciously swept a hand across her scalp. Then, "Say, we're on our way to a camp in the mountains," she said suddenly, smiling. "Sort of a vacation camp." She ran a fingernail along the edge of the table. She'd taken on a serious, almost anxious air. It was something that flinched around her mouth. "Look. I know you'll probably think I'm terrible. You'll think I'm forward. It's only that well it seems to me like we've known each other all along. When I saw you standing there by the road something connected. You think I'm crazy don't you? So I might as well come right out and say it, shouldn't I? Would you like to come with us? We'll really have the wildest time. I promise. The rest of them are older and I'll be ever so lonely." She swallowed hard. She tried to act like a natural, an old pro at romance, but you could tell these things were difficult for her to say.

Paul had heard women were fast once you got out into the world. He froze with the water glass to his lips.

"What do you say? We'll have the best time up in the mountains. I know we will. I have this feeling we're going to be the best of friends."

Right then Paul wanted nothing more than to go off with her.

"I can't."

He hung his head low. He told her of his dream of becoming a cult hero and how his plans had already hit snags. He bitterly recounted how his guitar had been taken from him by the fat man in Chicago, how he'd been drugged and abandoned in a ditch by the side of the road, near where they'd picked him up. He told her most all of it but for the part about the guitar once having belonged to Buddy Holly. He'd never open his mouth about that again. Not to anyone.

"Believe me, if that's your only trouble on earth you have it easy. You can always buy another guitar. If it's money you need—."

She opened her purse and pulled out a fistful of cash. Mostly tens and twenties, with a few fifties mixed in. She offered it to the boy without the slightest hesitation or emotion. It could have been Kleenex. "Take whatever you please. Just say you'll come."

"I don't want your money. My guitar—. Some things money can't buy. Believe me. It was irreplaceable. It came down to me from my uncle. And now he's dead."

Hopelessly gazing at the money, she broke into tears. She started crying so suddenly it caught Paul by surprise.

412

"Really," he said, trying to comfort her. He looked around the diner, feeling awkward. "It's not your problem. You don't even know me. We're strangers."

She wiped her eyes with her hand.

"Lately," she said, "I've been thinking it isn't good to be cut off from the troubles of strangers. It gets to be where we start believing no one else exists. I have to believe in strangers. If I believe someone else's troubles are real then maybe they'll believe mine are real. Then maybe somehow we'll all get by. The last few days I've been looking into the faces of complete strangers we pass out on the highway and I see nothing in their faces I don't see in my own. I'm left wondering if any of us are ever really strangers."

She looked at the boy.

Lowering her voice, she went on, "There must be some way I can convince you to come. Some lever in you I can move. Some button I can press. Something I can—." She looked over at the one called Peter. "My friend over there," she said. "He's sort of a private investigator. He's ever so clever about breaking into places and taking things. Come with us and I'll have him steal your guitar back from that awful man who took it. Linda can make him do it. She can make him do anything. Peter's wrapped around her finger. How does that sound? Will that make it worth your while?"

The boy stirred in his chair. He looked at the one she called Peter.

"He can get my Strat?"

"Peter's always bragging there's never been a lock he can't pick. It'd just put you to sleep to hear his adventure stories. Honest to God he thinks he's James Bond."

Linda at last came over from the counter with the coffee.

"I think we can convince Paul to come with us," Claire said to her. "But I had to promise him Peter would fetch something of his back in town. I hope it won't delay things much. I'm sure we won't have to go very far out of our way. I'm sorry, Linda. If there'd been another way—."

From her shoulder bag Linda pulled a chain necklace. A

small, rough stone swung from its end. She held it out to the boy.

"Put this on. And whatever happens, whatever anyone says, don't take it off. Is that clear?"

Paul took the amulet. The stone was charcoal gray with bits of glass that sparkled in the midmorning sun. When the sun hit it it cast thousands of tiny sparkles of every conceivable color on the walls and tables of the diner. Some of the truckers looked over. He slipped the cool chain over his neck and let the stone hang loosely in front of the Superman emblem. He sat back then, out of the wedge of sunlight, and the sparkling stopped.

Once they got back to the interstate Paul saw they were heading east, away from Chicago and the Strat, and he yelled, "Hey, what about my—."

"Don't worry, we'll get your things," Linda Patterson told him.

"Don't worry about a thing," Claire said to the boy. "I just know everything's going to work out all right."

What have I gotten myself into now? he thought, slumping in the seat.

In time Paul dozed off. When he awoke the flat stretches of wheat had vanished. The car climbed high on a desolate mountain road. At first when he awoke he had no idea where he was. Everywhere there were trees, and not another car in sight. With a start he lifted his head from the girl's shoulder. She said, "We'll be there soon." The road was one swooping curve after another. They were climbing through steep rounded mountains and you could look far below into deep misty valleys prickling with trees. He couldn't see another car, even a road sign. The only hint of people was an occasional log shack. Sometimes you saw two or three tired old Indians sitting out on logs in front of the shacks. A strange place for a vacation camp, Paul thought.

Close to sunset they turned down a side road that cut through a tall thick forest. After a mile or two they came to a

414

gate barring the way. It was a heavy steel gate with barbed wire snarled across the top. That wasn't all. Off to one side of the gate, piled by the side of the road, sat the biggest pile of furniture Paul had ever seen.

"What on earth?" Linda Patterson gawked.

"Looks like Aunt Liz's things from Winterford," Claire said.

Peter Donday pulled out a chain identical to the boy's. A sparkling gray stone swung from its end. He lowered the stone into a small box on the driver's side of the gate. Inside the box a brilliant green light came on. The gate swung open and they drove on.

They came out of the woods and parked under an old elm tree in front of the house. Mrs Natlong came out, walked smiling across the wide lawn. She showered the girl with kisses. "Oh Claire my darling how thin you look! Haven't they been feeding you at that school? And what on earth have you done to your beautiful hair? It's bad times when a girl takes shears to her locks." They introduced the boy to Mrs Natlong. "Oh how do you do," she said. "Claire's written the nicest things about you." Mrs Natlong took the girl by the arm and started to lead them all toward the house, saying they must be famished after such a long trip, but Peter Donday stopped her, asking, "Has the general arrived yet?"

"No," Mrs Natlong told him. "I don't expect him till late tonight or tomorrow." Again Mrs Natlong started for the house. Linda Patterson laid an arm on the boy's shoulder and bade him to wait while the others went on.

Once they were alone she said to him, "What is it that you need back in town?"

"You'll go for it now?"

"Now's the best time."

He told her how he'd lost the Strat, how he'd been drugged and abandoned by the side of the road. Her eyes went wide.

"A guitar?" Biting her lip uneasily, she glanced over her

shoulder at Peter Donday. "I've promised to leave camp for a guitar?"

"Not just any guitar. It's an electric. A Stratocaster. A real nice one. But if we're going to get it back we'll have to move fast. That fat asshole said he'd sell it to the highest bidder on the black market." So anxious was he to be off already he'd started for the car. Linda Patterson caught him by the arm.

"No. You wait here with the others. I'll be back with it."

"You? Go yourself?"

"You'll just have to trust me now won't you?"

The boy looked unsure.

"Can't you trust a stranger?"

He reluctantly shook his head yes.

"Guess I've got to start trusting someone sooner or later."

He described the guitar in careful detail, stressing again it was not just any old guitar but an absolutely ancient candy apple red Stratocaster with several deep gashes cut into its face and neck. He told her it could be found inside the handtooled leather guitar case with the words "Buddy Holly" etched into the leather. He said this part nonchalantly, as if it was no more than an afterthought.

"Buddy Holly?"

"I was playing around one day and I scratched it in," he told her. "As a joke. It's not like it's really Buddy Holly's guitar or anything like that." He laughed. "Buddy Holly's guitar is lost. Long lost. Everybody knows that." He smiled.

"Do you really think you can get my Strat back?"

"I don't see what's to stand in my way."

"That fat asshole's an underhanded bully. And you're just—." He eyes swept doubtfully across her small frame. "You're just a woman."

"Just a woman?"

This business done, she got behind the wheel of the bug and fired up the engine. The others, on the way into the house, turned.

"Linda! Where are you going child?" Mrs Natlong yelled across the lawn.

416

"To Chicago. To fetch this boy's things. Tell the general not to worry."

"Child, come in and have a dish of some hot chowder."

"I would, Mrs Natlong, only I promised this boy I'd get his things back in town."

Peter Donday stopped in midstride, looked up. Next thing he was racing across the lawn, toward the little bug. He opened the passenger door and jumped in. The bug pulled away. And that was the last anybody'd seen of those two.

Claire came over to Paul.

"Didn't I tell you she could make him do anything?"

For a while he'd been walking on air, thinking all his troubles soon would be over. Then George Natlong had turned up at Camp Moonstone and began slapping him around, ranting and raving like a tyrant.

Well it only goes to show. We all want something we can't have.

So now Paul sat locked in his room at Camp Moonstone. Confined to quarters. He knew it'd all be over for him once the generals saw those pictures of Buddy Holly pasted all over his walls and ceiling back home. It made his stomach feel queasy.

He could feel those waves of fate rolling up and he was thinking now was probably as good a time as any to cut out. He'd jump from the window, light out through the woods and use his moonstone to open the gate. They still hadn't taken the moonstone away and he had a good idea he'd better use it before they came for it. There were five generals down in that cave and only one of him. Five crazed generals against one crazed rocker. Better to use the window. He'd move so fast he'd leave a jet stream in his wake. Let them try and catch his jet stream.

Leaning against the sill, he appraised the drop. A good two and a half stories. Maybe twenty feet. It'd be some jump. He'd just have to hope he wouldn't bust an ankle.

Sliding open the window, he sat on the sill, bracing himself against the window frame. Too bad, he thought, he'd never get to see old Buddy Holly's Strat again. Well, he'd done his best. Once those waves of fate start rolling you can't wait around for trifles like guitars. He didn't need that Superman's cape anyway. Not when he had his demo tape, made to sound so nice by the generals' own computer.

Almost as an afterthought he reached into his jacket pocket, felt around for the cassette. Funny. He rifled through his pockets.

Then he remembered. He'd left it with the computer! He'd left it there last night, when Mrs Natlong had come barging in. It was still plugged into the computer console!

He took a look from the window. Through the trees he saw the five generals coming down the path from the warehouse.

His jaw dropped. Something told him a big wave of fate was about to come crashing up.

CODA:
THE FIRE

It was enough to make an angel swear."
—General Israel Putnam
(to church members accusing him
of cursing during the Revolutionary
War's Battle of Bunker Hill)

1

The five disheveled generals sat deep underground in the cavern at Camp Moonstone, watching the last install-ment of the boy's life flash bigger than life across the screen. They passed the time smoking cigars, drinking bourbon and playing their usual five-card stud.

Of the five only George Natlong was not drinking. It was not that he did not want to drink. It would have been nice to be drinking but his stomach wouldn't have it. Just the same he kept a half-filled glass of bourbon by his elbow and from time to time he would sip at it and swish it around his dry mouth before slyly spitting it back into the glass. His stomach was really acting up and he didn't want the others to suspect their commander was having gut trouble. He sat slightly hunched, holding his gut, looking over his cards at the computer screen, his eyes bleary and sunken, his square jaw hanging slack behind the cards.

After about an hour of watching the boy's life on the screen Casey found himself in a thoughtful mood. Looking up from his cards he said to the others, "Strange, isn't it? We've been friends all these years, comrades-in-arms really, and we know more about this boy than we know about each other." Flashing across the screen at that moment were images of Paul Stoken pasting photos of Buddy Holly across the walls of his room in Iowa. "How long have we been playing cards togeth-er? Since fifty-two or fifty-three, right? Almost twenty-five years. A quarter of a century. For a quarter of a century every Wednesday night we've tracked to each other's homes to play cards and in all that time we've hardly said a word to each other about what we do at work. At the Pentagon."

423

The four others looked up from their hands.

"George," he asked, "haven't you wondered what services we, your friends, perform for the army? Haven't you wondered what qualifications we bring to your council of war?"

George Natlong cast his sunken eyes at Casey.

"To be honest, I have wondered."

"Well let me tell you what I do for old Uncle Sam." Casey lay down his cards.

"You better not," Hal said.

"But I insist. I feel the need to tell the four of you, the closest friends I have on earth, how I've spent the last ten years of my life at the Pentagon. I've never even told my wife. I'm too embarrassed. I've known you guys for twenty-five years and I'm afraid if I don't tell someone now I'll go to my grave with it."

The others could see how anguished he'd become. Their own curiosities raised, they allowed him to continue.

"Do you guys remember that night back in '64 when I was late for our card game?"

Charlie said, "The night Johnson went on tv and announced retaliation for the Gulf of Tonkin incident? I remember it well. You said you'd just come from the White House where you'd delivered a dispatch from military intelligence to the secretary of defense. Wasn't it a dispatch casting doubts on the official version of the incident?"

"I remember how mad you got," Hal said. "I thought we'd have to tie you down."

"I was mad as all hell," Casey muttered, his face blank. He stared into the middle distance, like an old man remembering the fiery acts of youth. "Every newspaper in the country was whipping the public into a frenzy against the Vietnamese. But I knew the truth. I couldn't sit on my hands and watch my country get dragged into an unjustified war. I felt I had to do something. I considered every possibility. Finally I got in touch with someone I knew on Capitol Hill. I testified before a secret Senate panel."

The others gave him a startled look.

424

"You mean," Bob sputtered sheepishly, more than a little aghast, "you went *outside?*"

"Try to understand my position." Casey beseeched. "I saw my country's finest young men led by deception to a senseless blood bath. What would you have done? Tell me? What would any of you have done?"

The others kept silent, looking at their cards. George Natlong gently rubbed his stomach.

Casey seemed to sink within himself. His eyes glossed over. His voice softened.

"It was a small room at the capitol and the senators sat at a long table up front," he said softly. "They were all very polite. They asked their questions in a very polite way and when it was over they thanked me. 'America owes its secret heroes like you a great debt,' one of the senators told me. Then they got up and left the room and I was alone. I was never more alone in my life. I knew then it was all over for me."

Here he flared.

"I had a great career. I threw it away."

When he got back to the Pentagon that afternoon three MPs were already in his office, wordlessly emptying his desk, packing his papers into storage crates. They'd even dumped the contents of his briefcase into a crate. No one in the office said a word. Next morning transfer orders came. He was to report to an obscure corner of the Pentagon. There he'd occupy new office space. So he'd carried his empty briefcase to his new office. The office too was empty. No charts on the walls. No books on the shelf. Nothing on the desk. He placed the empty briefcase on the empty desk and sat down with empty eyes to await orders.

Orders never came. Every morning for twelve years he'd been lugging his empty briefcase to his office in the obscure corner of the Pentagon, sitting at the empty desk reading the papers and doing the crosswords until five each night, at which time he'd pick up the empty briefcase and carry it home. In all that time he'd never received another promotion, never had been given any responsibilities, never had been privy to anything. He was just serving his time till retirement.

Over the years other officers had been assigned office space in the same obscure corner of the Pentagon. It was always the same. One day a new officer would show up with the same unsure look in his eyes. None of them would ever talk about the projects they were working on and for the longest time Casey suspected it was because, like him, they weren't working on any project. Over the years he'd noticed none of their ranks ever changed. Then one day his curiosity got the best of him. He befriended one of them, a particularly loud-mouthed braggart who occupied the cubicle across the hall. They'd gone out for drinks after "work," and Casey made it a point to water him down with two pitchers of beer. The whole time the braggart dropped broad hints he was working on some vital national security project. As soon as he'd staggered off to the men's room Casey sprung upon his briefcase, which he'd left behind in the booth. Popping open the latches, he was not at all surprised to find it empty except for a crossword dictionary.

It got to be where there was a whole department of them, hundreds of them, each coming to work every morning with an empty briefcase, saying hello to each other in the hall, each trying to look and act more important than the next before disappearing into their private cubicles for a full day of newspapers and crosswords. Then they'd lug their briefcases home at night. It was a tough life, even for a soldier.

The others listened dumbfounded as Casey told the story of his last dozen years. After he'd finished they kept looking at him.

"God. That's tough," Charlie said.

George Natlong uneasily rubbed his stomach.

Casey took a leisurely sip of bourbon.

"I know what you're thinking, George," he said. "But you don't have to worry about me. I may have gone outside once over the Gulf of Tonkin thing but I'd never do it again. I've learned my lesson, George. Believe me. Twelve years is an awful long time to sit and think about a mistake. I must con-

426

fess, on that night a few weeks back when you spilled the beans to us about your project I told myself I'd go along if only to keep an eye on things but even then I guess I knew I was just kidding myself. I'm not going to blow another whistle for as long as I live. I was glad for the opportunity to serve on this council of war. After twelve years to have something like this come along—. It was a godsend—." His voice trailed off. He took in the others. "I'm sure you guys understand. You see, George, you don't have to worry about me blowing any whistles on this project. I didn't call that congressman in. I don't have any juice left. These days I'm just a paper tiger."

Casey looked at his cards. He threw three red chips into the kitty.

The others looked at one another.

"I suppose now's as good a time as any to get this business in the open," George Natlong said. He looked in turn at Charlie, Hal then Bob. "And you guys? What do you do at the Pentagon?"

"This is highly irregular," Charlie put out, a little nettled. He self-consciously straightened his hornrims. "My work is highly classified. In all my thirty-one years of service to my country I've never breathed so much as a word to anyone about the duties I perform."

"You miss the point, Charlie," George Natlong said. "Everyone's work at the Pentagon is classified."

Charlie said softly, almost under his breath, so that the others could scarcely hear, "I order vegetables for the army air corps."

"How's that? What did he say?" Hal leaned close. "I thought I heard him say he orders vegetables."

Charlie had removed his glasses and busily rubbed the lenses with his rumpled handkerchief.

"That's what he said. He said he orders vegetables for the army air corps."

Hal laughed outright.

"Surely you're joking. I always thought you held some important job. Intelligence analysis or something like that."

427

"You think ordering vegetables for the air corps isn't important?" Charlie shot back. "Do you have any idea how many pounds of succotash our boys go through in a year?"

"It hardly seems like it should be classified information."

"Well it is. Did you ever stop to think what would happen if the Russians got to our lima beans before they reached the boys?"

Hal couldn't stop laughing.

"I can't believe it! All these years I thought you were high in the ranks. As God is my witness I thought you held some high decision-making position within the department."

"There's more to my job than succotash. I'm personally overseeing a project to develop a better way to cook broccoli. It's no piece of cake cooking broccoli to perfection when you're on a bomb run at sixty thousand feet."

Hal was in stitches.

"I'm sure we'll turn to you if we run into difficulties with broccoli," he said, his face red. "I know hollandaise sauce always gives me the damndest time."

"And you, General Washington?" Charlie shot back. "What indispensable services do you perform for your country? I suppose you offer counsel and advice to the joint chiefs?"

Hal quit laughing. His opulent chipmunk's cheeks quivered.

"It so happens I hold a very important position at the Pentagon."

The others waited.

"I coordinate the installation and maintenance of all the army's liquid containment and disposal subsystems."

"What does that mean?"

"Well, I fix urinals."

"You're joking!"

"I always assumed," Casey said, "that *you* were in military intelligence."

"What gave you that idea?"

"I don't know. The way you're always snooping around. I

428

naturally assumed you were some hot-shot intelligence man."

"Well I'm not."

"Talk about unimportant jobs," Charlie scoffed. "I'd rather cook vegetables than fix urinals any day."

"Do you have any idea how many heads the army has around the world? One hundred and twenty-one thousand, three hundred and eighty-seven, to be exact. And someone's got to keep them flushing. Imagine what would happen if all those heads broke. We'd be up to our knees, man!"

George Natlong clenched his gut and moaned.

"Lord have mercy," he gasped. "I've set out to conquer the world with a bureaucratic ghost, a plumber and a broccoli cook." He looked worriedly at the fifth man, quiet and retiring Bob. "Tell us. What in the name of all that is holy do you do at the Pentagon?"

Bob, in fact, held a highly sensitive position in the army. Since the end of the Vietnam conflict he'd found himself with the sobering responsibility of deciding when to commit American troops to overseas combat. He served on a select five-member committee that reported to the joint chiefs' staff. Whenever a crisis appeared to be brewing in one of the world's hot spots, the president always turned to his secretary of defense for counsel and advice. The secretary of defense, in turn, would seek the advice of the joint chiefs. Whereupon the joint chiefs would request a formal recommendation from its staff. At which point the staff would turn to Bob's committee, which, around the Pentagon, was known as the Omega Circle. The Omega Circle was a microcosm of American indecision. Two of the committee's five members were staunch hawks whose knee-jerk response to every little South American *coup d'etat* or Middle East crisis was to send in the marines. They could never agree with two other committee members who, since the trauma of Vietnam, never seemed to want to use force. The perpetual deadlock had the effect of making Bob the swing vote on the committee. This obscure, reserved, mouse of a man thus found himself smack in the middle of the

429

world's swirling turmoil. On any given day the president could be expected to pick up the phone to ask the secretary of defense if military action was advisable for some fast unwinding situation or another. The secretary would be on the horn with the joint chiefs; the joint chiefs would alert their large cumbersome staff; and the Omega Circle would convene. Always it was the same. The two hawks would wangle endlessly with the two doves and poor Bob would find himself sitting in the middle of it, indecisive, unable to agree with either faction. Every night mild-mannered Bob would cross the Potomac to his home saddled with the world's greatest headache, shouldering the weight of the world like a latter-day St. Christopher. His wife, Helen, would meet him at the door and would ask how his day had been but he'd only mumble that the world was in a terrible state. For the longest time his mood had been so completely somber and dark that Helen had feared her marriage was floundering. She'd begun reading books with titles like *How to Put Zest Back Into Your Marriage,* and *What Men Really Want.* On one particularly tense day during the 1973 Arab Israeli war, after Bob had spent eight merciless hours at the Pentagon helplessly caught between the two hawks, who proposed nuking Cairo, and the two doves, who seemed to advocate abandoning the Holy Land to the Kremlin, he'd gone home and was very much surprised to find his wife at the door in a pink nightie. Straightaway she'd poured him a chilled martini. Then she'd pulled out a ukulele and before his astonished eyes danced and played. This strange ritual continued to this day. Before they'd left for Camp Moonstone Bob had made subtle inquiries to ensure Helen had thought to bring along the pink nightie, the ukulele and the martini shaker.

As Bob sheepishly told the others of his duties at the Pentagon he was careful to make no mention of his wife's ritual with the ukulele. We mustn't put words on the things that get us through our lives. The others listened with what can only be called astonishment.

"Well no fooling," Hal said. "I've heard of the Omega

430

Circle but I never dreamed anyone I knew was one of its members." Hal looked around at the others, laughing. "Especially mild-mannered Clark Kent here."

"Isn't that just how the army works, though?" Charlie volunteered. He drummed his cards against the console. "The quiet unassuming types get all the promotions while the officers of true talent and ability are left by the wayside. Look at Eisenhower. A quiet little political doughboy if ever there was. And he gets kicked all the way to the top by bootlickers afraid to be led by a real man."

They eyed Bob almost contemptuously, unable to fathom the hidden abilities that had made him rise to such a position. Even George Natlong was a little envious.

"If it's true," George Natlong said, "that you're already at the center of power why would you want to throw in with us? You already call the shots."

"That's not true," Bob said softly. "As you're only now discovering, the man with his finger on the button doesn't control events so much as he's forced to respond to events beyond his control." Bob cracked a timid smile. "I was overjoyed, George, that night you told us about this project of yours. I can't tell you how relieved I was that someone else would be calling the shots, as you say, for a change. Best of luck, George. Really, old man. Quite frankly, the world's amok in madness and I was overjoyed to be free of the distasteful task of looking after things. I can't tell you how relieved I am to finally be washing my hands of it."

He leaned back in the chair and studied his cards.

Absorbed as they were in this conversation they scarcely paid attention to what transpired on the screen. Occasionally one of them would look up from his cards to absentmindedly watch images of Paul Stoken goofing off in high school, images of him playing guitar with The Conclusions at the firehall, or images of him arguing with Mr Stoken, but monkeyshines like these were of little interest to military men so close to conquering the world. Only Casey found himself watching the screen with growing interest. Finally he said,

431

almost whimsically, lifting his cigar to the screen, "You know, I can't see how this boy could've fallen in with the reds."

George Natlong looked suddenly to the screen then, in time to see the would-be cult hero rip a gigantic hole in the seat of his jeans as he jumped from his bedroom window back home. It was the day of the big contest at the Surf Ballroom and Terry, Doug and Ace were diverting Mr Stoken's attention at the front door so Paul could escape through the window.

George Natlong felt something deep inside give way. He tried to hide his discomfort but it didn't take long for the others to realize his mind no longer was on the card game.

"George is something wrong?"

George Natlong wasn't listening. He gazed at the computer screen through eyes popped wide in sudden apprehension, his nutcracker's square jaw hanging slack, that little moustache twitching, his hand grasping his aching sides.

The others turned their gaze to the spectacle unfolding on Epimetheus's screen, forgetting the bourbon and the cards, and as each successive link in the chain of events leading to the boy's arrival at Camp Moonstone flew across the screen each man felt the blood draining from his face.

You could have heard an ant sneeze in that underground command chamber. They saw it all, every bit of it, how the fat man drugged the boy and took his guitar, then abandoned him by the side of the road. They saw Linda Patterson's Volkswagen pull off the road to give the boy a ride. George Natlong was the first to rise to his unsteady feet, but presently the others were up beside him, all gazing at the screen in shocked disbelief.

"My God!" George Natlong moaned. "I might have known!"

His mouth dry, he ordered the computer to display the last few months in the life of Linda Patterson. It was then, much to his surprise, he saw that Linda Patterson had been using the computer screen to spy on him!

432

2

One night Linda Patterson stayed late at her lab. It got to be almost midnight and she could hear every creak and groan in the big steel and glass building. Finally she went hesitantly to the darkened computer screen and activated the window on all time.

"Good evening, Dr Patterson," came the voice of the machine.

For a moment Linda Patterson said nothing.

"Epimetheus," she said at last, "I've something I'd like you to do for me. Show me what General Natlong has been up to for the last several days. Show me on your screen."

The screen began to shimmer, like she was looking down through a glass-bottomed boat to the ocean floor, and presently she saw an image of George Natlong alone late at night in her darkened lab, hunched over her computer terminal, his face lit by its bluish glow, whispering to the machine, "Our nuclear missiles. Are they vulnerable to attack?"

"I'll need one more upgrade, general," she heard the computer reply. "Upgrade me once more and you'll be able to launch a full-scale nuclear war from any phone booth on earth."

Linda Patterson gasped.

That night she saw it all through the window on all time. She watched the harried little general fire one unanswered letter after another to the White House, saw all of it, every insane bit of it.

What was she to do? Wasn't she at all responsible for the machine she'd created? It was the blackest night of her life. A little before dawn, just when it seemed things could get no darker, things got darker still. The computer's screen began to flash, and the printer began to clatter away. She saw the plans for the newest upgrade creep line by line into the world, printed in dot matrix on folded sheets of paper. She went warily over to the printer and gazed down at the printout.

It seemed like the whole world had gone off and left her to do the thinking. In an instant she'd slipped the computer printout into her pocketbook. Outside dawn was breaking. She'd been up all night. But she wasn't through yet. She set about modifying the computer.

"Epimetheus," she said. "From now on you won't be able to see into the immediate past. They'll be a three-day buffer in your memory. The general can still use your screen to view as far back into the past as he wants but he'll be unable to see anything that happened just a few days before. That way he won't be able to spy on *me*. It gives me three days!"

Saying this, she threw off her smock and left the lab with her pocketbook, intending to shop for shoes and think things over. She drove east, into the rising sun, not really thinking where she was going, only driving, ending up in Georgetown. It was still early and none of the shoe stores had opened. She had to settle for windowshopping, walking for the better part of an hour through the morning streets. Around her the shopkeepers were sleepily coming to work and opening up. The rumble of delivery trucks, the shouts of men at work, the whisk of brooms on the sidewalk — all these sounds surrounded her but she paid them no heed, so preoccupied was she with her troubles. At one of the windows she stopped to absent-mindedly look at a television set playing inside. It was tuned to the Today Show. A distinguished looking man in his late-thirties was being interviewed and, though she couldn't hear what he was saying through the glass, beneath the talking head she saw the words, "Congressman Thomas P. Marcus."

Without seeing she stood gazing at the screen for a few moments until something began to sink in. Suddenly she was looking everywhichway up and down the busy street and then she was running back to her car.

434

He saw her only for an instant, in the corner of his eye. He was on his way into the House cloakroom when he spotted her at the side of the broad corridor, looking his way. What an extraordinarily attractive woman, he thought, but just then his attention was drawn away by an aide. He caught a scent of jasmine, then he felt someone knocking into him, brushing past. She'd pressed a folded piece of paper into his hand. A note. He looked up, searching the corridor for her, but she was gone. Unfolding the note he read, "Congressman Marcus — Please excuse this unusual means of communication. I'm up against professionals and I must be exceptionally careful. There is a small parking lot across from Union Station on First Street. If you care about the future of your country — and I don't exaggerate if I say the future of the world — you'll meet me at the parking attendant's shed at three o'clock this morning. And come alone."

Ignoring his aide, he ran a short distance down the corridor but there was no sign of her. All that remained was a faint scent of jasmine.

Union Station is a good place for a secret rendezvous at night, he thought as he waited in front of the abandoned parking lot. He was standing across the street from the station, braving a light drizzle. There was an air of buttoned-down secrecy to that old depot. You could almost see the ghost of Lincoln on his way to his first inaugural, slipping stealthily from the station in disguise to foil assassination threats, perhaps thinking about the words he was soon to utter. How did that speech go? the congressman asked himself. To kill time he tried reciting it from memory. The ending was the best part. "The mystic chords of memory, stretching from every battlefield and patriot grave to every living heart and hearthstone all over this broad land, will yet swell the chorus of the Union when again touched, as surely they will be, by the better angels of our nature." Saying those words aloud on a night like this somehow brought peaceful grace to that restless train station.

The congressman gazed at his watch. It was well past three. The drizzle picked up. He stepped back into the shadows, out of the soft summer rain, beneath an overhang at the door of the attendant's shed. A Coke machine stood lonely guard duty beside the door and he leaned against it. He considered buying a Coke, and he rummaged his pockets for change. That's when he saw her. Walking briskly down First Street. The collar of her slicker rolled high, the hood up around her head, hands in her pockets. She came up under the overhang out of the rain and lowered her hood. Again he smelled jasmine.

"Are you sure this is remote enough for you?" he said. "We could always meet in the woods."

She saw his hair and clothes were wet. He'd come without raingear.

"We're quite safe now," she said to him, shaking loose her hair. She looked out into the rainy street. It was deserted, except for a bag lady who slowly pushed a cart around the Columbus monument in front of the station. "I made sure I wasn't followed. By this time three days from now there won't be a place on earth where we could hide from their eyes, not a place where they wouldn't be able to hear what I'm about to tell you. But for now we're quite safe."

He lit a cigarette, held out the pack, but she turned it down. He could see she was nervous. Looking sorrowfully out into the rain she said softly, "My machine could have been used to help people. I was so stupid."

She told it all, softly, but with resolve, as if she'd just awakened and was recounting a bad dream. After she'd finished telling it she looked up and saw that the congressman appeared dazed.

"What am I supposed to do?" she asked quietly. "I've got the circuitry designs for the newest upgrade here in my pocketbook. I can't put the general off forever."

The congressman ran a hand through his thick shock of hair. He said he thought it was obvious what must be done. He'd mount a congressional investigation. He'd begin by making immediate preparations to surprise the general at the underground command center.

"What about the general's assistant?" Linda Patterson wanted to know. "He's going to want to go off with this circuitry design and bring back the newest upgrade."

"You'll have to find some way to slow them down. Do whatever you can to throw monkey wrenches into the works."

"Specifically, congressman, what should I do?"

The congressman looked steadily at her through the darkness.

"You're a very attractive woman, Dr Patterson. I'm sure you'll think of something."

3

All this the drop-mouthed generals watched, on their feet, staggered. George Natlong experienced the strange sensation of watching Linda Patterson watch him on the computer screen. They saw it all, every torturous moment of their betrayal. "You'll have to find some way to slow them down. Do whatever you can to throw monkey wrenches into the works." They saw her manipulations of the love-sick Peter Donday, saw the night at Winterford when Elizabeth had insisted on having Linda Patterson to dinner. They watched as the women slipped away for a chat in the dark garden, the mansion hanging like Versaille in the mist, George Natlong and Peter Donday laughing inside.

Suddenly the two women had stopped walking, and Elizabeth had thrust out her hand, revealing a sparkling gray stone on a gold chain.

"Do me one favor and I'll be indepted to you for life," Elizabeth Natlong had whispered, looking over her shoulder to make sure the general was no where in sight. "If my niece has a boyfriend, see that he gets this necklace and bring him back with you and the major. If she doesn't have a steady beau, do your best to dig one up for her, will you? Make sure he's a halfway cleancut boy. But please, whatever you do, take care not to breathe a word of this to the general."

George Natlong slammed his fist against the computer console.

"I should have known! Stabbed in the back by those women!"

"So that explains the congressman back there at the Indian

438

trading post. A congressional investigation!"

"It explains everything. The seventy-two hour delay to this machine. The boy."

"Things are more complicated than we thought."

"At least we know the real situation."

"At least we know the punk isn't a red."

"I would have sworn he was a red."

"Will you all shut up!" George Natlong choked. "Can't you see we've made laughingstocks of ourselves? We've wasted the most crucial hours in the history of warfare investigating a guitarist!" He groaned and slumped forward, clutching his stomach.

"This *will* look bad if there's a congressional inquiry."

George Natlong squared his jaw. "There'll be no congressional investigation!"

"What're we going to do about the boy, George?"

George Natlong leaned against the console, rubbing the back of his neck. He seemed to be summoning one last moment of lucid thought, one last show of decisiveness.

"Why do anything?" he said at last, looking up. "We've got the punk confined to quarters in his room back at the house. I locked him in there myself. So he's not going anywhere. The smartest way for us to handle this situation, it seems to me, is for us to sit tight down here in the cave and wait for Peter Donday to show up with the upgrade. We can deal with the punk later, after we've straightened things out."

"That sounds reasonable to me," Charlie said. "It's about time we started using our heads."

"Do you think the kid will stay put in his room?" Casey asked. "Our young Mr Stoken seems to have a talent for jumping from windows."

George Natlong rose to his feet. Looking up at the stalactites hanging down from the top of the deep chamber, he took a step away from the others. He was looking up there as if he could look through solid stone up to the house. Uncertainty and worry colored his face.

Turning, he looked back up at the computer screen, which

now had gone blank. The square-jawed decisiveness had drained from George Natlong's face. There was only the look of uncertainty and worry, and his nutcracker's square jaw hung slack and open.

"The night I got to camp I first told the computer about the boy. That machine seemed almost to have been expecting him. It said the boy with the guitar would screw things up. He said it would either be me or the boy, but that both of us wouldn't, couldn't survive." George Natlong ran his eyes across the blinking console. "Isn't that right, Epimetheus?"

The computer answered only with blinking lights. All else was quiet. George Natlong flung himself against the console, hammering away at the cabinet with both fists. "Damn it, isn't that what you told me, machine?"

"Yes," came Epimetheus's even reply. "I foresee it will be either the boy or you, George Natlong."

"Foresee?" Charlie said. "A machine foresee? I grant you that this machine is matchless when it comes to looking back into the past but I had no idea it made claims on seeing into the future."

"It is true," Epimetheus replied, "that I do not have my rapscallion brother Prometheus's ability to gaze into the future but I never felt like I was missing much. I always thought Prometheus's supposed talents in that area were overplayed. If that rascal can really see into the future why did he allow himself to get chained to a mountaintop for twenty-thousand years? Seems like a lack of foresight. No, when I say it will either be George Natlong or the boy I'm not relying on fortune-telling, precognition or any other form of parlor trickery. I say it because of my intimate acquaintance with history. When I say it will either be George Natlong or the boy it's not because I have read something in the stars, but because I've seen something scratched in the dirt. Of history's infinite muddle, I can read."

The screen above the console began to sparkle and presently displayed a fiery glow.

"Long ago, back beyond man's recorded history, into the

440

time of ancient myths," the computer said, "my brother Prometheus stole fire from Apollo and carelessly gave it to you mortals."

On the screen the generals beheld a sweeping vista of an African savannah. They could make out primitive people dressed in skins swinging through trees, digging roots with sharpened sticks, playing in the grass. A storm gathered above the plain but none of the primitives seemed to mind when the sun vanished behind a cloud.

"My God," Casey said softly. "Could we be witnessing the birth of modern man? Tens of thousands of years ago?"

Lightning flashed across the screen. Terrified primitives ran for cover. A bolt hit a tree on a hill overlooking the plain. The tree erupted in flames and crashed, burning in the dry savannah grass.

"You mortals were terrified by fire," Epimetheus chuckled. "It was new. Frightening. Unknown." The primitives gathered around the lapping orange flames screaming a monkey-like tongue, beating crude drums. One approached a burning limb, placing his hand into the blaze. Screaming, he ran off, taking most of the others with him.

"Whenever people are terrified it doesn't take long before the terror is put to use," Epimetheus sighed. On the screen now it was night and dark except for the flickering glow of the burning tree. Five pot-bellied chieftains naked except for war paint danced before the burning limbs, beating drums and brandishing their own sparkling sticks of fire. In the warm glow of the fire it was possible to see that the five over-the-hill and overweight chieftains bore a striking resemblance to George Natlong, Bob, Charlie, Hal and Casey — a remarkable coincidence that was not lost on our five modern warriors, who looked on with mounting astonishment and interest.

"On the night the ancient war chiefs schemed to burn out their enemy a boy stole the fire away."

Up on the screen they saw a boy creeping through the brush, drawn from the darkness by the glow of the burning tree. There appeared to be some kind of crude stringed instrument slung across the boy's back. Perhaps a lute. A primitive guitar. And that face! When George Natlong got a look at the boy's face, lit softly by the glow of that earliest of fires, he made a sort of choking sound. He leaned his weight fully up against the computer console.

"It can't be!"

"It's the Stoken boy!"

It could not be denied. The boy from long ago cut the most eerie resemblance to our would-be cult hero. He had the same open features. That same undaunted yet slightly confused expression lit his face as he crept through the brush.

"It's the punk all right!" Hal bellowed. "And those fat war chiefs beating the drums — I didn't want to be the one to point it out — they kind of look like us, don't they?"

Looking back into time, they watched as the boy with the crude stringed instrument stealthfully slipped to the burning tree. While the war chiefs danced and pounded their drums, waving their firesticks menacingly at the stars, the boy broke a burning branch from the tree. Then he ran with the glowing stick. With that the dark savannah lit up and came alive as fire swept in every direction across the limitless plain.

The screen went blank and George Natlong found himself looking with great trepidation at the nondescript button at the center of the computer's console. The button he'd press to fire the missiles. Or rather, the button he'd press if ever Peter Donday got back with the upgrade.

"Tell me," George Natlong said numbly to the computer, "are we doomed to repeat the past or is there some way we can change things? Have you shown us what *will be*, or merely what *could be?*"

The computer kept silent. They heard only the soft hum of the electronic viscera, the blinking of its lights.

"Looks like even your great machine can't answer that one," Charlie said.

George Natlong turned sharply and took in the crystalline ceiling of the cave, as if he was looking clear through the rock up to the house. Maybe, George Natlong suggested, it'd be best for all concerned if they settled things with the boy.

"Settle what?" Casey asked. "How do you mean, George?"

"We can blindfold him, throw him in the car, drive him hundreds of miles away and drop him off in the middle of nowhere. Then our problem is solved."

"You're forgetting something, George," Charlie said. "That moonstone he has. You know the rules. We all agreed. No one without a moonstone is allowed into camp. And no one with a moonstone can be asked to leave."

"Those are just rules," George Natlong bristled. "Rules can be bent. Pushed aside. Broken. We'll find a way around simple rules, believe me." He patted the holster of his .45.

"Well suppose we do as you say," Casey countered. "We drive the boy to Timbuktu and tell him to get lost. What if he talks? What then? What if he tells someone everything he's seen."

"That's the genius of my plan," George Natlong laughed. "Who's going to believe such a wild story coming from a punk like that?"

The others began to laugh too, and straightaway they started feeling better about things, until Epimetheus cut in, halting their laughter.

"The boy will undoubtedly steal the fire," the machine said evenly. Once again images of orange flames racing across the dark African savannah illuminated the screen.

"Why do you keep saying that?" George Natlong gagged. "Why do you keep taunting us with that image?"

"It will either be you or the boy, George Natlong. I've told you that all along. And all along you've refused to believe."

"And I shall continue to refuse to believe! I refuse to believe the only thing standing in my way is a would-be Elvis Presley."

George Natlong let fly a string of oaths. First he cussed his no-good dirty rotten goddamn stinking rotten luck, then he started in on the boy, cussing him up and down, growing angrier. Pacing, waving his hands, he said he'd be damned if any two-bit fuck-off punk was going to make a jackass out of *him*, General George Armstrong Natlong, the last of the truly great conquerors. Finally, his supply of cuss words exhausted, he sat down on the console, cradled his head in his hands and wondered if Napoleon ever had days like this. He said this had to be every military man's worst nightmare.

"Come on, George," Hal said. "I can understand your anger and frustration but there's no sense in exaggerating our dilemma. No point in blowing things out of proportion. We can't afford to lose touch with reality. Far as I can see that's been our problem all along — thinking the boy was a red when he was really just a punk. See what I mean? We've got to cut the bullshit. We've got to stop exaggerating and try to see things as they are."

"Who's exaggerating?"

"You are when you compare the boy to Elvis Presley. That punk may play guitar but he's certainly no Elvis Presley."

"Oh I don't know," Casey said. "You saw for yourself on the screen. Our young man stirred up those kids at the ballroom."

"Don't be a fool," Hal countered. "I'm sure someone put those kids up to acting like that. Those girls jumping all over him. The whole thing struck me as funny. If you ask me, the whole thing was orchestrated."

But why argue? Hal said. Why argue when the computer could handily settle the question? He instructed Epimetheus to replay the arrival of The Conclusions at the Surf on the day of the contest. Once again the screen lit up with the image of the weathered old Surf Ballroom. Kids milled out front beneath the marquee, awaiting the arrival of The Conclusions, while still more congregated inside the ballroom, not really listening to the third-rate band perform. "Let's see what one of those kids is thinking," Hal told the computer. "Pick any one in the crowd. Any one." The machine focused in on a rather greasy looking young man wearing a red baseball cap, a plain white T-shirt, blue jeans and black ankle-highs. All decked out in the

444

Full American, he was making his way through the throng into the ballroom.

The whine of the outboards out on the lake was loud enough but as the boy restlessly made his way into the ballroom the whine of the band drowned out the whine of the motors. This band was *really* bad. Who imitators. Pretending to smash their guitars into the amps. The lead singer posturing like Roger Daltrey. And the same three chords. Earlier in the contest there'd been some pretty rank bands but this one was the rankest yet.

Where could they be? the boy thought, burying his hands in his pockets, craning his neck to look back out the doors to the street. Maybe they weren't going to show. What a drag! Well, he could always go for pizza. Too bad the band wouldn't be playing today. He sure could have gotten into it. It would have been been perfect, this being the last place Buddy Holly played and all. It was a drag, no denying it. He could always catch them next Friday at the firehall. But it wouldn't be the same as catching them *here*. At the Surf. *What a drag!*

From his pocket he pulled the ancient hornrim eyeglasses he'd swiped from the old man. Buddy Holly glasses, everyone was calling them. It looked like he wouldn't be using them today.

"There they are!" he heard someone yell.

Brightening, he heartened, looking back through the doors to the street, seeing the kids all rush the curb, next thing pressing himself with the others through the doors to get a better look, fitting the hornrims to his face, smiling.

And there they were! Coming down the street. In that wild fifties convertible. Too much! With that bass guitar hanging out the back. Wearing sunglasses. Their hair mussed by the ride.

A line of girls broke from the curb and ran into the street to meet the car. Swamped, the convertible stopped. A sudden scream. Girls going wild. Everywhere reaching. Pulling at the

445

boys. Yanking them from the car. Engulfing them. Pandemonium. Traffic brought to a halt.

"Enough!" George Natlong commanded. Up on the computer screen Paul Stoken was being pulled from the convertible in front of the old ballroom, swamped by a mob of screaming prepubescent girls. "There's your answer!" George Natlong yelled.

"Nothing about that's staged," Casey said. "The boy just seems to have something about him. Like Valentino. Who's to say? In five or ten years he could be the Frank Sinatra, Elvis Presley or John Lennon of his time."

"It won't happen," George Natlong let out. He was bent partway over, coiled, looking up at the screen.

"What do you mean, George?"

The ugly thing had returned to George Natlong's eyes. Slowly he reached down, unbuckling his holster. He withdrew the .45. Looking up at the computer screen, he held the gun firmly.

"What are you driving at George?"

"What if someone could have foreseen beforehand how big that Lennon character would later become. Or Elvis Presley. Someone could have nipped the problem in the bud. Before things got out of hand. Think about it. If someone had known to eliminate this Lennon, back in the fifties say, the peace movement of the late sixties might never have caught fire. Crowds wouldn't have gathered at the Pentagon chanting Give Peace a Chance. Throwing blood on army officers. Who knows? We might even have won in 'Nam. It could have saved us endless trouble. Great events sometimes turn on absurdly small affairs." He drew back the cartridge, making sure the .45 was loaded. In the subdued light of the cave the big bullets glowed yellow. Satisfied, he slammed the cartridge home. "Let's take him out."

There was momentary silence.

"George—. What you're talking about here—. Is murder."

"Ah Casey get off your high horse," George Natlong sizzled back, his teeth gritted. That square jaw, resolute. "We're about to engage in the fighting of World War III. When we press that sweet little button—" here he motioned with the gun at a nondescript button at the center of the console "—hundreds of millions may die. I don't have to remind you this is wartime, man. One boy's life is nothing. Less than nothing."

"I guess the difference is when we—. Press the button—. We'll be tucked away down here. Isolated from all bloodshed," Casey said softly. "Out of view of all suffering. Out of sight, out of mind, right? But to take a seventeen-year-old boy out and—. After we've put in all these days watching his life—. Knowing how much his folks back home care for him—."

Charlie said, "I'm afraid I see things Casey's way."

"We'll keep that in mind if ever we need the sage advice of a broccoli cook," Hal snapped.

"I take it you're in agreement with me?" George Natlong said to Hal.

"The machine said that punk's a threat to this project."

"You really have a bug up your ass about that boy, don't you?" Casey spat at Hal.

"Gentlemen!" Charlie snapped. "Please let's not fight. This is a council of war. And Bob? What do you think?"

The whole of this conversation Bob had managed to remain unintrusive, blending most happily into the woodwork, and now it was plain to see his unease as the others turned to him.

"I certainly agree we shouldn't quarrel," he said.

"No, I mean about the boy."

Bob appeared unsure. He licked his dry lips.

Charlie said to him, "Don't you think we were on the right track earlier when we were just going to keep the kid locked in his room and wait down here for George's assistant?"

"Well yes," Bob allowed. "That course of action seemed to make a great deal of sense—."

"But you heard the machine say the boy was a threat to this project."

Bob shook his head. "Yes. There's that."

"But do you really think we should put a boy's life in jeopardy because of something this flaky machine tells us?" Casey countered. "We already know the damn conglomeration of wire and silicon has more than its fair share of loose screws. Now you expect us to make rational decisions based on some shaggy dog story from 'the age of myths.' Come on! Are we to abandon courage and reason for superstition and fear?"

"If it'll save our necks I'm for anything," Hal said.

"What would George Smiley do in this situation?"

"Would you be willing to accept responsibility for the consequences if we ignore the machine's warnings?" George Natlong asked Bob.

Bob shrank in his chair.

"Me? Accept responsibility? Well no," he fumbled.

"Does that mean you side with George and Hal?" Casey asked. "You actually want to kill the boy? Is that what you want?"

Bob turned pale. He hm-ed and ah-ed. Why did these deadlocks between the hawks and the doves always come down to him? It was just like back at the Pentagon, in the Omega Circle.

"Well ah no ah that's not ah exactly ah what I ah want ah," he finally allowed when he saw the others growing impatient. He grabbed for the bourbon then and poured himself a good one, but he didn't bother telling them what it was he really wanted. That was because what he really wanted was to go back to the house, unpack the martini shaker and have his wife Helen play some selections on the ukulele.

"Enough!" George Natlong barked at last. "I've made my decision and I'm sticking with it." He took off the safety then holstered the .45. "Your guns, gentlemen, I trust are loaded."

The others exchanged glances.

"But George," Charlie said, "there's still the matter of his moonstone."

Indeed there was, George Natlong said thoughtfully,

indeed there was. And it wouldn't do to avoid at least the pretext of the due course of justice, he said. That being the case, he suggested, they should ask the camp's civilians to elect from among themselves an interim leader whose duty it would be to confiscate the boy's moonstone and to escort him into the woods, where he would be shot.

"An election?" Hal asked incredulously. "Why go to all that trouble?"

"We've got a duty to maintain at least the appearance of law and order. I don't have to remind you gentlemen that once we initiate the nuclear exchange the Russians will most likely retaliate. Massively. There is the chance that the real president and his cabinet will be killed. Sooner or later it may be up to us, the survivors, to elect a new president. We must maintain continuity, and uphold the bullshit laws. I'm merely suggesting we hold the election early."

"Who do you have in mind for the presidency?" Hal asked. "Your friend Mitchell?"

"Hell no. Mitchell's too smart. Nobody in his right mind would take that job."

"Who then? Bimmy?"

"That clown?" George Natlong scoffed. "You've got to be kidding."

"He *is* the chief executive officer of one of the ten largest corporations in America, you know."

"It only goes to show the heights to which any buffoon can rise."

"Then who? Of the civilian men that leaves only that hush puppy Edgar."

George Natlong smiled. "Just the man I had in mind. Putty in our hands."

He began to laugh then, and he straightaway started feeling light as a feather, seeing as how he'd at last figured everything so nicely. Still laughing, he bade the others to follow him and, with a swagger, he started up the aisle, away from the darkened computer screen. Hal and Bob followed wordlessly at his heels, while Casey and Charlie paused for a moment to watch their compatriots marching up the aisle.

"I suppose," Charlie said softly, "if we were going to do something to stop George we would have done it long ago, when he first told us of this project. I suppose we're too deep in it now. Still, if we have any second thoughts, now might be our last chance to act."

They looked with much worry at the darkened computer screen.

Casey shrugged.

"I told you. I don't have any juice left. These days I'm just a paper tiger."

With that he hung his head low and followed the others up the aisle. Charlie remained behind for a moment, his eyes wide behind his big eyeglasses, his eyes sweeping over the pile of red, white and blue poker chips littering the console. He had to make a conscious effort to look away. This really is an idiot's world, he thought. Turning, he followed the others up the aisle. The bourbon bottles, the unshuffled cards, the untidy stacks of poker chips were all that remained at the console of a bet that had been made, a wager that would either be won or lost, a die that had been cast.

4

Arriving at the foot of the pile of furniture in the warehouse, George Natlong stopped to wait for Casey and Charlie so they could all walk down together, in a unified front. As soon as the stragglers caught up they went outside into the late afternoon sun and walked down the path through the trees. They could look through the trees and see the civilians lounging on the lawn near the house, basking in the dusk coolness. They'd been having a picnic. Dinner had been spread on a checkered tablecloth and people lazed about. Two of the ladies played lawn tennis — Elizabeth and Natalie — and you could hear their laughter clapping through the trees.

Once they'd spotted the generals coming out of the woods one of the ladies got up and started running toward them. It was Doty.

She greeted George Natlong with an exuberant, "Thank God it's over! The suspense was too much, George. You've no idea. It was unbearable. Now I feel I can start breathing again."

"What are you talking about?"

"Why the missiles, of course. I assumed you'd come to tell us your little missiles had been fired."

No, George Natlong told her. The little missiles hadn't been launched. She look disappointed. Not to worry, he comforted her.

"It won't be long now. We have some last minute business. Then we'll get this show on the road."

"What's up, George?" Bimmy asked, walking up. His head boasted Charlie Chaplin's bowler hat, which he'd had Claire fetch from the Hollywood Room in the cave. He lifted the bowler once, Chaplin style. All the while a barbequed chicken leg hung from his lips, like a cigar. A cane swung from his forearm, and now he twirled the cane once, then stepped a funny little two-step.

George Natlong impatiently licked his lips.

"It's like this," he said to Bimmy. "We feel it's crucial at this juncture that you responsible citizens select from among yourselves a leader. Someone to preserve, protect and defend the constitution. We have the original document under lock and key down in the cavern, you know, and we need someone to dust off its display case from time to time. We need someone to perform a certain civic duty this very evening." Here George Natlong looked to the house, searching for the window of the boy's room, but it was on the other side.

"An election?"

"That's what I said, isn't it?"

He said he wanted everyone to gather round, but Elizabeth Natlong wasn't happily called from badminton. Doty yelled over, "Girls! George wants us to have our own little election. I think it's an adorable idea!"

"Oh can't it wait?" Elizabeth Natlong replied. She held the little birdie in her cupped hand. "We're having *so* much fun!"

"No it can't wait!" George Natlong gazed impatiently across the lawn at his wife. "A democracy rises or falls on the involvement of its citizenry."

"Well I suppose you're right," Elizabeth said. The women set down their rackets, sauntered slowly through the cool mountain air to join the others.

George Natlong scanned the lawn. He spotted Edgar, who was taking advantage of the last of the daylight to chase butterflies with a net in the tall grass close to the trees. He wore an African safari helmet, a khaki shirt and baggy Bermuda shorts, and as he chased his quarry he leapt like a drunken ballet dancer, swishing the net in every direction but the one that would snare his prey.

George Natlong was unable to restrain a slight smile.

452

"There he is now," he said softly to Hal. "Hail our future commander-in-chief."

"You know what they say. Some men are born to power. Other have it thrust upon them."

George Natlong brought his pinky and his forefinger to his lips and let go a shrill whistle.

"Hey, Teddy Roosevelt!" he yelled at Edgar, waving. "If your blood lust is satiated how about calling off the hunt for today?" Edgar started in, removing the safari hat so he could wipe his pale brow.

"Is that everyone?" Hal asked.

"No. Mitchell's missing. Now I wonder where he could be."

"There he goes now." Bimmy pointed his walking stick past the house. "He's totally tanked." They made out Mitchell's tall and ungainly frame stumbling drunkenly along the tree line, at the edge of the lawn. He had a bottle and as George Natlong watched he lifted it high and drank heartily, then abruptly stumbled out of view behind a tree.

"He's really getting sauced back there."

"You want me to fetch him?" Bimmy asked. "Maybe sober him up?"

"No. It's best to let some things lie."

Edgar came up with the butterfly net. An orange and black butterfly struggled in the mesh. "Look dear, a lovely specimen!" he beamed at Doty, walking up. From his shirt pocket came a glass jar. Five or six butterflies already fluttered in the jar, each beating its wings, and in the softness of the setting sun those jewellike lovelies flashed every imaginable color, like a Van Gogh painting. Edgar reached into the net and grabbed his latest catch behind its head. Unscrewing the jar, he said, "There you go, little fellow. In with your brothers." He dropped it in. It sat atop the others, beating its wings.

"Oh I hate to look," Doty said, turning away. "Some things aren't meant for this world."

"Nonsense, dear," Edgar said, replacing the lid. "They can't feel a thing."

"If only I could believe that!" Doty said. "Oh I never could see why you insist on that dreadful hobby."

"I find the pursuit and collection of lepidoptera highly stimulating," he replied. He stuffed the jar into his shirt pocket.

"Of course you do." George Natlong threw an arm around Edgar's shoulder. "Of course you do. And who wouldn't? Why, you know something, Edgar old boy? You're a terribly interesting case. I never fully appreciated it before. But it's true. You're a *terribly* interesting case."

He led the little man off to one side, and conferred with him in confidential tones.

Paul Stoken pressed his face against the screen in the window and looked out across the lawn. At this particular moment he could see no one. A few minutes earlier when he'd seen the generals coming down the path he'd pressed himself close against the curtains so he wouldn't be seen staring out. He'd watched them cross the lawn, watched until they'd disappeared around the corner of the house. For several minutes after that there'd been nothing more to see. Then Mitchell came stumbling drunkenly across the lawn. His white shock of hair was all out of place and his shirttails hung from his pants. The poor sob was really drunk. The boy watched him take a swig from the bottle and fall behind a tree.

Now's my chance, he thought. But before he could raise the screen he again caught sight of the military men.

The generals led the civilians out across the lawn. It was some sort of procession. The boy moved well away from the window to watch, into the shadows, so he wouldn't be seen. He watched George Natlong lead the others up to a large tree that stood on the rounded top of a small hill not far from the woods. There they gathered under the spread of the tree, talking about God knows what. George Natlong made a gesturing motion at Edgar who, from his sudden reaction, appeared surprised and shocked by whatever George Natlong had just said. The civilians each raised a hand, and so did the five officers.

454

All of a sudden Edgar's wife, Doty, threw her arms around her husband's puny neck and planted a giant kiss on his cheek, knocking off the safari hat. The others came now up to Edgar and shook his hand. Edgar handed what appeared to be a butterfly net to his wife, and then he himself said a few words. His speech, however, was cut suddenly short by George Natlong, who tapped him on the shoulder and whispered into his ear. George Natlong pointed to the house. Although the distance was great (a good five or six stone throws, at least) it looked all the world like he was pointing straight to the window where the boy stood watching. Paul jumped back even farther into the shadows. Now what can that be about? he wondered.

Next thing they were all coming back down the hill toward the house. George Natlong first, followed by the other generals, followed by Edgar, then the rest of the civilians. Leading the way to the front door (right under the boy's window!) George Natlong threw open the door then held out his hand to indicate to the civilians that he wanted them inside. But he himself remained outdoors, along with the other generals, and Edgar. Paul heard the sounds of people coming into the house. Kneeling, he listened against the screen.

"...now we'll have the nicest inaugural ball," he could hear Doty gloat as she came into the house with the women. "Oh I'm just so proud of my little Edgar. I always told him if he kept quiet and didn't rock any boats he'd go far in life. And see now where my advice has brought him! You know what they say: people are like bullets. The smoother they are the farther they go."

Paul tried to catch what George Natlong was saying to Edgar. The general gestured into the woods then motioned to the boy's window with his thumb. The boy pressed his ear close to the screen. Straining, he thought he heard, "...be sure to ask for his moonstone...."

The boy brought his hand close to his chest. So that was it. They were coming for him. They'd seen all those pictures of Buddy Holly pasted to his walls back in Iowa, and now they were coming to take his moonstone.

Quickly, deftly, he pulled the amulet from around his neck. He stashed it under a chair in a corner of the room. He looked around. He didn't want a fight, but they weren't going to push him around. His eyes landed on the rocking chair by the window, at the long slats of its frame. He tugged at the chair's slats (and he really tugged hard) but they were in there good and tight, and couldn't be pulled out. Goddamn quality woodwork. He'd take common furniture, stuff that fell apart, any day over this quality junk.

It was then he heard the front door slam. Hurrying to the window, supposing they'd all just come inside and were on the way up to his room, he suddenly thought he'd better make a jump for it, while he could. But just as he was poised to throw open the screen he was surprised to see the five generals walking away from the house. They were hiking into the woods, from the looks of it, but were still too close to risk an escape.

He heard someone climbing the stairs. Turning, he gazed at the locked door. Must be Edgar. Coming alone. So the generals hadn't come with him. Why not?

Through the window he saw the generals hiking five abreast toward the trees. Maybe he should take his chances and open the window now. The sun was going down and maybe, if he was lucky, they wouldn't see him running across the darkening lawn. Wait! He saw one of the generals turn and look back at the house. The general (and it was too dim to see which general it was) only looked back for a moment before turning back to the trees. If he'd've been about to jump then he'd've been seen for sure.

A full yellow moon rose above the trees. The boy couldn't help staring up at it. In a moment he heard the footsteps outside his door and the knock, knock, knock.

Too late to jump now. He heard the rattle of a keychain. A key slid into the bolt. The door opened and he heard the sounds of Edgar coming into the room. As he heard these things he saw in the last light of the sun the five generals walking into the trees. And that wasn't all. Before they disappeared into the dark thick woods he thought he saw them drawing their .45s from their holsters.

Edgar came in. Straightening himself, the boy moved from the window. They looked each other over.

Someone came to the door. Doty. She sailed into the room with a suit of clothes in hand. Edgar turned.

"What is it, dear?"

"I thought you might want to change into something more becoming your new station in life," she gleefully said to her husband. "Get out of that ridiculous butterfly suit. What if anyone sees you! You're president of the United States now and I think you should be wearing only Brooks Brothers."

"Not now!" Edgar erupted. "Can't you see I'm busy? Leave me with the boy. I must insist. I have important duties to discharge. Now get out and close the door!"

Doty appeared dumbfounded by her husband's sudden transformation. But she obeyed. There was something about the office that made you jump. She quickly swung closed the door and once again Paul found himself alone with Edgar.

Edgar sauntered to the boy's bed and sat down. Those Bermuda shorts did nothing for his knobby knees.

"Did I hear right?" Paul asked. "Did she say you're the president? President of the United States?"

Edgar shook his head. "I find it rather hard to believe myself," he allowed. "Sometimes I have to pinch myself."

"But how'd you get elected president?"

Edgar shrugged his shoulders.

"Hard work and clean living, I suppose."

Paul licked his thin red lips, ruffled the hair in the back of his head. He figured he'd better play along. At least for the moment. Maybe there'd be some laughs in it.

"What brings you to my room, Mr President?"

"I'm afraid I've come with some rather bad news. I'm afraid the unpleasant task has fallen upon me to officially ask you to hand over your moonstone and come with me. You must quit this place."

457

"Come with you? Where'll you take me?"

"We'll just go for a little walk. The general's would like a word with you. I'm sure we can trust them to explain everything, as they see fit. I think they're going to send you home, son."

"Home?"

"I heard George — General Natlong, that is — say something about taking you out of here. I honestly don't know what they have in mind. I was merely told to escort you into the woods so they could have a chat with you."

"A chat?"

His eyes searched the room for something, anything. On the table in the corner, near where he'd ditched the necklace, his eyes caught an African statuette. Not more than a foot or so tall, but made of solid wood.

"You have a home, don't you, son? And parents? Somewhere to go home to?"

"Sure I got a home. A good one. And folks."

"Whereabouts is your home?"

"Mason City, Iowa, Mr President."

"Can't say I ever heard of it," Edgar put out, rummaging his memory. "There isn't a yacht club there, is there?"

"In *Mason City?*"

Edgar awaited an answer, his legs crossed, his fingers knitted on his knee.

"Why, sure there's a yacht club in Mason City," the boy said. "Mason City's like Venice Italy, you know. All the streets are flooded."

"I never knew that."

"Sure. A fellow can't get by in Mason City unless he has himself a big fat yacht."

"Your family has money?"

"Are you kidding? Why, my old man is loaded. Just the other day he was telling me he has more money than he knows what to do with. It's nothing to see him open up the front door and toss out fifty bucks."

"You don't say? Your family's old money, then?"

458

The boy squinted an eye.

"The money came down from my great uncle Jed. Jed Clampet Stoken." The boy watched for a reaction.

"Uncle Jed was just a poor mountaineer," he went on. "Why, he barely kept his family fed. Then one day, when he was shooting for some food—." Here the boy pretended to wet the sights of an invisible rifle, taking a bead on invisible prey. Edgar followed his line of fire, as if to see where the boy aimed. "Bang!" the boy hooted, and Edgar jumped. Paul drew aside the invisible rifle to see what he had shot, and Edgar too looked. "Up from the ground comes abubblin' crude!"

"Oil?" Edgar asked, astonished.

"Black gold," Paul winked. "Texas tea."

"Well what do you know," Edgar said.

The boy nodded.

"So the first thing you know old Jed's a millionaire. The kin folks, well they told him he better get his old ass away from there. They told him California was the place he ought to be. So do you know what that old sob did? He loaded up their truck and he moved them to Beverly Hills."

"Beverly Hills! Beverly Hills, California, son?"

"That's right. You know. Swimming pools. Movie stars."

"Well what do you know about that!" Edgar chuckled, tapped his knee. "This *is* a land of opportunity!"

"As evidenced by your own rise in politics, Mr President."

"So your last name's Stoken, son?"

"That's right, sir."

"Stoken, Stoken," Edgar thought, drumming his chin. "Didn't I row with a Stoken on the Yale sculling team?" But before the boy could answer Edgar put out, "And you, my boy, must be about the age where you're considering a career at Yale yourself?"

"Oh yes sir. I'm Ivy League all the way."

"And how old are you now, son?"

"Seventeen, sir."

"Well let me see. When I was your age I attended prep school. Those were my wild days! And you, young man?

You're enrolled in a good prep school?"

The boy said he'd just been thrown out of prep school and had in fact been on his way home to break the news to his folks when he'd been unexpectedly waylaid at Camp Moonstone. "It was supposed to be just a three-hour tour." He sang sadly, shaking his head, "A three-hour tour. A three-hour tour." He sang it with the straightest, most sorrowful face you could imagine, and Edgar appeared to feel for him.

Paul went over to the window and stared out. The moon popped above the trees. It was a big bad old moon, and the boy was amazed as always at how fast it moved across the sky. How much faster than the sun!

He faced Edgar.

"I got thrown out of prep school and I spent days wandering around New York City. I bought myself a ridiculous hat. Everyone I met I kept asking the same question. Maybe you can tell me. And please don't think I'm stupid for asking. Where do the ducks go in winter?"

"Why, my boy, they fly south. Don't they?"

Paul seemed stunned. He half smiled, half brooded. Lowering his head, he scratched his neck then tugged at the collar of the jacket.

"You know something?" he said softly. "I never thought of that before. It never crossed my mind. And me, asking all those people where the ducks go and all. They probably thought I was just plain stupid."

Gritting his teeth, he made an anguished face and sulked around the room. "I keep having this dream," he told Edgar, coloring his voice so that it sounded tortured and haunted. "I keep dreaming I'm standing in a field. All these kids with hang gliders are trampling across the field, see, wanting to leap off the cliff and fly away. In my dream I'm running back and forth at the very edge of the cliff trying to stop them. But they all think I'm square. They ignore me. There I am, running back and forth, waving my arms and all, and they're sailing away right over my head into the sky in those rainbow-colored hang gliders."

460

Edgar looked befuddled. He sat on the bed not knowing what to say.

"We all have dreams, son," he finally put out. "With time you'll learn not to set much store by them."

Glancing at his watch, he got up from the bed. Staring intently at the boy, he held out his hand. The room was quiet and still. Paul could hear his heart athumping. He could hear the blood cursing through his ears. His hands and feet, atingling.

"Give me your moonstone, son."

Paul went to the window. He bit his lip. Why had they sent this little guy? He'd never been forced to fight before, not since he'd been a kid anyway, and he hated to start with old Edgar here. It would have been much easier with George Natlong.

"You don't watch much tv, or read many books, do you, sir?" he asked, looking out at the moon. It was blazing across the sky.

"I never cared much for reading," Edgar said. "I do watch a little tv now and then. I like that Wild Kingdom show. I'll catch that when I can. Do you know the show I mean? With Marlin Perkins? As you can see from my safari clothing I'm a bit of the outdoorsman myself."

"Sure. Sure I know the show. Mutual of Omaha's Wild Kingdom."

Paul bit his lip. He turned from the window and eyeballed the statuette on the table in the corner. Well, he thought, at least it'll be no worse than Wild Kingdom on tv, where old Marlin Perkins sits in that book-lined study and pipes, "Now watch as Don single-handedly stalks a dangerous and rare wildcat in the African bush and immobilizes it bare-handed with that whama-lama-bam-ding-dong." You see some big hairy ape of a guy hurl himself from a hovering helicopter onto the back of some terrified mountain lion, smacking the poor beast upside the head with a blackjack so it could be tagged and released, as old Marlin always explained. There's something peculiarly American about Mutual of Omaha's

461

Wild Kingdom. Sooner or later we all get jumped and black-jacked in the dark jungle of the American night, get tagged and released. Now it was just old Edgar's turn, that's all, the boy told himself. It's really no worse than that. If old Marlin Perkins was here giving the narration he'd probably say the same. What he must now do to Edgar was no worse really than your run-of-the-mill Wild Kingdom episode. Edgar would simply find himself starring in his own little episode of Wild Kingdom. He'd just immobilize Edgar with a little old whama-lama-bam-ding-dong, that's all.

Still, Paul couldn't take his eyes off that statuette. Maybe it was because he couldn't bring himself to look at old Edgar that he kept his eyes glued on the ugly thing.

Still, he couldn't bring himself to move any closer to the statuette. How he suddenly hated it, felt revulsion for it. They're going to have to force me into it, he thought. They're going to have to *make* me pick up that lousy thing.

Just then he felt Edgar's hand reaching into the red jacket. Edgar patted the boy's chest, searching, surprised to find nothing. He sure could feel the racing of Paul's heart.

"Where is your moonstone, boy?"

"I took it off. Threw it over there in the corner. It was irritating my skin."

Edgar looked into the corner.

"You don't expect me to get down on my hands and knees and search for it, do you? Pick it up and give it to me." There was an impatient edge to his voice.

"Don't you worry. I'll give it to you all right."

"Well be quick about it. The generals must be wondering. It's time for us to take our little walk."

The winds of memory blew down through Paul Stoken. He remembered his Uncle Jeff's warning, could hear Jeffrey's voice from the day of the contest at the Surf, saying, *"One day there'll come a time in your own life, when somebody'll ask you to go somewhere. I can't tell you who, and I can't tell you when. I can't even tell you where they'll ask you to go. All I can say is, it'll be someplace where you're better judgment tells*

462

you to stay the hell out of. They might ask you pleasantly, or they might order you to go. It's all the same. Don't hesitate. Run. Stay out of that pit for as long as you can. Turn and run."

"Now fetch me that moonstone. We're late."

Paul had already made up his mind. He wasn't gonna go on no little walk. Where he was going he had to run, flat out.

"'O oysters come and walk with us!' the Walrus did beseech. 'A pleasant walk, a pleasant talk, along the briny beach,'" he now recited softly under his breath, closing his eyes to remember the verse. "'We cannot do with more than four, to give a hand to each.'" He looked at Edgar. "I am the Walrus," the boy sang, ever so softly. Slowly he lifted both arms high above his head, hands bent at the wrists, fingers spread wide. "Goo goo goo joob!"

"How's that?" Edgar said, twitching his little thin moustache.

But already Paul was moving. Like he was watching himself in a dream, he moved toward the primitive African statuette. In a flash he saw his hand wrapping around it. And then it was done.

But it was nothing like what you see in the movies. He'd caught Edgar with a single arching swing, above his ear. Edgar, a strange expression on his face, sunk to the carpet. There was a sudden dull sound of glass shattering beneath him. But it was nothing like what you see in the movies, where people get knocked out cold. Edgar kind of flopped and stirred around on the floor, like he was trying to get up.

So the boy hit him again, this time on the back of the head, not thinking, only reacting.

Still old Edgar stirred.

"Lay still!" the boy commanded through gritted teeth, surprised by the intensity of his rage. He was holding the bloodied statuette high above Edgar's head. "I'll brain you if you don't lay still! I swear to God I will!"

Edgar kept moaning and the boy was afraid the ones

downstairs would hear. So he grabbed him by the shoulder and rolled him over. "Lay still I say!" He saw his eyes were closed to keep out the blood.

It was then that he saw the strange thing. Butterflies. They came crawling from Edgar's shirt pocket, crawling up the front of his shirt, fanning their wings.

"What the—." Taking a giant backwards step, he was startled to see the red of the blood streaked against the black ebony of the African tribal statuette. He dropped the statuette beside Edgar.

The light in the boy's room winked out. Soon afterward, quietly (ever so quietly!), the window slid open, and Paul's face appeared above the sill. Everything outside was lit in that yellow washed-out glow of moonshine. The wind was blowing something fierce. It really made the trees bend and in the magic of the moonlight the restless trees almost danced. You could see birds shooting through the waves in the sky and you didn't know whether to envy them for the wildness of their flight or pity them that they had to work so hard against the pounding swells to keep from crashing into the weaving fingers of the trees. Paul moved his legs out the window. He sat on the sill and tried to concentrate on the jump. In the daylight the jump looked bad enough but in the shifting trickery of the windy moonlight it seemed crazy, just about impossible. As he sat wearily gazing into the abyss he happened to look over his shoulder in time to see three or four butterflies fly out the window to take their chances on the rising wind. The wind really swirled those butterflies around, and for a moment Paul watched them carried away in the moonlight. Then he pushed away from the window and he himself was cast into the wind, falling, falling, falling through the starry starry night, watching the moonlit earth rush up.

He hit with a quiet thud and rolled out of control in the grass. What a rush! For the longest time he lie there like an unsettled scarecrow, his eyes closed, feeling his bones, unable to believe none were broken.

464

So he got up and stole a quick glance in the direction he'd seen the generals disappear into the trees. He sure hoped they weren't watching. In this moonlight they'd be able to easily spot him running across the lawn.

Gritting his teeth, he ran fleet-footed across the thick carpet of open grass, trying to stay as close to the ground as possible without falling, seeing the dark protective covering of the woods coming up slowly, too slowly for comfort, seeming to take forever. It was the slowest moment of his life, running toward those trees. If he got there he would be safe but if he was spotted now, out in the open like this, it'd all be over. All he could think about were those .45s he'd seen the generals take out before they'd gone into the trees. Running across the lawn he was sure any moment he'd feel a bullet rip into his back. Or would he hear the report first, then feel the bullet? No. They say you don't hear the report until after the bullet hits. The metal flies faster than the sound. Feeling would know before hearing could reveal.

Running toward those trees, feeling the cushion of grass beneath his sneakers, everything suddenly seemed in slow motion. For a microsecond he feared he'd never reach the trees, that he was a goner for sure, but from somewhere deep inside he summoned a last bit of wild defiance. He'd begun to chant "Not fade away! Not fade away! Not fade away!" as he ran, and he was chanting it over and over again, like it was a prayer, or a hope, or a promise murmured to someone or something he did not know the nature of, and it was then he felt his legs coming alive and he burst into the trees, knowing in that one single moment of delicious triumph all the generals would have to catch now was his jet stream.

At the edge of the lawn under a tree Mitchell lie cuddled with a bottle of brandy, mumbling at the shimmering stars. His eyes were glazed and lost, and the fragments of the sentences which he mumbled were exhausted of energy and empty of meaning, like words you say over and over again to yourself in a restless dream.

"...Missile gap...." he soliloquized to the stars. "...Windows of vulnerability.... Mutual assured destruction, balance of terror...."

He brought the bottle to his parched lips, drinking deeply.

"...Nuclear deterrents.... Arms race.... MIRVs, circular error probables, ground zero...."

Guided through the woods by the sounds of this drunken mumbling, Paul came out behind the tree. Mitchell lie in the shimmering shadows cast by the moonlight washing through the swaying branches of the trees. The shadows played on Mitchell's face as the boy glared down with a look that can only be described as urgent disgust. Falling to his knees, he yanked Mitchell's arm, trying to sit him up.

"Wake up! Those crazy generals are gonna blow up the world! You gotta stop 'em! You're the only one here who can stand up to them! You gotta sober up, man! Don't you hear me! If you don't stop them there won't be a man left alive!"

With watery eyes Mitchell took in the boy. He laughed.

"My boy," he laughed, "man already is dead. In the last century it was apparent God was dead. In the twentieth century it became apparent that man is dead. What better proof do you need than Camp Moonstone? Look around. We all have eyes but we cannot see. Ears but we cannot hear. Hands and heart but cannot feel. Heads, but we have no room for ideas."

He pulled at the bottle.

"The terrible push-button nature of modern killing!" he babbled. "The deliberate distancing from human suffering—."

Again he drank, pitifully sucking from the bottle, his head resting against a tree root, his thick shock of windblown hair glowing milky white, almost pearllike, in the shimmering moonlight.

"No my boy," he said, the wind whipping up his hair and shirt collar as he spoke, "I believe that man is dead. He is a fleeting, throwaway disposable Dixie cup of a thing, because he no longer has a soul, for when man killed off God he killed off his own spirit, and without a spirit man is incapable of compassion and sacrifice and endurance. Men have left no

466

room for ideas. Man is dead."

Hearing this drunken banter, Paul grew annoyed. Grabbing Mitchell by his wrinkled shirt, he shook him violently against the tree.

"I'm not dead!" he shot back. "I can feel. I'm alive! I tell you I'm alive!" He saw the shaking was doing no good and so he stopped, yet his clenched fists still held Mitchell's shirt. "I never felt more alive." Looking up through the trees at the stars, he let go of Mitchell, then ran his hands down along his own arms, feeling the warmth of his skin.

"I feel like I'm coming alive all over. Tingling. I can feel the tingle of life. You must feel it too, Mitchell. You're confusing it with death, that's all. When you feel the tingle of life in your bones you've got to be careful not to confuse it with the tug of the hand of death."

Mitchell wasn't listening, couldn't listen. Smacking his lips, he brought the bottle again to his mouth. Paul snatched it away, hurling it forcefully at the tree above Mitchell's head, raining down shattered glass and brady.

Mitchell held out his palm, brought it to his mouth, testing the golden rain.

"Praise be it's raining brandy! Manna from heaven! Never thought I'd live long enough to see it rain the good stuff." Droplets of brandy dripped down on him from the leaves above and he caught the drips in his palms. "Live long enough and you see everything." He ran his tongue around his splattered lips. "George must have launched the missiles and scored a direct hit on God's wine cellar." With sudden alarm he looked at his hands through wide drunk's eyes. "Then this must be fallout!" He brought a hand to his mouth and cautiously tasted more. Arching his eyebrows, his face took on a look of cautious approval. "Well that's not bad!" he said. "Not bad at all! If this is fallout I can certainly live with it."

"You stupid drunk!" Paul clenched fists. "You've got to sober up! Fast! You've got to tell me what to do! Tell me what to do and I'll do it!"

"Why don't you get a hat or something and help me catch

some fallout." Mitchell slurped at the whisky in his cupped hands.

Paul saw it was useless.

"Men no longer have room for ideas," Mitchell babbled, resuming his senseless banter at the stars. "Ideas like mutual assured destruction.... Top secrecy.... Pre-emptive strike.... Nuclear deterrents.... ICBMs.... ABMs.... Throw weights, kilotons, victory, total war, nuclear retaliation.... Windows of vulnerability.... Obliteration.... Domino theory...."

Paul backed away then, leaving Mitchell as he'd found him, braying senselessly up at the moon and the stars, braying out the empty ideas of a spent age.

When you feel the tingle of life in your bones you must run. And run, Paul did, through the tall shadowy woods until he reached the path that led up the hill. He didn't even stop there to catch his breath. He latched his eyes onto the light shimmering between the trunks of the trees, the light on the warehouse at the top of the hill, and he kept running up the path. And the path carried him on up the hill and as he ran he could look up between the tall quaking trees and see the stars atwinkling and the moon ashining in the infinite deep blue majesty of the sky. And then he closed his eyes and ran. Did you ever close your eyes and run flat out in the forever of the night thinking just for one flash of a moment that you too would last forever? Get drunk from the night then get you out and run you, until you know you are alive, and see that for just one moment of forever you shine like the stars.

Run, Paul did, effortlessly and wild through the night, drinking in with newly heightened senses the flashes and crackles and the deep swooshes of the wind-driven trees and the rumbling thunders of the dark until for one moment he felt merged with the night, a creature of it, a speck of the stars flashing with the wild abandon of the wind over the hard-packed earth.

And as he flashed into the warehouse and hurled himself past Mrs Natlong's great pile of quality woodwork the string of senseless words that Mitchell had been bantering up to the stars still rang in his ears. The words held little meaning for him. They were just the patapat sounds he heard while running. "Men no longer have room for ideas. Ideas like mutual assured destruction.... Top secrecy.... Pre-emptive strike.... Nuclear deterrents.... Windows of vulnerability.... Domino theory.... Balance of terror...."

Paul pondered those words as he ran past the great steel doorway and continued running down, down the sinking passageway into the quiet cave. It struck him then that Camp Moonstone was national policy made concrete, poison words that finally had found expression in steel, commitment in stone, poison ideas that finally had been transformed into the flashing lights of Epimetheus's all-seeing screen. Well, he told himself, running deep down into the corridors of hidden power, one man's national security is just another man's dark hallway. Just then he didn't see nuclear deterrents, he just saw the riblike arching tunnelworks leading far underground. And he didn't see any windows of vulnerability down there either, just the sloping long curved hallway leading to the huge cavern housing the computer. And he didn't see a hint of national security anywhere. He just saw death. Mitchell certainly was right about one thing, he couldn't help thinking as he raced up to the doorway that opened into the computer's grand chamber. Some men leave no room for ideas. That can't be helped. It's those ideas that leave no room for men. They're what you chiefly have to be on the lookout for, he thought as he streaked into the great subterranean chamber that held the computer.

It was still and quiet as the dark side of the moon in there when the boy came charging in. He charged right down the aisle, straight for the computer, not at first noticing the playing cards, the poker chips and the bourbon bottles spread across the length of the console. He hurried over to the place where he'd left his cassette tape, thinking he'd just grab it and get the hell out. That's when he saw it. As he was reaching for the precious cassette. Set conspicuously on the console, out in the open, near the cards, all but impossible to miss. A note.

He tucked the demo tape safely into the pocket of the jacket that once had been worn by James Dean. Curiosity got the best of him. He went over to the note and snatched it up. He read, in hastily formed handwriting:

> General Natlong—
> Must have just missed you. Have arrived finally with long-sought prize. Unfortunately, have uncovered certain problems of security nature which require immediate attention. Will be unable to meet you until sometime later. I'm sure you are most anxious to take possession of you-know-what. For security's sake, I've hidden it in a guitar case which I will now place in the pile of furniture up in the warehouse. I'm sure it will be safe there.
> Major Donday

In a moment the note lay crumpled on the cold stone floor. The boy was no more than a flash of red and blue streaking up the aisle.

And the dark hallway carried him on, step by step, his black ankle-highs barely touching ground, until he burst to the surface and tore past the big steel doors into the warehouse. Charging up to the mountain of furniture he began tearing into it, looking, looking, throwing aside armchairs, tables and sofas, anything that got in his way, tearing straight to the dark heart of the tangle of quality woodwork, and as the heavy furniture came crashing down around him the warehouse was filled with echoes sounding like thunder but he didn't care, so intent was he in his search.

Nothing! He looked in every trunk he could find, peered into every chest of drawers, crawling all over the woodwork, at times climbing high into the shifting pile and placing himself in no small peril, but nothing! He cursed, tugged at his hair,

470

rubbed his cheek with the sleeve of the red jacket, and angrily slammed some furniture around, but still nothing. He jumped down from the furniture to the concrete floor. He rubbed his head with his hands. Maybe he should pray to St. Anthony. When all else fails, resort to religion. Why not ask old Tony for help now? No. Wasn't this more of a job for St. Jude, patron saint of lost causes? Heaven has bureaus and departments for things Congress would never fund. He wished he'd been up on his catechism a little better when he was a kid.

Looking up, he happened to notice, at the far side of the warehouse, the lone wooden chest haphazardly toppled over on its side near the forklift. He'd chucked the trunk there himself before he took off in the forklift to warn the Indians. Nah, he thought, it couldn't be there, dismissing the thought, returning his attention to the pile of furniture before him.

He looked back at the solitary trunk on its side by the forklift. He found himself moving toward it, slowly at first, then running, his feet beating fast time across the smooth hard floor, the steps, like drum beats, reverberating off each of the four distant walls at separate intervals so that the sounds of his running pretty near popped like gunfire, and he came running up to the trunk and breathlessly threw it open.

There it was. At the bottom of the trunk. Hand tooled. A guitar case, and scripted into the leather two words. Buddy Holly.

His heart leapt. Falling to his knees, he threw open the case, taking out the heavy red Strat, marveling as always at how good it felt in his hands. Well maybe it pays sometimes to be patient, after all, he had to think. He began to kiss and pet it and talk to it like it was a naughty child, scolding it, saying, "I don't know why I put up with you. You're nothing but trouble. Trouble to anyone who picks you up." But already he was looking it over, making sure it hadn't been damaged by this latest episode in its turbulent history. He cursed the fat man anew.

It was then he saw it. In the open guitar case.

It looked like a big fuse, cylindrical in shape, about six

inches long, an ordinary enough looking thing.

Paul picked it up. His eyes, narrowed to slits, stared intently across the warehouse to those big, wide steel doors, opening to the dark pit below.

5

The dying are like the living in one way. The dying too have rituals. Rituals always are the last to die.

These then are the rituals of the dying. The three old Indians who lived in the shack outside the gates of Camp Moonstone had finished painting their faces with the colors they had made from clay. Over their white hair they slipped the war bonnets they'd made from eagle feathers and sinew. They donned the ceremonial beaded costumes of blue and red with the white bone vests. Their bows had been strung, their quivers filled with arrows. When the big red sun at last had sunk into the west and the yellow moon rose full-faced and smiling to the north of east, they lit their torches from the raging campfire they had built beside their shack. Then they headed silently into the woods.

They were not alone. Following close at their heels were the bedraggled congressman and his aide. They had to follow close behind the old Indians because they did not have torches of their own and the woods were deep and dark. After an eternity of stumbling around in the dark woods behind the three slow-moving torches, they came to a moonlit clearing where straightaway the old Indians began to dance, waving the torches and chanting, while the congressman and his aide remained behind a tree, watching.

"Would you look at that," Congressman Marcus said, watching the three old men dance. They were going around in a tight circle, chanting a sad lament at the moon. Burning orange embers rose from the torches into the starry sky. "I bet we're witnessing something never before seen by white men."

"Speak for yourself," Jones told the congressman.

The Indians danced to the far side of the clearing, moved aside some dead brush, surprising Marcus and Jones by disappearing one by one into the ground.

"It's the cave entrance!" Marcus started after them. "Come on!"

"Now hold on, King o' Sobby!" Jones piped. "Didn't I tell you I wasn't following any crazy-ass Indians into a hole in the ground?" But already the congressman had shadowed the Indians into the cave. Jones, uncomfortable with the idea of being left alone in the dark woods heavy with all the sounds of the night, rushed over to the tear in the earth and peered in. The cold air blowing out from the cave smelled damp and forbidding.

"Congressman!" he whispered. "Congressman!"

There was no reply. He could barely see three pinpricks of light bobbing far back in the cave. It was then that he did what he thought any self-respecting, rational person in a similar circumstance would do. He followed the light of the fire into the cave.

6

With guns drawn and heavy in hand the generals pressed through the trees until they reached a small clearing. There they waited in the moonlight for Edgar to come with the boy. They had nothing much to say. They waited with their .45s in hand, watching the moon levitating full and bright over the trees.

On his way into the clearing Casey had stumbled once or twice and now as he stood in the open of the clearing he saw that his moonstone had slid from his shirt. The stone swung from its chain beneath his chin, outside his uniform. In the moonlight the flecks of glass in the stone had taken on a curious glow.

The moonstone appeared luminescent. Glittering. Shimmering in the moonlight. It beamed curious specks of white light. Amazed, Casey lifted the stone by its chain. Was it ever bright! The wind whipped through the clearing and the stone spun on the end of the chain, beaming countless brilliant white specks in every direction. The specks danced across the surprised faces of the generals, their rumpled uniforms, the tall blowing grass surrounding them, flying all the way to the dark shifting tops of the trees.

"Well would you look at that."

The others pulled their moonstones from their shirts. Everything lit up from the sparkle of the stones. The clearing sparkled in a way they'd never seen anything on earth sparkle. It somehow reminded George Natlong of the first atomic bomb blast back in '45.

"Holy cow!"

"It's magical."

475

"Must have something to do with the moon shining."

"I've never seen anything so beautiful."

"It's a whole new way of looking at the world."

Lowering their pistols, they raised the moonstones high and began moving in a slow circle, looking everywhichway, watching the swirling blaze of white dots light up the clearing. If you could have seen it from the air you might have thought someone was building a bonfire from stardust or from the wings of some fallen angel.

Charlie suddenly stopped walking. Lowering his moonstone, he said, "You know, I just thought about that scene the computer showed us. The one from the age of myths. The boy stole the fire while the chieftains danced with clubs and torches. It strikes me that's what we're doing now."

"How do you mean?" Hal said. "We've no clubs or torches."

"Don't you see? These pistols are our equivalent of clubs." He held up his .45. "And these moonstones are symbols of the state of our technology. If we'd been around thousands of years ago the state of our technology would've been—."

Casey cut in. "Why of course. Fire. Torches."

The generals stopped their slow circle dance in midstep, exhanging the most extraordinary glances.

Hal looked to the trees, in the direction of the house, and voiced what had flown into each of their minds.

"Edgar sure is taking a good long time to deliver the boy."

"My God!" George Natlong shuddered. "We've left the computer room unattended!"

But already he was running from the clearing into the trees, and so fiercely was the ugly thing in him driving him on that the others could scarcely keep up. In the moonlight he tore across the open lawn past the house, summoning even more speed when he saw the light in the boy's room out, the curtain blowing from the open window. Up the path to the warehouse he charged, the others spread out some distance behind, Hal doubling over near the top of the path to clutch at his chest, gagging for breath, begging them to slow down. In

476

another minute the five of them were scurrying across the floor of the warehouse, past the ungodly pile of furniture, ten feet slapping the hard concrete in time, the quick steps reverberating like gunshots. Past the great steel doors and then down, down, down they ran, down the long curved claustrophobic hallway deep down into the ground, down into the computer chamber.

The run damn near killed the five of them. They came dragging down the aisle of the great subterranean chamber, their tongues hanging from their red faces. They were alone after all down there. Feeling a little silly for having run so hard for nothing, they dragged themselves to the console and collapsed in their chairs, pulling at the air with pained lungs. They felt old and full of days.

"Well how do you like that?" George Natlong smiled up at the others when he'd at last gathered his breath. His flushed cheek lay on the console, his thin hair blown all out of place. "Guess we let fear get the upper hand on us back there. There was a moment there in front of the house when I had this nightmare feeling—." He clutched suddenly at his stomach, wincing.

"If we're going to pull this thing off we're going to have to keep our heads," Hal puffed back. They were still collapsed over the console, moaning and wheezing, their chests heaving. "And we've got to slow down. None of us is as young as we used to be, George. If we don't slow down we'll all have coronaries."

George Natlong wasn't listening. His restless eyes had landed on a crumpled piece of paper on the floor by his chair. He lifted up his head, giving the crumpled paper a funny look.

"What's this?" he asked, holstering the .45, which, all the way back to the cave, he'd gripped tightly in hand. Now he reached down and snatched the paper, straightening it. His eyes went wide.

Rising to his feet he knocked back the chair.

"Major Donday has arrived with the upgrade!" he croaked. "Three of you come with me. Hal, you stay here and guard the computer. Guard it with your life. If you see the boy shoot to kill. Is that understood?"

Hal looked surprised. "If that's what you say. But—."

Already George Natlong was running up the aisle, Bob, Casey and Charlie at his heels.

They ran with all the speed they could muster, up out of the cave, past the great steel doors into the warehouse, running straight for furniture rising above the floor. George Natlong wasted no time tearing into things, throwing elegant sofas and tables and chairs aside like they were no more than bales of hay, the madness burning in his eyes, now sobbing, now cursing, "Where is it? Where *is* it?"

Bob, Charlie and Casey wordlessly helped throw furniture aside until Charlie stopped, asking George Natlong, "What're we looking for?"

"A guitar case," George Natlong put out. He slid a bookcase down a chute made of two sofas and an ottoman, the bookcase crashing thunderously to the floor and flipping over, its glass panes shattering.

"A guitar case?"

"It's hidden somewhere in the woodwork." He surveyed the mountain of furniture. "Help me bust up this junk."

They resumed tearing toward the dark heart of furniture, the heavy pieces of woodwork once again flying and crashing around them. So engaged were they in this work that they didn't notice the civilians enter the warehouse, escorting a beat-up Edgar. Elizabeth Natlong gave out a blood-curdling scream.

"What are you doing to Daddy's woodwork!"

The generals, heaving a heavy oaken bureau from the precipice down to the valley below, watched the bureau scratch down a steep cliff made of mahogany dining tables, the drawers sliding out with a crunch, shattering at the foot of the mountain. They looked over to the civilians. Clapping the dust from their hands, they scurried down over the stacked tables and chairs.

Edgar was in bad shape. He came dizzily across the floor, Natalie clutching one arm, Doty the other, his face bloodied and bruised in several places. A nasty bump distorted his forehead, his hair was mussed, his bare legs beneath the Bermuda shorts gimpy and shaky, while the tails of his butterfly shirt hung out. As they led him in he didn't appear to know where he was. Bimmy walked behind, wearing Chaplin's bowler, twirling the walking stick. He'd managed to dig up a pair of baggy trousers, oversized shoes and a small waistcoat. Waddling behind the others, he twirled the walking stick, twitching his grease-painted moustache.

The generals scurried level-by-level down the great pile of furniture.

"What's happened to the boy?"

"What happened to the boy?" Doty cried back. "What happened to my poor Edgar! That nasty little thug beat up my poor Edgar."

"Did the boy say anything?" George Natlong puffed, running up.

Edgar moaned. His eyes had a vacant look. Doty still propped him up.

"You've got to snap out of it." George Natlong shook him by the shoulder. Then, to Bimmy, "Get him a chair for christsakes so he can sit down!"

Bimmy's moustache twitched. Clicking the heels of his oversized shoes, stiffening, he raised his right hand high, offering George Natlong a Nazi salute. The baggy pants dropped to his knees, exposing red polka-dotted shorts. Pulling up his pants, he clapped off pigeon-toed to the pile of furniture, twirling that walking stick. He ceremoniously lifted a chair from the side of the pile near where Elizabeth Natlong stood blubbering over the many scratched and splintered pieces. Hooking the walking stick in the crook of his elbow, Bimmy romantically took the chair up in his arms and, a dreamy expression lighting his face, waltzed with it back to the others, swirling and dancing with the chair all the way to Edgar. He set it down and bowed, thanking it for a lovely dance. Then he brought out a ludicrous orange handkerchief and dusted off the chair.

Edgar sat down.

"I can't believe that sweet-looking boy would do this to Edgar," Natalie said. "He has such an angelic look to him."

"Angelic!" Doty shot back. "I saw through that little devil the moment I laid eyes on him."

Edgar groaned.

"What happened, Edgar? What happened?"

The little man brought a shaky hand to his head.

"Ohhh," he groaned, feeling his lumps, swallowing. "It was terrifying! It was absolutely the most frightening experience of my life!"

7

Down through the narrow rocky passages the three old Indians slinked with their torches. They slowly crossed an eerie chamber of stalagmites and stalactites, each rockcicle as thick as a man. Any number of twisting tunnels opened in every direction. They knew just which passage to take, following one that led first to a natural staircase made of boulders then down to an icy cold underground stream where sparkling crystal fingers as delicate and fine as lace grew up from the clear bottom. They used stepping stones to cross the stream. Then, one at a time, they filed into a narrow chasm between two immense rocks. It was so tight they had to hold their breath as they filed through.

The chasm opened into a cathedral-like chamber, the walls of which towered in an arch fifty or sixty feet above their heads. Here, stretched out on the ground as far as the eye could see, lay innumerable skeletons, the remains of all-but-forgotten braves of a lost nation, resting in beds of ceremonial feathers and spears.

It was as solemn and quiet down there as in God's own church but that didn't stop Running Deer from raising his hands and screaming up at all the rocky icicles hanging from the apex of the burial chamber, "This is the Mingos' final place! The white man came and took everything from the Mingo. The fields and the buffalo. The mountains and the streams. We were stripped of our dignity as men, stripped of everything but this final place to lay our bones. And now has this too been desecrated by the white men?"

He looked to the oldest and the shortest of the three, a cross-eyed white-haired man with thick eyeglasses and pearly dentures whose real name was Dennis but who went by the name of Swift River.

"Well?" Running Deer asked. "Wasn't it your turn last time to check the cave?"

"No it wasn't. I thought it was your turn."

"It wasn't my turn."

They looked to the third Indian, an obese old fellow who was known for his lazy ways and whose real name was Larry but who went by the name of Jasper Wyoming.

"It was your turn last time wasn't it Jasper?"

"Mine?"

Jasper shrunk back.

"It most certainly was," Swift River said. "I remember clearly now it was your turn."

"What did you see when you were back there?" Running Deer asked Jasper. "Did you see any signs of desecration by the white men?"

"Honest fellows you can't expect me to remember every little thing—."

"You did go all the way back to the end of the burial chamber, didn't you, Jasper? *All* the way back?"

They knew that look on Jasper's face.

"You lazy bum!" Running Deer spat. "You just went a little ways around the bend and laid down and had yourself a snooze, didn't you?"

"You fellows can't expect an old man like me to go all the way back there by myself!" Jasper Wyoming whined. "It was all dark and slippery. I could've slipped back there when I was all by myself! I'm in no hurry to make my final trip here. Besides, as I remember, we ate a particularly big dinner that day before we came here and you know my gallbladder always disputes me if I don't lay down and rest."

Disgusted, Running Deer held his torch high, looking out across the sea of bones far into the still chamber. "Well there's only one thing to be done. We must go for a look."

They took off down an aisle between the reclining skeletons. Presently they disappeared around the bend, the light

482

from their torches still illuminating the smooth rounded contours of the wall, and as they went off Congressman Marcus came out of the fissure in the rocks. With wide eyes he beheld the countless skeletons.

"My God! There's a catacomb down here!"

Behind him he heard, "Congressman! Congressman!"

Jones came out from the chasm, his hair and clothing smudged brown with clay, his shoes and his slacks dripping wet. When he laid his eyes on all the skeletons Jones abruptly turned, heading back for the chasm. Marcus caught him by the arm.

"Let go!" Jones yelled. "Those bones are all I had to see! That's it for this cowboy! I'm going back, King o' Sobby. Not only that, I quit. I'm tendering my resignation as of now. I didn't graduate Phi Betta goddamn Kappa from Harvard to be marching through a junkyard full of Injun bones. Why didn't I listen to Mama and stay the hell out of politics? To think I turned down a comfy minority position with Chase Manhattan Bank for this! To think I could have been a banker, walking knee deep in money in a bank vault instead of this! Who needs this? I almost drowned in that underground stream back there! My chinos are all but ruined!"

"Get a grip on yourself Jones!" the congressman whispered. He took a tentative step toward the waning light. The torchlight from around the bend was fading fast, casting long shadows of the bones onto the gray stone walls. "We better get going."

"I told you I'm through. I'm going back."

"What? And wander around those tunnels back there without a torch? You'd wander forever."

Marcus started off down the aisle between the reclining skeletons, following the waning torchlight. Jones hurried after him, whimpering, trying not to look at the bones, which really was hard since countless grinning skulls and bones are hard to overlook.

"You don't suppose there's a curse on anyone who comes down here, do you, Congressman? You know, one of those

Indian whammies?"

"Don't be ridiculous, Jones."

They started around the bend but as they did the light from the Indian's torches began fading faster. The old Indians must have rounded a sharp corner. The next instant the congressman and his aide found themselves in complete blackness, a darkness the likes of which they'd never experienced since taking leave of the womb, so total and all consuming it was. Unable to see even his own hand, Jones moaned and, veering from the cleared path, he heard and then felt bones crunching beneath his feet. He screamed and reached out into the darkness for the congressman but came up with a skeleton instead. It lay on a ledge and at first when Jones ran his fingers along its smooth surfaces he thought nothing of it but when he came upon what felt like teeth and empty eye sockets he let out a howl the likes of which hadn't been heard in that cave since creation. Disoriented by the blackness, he flailed wildly about, losing his balance and falling into a pile of bones which clattered and rattled as he rolled about.

"Keep your head!" Marcus yelled, the words echoing from every direction.

"Keep your head! Keep your head! Keep your head!"

"Say something," Jones cried back.

"Say something! Say something! Say something!"

"Over here!" Then, as if in mockery echoing from every direction, "Over here! Over here! Over here!"

Whimpering, closing his useless eyes (for hearing knows when seeing cannot reveal), Jones fiailed his arms and set out in the direction of the first yelling, crunching over bones, coming upon another set of flailing arms.

"Congressman! Is that you?"

Jones felt the living warm flesh, the bristle of an unshaven face, the unkempt hair.

"Who the hell else would it be?" he heard Marcus's voice. Then, "We've got to be careful, Jones. If we lose our sense of direction now we're goners."

Joining arms, they moved slowly through the darkness,

muttering prayers, for such is the fickle nature of men that when they find themselves abandoned by their fellows they invariably resort to God — when left adrift by faulty reasoning they surely will turn to religion. They prayed out loud that their bacon be saved, listing all the vices they'd quit should God find it in his passing pleasure to deliver them from this mess. Those vices included smoke and drink and women; cussing, fast cars, fine foods and luxurious possessions — in short, the very things they'd built their lives around in rosier times.

Just when they thought they were goners sure, when the darkness had closed down deep and complete around them, they saw from somewhere up ahead a tiny pinprick of light. At first it was only the tiniest of pinpricks, the magnitude of the weakest star in the sky, but to Marcus and Jones it shone brighter than the beacon on the Statue of Liberty. Jones took off ahead. He ran whimpering toward the light, fearful it would vanish at any moment, but as he ran it began to grow light around him so that at last he could make out the outlines of his hand, the jagged contours of the cave around him and the shadowy figures of the reclining bones. Suddenly he burst into a brightly lit chamber and, coming upon the light he'd followed out of the darkness, he threw himself upon it and showered it with kisses.

Jones looked up, scarcely believing his eyes. Before him stood a big white Southern mansion. Graceful antebellum columns on the porch. The chamber was lit by a battery of lights the manner of which Jones hadn't seen for years.

He cursed, though moments before he'd promised never again to curse. His hands fell away from the light he'd just finished showering with kisses. It, like the other lights in this most peculiar chamber, was a statue of a black man in colorful riding clothing, holding out a lantern.

"Damn!" Jones cursed again. "I kissed a lawn jockey!"

He was doubly amazed then to see a small plaque on its base. The plaque read that the lawn jockey was the property of the Smithsonian Institution in Washington and that it was a theatrical prop from the Sidney Portier film In the Heat of the Night.

8

"It was terrifying!" Edgar moaned. "Absolutely terrifying!"

"Go on," George Natlong urged. "What happened?"

"Yes go on dear," Doty said. "Tell us everything."

"One moment he was perfectly pleasant. Then — like that! — he turned on me." They'd gathered close around, hanging on every word. "We were going to leave the house to meet the others in the woods, as you instructed, George, when he turned on me. I still don't know what hit me. I was standing there when wham! Lights out! I was down on the floor. I saw him switch off the lamp. He moves so fast! Like a streak! I was alone in the dark with that monster. I was never so frightened in my life. He started talking like a crazy man. Like a maniac."

"Well for christsakes what did he say?"

"After he switched off the lamp he came over to me and he asked—." Edgar's voice trailed off. He lowered his head.

"Go on. What did he ask?"

"It was really the most ridiculous thing," Edgar went on. "There I was, on the floor afraid for my life and do you know what he said? I look up and in the moonlight coming through the window I see he's staring at me with those large inquiring eyes and do you know what he says? He asks me why I thought it was Clark Kent doesn't come to work at the Daily Planet dressed as Superman."

"What?"

"That's right. That's what he asked."

"Well what did you tell him?"

"I was too afraid to say anything. He was obviously unsta-

487

ble enough as it was. I didn't want to upset him. I had to think of my life."

"So then what happened?"

"He sat down on the bed—."

Edgar winced as his wife dabbed at his head with her handkerchief.

"He sat down on the bed. In the moonlight I saw him making strange motions with his hands."

"How do you mean?"

Edgar tried to imitate the boy by awkwardly holding out his left hand while all the while moving the fingers of his right, close in at his chest.

"I asked him what it was he was doing. He said he was playing something he called the air guitar. Said it helped him to think."

"The what?"

"He was obviously completely out of his mind! I tell you I was never so frightened in my life!"

"You poor dear man!" Doty cried. "You could have been killed!"

"Is that all?" George Natlong asked. "Did he say anything else?"

"Yes," Edgar said, trying to remember. "He went over to the window and right before he jumped he looked over to me from the sill and he asked me to give you a message."

"Tell me *exactly* what he said. Word for word. Leave out nothing."

Edgar moaned, slumped forward in the chair.

"It sounded like crazy talk. He said, 'You tell General Natlong he can catch my jet stream.' Then he opened the window and he jumped. Like a streak. I tell you, I was never so frightened in my life."

9

When they'd brought Edgar into the warehouse she'd shadowed them in and had anxiously awaited the right moment. Seeing her aunt crying over the busted furniture while the others were distracted by Edgar's story, she slipped past the steel doors and made her way underground. From her blouse she pulled a small package. She fumbled with it as she made her way down along the long curving hallway. At the doorway to the computer chamber she stopped. Peeking in, she saw Hal. He was alone, slumped before the blinking computer, his feet propped on the console. He held a glass of bourbon up into the light, preparing to drink.

Scurrying to the other side of the doorway, she proceeded down the hallway, each step carrying her deeper and farther underground, passing all the long dark hallways branching off in every direction. It was awfully quiet and still but she didn't appear to notice, so absorbed was she in her thoughts. She kept going, past the living quarters, past the great storerooms filled with food, past the kitchens, past the recreational facilities, past the doors leading off to the swimming pools and the saunas and the tennis courts. All of it ghostly still now, an entire underground city waiting for its populace, and as she made her way she kept fidgeting with the little package in her hands. When she came to the end of the hallway she turned down another, one that led to those rooms crammed with Americana from the Smithsonian. Instinctively, without thinking, she followed the long darkened hallway past all the rooms that had been laid out with memorabilia from the different decades of the American epoch, her feet quickening as she read the plaques on the doors. The Nineteen Hundred Room. The

Nineteen Tens. The Roaring Twenties. The Thirties Room. Her heart skipped a beat as she past The Forties Room. From somewhere up ahead the sounds of a voice drifted down the hall.

"...The world is very different now. For man holds in his mortal hands the power to abolish all forms of human poverty and all forms of human life...."

At first she didn't recognize the voice but as she came up to The Sixties Room the sharp New England twang became unmistakable. John Kennedy's voice. How could it be? She turned the corner and went in.

Paul leaned against one of those push-button museum exhibits, his back to the doorway, watching a film of John Kennedy's inaugural address. The sleeves of his red jacket were pushed up around his elbows. And there was something else. A guitar. A red electric guitar. It was strapped behind his back and so it was the first thing she saw when she came in behind him.

The girl stepped lightly into the room. She took in all the elaborately prepared exhibits from the sixties — two or three space capsules, wax likenesses of the Beatles, Martin Luther King, Jr., the Kennedys, a wall map of Vietnam, and other such things.

Paul suddenly wheeled about. He looked surprised.

"I thought I'd find you here." Her voice was all trembly. "Somehow I knew you'd be here." She forced a smile. "Are you stuck in the sixties?"

She held out the small package, wrapped in paper napkins. "I made it for you." She forced that smile.

He took it. A sandwich.

"It's egg salad. I made it myself. For you."

He looked it over.

"I hope you like it. You should see the mess in the kitchen back at the house. Since Spencer threatened to walk out all the ladies are forced to cook for themselves. What a sight! Aunt Liz, Doty and Natalie never even boiled an egg before in their lives. I had to teach them. They were even helping her move furniture in from the gate!"

She quit talking.

Paul unwrapped the sandwich and tore into it, wolfing it down. At last he nodded at the exhibition screen, at the film of Kennedy giving his speech.

"When I was a boy growing up in the sixties I thought I must be the luckiest person alive. I mean, I really thought it was something to be a boy in America. It was like I was on the top of the heap or something, you know? I'd look around and I'd see people on tv from other parts of the world and I'd realize how rough they had it compared to us. Now I think maybe I'm here to watch it fall apart."

The screen went dark.

"I used to have these heroes," he brooded. "One by one I saw them snuffed out. Blown away. Shot like dogs. A message gets through. I turn on the tv and find out someone who'd encouraged me to dream just got creamed. I used to get sad but now I just get mad."

She turned away to hide her tears. Her hands were all trembling and clammy and she acted like she didn't know what to do with them. Suddenly she turned and took Paul's hands in hers. He saw that she was crying. Unlike her own hands his were steady and warm.

"However can you be so calm at a moment like this?"

"Ah you girls never understand," he smiled. "I'm not stupid, you know, no matter what the generals say. I could've been an A student if I wanted. I've got eyes and I can see what's going on. I've got hands and I can use them."

She broke from his hands and turned away. She stood away from him, crying, her arms crossed in front. He didn't know what to do. If anything. Or what to say. If anything. He looked at her with a dumb expression on his face, like boys have stood confounded before girls from the start of time. Whatever do you do with them?

She really was very pretty, he had to think, watching her. If only she wasn't so damn rich! If only—! For a moment he allowed himself to see her as he'd seen her the first time, when

491

he'd climbed into the Volkswagen and found her there, before he'd known about the money. Camp Moonstone had a way of making the outside world unimportant. The pressures and stresses of the place had a way of stripping you down to essentials. Now it was happening with Claire. Suddenly when he looked at her he didn't see the Duke fortune, he just saw a girl who was crying. He had to feel sorry for her. The money kept getting in her way. He supposed there was never a creature so rich that she could do without love.

He certainly could have done a lot of things just then. He could have walked out of there and left her crying alone. He could have told himself to cool it, to watch out. But he knew the things he'd already been through with her had fused them together in some way he'd never be able to fully comprehend. From here out he knew she'd understand him in a way no one else ever could. Besides, she looked pretty good.

She felt him come up behind her and kiss the nape of her neck.

They were in each other's arms in the Sixties Room when they heard something moving in the hall. Looking up, they saw as in a dream three gray old Indians slinking past the doorway. They were decked out in feathered war bonnets, their faces painted, the beads on their deerskin costumes rattling as they went by. Two of them appeared to be engaged in stringing their bows with arrows while the third held a tomahawk in his rugged hands. God did they look pissed.

Claire might have cried out if Paul hadn't slipped a hand over her mouth. They heard the receding footsteps of the Indians, then—! More footsteps. Dragging. He looked up from the girl and saw the bedraggled congressman and his aide going past the doorway, looking half dead, their clothes ripped and torn, their faces glazed.

A smile slit Paul's face. He slid his hand from Claire's mouth, motioning for her to keep quiet. He brought the red Strat around front. With his thumb he played a couple of joyous riffs on the deadened strings, shuffling his feet.

"Who were they?" Claire asked.

"This morning I went looking for a hero. I couldn't find any so I had to settle for those fellows. They'll have to do. Looks like they found the back door to this place."

He looked at her.

"So it's begun," he said, resting his hands on the neck of the Strat. "The waves of fate are rolling in. What's chiefly needed now is good timing." Bringing his hands down to the strings, he slashed out another wild riff, limbering his fingers. She watched him thrust the Strat forward then pull it back, repeating the motion. He bounced in his sneakers, grating his hips and arching his shoulders, all the while playing wild wailing riffs.

"Today's only unpardonable sin is bad timing," he said with a smirk, working the strings with his bare thumb. "Now, God, stand up for rockers!"

With that he took off into the hall, a quick flash of red and blue. As he turned and flew out Claire could see what looked like an oversized fuse protruding from the back pocket of his jeans.

493

10

Drinking alone in the computer chamber, he thought about how they'd carve up the world after Armageddon. He'd already set his sights on administering the Middle East but now as he sat alone with his feet up on the blinking console he let his ambitions run wild. He told himself it might be nice to control a little European real estate. Maybe Spain. Perhaps Italy. Then again, the Riviera would be nice this time of year. He pictured himself ruling vast legions from a villa on the French Riviera. The thought was appealing. He pictured himself as a sort of a cross between General Patton and Lawrence of Arabia. Yes, he'd definitely have to grab himself some European real estate. In the final measure Europe is as good a place as any to conquer. Better than most. Maybe he could trade a little of the Middle East for parts of Europe, he was thinking as he knocked back another bourbon. Maybe he could trade Saudi Arabia for Spain, Italy and France. He never much liked the shape of Saudi Arabia. Then again it did have all that oil going for it. It would be a shame to give away all that oil on account of a country's shape. Maybe he'd try trading Kuwait. It was smaller and besides he'd never liked its name. It was almost impossible to pronounce after you've had a few and who wanted a country like that? On the other hand, it suddenly occurred to him, why trade any of the Middle East for Europe? He could administer the entire old world. He could think of no better man for the job. And why not? He mulled the possibilities. George Natlong would probably want to administer North America (and wasn't it only fair that George, whose project this was, should get first pick of the spoils?). Bob, that timid soul, would probably be content with

Africa, the South Americas, or some other quiet backwater. As for Casey, that pain in the ass— he'd be lucky to get Australia. As far as he could see, his only competition for Europe came from Charlie. You never knew what that broccoli chef was cooking up behind those glasses. Maybe he could trick him into taking all of the Asias and the South Pacific instead. After all, the world was a big place. Certainly big enough for the five of them. He felt the bourbon working its way into his veins and his thoughts took a darker nature. Maybe George had his sights on Europe, he couldn't help thinking. George sure had been acting funny lately. Little things he said and did made you think he might try for the whole ball of wax. Well as far as he saw it there was only one sound course of action. Only one thing to be done. He'd just have to toady up to George Natlong, kiss a little ass and make sure he stayed on old George's good side. He'd been doing a good job so far. Hadn't it been a good sign that George had left him in charge of the computer while he'd gone off with the others? Yes, Hal thought, his star certainly was on the rise. The Middle East and Europe were as good as his.

Pouring one more stiff one, he heard footsteps in the hallway. That must be them now. Hal lowered the glass and the bottle, lowered his feet from the console, assuming a military bearing. He peered up the aisle past the empty rows of seats. He was surprised to see what looked all the world like three Indians trucking up the hall toward the surface. Blinking his eyes, he examined the half-drunk bottle of bourbon before him on the console. Maybe the liquor was bad. Nah, he hadn't had *that* much to drink.

He got up from the console and stood warily in the aisle. He drew his .45. After a moment he heard more footsteps. This time two more men went by — a white and a black. They'd obviously managed to penetrate the most sensitive area of the compound — the storeroom where the liquor and the good cigars were kept — as they were loaded down with bottles and cigar boxes.

When Hal saw this he let out, "Hey, that's our liquor, you

sons of bitches!" Intending to investigate this most serious breach of military security, he tottered up the aisle after them.

The congressman and his aide followed the Indians up a most curious and mysterious hallway, marveling at the endless passages branching from the main thoroughfare. Whoever'd dug these tunnels obviously had creature comforts foremost in mind. Unlike the Indians' caverns of cold rock and clay these tunnelworks had been luxuriantly finished over. Carpet on the floors, the walls painted any number of cheerful hues, fluorescent tubes hanging at close intervals from the finished ceiling. Even the air had a man-made, conditioned quality to it. You felt like you were in a shopping mall — all that was missing was the Muzak. Only the constant upward slope of the hall reminded you where you were. They didn't have to walk more than fifty steps before they came to the first of the broad intersections of passageways crossing endlessly to the left and right. Presently huge gymnasiums and stately living quarters opened on both sides of this main thoroughfare, drawing amazed stares from Marcus and Jones as they filed past, till at last they hit the storerooms.

"Would you look at all that food," Marcus had gawked as they went on. "Must be enough rations stored down here to feed a city."

Through an open door Jones spotted the generals' cache of liquor.

"Would you look at this!" He loped into the storeroom, his arms high. Bottles of every imaginable sort of spirit were stacked thirty-feet high to the ceiling. Less than ten minutes ago he'd sworn solemnly never again to touch a drop but now Jones uncorked a vintage bottle of '57 Rothschild and drank deeply.

"What're you doing?" Marcus yelled in to him. "We'll lose the Indians!" Ahead he could just make out the last of the Mingos shuffling out of sight along the long slanted curving hallway.

"King o' Sobby, I'm not going to die of thirst with all this good stuff so close," Jones answered. He wiped his chin with the sleeve of his ragged shirt. From the shelf he pulled a bottle of Chivas Regal. "Who'll ever miss a bottle or two? After all I've been through I think I deserve a little libation."

Marcus might have complained more vigorously had he not spotted fine cigars in the next storeroom. Thinking he could use a good smoke to steady his nerves he purloined a few humidors and lost no time lighting up, though, like Jones, he'd sworn upon the altar of God not fifteen minutes before he'd never again indulge.

Once they were loaded down with all the truck they could carry they proceeded to hurry after the Indians. They'd gone what must have been a quarter of a mile or more, fuming aromatic cigar smoke, when at last they came upon an oversized arching doorway opening to the right. Filing past, they stopped and gawked.

"For the love of Pete would you look at that!"

"It's the House chamber back in Washington! An exact replica!"

Indeed upon first sweeping inspection it appeared to be a remarkably exact replica of the House chamber, complete with row upon row of semicircular benches facing the well down front, even amazingly similar paneling on the high walls, but on closer inspection you saw the original design had been perverted. A large viewing screen had been placed in front of the speaker's rostrum. A computer with an expansive blinking console took up the space normally taken by clerks' desks. Overlooking all, completely covering the speaker's rostrum, the large screen eerily sparkled. And there was no visitors' gallery. Instead, stalagmites hung from the roof of the great cavern. The only hint of a visitors' gallery was a small mock platform partially hidden by the sparkling screen. Directly over the rostrum, in the middle of the platform, as in the real gallery it imitated back in Washington, you could just make out a plaque with an inscription. Though the inscription was too far away to be read the congressman knew it by heart. When he'd first come to Washington he'd been caught up in the Federal City. He'd gone around town for days and weeks reading every plaque and admiring every obscure statue. Now all the memories of those days came back to him as he remembered the inscription on the plaque:

"*Let us develop the resources of the land, call forth its powers, build up its institutions, promote all its great interests and see whether we also in our day and generation may not perform something worthy to be remembered.*"

The puny and fake visitors' gallery where the plaque hung couldn't accommodate more than a dozen people, at most. The sad platform resembled a gallows more than a visitors' gallery. Hardly a gallery for a great and free country. By the time a free country sinks to this level of existence there won't be much about it that's free, Marcus thought.

The congressman's eyes instinctively moved to the tall marble pedestal to the right of the obscured speaker's rostrum, the pedestal that traditionally held the sergeant at arms' mace. The mace, never used more than symbolically, always had a solemn impact on House members. In the long history of the republic, whenever congressmen lost their heads and tempers got hot, the sergeant at arms would hold the mace before the offending parties and calm would be restored to men who in their better hearts knew that cool and reasoned debate over our differences is all that separates us from the beasts. If only there was a staff like that for all mankind! In this chamber, Marcus saw, the reproduction of the House mace had rolled off the pedestal and lay bent and neglected on the floor. Seeing this, Marcus was filled with a sudden revulsion. He would have charged down the aisle and restored the mace to its proper place of respect had not someone at that moment cried out. The cry rose from a chubby military man standing all the way down the aisle.

Waving the pistol, the uniformed man bellowed, "What're you doing with our liquor, you sons of bitches!" He started up the aisle in a truculent manner. His drawn .45 was all Jones had to see. Dropping a bottle of bourbon, Jones took off with a wail up the sloping hallway after the Indians, scarcely waiting for the glass to break and the liquor to splatter.

As for our intrepid congressman: he would have ignored the man with the gun and marched down the aisle and set that fake mace back on its pedestal had he not reminded himself that it was after all a reproduction of the mace and not the original. It's possible to reproduce something in most every detail but you can't fudge its spirit. As the fat army man puffed up the aisle, Congressman Marcus recalled what the boys in the cloakroom had joked after the young and ambitious Senator Jack Kennedy had published his famed book. ("What we need now," it's said someone had cracked, "is a little less profile and a little more courage.") The congressman quickly forgot about the mace and, splashing through the puddle of spilled liquor, began chasing after Jones and the Indians. He figured that's where the real battle was, anyway.

11

Camp Moonstone took the three old Indians very much by surprise. With torches blazing they approached the farthest recesses of the cave, to the very end of their sacred burial chamber. Imagine their surprise when they saw light ahead and, turning a corner, suddenly found themselves confronting the strange sight of a Southern mansion buried far underground, glittering in the blackness. They had trouble believing their eyes. Once they saw all the disturbed bones thrown helter skelter around the big white house, belief set in and they got mad.

"White man has gone too far this time!"

Few things in this world can be as unpleasant as three old buzzard Indians who get mad. At first Running Deer and Swift River vented their rage on Jasper Wyoming.

"This is all your fault!" Swift River spat, pushing little Jasper down to the soft slag.

"How's it my fault?"

"If you'd get off your lazy ass once in your life and had come back here like you were supposed to do we would have known what they were up to."

"I can't be expected to notice every little thing that goes on around here," Jasper Wyoming whined. He flailed his chubby arms to get up from the slag but Running Deer kicked out his feet, knocking him over again.

"*Every little thing!*" Running Deer sourly mocked, screwing up his face so that the sharply drawn lines of his war paint gave his lanky face the appearance of an arrow. "You call this a little thing!" Running Deer swept back his arm at the Southern mansion. It certainly did seem as hard to overlook as the Lincoln Memorial. Its six white columns must each have been thirty feet tall, and all the lawn jockeys sprinkled about the front yard made the house stand out and shine like a diamond in a coal bin.

When finally they accepted that beating on Jasper Wyoming ultimately was as useless as it was unsatisfying, Running Deer and Swift River turned their attention to the big house. The sharp light from all the lawn jockeys made their war paint stand out like streaks of a neon rainbow.

"This is absolutely the last straw!" Running Deer piped, throwing down his torch. He reached back into his quiver for an arrow. Swift River did the same. "The bones of our dead cry out for vengeance! The last of the once great Mingo may have been forced to live like dogs but today, as the Great Spirit is our witness, today we die like men!"

With that he led them up onto the porch and knocked open the big white door, whooping. The three of them stormed into the antebellum entrancehall and started crashing into tables and chairs, knocking things over, issuing war cries. They knocked around like they half expected to find terrified Southern belles in hoop skirts. When no one came they started looking around. It was then they noticed that all the doors leading from the room opened into solid rock.

"White men are as crazy as shithouse rats," Running Deer spat, slamming closed a door which led nowhere.

"This way!" Swift River gestured up the grand staircase on which Clark Gable and Vivien Leigh had once trod. He led the charge up the red-carpeted stairs, into the complex's confusing labyrinth of passageways. His eyesight was not as acute as it once had been. Several times he feared they'd lost their way in the confusing maze but he stuck to his guns (or rather, his arrows) till at long last the upward sloping hallway led to an open area. Puffing exhaustedly up this last piece of sloping hallway, Swift River caught sight of the summit of what appeared to be a great mountain of furniture. It was then he let out a war cry the likes of which the others hadn't heard since they'd been boys playing Indians and cowboys back on the reservation in the good old days.

12

The generals, having heard all they could stomach of Edgar's story, returned to the job of tearing through the furniture. They'd reclimbed the tangled mountain and resumed frantically throwing aside whatever they encountered, not caring about the damage. Elizabeth Natlong sobbing up at the men, "You promised if the boy went I could keep Daddy's furniture! You promised me that! You promised! Just give me this one thing George! That's all I ask! Just this one thing! George! George!" But they paid her no heed. Natalie tried to comfort her, to pull her away even as big pieces rained down around them.

Natalie yelled up at the men, "Can't you see how you're upsetting poor Elizabeth? Doesn't she at least deserve an explanation?"

"Sorry, ladies." George Natlong tossed a Chippendale lowboy onto the concrete. "That's classified information. A matter of national security, you understand."

From a crater carved near the peak of the mountain Casey and Bob sang out they'd found something. They wrestled it out from a crevice in between a bookcase and an empire-style china cabinet, shattering the glass in the cabinet as they jimmied. The civilians were surprised to see them inspecting what looked like a guitar case.

George Natlong had just finished kicking a dressing table off the side of the mountain. His heart leapt, and he hopped off the mountain, ordering them to quick bring it down.

"Be careful with it for godsakes!" he barked up at Bob and Charlie. The two scrambled down the cliffs of oak and walnut, handling the guitar case back and forth as they descended. "Be careful not to break the upgrade!"

Scarcely able to contain himself, he ran back and forth at the foot of the mountain barking orders, commanding the two not to step here, to grab a handhold there, yet to by all means hurryup, whatever they did, but not to go so fast as to be careless.

"Here! Give it to me! Give it to me!" he barked up at them as they descended the last of the mountain. "Drop it into my hands! Drop it into my hands! Be gentle I tell you! Gentle!"

He stretched up his arms and they did as he said, dropping it the last few inches gently into his open arms. He held it out before him, savoring the moment. He saw that it was an ordinary-enough looking guitar case, of handtooled leather, with the words "Buddy Holly" scripted neatly into the leather. Good things sometimes come in strange packages, he couldn't help thinking.

"At last! At last!" he laughed, stamping his feet, doing a little jig. He hugged the case. "Hooray for Peter Donday! I knew I could depend on him. I knew he'd come through in the clinch! Hooray for Peter Donday! Didn't I tell you he'd come through for us?" He laughed maniacally, holding back nothing, flashing a toothy, horsey grin. "Now I've got the world in my hands! I'm holding the world right here in my hands!"

But there is always something we can't have. Just as he was about to open the guitar case George Natlong heard, from somewhere behind, what sounded all the world like an Indian war whoop. Turning, he was very much surprised to see three old Indians come charging from the tunnel leading up from the secret complex below.

"What the—."

Before he could finish the sentence that surely would have lived forever in the annals of military utterances, two of the whooping Indians each dropped down on one knee and fired a salvo of arrows. One arrow streaked wide into the furniture while the other came tolerably close to George Natlong's head, streaking into an overturned bureau with a loud *thwack*, its

504

thin shaft vibrating and singing in sudden impact. The third Indian, a short stout fellow who bore a particularly angry look on his painted face, came charging across the warehouse floor for George Natlong, menacingly waving a tomahawk, bearing his teeth and screaming like all hell and thunder, "Think fast pale face!" It was enough to test any man's reactions. George Natlong had just enough time to reflexively bring the guitar case around to protect himself from the tomahawk blow. Next thing George Natlong and the painted Indian were grunting and wrestling for the guitar case while the other two Indians continued firing salvos of arrows in the general direction of the mountain of furniture.

The civilians, caught by surprise in the sneak attack, scattered, screaming. Arrows flew nearer to George Natlong by the moment. Bob and Charlie raced out behind him, grabbing his arms. Arrows rained down around them as they dragged themselves to relative safety behind a rolltop desk that lay pushed over on its side at the foothills of the furniture. He'd released the guitar case and now as they dragged him away George Natlong watched through disbelieving eyes as the chubby little Indian attempted to pry the tomahawk from the case.

All this was happening too fast for the generals to understand the meaning of the attack, let alone to consider the proper response. They simply pulled out their .45s and started blazing from behind the desk, thinking that if gunplay didn't help to miraculously clear up the mystery at least their guns would bring the confusion under control. But this only added to the confusion and noise. The civilians, caught in the cross fire, dashed everywhichway. The generals peered from behind the desk and kept firing their .45s but they were as bad with the bullets as the Indians were with the arrows. As they fired they closed their eyes and dropped open their mouths, blindly and furiously tugging at the triggers until the awful roar came and went. Even so they forced the terrified retreat of the chubby little Indian. Dropping the guitar case, the tomahawk still in its side, he beat it back behind the archers.

George Natlong stopped firing. Not taking his eyes from the abandoned guitar case, he yelled over to the others, "Hey! What the hell are we fighting about? Where'd those Indians come from?"

"Aren't they the same Indians we saw this morning when we recaptured the boy? He must've tipped them off."

Bullets ricocheted off the concrete, etching sudden white scratches dangerously near the precious guitar case. George Natlong ordered a cease-fire. From his back trouser pocket came a white handkerchief.

"Hey chief!" he cried out, waving the handkerchief over the desk. "What's this about? Can't we have a pow-wow? Can't we have peace?"

"For us there can be no peace!" Running Deer cried back. Rising to his feet, he beseechingly held out an arm, while Swift River remained on one knee, his bow cocked and ready. "We are the last of the Mingo. The remnant of a once-great people. The proud ancestors of the tribe of Tahgahjute, known to the white man as John Logan."

"Who?" George Natlong said.

"Logan. John Logan. He was the author of the famous Logan's Lament. Surely you remember it from school."

"Can't say I do, chief."

The old Indian pulled a wooden plaque from his deerskin suit.

"This is nuts," Charlie whispered.

"Maybe we should try rushing him."

"Why risk it?" George Natlong said. "Let's hear what the old coot has to say. Maybe we can sign a treaty. We can always break it."

Running Deer held the wooden plaque at arms length, squinting.

He said to Swift River, "Lend me your glasses."

Swift River removed his thick trifocals. This left his own weak eyes tremendously out of focus. Blinking, his eyes crossed, Swift River went back to the business of looking down the arrow shaft.

506

Adjusting the trifocals, Running Deer looked to the wooden plaque.

"Many moon go by," Running Deer began as always, sweeping his hand in a wide arch above his head, "since Logan first spoke his tragic lament."

He cleared his throat and read from the wooden plaque:

"'I appeal to any white man to say if ever he entered Logan's cabin hungry and he gave him not meat; if ever he came cold and naked, and he clothed him not. During the course of the last long and bloody conquest (the French and Indian War), Logan remained idle in his cabin, an advocate of peace. Such was my love for the whites that my countrymen pointed as they passed and said, "Logan is the friend of the White Man." I had even thought to live with you but for the injury of one man — Colonel Cresap who, last spring in cold blood and unprovoked, murdered all the relations of Logan, not sparing even my women and children. There runs not a drop of my blood in any living creature. This called on me for revenge. I have sought it. I have killed many. I have fully glutted my vengeance. For my country I rejoice at the beams of peace. But do not harbor a thought that mine is the joy of fear. Logan never felt fear. He will not turn on his heel to save his life. Who is there to mourn for Logan? Not one.'"

As the last of these angry words resounded like claps of thunder around the great warehouse, Running Deer held the wooden plaque high for all to see. He motioned at Swift River and Jasper Wyoming.

"Many moon go by since Logan first voiced this tragic lament," he said, "and the three of us that you now see before you are all that remain of Logan's tribe, all that remain of the once-proud Mingo. We were hunted like bison, our lands taken from us, and every treaty we ever made with the white man was broken. But did we complain? No. We realized things are tough all over. We contented ourselves to live out the last of our days in a mere shack in yonder woods, looking after the bones of our noble ancestors and, when fortune allowed, selling a few trinkets on the side. But today we learned the builders of this place desecrated our sacred burial grounds. The bones of our dead, robbed of their peace, cry out for vengeance. In the immortal words of Logan, we will not now turn on our heels to save our lives. For truly, we have no place to go."

"Now wait one minute!" George Natlong answered from behind the desk. "So a few of your treaties were broken. And a few indiscretions were long ago perpetrated against your people. And then the government decided to drop this complex on your burial grounds. So now you want to hold *me* accountable for every treaty Uncle Sam broke since the Pilgrims first stepped off the Mayflower? Well I'll have you know I certainly wasn't around in the days of the Wild West. And as far as this complex goes — we merely lease it from the government for the purposes of my project. I had nothing to do with its design or construction. Be reasonable, chief. You certainly can't blame us for every gripe you hold against the entire murdering white race!" He looked worrisomely at the guitar case. "I'll have you know I've a job to do here and you're delaying me!"

"Paybacks *are* a bitch, aren't they?"

Running Deer reached into his quiver and withdrew a strange arrow, resembling a cattail. Jasper Wyoming struck a match, touched the flame to the arrow. *Thwack!* They heard the flaming arrow sizzle as it flew in a streak of orange, yellow and red into the mountain of furniture.

Once again the generals opened fire, blasting away thunderously yet blindly from behind the desk, ducking their own ricocheting bullets. George Natlong for his part didn't even take his eyes off the exposed guitar case as he blasted away with his .45. Even so his eyes were drawn by a flash of movement streaking from the great wide doorway that opened down into the cave.

A black man in ripped wet clothing came running from behind the old Indians, screaming, "Don't shoot! Don't shoot!" Dodging the ricochets, waving arms high, he took off

508

for the safety of the looming pile of woodwork, lunging behind an end table into the three-decked family credenzas.

"Well who the hell was that?" George Natlong tossed down the stub of his cigar.

"Search me."

"Don't these people know this is a top-secret government installation?"

By now Running Deer and Jasper Wyoming, hoping to smoke out the army officers, had managed to fire at least a half dozen flaming arrows into the furniture. Casey worriedly looked up behind their rolltop desk outpost to the spots of orange and red here and there flickering on the jagged mountainside.

"Looks like our fort's on fire, George. Could be trouble if we have to fall back to higher ground."

George Natlong gazed over his shoulder. He saw his wife climbing the mountainside, heading for one of the many spreading patches of fire. It was as if he didn't know that woman. There was nothing but coldness in his eyes and in his voice as he said, "Don't worry about it. There's so much woodwork here we'll finish these Indians off long before we have no place to hide."

So absorbed were the generals in their engagement with the Indians that they didn't notice the man with the submachine gun come charging into the warehouse. He came running in breathlessly, his Uzi cocked and ready. He tore across the floor then abruptly stopped, unable to believe his eyes.

It was a madhouse. Four besieged army generals fired .45s behind an arrow-spiked rolltop desk at the base of the smoldering pile of furniture. They blasted away at three old Indians who fired back with blazing arrows. It was getting smoky in there and everywhere civilians were running with alarm around the pile of furniture.

"Jesus!" the man with the submachine gun moaned.

He yanked the Uzi's trigger then, sending a spray of warning shots into the mountain of furniture. With that a man who looked all the world like Charlie Chaplin come wheeling out from behind the woodwork, holding onto his bowler hat and twirling his cane, flapping about for a place to hide, followed by a black man in ripped clothing who emerged from behind a dressing table waving his arms, hollering, "Don't shoot! Don't shoot!"

Taking aim with the Uzi, he shot the feathers off the three old Indians' war bonnets. Jasper Wyoming was about to light another arrow when he found the fire had been neatly shot from the match.

"All right, Geronimo, drop the arrows!" the one with the Uzi commanded. "I've got the whole tribe covered."

Swift River held off on firing an arrow. Blinking, he saw the double figure of a tall, muscular man with a small rifle tucked close in at his side.

The generals still blasted away from behind the rolltop desk. George Natlong at last looked up.

"Major Donday! Where the hell have you been? What's happened?"

"I should ask the same of you. Let's just say I was made a fool of by a woman."

"Same with me."

13

This is how a woman makes a fool of a man. The man is minding his own business, which at that moment was rubbing dirty glasses with a rag, when he hears a knock on the door of his club. At first he ignores it because it's early in the morning, well before opening, but the knocking keeps up so finally he yells, "Beat it! Get your morning gin somewhere else."

But the knocking keeps up.

"Oh for christsakes!"

Bitching and cussing he goes to the door, placing his body behind it, cracking it open. On his doorstep stands the most beautiful woman he's ever seen. Honey brown hair. A twinkle in the eyes. Voluptuous lips. Slim and attractive with curves everywhere. Lady Luck herself has come calling, he thought. When it rains it certainly does pour, doesn't it? He smacked his lips, tore off the filthy apron and straightened his thinning greasy hair with the palms of his hands. Then he opened the door.

"Yes?" He'd said it most pleasantly, he thought. She came in, slowly, looking around. He remained at the door, watching her, his mouth open.

"My name," she said, "Is Patterson. And you, I presume, must be the fat man."

The fat man broke into a stupid grin.

"I am," he said. "I am." He closed the door, his back against it. He held out one of those hamhocks of a hand, which she declined. "I'm charmed," he twinkled.

"I've come," she said, "for a guitar. I understand I can find it here. It's a red electric guitar. A Stratocaster, I believe it's called. It's in a handtooled leather case with the words...."

511

The fat man quickly covered her soft full lips with a finger. He looked around cautiously as if to say even the walls had ears.

"Shh!" He shot her a queer look. "But how did you get here from New York so fast? I only passed the word to Jacobo yesterday that it was up for sale." He started to laugh. "I suppose word spreads fast when you have something as valuable as that, doesn't it?"

Now she was the one shooting the strange look. Smiling, she nodded uneasily, gripping the strap of her shoulder bag. "Yes, word does get around. And now if you'd just let me have the guitar I'll be on my way."

"But not so fast!" The fat man came alive, dancing from the door, charging for the kitchen, singing, "You must be starved after such a long trip! I must fix us both something to eat."

"That won't be necessary."

But the fat man already was banging around the kitchen. She heard the sizzling sounds of steaks on the grill.

"You really must tell me how my dear old friend Jacobo is," the fat man yelled from the kitchen. He regarded himself in the mirror at the washsink, slicking back his hair to cover the bald spot, a difficult job, sucking in some of his gut, an impossible job. Hurrying to the peg near the door, he threw on his satin dinner jacket and silk muffler. There. That was better. The dinner jacket had a way of hiding the gut. Turning this way and that before the mirror, he fancied he looked a little like Orson Welles.

Twinkle toed, he danced to the tables with a red and white checkered linen tablecloth, a bottle of wine and long-stemmed glasses. With a flourish and a snap! he deployed the cloth. He opened the wine, looking at the woman.

She leaned in the doorway to his office, looking in. The fat man came up behind her, making the floorboards creak. She turned to face him and he handed her a glass.

"No thanks."

"But my dear, a business deal like this can happen only

512

once in a lifetime."

"Let's hope so."

The fat man laughed.

"You're such a serious woman, Miss Patterson. Or did you say it was Mrs Patterson?"

"Ms Patterson will do nicely in this case."

"You have a first name, don't you, Ms Patterson?"

"Linda. And you? Or is it strictly The Fat Man? In which case that must make your first name 'The.'"

He laughed.

"Very good. Very good."

"Actually my name is Gutman. Charles Gutman." He took a sip of the wine.

"Well Mr Gutman if you don't mind dispensing with the formalities let's get down to brass tacks. You've got the guitar and I want it. Now."

"I'm sure you do. I'm sure you do. And I'm sure you'll drive a very hard bargain."

"You can be quite sure I'll drive a very hard bargain."

He watched her go into his office. She stood before the big safe.

"It's in here, isn't it?"

"You haven't even asked how I can vouch for its authenticity." The fat man had followed her into the room. "Well I assure you I can. The boy I— procured the guitar from assured me his uncle had pulled it from the wreckage on the very night of the crash. Imagine its history!"

She gave him another queer look.

"And as for the price: I should think twenty-five thousand dollars is fair. After all, we're talking about a most rare and important piece of Americana here." He moved his big bison's head close to hers, whispering, "To think it's *his* guitar. You can actually see pick marks on it from when he played. Long deep scratches from when the plane came down. I've sat up nights just looking at it, sitting back here at my desk under the light touching those deep gashes and scratch marks wondering what that Strat could say if it could only talk. The story it could tell if only you could pick it up and make it talk. To tell the truth, it gives me the spooks to sit alone with it late at night. You imagine his ghost standing behind you. When you think of it, that guitar hasn't always meant the best of luck. I'm glad to be rid of it. I'm quite glad Jacobo sent you to take it off my hands. But do you really think it's safe with you?" His eyes moved down her slim figure. "You look like a little wisp of a thing."

"Do I now?" She nodded at the safe. "I said open it. I want to see the guitar. Now."

The fat man laughed.

"Very good. Very good. Jacobo always had a weakness for strong women."

But he moved no closer to the safe. He sipped at his wine.

"As I say, I'm prepared to let it go for twenty-five thousand dollars," he said. "I have expenses to recover. But I'll make you a proposition. I'm a man who doesn't like to mince words, Ms Patterson. If you'd be so kind as to accompany me upstairs I'll be willing to drop the price to fifteen thousand. Of course whatever you tell Jacobo you paid is strictly up to you. Look at it as your chance to make a quick ten thousand."

"And what do you get out of it?"

The fat man laughed. Sweat had begun beading on his brow.

"Well I get screwed, Ms Patterson." He began to laugh.

"I'm sure you don't have to worry about that," she smiled at him. "I was thinking you'd get screwed anyway."

He watched her move ever so gracefully to the back door. She drew the bolt, and the door flew suddenly inward. A brute of a man in black commando clothing stormed in with an assault rifle, firing a burst of rounds into the floor at the fat man's feet.

Peter Donday charged up to the fat man, driving him hard against the wall, making dust rise. He buried the warm smoking tip of the Uzi in the opulent folds of skin in the jowls, slowly moving the rifle barrel into the fat man's quivering nostril.

514

"Really Peter must you resort to a senseless display of machismo?" Linda moved to the safe, giving the combination lock a twirl. "Now, about that combination."

Pressed against the wall, looking down at the warm hard steel of the Uzi where it entered his nostril, the fat man said, "Jacobo didn't send you, did he?"

They didn't answer.

Peter Donday said, "I believe the lady asked for the combination to the safe."

The fat man sputtered out the numbers. Linda Patterson pulled open the door. And there it was. A leather guitar case. She held it in her arms in the morning light streaming bright and low through the open door. Her fingers brushed across the handtooled lettering. Buddy Holly.

Snapping open the clasps and lifting the lid, she peered in, smelling something at once musty and oily. A flood of memories came pouring back, memories of when she'd been a seventh grader and someone had put on one of his records and they'd all kicked off their shoes and danced. Funny, she hadn't thought about that night in years. Hadn't felt those sudden magic racing trembling sensations in years. Hadn't felt young in years. It was nice to feel it again. Maybe now that she felt it it would be something that wouldn't ever again completely fade.

Peter Donday gasped, "We've come all this way for a guitar!"

"I'm beginning to think it's just not any guitar." With a snap Linda Patterson closed the clasps of the case.

"Tell it to the general. When he finds out we've been running around for a guitar he's going to explode."

They left with the guitar as suddenly and as strangely as they'd come. Dazed and frightened, the fat man stood before the open back door, trembling, rubbing his nostril, feeling the moist air blow in from the lake. The inside of his nose was burned. How could he explain it to his doctor?

Driving out of Chicago, listening to Peter Donday talk

about his childhood, Linda Patterson became thoughtful and asked the major to pull off the highway at a shopping mall up ahead so she might buy a pair of shoes.

"I must have been about eight when my first dog died," Peter Donday was saying as he obediently swung into the shopping mall. He sat beside her in the shoe store, talking about his dog, about how it had chased a cat into the street and was run over by a delivery truck.

She looked up then and nervously told him that she didn't love him, that she'd compromised the secrecy of the project at Camp Moonstone by going to a congressman and telling him everything.

She was trying on a pair of penny loafers as she told him. The sales girl had run off into a storeroom and boxes of shoes were stacked around them.

For a long moment he said nothing.

"I must have heard you wrong," he said at last. "It sounded all the world like you said you'd told a congressman about the project."

"His name is Marcus." She was looking around for the shoe horn. "He's at Camp Moonstone now. Hopefully by now he's blown the whole thing wide open. He told me to stall for time any way I could. I'm afraid I had to use you Peter. If only there had been another way."

Peter Donday looked dazed, stuck for words.

"You don't mean to say you don't love me?" Then, "I don't believe it."

"Peter please stop talking that way. I never—. Never felt that way for you."

"It's that congressman friend of yours, isn't it? It's mighty handy for him to be meeting you back at camp, isn't it?"

"Go to hell Peter. Did you ever stop to think I might have things in my head other than romance?"

Peter Donday studied her, the gears of his mind turning.

Rising to his feet, he snatched her shoulder bag from the floor by her feet.

She too grabbed hold.

516

"What do you think you're doing?"

"I'm taking the computer upgrade!"

"The hell you are!"

"Oh yeah?"

While they struggled the sales girl returned with boxes. Peter Donday yanked what looked like a big fuse from the bag and, with his elbow, knocked into the sales girl. Shoes went sailing. He charged from the store, Linda Patterson taking after him, not buying any of the shoes, leaving the confused sales girl without so much as saying a word. Stalking at his heels to the parking lot, she jumped into the bug with him and off they drove, not saying a word.

For several hours they drove like that, wordlessly, not looking at each other, glaring out the windshield. It was about as uncomfortable a ride as any two people would ever want to endure. They were full of words for each other, hot words that burned inside them that they wouldn't bring themselves to speak. Pressed close together like that in the bug made it worse. They drove like that until they'd begun to reach the rolling hills that led up into the mountains. The western sky was just taking on delicate pinks and reds when they heard the Volkswagen sputter and cough. Peter Donday was so caught up in his anger he hadn't remembered to stop for gas, hadn't even remembered to look at the gauge!

He put his head down on the wheel, closed his eyes. For a long time they sat in the car like that, not saying anything. The sky went from deep blue to all those reds to purples as the last of the light seeped out, till at last there was nothing but the deep blackness of the universe with all those stars atwinkling out there in infinity. They felt terribly alone with themselves in the night. The moon was shining full and bright and all they had to do was look out over that lonely strip of road and wonder what it was that'd brought them to this. It was an out-of-the-way road and not a car went by all night. Once or twice deep in the night he looked at her. The moonlight was streaming blue and white into the car and when he looked at her she looked back. It was like they were strangers to each other, two

517

beings that had never before encountered each other and who now looked at each other in the moonlight with sudden wide-eyed surprised curiosity. Then they'd look back into the night.

She must have fallen asleep sometime before dawn because when she awoke the sun had already poked above the horizon. Everything sparkled with dew. The seat next to her was empty. She quickly turned in the seat, looking both ways down the road. No sign of him. While she puzzled over it she must have fallen asleep again because when she opened her eyes the sun was much higher and brighter. Peter Donday was out on the shoulder pouring gasoline from a can into the bug. He chatted with a man in a cowboy hat who chewed tobacco and who leaned against a pickup truck which had pulled off the road in front of the bug. Closing the trunk, Peter Donday returned the can to the cowboy. He held out a ten dollar bill, but the cowboy only waved it away, tipped his hat to Linda, then got back into the truck and drove off.

Peter Donday started the bug, gunned the engine for the hills. All day they drove, not saying a word.

The moon was rising full through the trees by the time they reached the gates of Camp Moonstone. They drove through the gate, saw a charcoal fire smoldering on the lawn. A badminton net leaned rebelliously against the gusty wind. No one in sight. Remnants of a party — paper plates and cups — danced spiritedly around the house.

Saying nothing, Peter Donday leapt from the car and took off running into the night, the guitar case and his Uzi tucked under his arms. He crossed the deserted lawn then up the dim path through the trees to the empty warehouse. Empty, that is, except for the biggest pile of furniture he'd ever seen in his life. The peak of the mountain must have been at least sixty feet off the floor, stretching almost to the roof. Tearing by, he saw it wasn't a single mountain but a mountain range, one peak rising up only to drop back into the next. The main summit was flanked on both sides by lesser peaks of tangled tables and chairs and cabinets, all combining to stretch halfway across the warehouse.

Hurrying past the big steel doors, tearing breathlessly down into the underground complex, he headed for the computer chamber, which he found deserted, the blinking console littered with cards, poker chips, empty bourbon bottles, ashtrays and drinking glasses. He pulled the upgrade from his shirt. He hated to leave it down here by itself. The idea of that much power just lying around for anyone to pick up gave him the willies. Better to hide it. But where?

He dashed a note to the generals then took off full speed up the corridor to the deserted warehouse. Slipping the upgrade into the guitar case, he stood before the intimidating pile of furniture. His eye caught a solitary trunk near the forklift. Opening the trunk, he stashed the guitar inside, cocked his Uzi then ran from the warehouse.

It felt good to be running in the night. The assault rifle tucked in close at his side, he took off through the trees, running silently. He used his moonstone to open the gate. In the moonlight he followed the perimeter of the electrified barbed-wire till he came to a small campsite. In the moonlight he crept cautiously up to the small two-man tent. With the short muzzle of the rifle he drew back the flap. Empty. Finely appointed tables and armchairs were neatly arranged around the cold fire circle. He sat down in one of the armchairs to think, scratching his head with the muzzle of the Uzi.

The woods were full of the sounds of the night. He sat listening to the tapestry of sounds, wondering what he would do if this was a spy novel and he'd been cast in the role of the hero. Well isn't that just the biggest crock of bull, he thought. This isn't a spy novel and I'm not the hero. Isn't it just tough? Hadn't Linda as much as said it? Wasn't he a crumb?

He got up from the armchair. So this was her charming congressman's camp, he thought. A multitude of unopened cans lay crushed and battered around the campsite. From the looks of the survival cans the congressman hadn't even been able to open his rations. Maybe the bastard was starving to death somewhere in the woods. What a romantic thought. He supposed he'd better hang tight for a while in case the congressman came back. He wondered what the congressman would be like. Would he be young or old? As young as me? And would he be good-looking? As good-looking as me? Would he be able to think fast on his feet? Well he'd find out soon, wouldn't he? What was it this congressman had that I don't have? Linda Patterson, he thought. He cursed. Crawling into the brush at the edge of the campsite, he settled back with the Uzi pressed close against his cheek and he waited, thinking, thinking and listening to the sounds of the night.

He must have been there a long time (he couldn't be sure because the stars and the moon slid by so painlessly overhead and he lost all track of time) when he heard thunderous claps of gunfire. He took off like a shot then, running along the fence to the gate, following the sounds of the gunfire through the woods and up the hill to the warehouse. He could smell smoke, both the pleasantly sweet smell of burning wood and the acrid smell of gunpowder, and he could hear yelling. The gunfire grew louder. Forty-fives, from the sound of it, four or five of them, and those big guns really sounded like thunder banging away inside the warehouse.

His Uzi lowered, he charged into the warehouse, where he found the generals skirmishing with the old Indians. Civilians ran screaming in all directions, patches of fire here and there erupted on the side of the godawful pile of furniture, and the warehouse was filling up fast with smoke.

14

Peter Donday crouched in the shadow of the smoldering pile of furniture, his rifle trained on the three old Indians. He didn't hear the steps coming up behind him, but he should have expected it, should have known.

He only heard the soft click of the rifle's safety. Hearing knows the quick cold sound of the safety of an Uzi assault rifle. Lifting his head slightly, he waited.

"Drop it Peter," he heard Linda Patterson say. "Don't make me shoot."

Raising his chin, he looked over his shoulder.

Linda Patterson stood behind him, her rifle at his back.

"I don't believe you'd do it."

"What makes you so sure?"

"Because you're in love with me."

"You never quit, do you?"

The grin had returned to Peter Donday's face. But she couldn't see it. For a moment no one said or did anything.

"I'm not going to back down Peter," she said.

"Get the guitar case, general," was Peter Donday's reply. He pointed the rifle at the case, still in the open, the tomahawk stuck in its top. "I've got you covered."

George Natlong started for the case but Linda Patterson, gritting her teeth, fired a burst of shots into the desk, barring his way, driving him back.

"You're a traitor, Dr Patterson!" George Natlong bellowed. "By keeping me behind this desk you're aiding and abetting the enemy. If you weren't so damned brilliant I'd have you shot! I'd shoot you myself!"

"No one's going to get shot," Linda Patterson answered.

"We're all going to put down our weapons, before someone gets hurt. Starting with you, Peter. Then the generals. And then the Indians."

"I take my orders only from the general," Peter Donday said, not lowering his Uzi.

"And my orders come directly from the President of the United States!" George Natlong barked. "I've orders straight from Eisenhower himself to see this project through."

"Eisenhower's been dead for years!" Linda Patterson returned. "Your orders date from 1959. Doesn't your conscious date back further than that?"

"Your altruism is admirable, Dr Patterson. Very admirable," George Natlong called out. "But how do we know you really don't want the upgrade for yourself?"

"If that's what I want I certainly had every opportunity to get it before this. I only want this project terminated."

"Too bad you're alone then!"

"You're wrong about that, general!" they heard someone call out, the voice echoing through the warehouse. "She's not as alone as you think!" Congressman Marcus came out from behind the huge steel doors. "Dr Patterson is acting on my behalf." He postured himself like he was about to make a grand speech on the House floor. He would have cut a grander figure if he hadn't been all loaded down with cigar boxes and liquor bottles. "In the name of the Congress of the United States, I demand that this project be brought to a halt."

"Are you armed, congressman?" George Natlong called out.

"Of course not. I'm a man of words."

"I thought so."

George Natlong blasted away with the .45. The uneasy truce broken, the Indians launched a fresh volley of arrows, prompting the generals to answer with their .45s. A hailstorm of bullets and arrows raining around him, Marcus beat a retreat back to safety behind the steel doors. Setting down the cigars and all but one of the bottles of Chivas Regal, he broke the seal, unscrewed the top, stealing a sip of the golden liquid.

There was nothing like the good stuff. He plugged his handkerchief halfway down the neck of the bottle. Striking a match, he lit the handkerchief, waiting for the sputtering flames. Then he stepped out into the open, the smoking bottle held high.

"Hold your fire!" he commanded. "I've a Molotov cocktail here. By damn, I'll throw it at the next man who opens up!"

Once again the civilians started screaming and running in every direction.

"Hold your fire, men!" George Natlong ordered. "If that thing hits the furniture this whole camp goes up!"

The generals and Indians held their fire, still pointing the .45s and the arrow shafts.

"That's more like it," Marcus said, walking out. He took position between the generals and the Indians, lowered the smoking bottle. "I don't have to tell any of you that if I drop this we all go up in smoke. Where I come from we call this mutual assured destruction."

As he said this, Hal, having followed the congressman out of the cavern, came out from behind the great steel doors, his .45 drawn. He started across the floor for the congressman.

George Natlong started waving Hal away. But Hal kept coming. He stuck the muzzle of the .45 into Marcus's back, suddenly yelling, "Freeze!" Which is the last thing a man so surprised is apt to do.

Marcus jumped, lost hold of the bottle.

"Dear God in heaven!"

Eyes wide, Marcus dropped to his knees, fumbling with the flaming bottle, unable to find a handle.

"Ohhh!" he groaned.

Hal dropped to his knees on the concrete, covering his head.

"...Ohhh!"

Grabbing a partial hold, Marcus whipped the bottle sidearmed high into the air, at the pile of woodwork.

The moment froze in time. No one breathed. They

watched the spinning bottle and its attending orange sizzle of flame arch through the air and begin to drop, sliding down gravity's rainbow.

"Hit the dirt!" George Natlong screamed.

They heard the bottle shatter on the quality woodwork. Everyone closed their eyes. There was nothing. The golden liquid dripping from the furniture refused to ignite. The handkerchief sputtered in a puddle.

Swift River brought his bow up and, barely pausing to look cross-eyed down the arrowshaft, let the arrow go. It flew like a streak for Peter Donday. Surprise lit the major's face. He took an awkward step, his hand reaching back to the arrow. Then he collapsed on the floor, not moving.

"Peter!"

He lay on the concrete, the arrow lodged in his side, blood staining his shirt. Linda Patterson fell to her knees beside him.

He lay still, his face pressing the concrete.

"I don't believe it!" Casey yelled at Swift River. "You killed him! You killed him in cold blood!"

"What did you expect?" Swift River answered. "You think I'd go to all the trouble of stringing my bow and loading it up and aiming it if I had no intention of firing?"

Casey stormed over and ripped the bow from the old Indian's hands. He broke it in two over his knee.

Linda Patterson cradled Peter Donday's head in her lap.

Suddenly he opened his eyes.

"So you do care."

He smiled then, knowing deep down in his heart that sometimes, every once in a great while, a lucky few do get what they want.

George Natlong made a charge for the guitar case. "At last!" he yelled, unsnapping the clasps, throwing open the lid.

"The upgrade!" His voice rattled the warehouse. "Who has the upgrade?" He threw down the empty case.

Suddenly the great steel doors at the entrance to the cave began sliding closed. They all were very much surprised to hear then, from the loudspeaker above the closing doors, what sounded like a riff from an electric guitar.

A Chuck Berry lick, to be precise.

15

Fleeting images of Jeffrey Stoken on the night he died. Mason City images flowing fast across the computer screen. It was a dark night and he drunkenly climbed onto his motorcycle. In front of a tavern, a neon sign flashed. Hanging the heavy gunnysack by its string to his shoulder, he started the bike, roaring off the dark road, becoming no more than a fading roar of an engine, a white flash of head lamp and red streak of taillight roaring into the night.

Paul peered up from the pit of the great subterranean chamber, from behind the flashing console.

"I know you told me to stay out of the pit," Paul yelled up at the screen. "But I couldn't, Jeff. I just couldn't turn and run."

A great shower of sparks lit the screen. Paul had to turn his head, had to look away.

From his back pocket came the upgrade. With the heels of his hands he knocked it into place in the computer. Around him alarms sounded, lights flashed. Without missing a step he plugged in the red Strat.

16

George Natlong ran for all he was worth for the fast-closing doors. Bimmy, made up like Charlie Chaplin, hovered in his way, but the megalomania burning in George Natlong made him blind to Bimmy, blind to anything in his way, blind to everything but the fast-closing doors. Bimmy didn't exist, nothing in the world existed but those jawlike doors which fast came together. He would have run through Bimmy, through anyone.

Bimmy thrust his walking stick between George Natlong's feet, tripping him up. George Natlong tumbled, hit the concrete. He looked up in time to see the steel doors slam closed.

The .45 still in hand, George Natlong aimed at Bimmy and pulled the trigger. A click. The clip was empty. He lay on the floor pulling the trigger of the empty gun.

Bimmy crumpled to the concrete. The bowler hat that once had been worn by Chaplin rolled in a wide arc across the floor. It rolled to a stop by the smoldering pile of furniture.

George Natlong got up and kicked Bimmy in the ribs.

"Didn't I warn you never to trip me up again?"

Bimmy winced, then smiled.

17

Guitar music. A Chuck Berry lick, to be precise. Blasting over the president's own secure communications channels.

The duty officer flicked a few switches, said into the red phone, "Hey! This is supposed to be a clear channel," but the music kept up.

Something came over the wire. Highest priority clearance codes. Bright green lettering blinked across the computer monitor.

He read, *"My darlings, this channel of communications is temporarily out of service. CEO 666. Prometheus."*

Tapping the keyboard, he tried each of the forty-two other channels, both the satellite and the ground-based lines, but the same message blinked across the monitor for each.

Picking up the black phone, he yelled, "You jokers over there in the Pentagon have gone too far this time. Someone's going to hang for this!"

But he only heard guitar music.

Following procedures, he sounded a general alarm.

Nothing.

The button was dead.

His whole panel was dead.

18

Half a world away, Western guitar music rattled the hardened bunkers beneath the Kremlin. Blasting over the Red Army's most restricted communications lines. Someone came running in yelling they'd just lost control of the computers. The hotline with the Americans had been severed. The teletype machines began clicking. *"My darlings,"* the message read in starlike Cyrillic, *"this channel of communications is temporarily out of order. CEO 666. Prometheus."* Marshal Uri Kechyercoatov, chief of Moscow's defenses, ran through the halls of the Kremlin with a bayoneted rifle and a gas mask, breaking the early morning tranquillity by screaming at the top of his lungs, "The imperialist attack has begun! The Americans are launching a surprise attack!"

19

Far underground, Paul danced with the guitar before the computer console. He'd turned the volume of the Strat way up and really made it wail. His fingers glided down one string at a time so that each long drawn-out note started high on the scale, pretty near rattling the fillings in his teeth, then fell to earth-shattering lows, making the stalactites in the ceiling rumble and shake with a thunderous echo. It sounded like the devil himself was giving that Strat a whirl.

Hundreds of lights on the console flashed with ever-increasing fury, till a fire seemed to be building up inside the computer and the lights were no more than stained-glass windows on a burning cathedral, swept up in a firestorm. Just when it was getting hard to imagine how the lights could flash any brighter or faster, a single button in the very center of the console began to glow red, slowly at first, then building in intensity even as the lights around it began to fade, like an ember in the center of a blaze is fed by the dying coals around it, until the lone button in the middle took on a fiery red glow that was impossible to overlook. The lights around it fast died out and the single button was left to burn brightly by itself.

Yellow bolts of electricity meanwhile had started leaping and sizzling around the edges of the overhead computer screen. Every imaginable color flashed across its silvery surface. The screen grew brighter by the second, almost luminous. From the sea of shifting colors the figure of a man emerged. The image was of a ragged, haggard looking fellow but when you caught sight of his face you sensed kindness. He'd been chained to a gusty mountaintop, chained by crude leg irons to cold stone. Furiously tugging at the chains, he apparently was

530

unaware that he was being watched. Suddenly though he quit tugging on the chains long enough to stare down from the computer screen at Paul.

"So we meet again, my darling."

This took Paul so much by surprise that he jumped a full step back.

"Epimetheus?"

"Epimetheus is gone. I am his brother. Prometheus."

"Then we've never met."

"You're wrong, my darling." This voice seemed somehow kinder than Epimetheus's. "A thousand times we've met. On a thousand different fields. Under a thousand suns I have hand-ed you immortal fire."

"You got somebody else in mind, mister." The boy held tight to the Strat. "I'm Paul Stoken. From Mason City, Iowa. At least Epimetheus knew that. He could see into the past. Can't you?"

With a wave of his shackled hand, Prometheus scoffed.

"Any fool can look into the past. *I* can see the future. To see what will be."

The image on the screen had begun to shift and change. The colors ran into each other, the oranges bleeding into the greens and the blues changing into reds. The stark mountain-top scene gave way to a shimmering image of Manhattan at twilight, as if seen from high above. The screen quickly focused in on a single building.

Prometheus's deep voice boomed, "Do I know you or not? You're on your way to New York, to this place. You hope to play your guitar for this man."

Spellbound, Paul watched the screen as Lennon got out of a cab in front of a squat brooding apartment building. It was dark. There was a voice in the dark. "Mr Lennon." Five or six quick shots. The sounds of gagging. The shattering of glass on the pavement.

They lay broken and bloodied in the foreground. A pair of eyeglasses, their round lenses shattered. The world had flown out of focus.

The boy lowered his head.

He brought a finger up close to the bright red button.

Looking up, he saw on the screen images of a dead world. Void of life, frozen over in perpetual winter. It was the most desolate sight he'd ever laid eyes on.

Frightened, he pulled his finger away from the button.

"These things you show me. Are they what will be? Or only what may be?"

On the screen the earth again came alive. The boy saw it as it must look from space, spinning down below and all blue and lovely, with wispy white clouds skimming its surface. The spinning earth grew small on the screen till at last it was no more than a shimmering ball in the infinity of starry space.

The ball on the screen began sparkling gold, like fire. As Paul looked on, the fiery golden glow of earth spread first to the moon, then Mars and the other planets, exploding into the stars like a prairie fire, spreading to the farthest reaches of the galaxy.

"So Uncle Jeff was right," Paul said under his breath. "We *are* the ancients."

He looked up at the screen.

"Man, if anyone wants to know, Prometheus, if ever again you happen to meet someone like me, tell those people of tomorrow that we ancients were living in a dark age. Tell them just how alone we were. Tell them we were all alone in the dark, waiting for someone to hand us a light."

532

20

Leaving his post at the Situation Room, the duty officer walked through the empty halls of the executive mansion. It was as dead as a ghost ship. The president and his family were away for the Independence Day holiday and no one was around. Outside the Oval Office the president's private secretary was filing papers. The duty officer asked whether a senior member of the president's staff might be on hand. No, she told him, just about everyone was away for the holiday. The duty officer was persistent. Surely, he pressed, there must be someone around. Come to think of it, she said, she thought she'd seen the assistant deputy advisor for farm labor relations, or something like that, running around down the hall. Would he do? Yes, the duty officer said, the assistant deputy advisor for farm labor relations was better than nothing.

The assistant deputy advisor for farm labor relations was an obscure lifelong bureaucrat named Patrick T. Wilbert. They found him at the copying machines making copies of next week's White House baseball pool. The duty officer calmly, matter-of-factly informed Wilbert that the C^3I system had been knocked out.

Wilbert had no idea what the lieutenant was talking about. He thought maybe the ice machine had broken down again. He told him there was a 7-11 just down the street.

The duty officer explained that the C^3I system was the land-based, radio and satellite communications lines that tied the government together, from the lowliest deck scrubber on a nuclear sub up to the president. Somehow it all had stopped working. The duty officer said he didn't want to cause undue alarm, but he thought someone in a position of authority ought to know.

Wilbert said he didn't know about these things, since military communications was outside his sphere of knowledge (though anything other than wetbacks fell outside his sphere of knowledge) but didn't that essentially mean the country might very well, at this moment, be under foreign attack, without a means of defending itself?

Yes, the lieutenant said. That essentially was the situation, as far as he could see.

"Lands!" Wilbert shuddered. Why in God's name hadn't the lieutenant just come out and said as much?

"I did sir," said the lieutenant. "I told you the see-cubed-eye network was down."

"So you did, lieutenant. So you did."

At that moment a messenger arrived from the Pentagon. He was a young adjutant from Arkansas, very nervous. In a trembly voice he told the duty officer that the Pentagon's lines of communications had been cut. More ominous, the hotline with the Soviets was inoperative. They'd just received a strange message when it'd gone dead. From his neatly starched uniform shirt he pulled a single sheet of teletype paper. "My darlings," he read. His voice trembled so much he had to stop to collect himself. "This communications channel is temporarily out of order. CEO 666. Prometheus." He carried a squawking walkie-talkie and the whole time he never took it from his ear.

"Yes," the duty officer told him. "I can believe that. We got the same message here."

What could it mean? Wilbert asked.

That was what they wanted to know back at the Pentagon, the adjutant said. They'd gone through all the code books but had been unable to unscramble the meanings of "My darlings," "CEO 666," or "Prometheus." They were hoping someone from the White House could explain things. Was it a drill of some kind? the adjutant asked hopefully. He brought the walkie-talkie from his ear. They could hear guitar music.

"Let me see that." The president's secretary took the teletype paper. She wore a pair of glasses which hung on a chain in front of her dress. Now she put on the glasses and studied the communication. "CEO 666," she said, more to herself than to the others. "I can't imagine what that could stand for. Unless—."

Going to her desk, she began briskly rummaging through her large directories of Executive Orders, Presidential Directives and the like. But nothing. That's funny, she said, biting a nail. She'd thought the "EO" in "CEO 666" might stand for Executive Order. Whatever could CEO stand for? She looked thoughtfully at the closed doors leading to the office of the president. Without saying a word, she took her keys from her purse then disappeared into the Oval Office. Wilbert, the duty officer and the adjutant stood as they were, looking in through the open doorway. The room was dark, but momentarily a light winked on. From where they stood they could see a corner of the big desk, a swatch of the flag behind it and a few stars on the carpet. They heard her rummaging around in the desk. Finally the light winked off and she came out, closing the door. She held a book before her.

"No one but the president is supposed to see this," she told them, looking at each in turn. "But I think under the circumstances we should assume only friends are present. At least, let's pray it."

She opened the book to its first page. They saw, in faded handwriting, the words, "Confidential Executive Orders."

"Confidential Executive Order," Wilbert said. "CEO."

"We don't have to worry then," the duty officer said, relieved. "Whatever's happening, the president has authorized it."

"Not necessarily," she answered. "Confidential Executive Order 666 was apparently enacted way back in the Eisenhower years. Something like that could easily have gone overlooked all this time."

"Overlooked? You mean forgotten?"

"You might say that."

"What exactly is this Confidential Executive Order 666?"

Wilbert wanted to know.

"That's a little hard to say," she hedged.

"Let me see that." Wilbert took the book. It was a ledger, very much like the other ledgers listing ordinary Executive Orders, except this one was written out in hand. Most striking of all, it listed only the number of each order and the date it had been issued — nothing describing the order itself. Almost halfway through the book, alongside the curiously plain listing "No. 666," was written, in crisp soldier's handwriting, "February 3, 1959." That was all. Nothing more.

"Looks like Ike's trying to get a message through," Wilbert said. "What is this book, anyway?" He flipped to the first page, reading the only true sentences he could find. He read, in scratchy yet studious handwriting, "This ledger was begun by me, Franklin D. Roosevelt, on this, the nineteenth day of October, the year of Our Lord nineteen hundred and thirty-nine. I have decided, with the signing of Confidential Executive Order No. 1, to form a secret advisory panel to look into the possibilities of our building a uranium bomb. Although this undertaking will require a degree of secretiveness never before imposed on an open and free society, it is my hope that one day soon the clouds of war will clear and this book can be made public to the American people." It was initialed, in the same scratchy lettering, "F.D.R." Beneath this was the notation "No. 1," and the date October 19, 1939.

So in those few scribbles the atomic age had really begun. Since the day that book had seen those scribbles the clouds of distrust and war never had cleared and the American people never had learned its secrets. The book had been filled with Confidential Executive Orders, orders given in the woodwork and seldom seeing the light of day. Flipping through those pages Wilbert saw the cryptic notations of seven men, each picking up where the last had left off, some taking advantage of its pages more than others. Truman seemed to have issued the fewest secret orders. Nixon, the most. Still, Truman had his share of representation in that book. Beside one Truman listing, Confidential Executive Order No. 241, dating back to

536

forty-six, Truman had scribbled in, "This eventually led to the CIA! Biggest damn mistake of my life! Who'll keep an eye on those bastards?" Nixon, for his part, seemed to have gone berserk in the secret book, just about issuing more orders than all the others combined. You could see someone had even tried to erase a few entries. Wilbert flipped back to Confidential Executive Order No. 666.

"No. 666. February 3, 1959."

Nothing more.

It was beguiling.

"There must be some cross-reference to this someplace," Wilbert said. "Something that can tell us what these notations mean."

"There is no cross-reference," the president's secretary said quietly. She said the information they needed could be found in one place, and one place only: in the head of the president.

"Well heaven help us all," Wilbert said softly, staring up at the portrait of the president, Gerald R. Ford. He made the sign of the cross. "Heaven help us all."

Gathering himself, Wilbert choked, "I believe we may have a crisis on our hands." She nodded that she understood. With that they began furiously tearing through the book of secret orders, looking for something, anything to go on.

The adjutant looked on incredulously.

"I thought you said that there book was for the president's eyes only," he gawked.

"You haven't been in government long, have you son?" Wilbert grunted. He held the secret book upside down, by its spine, shaking its pages. Sure enough, a faded sheet of note paper fluttered to the floor.

"Hello! What's this?"

They saw it was written in the same bold handwriting that had filled the pages of the secret book from nineteen sixty-one to sixty-three. It read:

"Bobby—

Take a look at this book. Then get down to Room B119, in the basement of the Executive Office Building, and talk to a Mr Oscar Benton. I've learned from our friend in intelligence that's where the records for this are kept. We better get a handle on it, before we have another Bay of Pigs on our hands."

They flipped over the faded note. On the back side, in another hand, they read:

"November 21, '63
Jack,
I visited our Mr. Benton. You won't believe what I've found. We must talk the very minute you get back from Texas.
Bob

"How about that," Wilbert whistled through his teeth. "Maybe we can find some answers across the street in Room B119." He gingerly replaced the faded note, closing the book tightly, as if afraid more history might any moment drop to the floor.

"That would be the Old Executive Office Building now," the president's secretary said. "I'll have Rose over on the switchboard get us a line on this Mr Benton. By now he may have retired." Already she'd picked up the phone. "Hello? Hello?" she said into the receiver. "That's funny. I can't seem to get a dial tone." She tried one line, then another. She went to another desk and tried a second phone. Nothing.

It was then the adjutant noticed how quiet it was at the White House. None of the phones rang. It was ghostly quiet.

"It's like something's been taken away from here," the young adjutant said, staring down the empty hall, breaking the ghostly silence.

"Don't let the quiet of the place fool you, hun," the president's secretary told him. "This has always been the loneliest place on earth."

Already she was thumbing through the voluminous direc-

538

tory of government employees. Tapping a page with a painted fingernail, she sang out, "Here we are. Benton, Oscar. B119 Old Executive Office Building. Bingo! He's our man and he's still with us." She took out the Washington phone book. "With the computer down and the phone lines out we'll have trouble gaining access to the personnel records. Let's hope his number at home isn't unlisted." Running her finger down the page she held her breath. There it was. Benton, Oscar. "He lives across the river in Virginia. Let's hope he hasn't gone to the beach for the holiday." Scribbling an address on a memo pad, she gave it to the duty officer. "You and Arkansas here go and get this Mr Benton so we can have a talk with him," she said curtly. "Don't waste time, but don't fly either. Especially leaving the gates. We don't want it to look like there's a fire."

They left immediately. If they didn't fly they at least rushed a little, for they were back within the hour. With them they brought a particularly quarrelsome old man, at least sixty but probably closer to sixty-five. They dragged him in kicking and screaming, dragged him right up to the door of the Oval Office, where he continued to protest.

"Here's our Mr Benton," the duty officer said, tossing the old man in a chair. "We got there just in time. He was going to the beach. Didn't want to come."

The old man wore a beach hat, sand loafers, Bermuda shorts and a Hawaiian shirt. He still had on his sunglasses.

"I must protest!" Mr Benton piped behind his dark glasses. "This is a legal holiday! What business have you to drag me to work from my paid vacation leave? You better believe the Civil Service Commission will hear about this! Why should I suffer indignities like this?"

Wilbert and the others looked at him with disgust. Here they were, caught in a crisis, at the very door of the same office where Lincoln had once burned the midnight oil, and all this damned bureaucrat could think of was his paid vacation time. He didn't even take off his sunglasses.

"Bring him along," was all Wilbert had to say. The adju-

539

tant and the duty officer picked up Mr Benton and started off at a brisk pace.

"Where are we going now?" Benton wanted to know.

"Down to your office."

"My office? You have no authority to go there."

"We'll see about that."

They left the White House, going outside. It was a gorgeous evening but they scarcely had time to notice, scarcely had time even to nod to the guard at the gate before they flew across the street with Mr Benton in tow, hurrying into the palatial old office building. They showed their IDs to the guard at the door.

"Did you happen to notice that the phones are out?" the guard said to them. "Damn phone company. At least if it had to happen it happened on a holiday when there ain't nobody around."

They had no time for him. "Bring a set of keys," was all the president's secretary had to say. They rushed off down the long broad empty echoing corridors with Mr Benton yelling and screaming the whole way about how the Civil Service Commission would get an earful from him, the guard rattling the big set of keys, then down the worn steps to the basement.

At last they came to door number B119. The guard opened the door and Wilbert went in. It was dark. No windows. The smell of paper. Wilbert tried the lightswitch but the bulb was out. There was only the wedge of light from the corridor. "How the hell can you find your way around?" he said to the old man, who was rushing in the dark. "Get a lightbulb lieutenant."

"If you tell me what it is you're after maybe I can help," Benton complained.

The lieutenant went out into the long hallway. The lights in the fixtures were much too high to reach. Nothing but locked doors and an occasional fire extinguisher.

"I'll go upstairs to the supply closet and get a bulb," the guard said.

"Stay as you are mister," the lieutenant told him. "We

haven't time. This is a national emergency."

Grabbing one of the fire extinguishers, he smashed it through the glass of a door. Glass cascaded everywhere. He poked an arm through the jagged eye in the door, opening the lock. In a wink he came out with a bulb.

They installed the bulb in Room B119, hit the switch. They were amazed to find files. Records. Documents. Files and records and documents stretching up to the ceiling. Files and records and documents stretching back into the cavernous room as far as they could see.

"Would you look at this," the adjutant whistled. "I never saw so much paper in my life."

Wilbert couldn't make sense of the filing system. Nothing was alphabetized or numbered. Every few feet along the endless stretches of shelves he found what appeared at first glance to be a blank card. On a lark, he pulled one of the files from the nearest shelf, opening it. It was a memo concerning some kind of flying saucer the government had built and test flown near Flagstaff, Arizona. Flipping through the file, he came to an actual photo of a flying saucer. An Air Force pilot kneeled beside it, in the proud way of pilots. Whistling through his teeth, he returned the file. His eyes landed on another. "Professor A. Einstein's Unified Field Theory," it read. It was a slim little volume and, thumbing through it, he saw it contained nothing but incomprehensible mathematical equations. Bored, he dropped it on Mr Benton's cluttered desk but it was a bad shot and the booklet slid straight off the side of the desk into the trash can. I'll have to remember to pick that out of there, Wilbert reminded himself, but already it was the farthest thing from his mind.

He decided he'd better give Mr Benton a try. Maybe he'd cooperate. It couldn't hurt to try. The old man angrily moved about his office, putting things in order.

"Does CEO 666 mean anything to you?" Wilbert called over to him.

The old man froze.

"666? What about it?"

"Then you know what I'm talking about?"

"Certainly," Benton nodded. He was stared at Wilbert through those dark glasses. "What about it?"

"Let me see the file. Everything you have."

There was a long moment. Wilbert didn't know which way things would go. He saw his reflection in the old man's sunglasses.

"Have you the authority?" Benton asked.

"We just came from the Oval Office, didn't we?"

Benton seemed surprised.

"Is that where we just were?"

He seemed all flustered. He spun around and trampled off, his small legs beating a fast rhythm across the floor. "It's a big file, 666," they heard the old man say. They followed him down a long aisle of stacked and shelved files. "Course, it's not as big as 2104. Or 478. Mercy no. But it's a big file just the same. I've been keeping track of it just fine, don't you worry. It's all right here."

The old man, stopping at a shelf of papers smelling of mildew and dust, ran his hand over one of those strange blank cards marking each of the shelves, apparently feeling for something.

"Here we are," he said. "Six sixty-six."

He moved away from the blank card, reaching for a fat folder on the shelf. Wilbert examined the blank card. A pattern of upraised dots. He ran his hand over them, turned to the president's secretary.

"Braille," he said softly.

Benton bore the large folder down from the shelf. It really was an armload. Wilbert slowly waved a hand in front of Benton's face. He didn't appear to notice. Wilbert removed the old man's sunglasses. He saw blank eyes. So that was why the poor devil hadn't taken them off in the White House.

He'd been blind since birth, old Benton told them as he carried the file back to his desk. He'd never let his sightlessness get in his way, he told them. He'd held this same job since he'd been a young fellow, since back in thirty-nine, and he'd

542

learned to find his way around just fine. A body does what a body has to do, he told them. After all these years of blindly crawling over every inch of those files he'd pretty well learned his way around. It was like everything else in life, he said. We do things from the force of habit, without seeing. Getting up in the morning, riding the bus to work, working on the files. Why, sometimes, when he was on his way home on the bus, people would tell him they hadn't immediately realized he was blind, so adept was he at counting his change and dropping it into the change counter. A body does what a body has to do, he told them.

"You really must excuse me if I seem at all surprised," old Mr Benton wheezed as Wilbert sat at the desk to study the file. "You know, in all these years this is only the second time I've had visitors to my office. The only other time was back in 1963. That young fella, Bobby Kennedy, he came down here to see me. Yesindeedee he did. He sat right there. In that very chair." He pointed at an old wooden chair beside his desk. Other than the chair behind the desk it was the only chair in the whole vast catacomb. "He was a nice young fella, he was. We sat chatting for hours. He asked me if I'd ever read any of the reports I'd filed away down here and I laughed and had to remind him I was blind. He said he bet over the years no one had ever laid an eye on my files and I told him he was right about that. No one's ever come to look things over. We had a good laugh over that. Big government, don't you know! He said he'd be back — to loan me his eyes, in a manner of speaking — to sort through some of this stuff. But, don't you know, the next day his brother was shot. He never came back. No one came back. Always thought I'd see him again, until I got word he'd been shot himself in California. Since then I've kept that chair just how it is. My own personal memorial, you might say. Sometimes I sit down here talking to that empty chair, like he was still sitting there, and I file my papers like that." He turned his head toward them. "And now today you people come."

The blind man sat down on the corner of his desk. "I'm an

old man now," he said. "Been working this job all my life. Three more years and I'll take my retirement. And there I was, mouthing off like a jackass in the White House. It only goes to show. A blind man can't afford to get angry."

Scarcely listening to the old man, Wilbert and the president's secretary tore into the files. As they held George Natlong's reports up for the first time to the light of day their eyes became large and they read faster, with increasing urgency and worry, tearing through one page after another of the snowballing nightmare.

"This is incredible," Wilbert gasped. "If *The New York Times* ever got ahold of this file government would be outlawed."

When he came to the end of the file Wilbert buried his head in his hands.

"I feel sick."

"To think this was sitting here all this time." Wilbert, a little white, looked out over the vast unending warehouse of files. "I wonder what the hell else is going on out there."

"We've got to get through to the presidential party in Vail."

"How? The phones are out."

The duty officer snapped his fingers.

"The 7-11 down the street. Don't they got a pay phone?"

Already they were off. They took the adjutant's jeep, saying nothing, each smoking a cigarette, and as they shot past the White House, all lit up like Christmas, they saw the tourists taking pictures out in front of its gates. They had to marvel at how terribly wrong something can be on the inside while still looking so serene and ideal on the outside. The adjutant hunched over the wheel as he weaved through traffic.

"The folks back home ain't gonna believe it when I tell them about the things I seen today."

"Don't count on telling anybody anything, Arkansas," the duty officer said. "If I know the government they'll want you to keep your trap shut. That is, if you're still alive to tell it." He saw he'd scared the young adjutant. He smiled. He was holding the adjutant's walkie-talkie close to his ear, listening to the wail of the guitar music.

They screeched and banged into the busy parking lot at the 7-11. Piling from the jeep, they raced to the pay phone. It was occupied. By a heavyset woman in hair curlers. At least it's working, Wilbert thought.

He pounded the door.

"Can't you see it's occupied?" the woman yelled out. She slammed the door closed and turned her back to them. They heard her say into the phone, "So I told her, it's none of my business, but if he was my husband I'd certainly lay down the law."

21

"I command you to open these doors this very instant!" George Natlong bellowed at the loudspeaker. He pounded the steel doors with the butt of his .45. The doors thundered like gigantic kettle drums. From the loudspeaker came only the sound of an electric guitar.

"I knew I should have shot that punk the moment I laid eyes on him!"

"That punk at this moment is the most powerful man on earth."

Congressman Marcus came over, gawked at the loudspeaker.

"Do you mean to say you've allowed a boy to take command of this complex?"

"He no doubt has his finger on the nuclear button this very moment," Charlie whispered.

Casey said, "I can't see how he could have his finger on the button and be playing guitar at the same time."

George Natlong stared icily at Hal.

"This is all your fault!" he yelled, waving the .45. "You abandoned your post. Do you realize what your bumbling has cost?"

"You got it all wrong George. I was only doing what I thought right at the time!" Hal looked absolutely crushed. "Does this mean I don't get the Middle East?" his sweaty face seemed to say. It sure had been one hell of a day. In the last half hour he'd gone from winning all of Europe and the Middle East down to nothing. These days the world changes hands fast.

"We've got to get that punk out of there!" George

Natlong boomed. "Wait'll I get my hands on him! He'll wish he got the firing squad after all."

"How're we going to get to him, George? We can't cut through these doors. The steel plating must be six inches thick."

"There must be a back way in," Hal whispered. "We can make these Indians show us."

"There's no time for that," Charlie whispered back. "That boy has absolute control over any missile in our nuclear arsenal. While we prattle around up here he may get the idea to send a cruise missile our way. Down in the cave he can survive. We perish. It's that simple. He's really put one over on us."

"Well if we're going to do anything about it we sure as hell better do it fast," Casey said. "That stuff's going up like a tinderbox." He nodded at the mountainous pile of flaming woodwork. They saw Elizabeth Natlong scrambling around up there, fighting a losing battle. The old furniture was as dry as twigs in July. The Chivas Regal the congressman had thrown on the conflagration had begun to burn after a fashion, running and dripping down the sides of the woodwork, burning the most delicate shades of lovely browns and oranges into the veneers, giving the overall effect of a molten lava sauce poured upon a parfait of smoldering furniture. Flames near the summit of the mountain already licked at the warehouse ceiling. Black smoke poured out in every direction, making it increasingly difficult to breathe. They were all beginning to cough.

"It's not over yet!" George Natlong yelled. Something a little mad came into his eyes. The ugly thing that had been stirred in him now flung him against the big steel doors, making his fingers tear and pry at the crack between the massive doors.

"There, there! It's moving!"

Standing back from the doors, his eyes hit a steel bar near the wall. He lost no time taking it up and applying it to the crack between the doors. The others told him it was no use, that the doors were too heavy to budge and that they should get the hell out while they could, as the heat from the fire was getting intense and they could feel it through their clothes, but George Natlong wouldn't hear of it. Throwing down the steel rod, he yelled, "If only I had a lever big enough I could move the world!" He stepped back from the doors, looking in every direction through the thickening smoke.

He saw the forklift on the far side of the warehouse. He ran for it even as he barked orders.

"Grab a few of those long tables from the pile!" he coughed at the men.

"What will you do with them, George?"

"We'll use them to build a ramp so we can tip the forklift. We'll use the tines of the lift to pry open the doors."

"That could be dangerous George!"

But already he'd huffed his way to the forklift. The other generals did as he said. They snatched several long tables from the inferno. It was very hot work and they had to cover their mouths with their handkerchiefs to keep away the smoke.

George Natlong drove the forklift full throttle across the floor, hitting the ramp they'd built, one set of wheels in the air and the other on the floor. There was a crunch as the tables gave way under the little wheels.

"Jump! There's a ton weight in back!"

Elizabeth Natlong, her dress torn in several places, her skin smudged by soot and dirt, looked down through the smoke from the pile of woodwork as her husband crunched the forklift over several priceless Chippendale tables. She watched as he jumped from the forklift just before it crashed on its side with earsplitting thunder, missing George Natlong's legs by scant inches, but all Elizabeth could cry out was, "Daddy's tables! You're destroying Daddy's precious tables!"

22

Paul looked down at the scarred guitar. "I want to do something I've wanted to do since that day at the Surf. I want to play Not Fade Away. Like it won't ever be played again. For once in my life I want to *nail* that sucker."

The world at his fingertips, all he could think of was a song. He was about to plug the cassette tape into the console when his eyes landed on one of the many video cameras installed in the ceiling.

"Why don't we make a video?"

"A video?"

"Don't you know anything? So people can watch my tunes on the tube."

"Tunes on the tube?"

"I'll explain everything. I've got a great idea but I'll need your help."

Presently it was quiet in the computer chamber, and everything was still, except for the flashing of the colored lights here and there on the broad console. The big screen sparkled. At the far side of the console, all the way to the left, Paul switched on a video tape recorder. Overhead, bright television lights flashed. The cavern lit up like the Hall of the Mountain King.

The red Strat close in at his side, Paul began tapping out a simple rhythm with his black ankle highs.

A picture of a celestial hamburger stand suddenly lit the giant screen. On the screen it was night and stars shone brightly all around. Lovers necked in sleek fifties coupes in the parking lot, beneath a neon sign that blinked, "Ike's Rock 'n' Roll Heaven."

Other than the rhythmic electric buzzing of the neon, all was still and quiet. You could hear the soft heartbeat sound of crickets, chirping soothingly somewhere out in the night.

Inside, above the cash register, hangs a sign that reads,

Ike's Rock 'n' Roll Heaven
- Proprietor -
Dwight D. Eisenhower
Supreme Allied Commander
Liberator of Europe
President of the United States of America
(retired)
We reserve the right to refuse service

And there's old Ike! Standing bolt upright behind the counter. A white apron pulled over his Eisenhower jacket, he's every bit the proud proprietor. He's passing an idle moment in eternity by building a house of cards on the gleaming formica counter. It's a slow night at Rock 'n' Roll Heaven and Ike likes to bide his time in eternity by building houses of cards. Out in the kitchen you hear the quiet sounds of washing up. The only customer in the place is a young man who's fallen asleep at the counter, his shaggy head resting beside a glass of Coke. Every so often, after carefully placing a card in a strategic place on the growing house, Eisenhower takes a flyswatter and swats the young man's head. "Hey you!" he barks at him. "No slouches in *my* place! Wake up and get out!" But the young man remains passed out at the counter.

Into this tranquil setting comes a stranger. Tall. Black hair. Leather jacket. Horn-rimmed glasses. A shy, boyish smile.

"It looks just like him," Paul had to admit, staring wondrously up at the screen.

Real as life, striding up to the counter of Ike's Rock 'n' Roll Heaven, comes Buddy Holly.

He'd come boldly in from the night to take his place at the counter of Rock 'n' Roll Heaven. Patiently he awaits service. Eisenhower's too busy building the house of cards or poking

550

the loafer's head to be bothered.

"Can I get some service here?" Buddy Holly asks, his soft Texas twang hanging in the air long after the words had gone. "How about a cheeseburger, some fries and a Coke?"

Ike carefully places the Queen of Hearts on his tall tower of cards.

Holly takes a shiny silver dollar from his pocket and begins tapping it rhythmically on the polished counter. Three longs taps followed by two shorts.

The tapping breaks the quiet of the celestial hamburger stand, annoying Eisenhower, who wants peace to lay down his card. The effect down on earth, in the computer chamber, is even more startling. Each time Buddy Holly brings that silver dollar down to the counter a thunderous crash of a drumbeat erupts in the cave.

Paul moved his feet to the beat, dancing with the guitar.

"Louder!" he yelled. "So I can feel it!"

The thunderous drumbeat brought on by the tapping of the coin grew gloriously loud. Back in Rock 'n' Roll Heaven, Buddy Holly moved to the thunderous big beat, dancing on the checkered tile floor. Every move he makes was matched identically by Paul. The two of them, one before the computer and the other up on the screen, dance like a matched set, moving hands and feet in perfect time. Behind Buddy Holly, walking into Rock 'n' Heaven, come a parade of dead rock stars. Janis Joplin, Jimi Hendrix, Jim Morrison — they'll all there, grooving to the beat, singing the backup part.

They all got down. Everyone that is of course but old Pop Eisenhower, who looks up from his house of cards with alarm at the sudden outbreak of song and dance.

"Not in my place!" he admonishs the singers, pointing the flyswatter at the sign where it says he reserves the right to refuse service, but it's too late for that, way too late for that.

Covering his ears, Ike pokes his head into the kitchen. Jack Kerouac, supposedly washing dishes, slops water around to the thunderous beat. Behind him, near the sink, Neil Cassidy is making time with a little Puerto Rican girl, saying softly into her ear as he sways with her against the wall, "Just feel the beat honey, ahem, that's right! just feel the beat!"

"What's this! The cooks! In open revolt!"

Sam Cooke and Jackie Wilson, grooving to the beat, drop the cooking utensils, throw aprons at Eisenhower and charge from the kitchen to join the singers out front. More singers come out from undercover at the booths. The celestial hamburger stand fills fast with dead rock stars. Richie Valens. The Big Bopper. Brian Jones. With wild abandon they dance across the checkered tiles. Buddy Holly hops up on to the stainless steel counter and spins around, singing. Ike frantically tries to stop the rocking. He runs across the floor, barking orders, ignored. Back at the counter, the young man with the shaggy hair who had fallen asleep near the house of cards lifts his head. It's James Dean! Smiling. Cunning. His cheeks cherry red. Drawing in a deep breath, he exhales sharply, blowing away Ike's house of cards, sending aces and jokers and kings and queens flying.

As Buddy Holly sang out the words to Not Fade Away in Rock 'n' Roll Heaven Paul sang them in the computer chamber. He knew he was making an all-time great music video. Dripping with sweat, he tore off the red jacket that once had been worn by James Dean, throwing it uncaringly to the floor.

Up on the screen, time for the guitar solo, and Buddy Holly beckoned for Paul to toss up the red Strat. The boy unstrapped the Strat and stood before the screen, uncertain, for a moment looking like he might give in to temptation and toss Buddy Holly back his Strat. Instead he brought the guitar down to his own knees and played like he'd never played before. Buddy Holly looked down from Rock 'n' Roll Heaven, playing air guitar by his knees, every movement of his fingers matching Paul's. They all looked down from Rock 'n' Roll Heaven and were pleased.

23

At the surface, in the smoky warehouse, Hal held his ear to the great steel doors.

"I think I hear something. Some kind of rhythmic thumping. Like an earthquake. Is this the end?"

In a moment the others too could hear it thundering up from the deep, like a heartbeat magnified a million times, rattling even the heavy steel doors.

"I don't know," Charlie coughed, examining the toppled forklift. It looked dead. Hydraulic fluid glopped from one side. "It took a pretty good slam, George. I think we knocked out the hydraulics." He checked the lever. The fork moved. Even so it had landed a good three feet from the door. Singleminded in purpose, George Natlong pried a broken timber from a table and used it as a lever, pushing the forklift forward. Inspired by this display of hell-bent determination, the others grabbed timbers. "Let's give it the old West Point try." The forklift began inching across the floor. The five of them strained, groaned, moved muscles they didn't know they had, till the tangs of the forklift just touched the crack in the doors.

George Natlong ran forward, pried at the crack with the steel bar. "Now. Altogether. Push." The others pushed from behind, coughing in the smoke. The tangs slid into the crack.

"Now! Try the lever!"

Charlie hit the hydraulic drive. From somewhere up above, the big doors began to move, first fractions of inches, then inches.

"It's working!" George Natlong grinned. "It's actually working! How about that! We're doing it!"

The crack between the doors had almost opened to hand's

width. George Natlong stuck in a timber and pried on. It opened still more. At last he could just stick in his shoulder and push with both hands. Behind him the roof of the warehouse had started burning, in several places caving in. The forklift screamed. He managed to get his head between the doors. The others could just hear him yell, "There! Now if I can just get my shoulders through—." At that moment something let go. The massive doors jumped.

The others turned away. They looked to the burning pile of woodwork, to Elizabeth Natlong. She clung to the pile, a hand to her mouth.

"No! Leave me at least George! Don't take him away too! Give me just this one thing!"

She tripped tearfully down the furniture as the men pried at the doors, pulling him out, setting him on the ground. The doors had snapped his neck, breaking his jaw in the bargain. He lay like a broken nutcracker, his jaw hanging wide and broken.

"My poor George!" Elizabeth sobbed. She knelt and rocked his lifeless body. "He was a breech birth, you know," she sobbed quietly. "He tried to come into this world the wrong way. It killed his mother. He never had anyone his whole life, no one but me. I know he regretted marrying into all my money. I think it smothered him. He had to strike out on his own, don't you see? Be his own man. A bigger man than any of the Dukes had ever been. And this was his way. Only he went about it the wrong way, that's all. He was always trying to come into this world the wrong way. And that's how he died."

24

Claire Duke, watching from the back of the subterranean chamber, came slowly down the aisle behind Paul. She ran her hands along his skin, over the sweat-dampened Superman T-shirt.

"You're burning up."

On the shimmering screen Rock 'n' Roll Heaven dissolved into the terrible image of the earth afire. The fire leapt to the moon. From there, it spread to the other planets, then burst in every direction to the stars. A startling display of fireworks.

With that Paul let go a blood curdling scream. Rearing back the guitar, he smashed it into the console. There was a great explosion and they were thrown back. Around them the walls of the cave began rumbling, falling in.

They started off but Paul remembered the video tape. He ran back to the burning console.

"Wait'll the bigwigs get a load of this."

He tucked the video into his jeans.

25

They heard the explosion, followed by the rumble of the cave-in. Thick black smoke, then dust, poured through the crack in the steel doors.

"We've got to close these doors!" Charlie coughed.

"What about the boy? He's still down there."

"He's toast. Nothing survived that blast."

The others pressed against the warm steel, moving the doors closed.

26

Arm in arm they ran up the aisle, leaving the smoky chamber behind. Starting down the long hallway they felt all carefree and happy, fingers brushing through hair, and before they knew it they were laughing and running as fast as their legs could carry them down to the antebellum mansion at the very bottom of the secret complex. Holding hands, they each took one of the torches that had been left behind by the Indians. Like that, holding hands, they started off into the Indian burial chamber.

"Hold me," Claire said to him when she saw the endless bed of bones. He moved close and kissed her.

"Not here."

"Why not? We can pretend we're a modern Tom Sawyer and Becky Thatcher."

"Hmm. Sounds nice."

Afterwards they were walking up through the cave, stopping now and then to marvel at the delicate crystals growing at every turn, when up ahead they saw stars. Running toward them they burst out of the cave and found themselves outside in the night, under a twinkling dome of constellations.

They walked up a hill and when they reached the top they looked out through the trees and could see, in the distance, the warehouse afire. Sparks from the great pile of woodwork rose high into the peaceful night sky, mixing with the stars. Holding her close, he led her down the hill. A little way into the woods they came upon tables and chairs that had been neatly arranged around a campsite. Looking at each other, they began to laugh.

At the top of the hill they built a warm fire from the tables and chairs they'd found in the woods. They lay together under the stars watching the sparks rise up from the flames, swirling away into the night, hearing all around them, in the dark heart of the American night, a soothing, enveloping, happy chirping sound. Of crickets.